Also by HEATHER GRAHAM

HAUNTED DESTINY
FLAWLESS
THE HIDDEN
THE FORGOTTEN
THE SILENCED
THE DEAD PLAY ON
THE BETRAYED
THE HEXED
THE CURSED
WAKING THE DEAD
THE NIGHT IS FOREVER
THE NIGHT IS ALIVE
THE NIGHT IS WATCHING
LET THE DEAD SLEEP
THE UNINVITED
THE UNSPOKEN
THE UNHOLY
THE UNSEEN
AN ANGEL FOR CHRISTMAS
THE EVIL INSIDE
SACRED EVIL
HEART OF EVIL
PHANTOM EVIL
NIGHT OF THE VAMPIRES
THE KEEPERS
GHOST MOON
GHOST NIGHT
GHOST SHADOW
THE KILLING EDGE
NIGHT OF THE WOLVES

HOME IN TIME FOR CHRISTMAS
UNHALLOWED GROUND
DUST TO DUST
NIGHTWALKER
DEADLY GIFT
DEADLY HARVEST
DEADLY NIGHT
THE DEATH DEALER
THE LAST NOEL
THE SÉANCE
BLOOD RED
THE DEAD ROOM
KISS OF DARKNESS
THE VISION
THE ISLAND
GHOST WALK
KILLING KELLY
THE PRESENCE
DEAD ON THE DANCE FLOOR
PICTURE ME DEAD
HAUNTED
HURRICANE BAY
A SEASON OF MIRACLES
NIGHT OF THE BLACKBIRD
NEVER SLEEP WITH STRANGERS
EYES OF FIRE
SLOW BURN
NIGHT HEAT

* * * * *

Look for Heather Graham's next novel,
available soon from MIRA Books.

HEATHER GRAHAM

DEADLY FATE

MIRA®

ISBN-13: 978-0-7783-3012-7

Deadly Fate

For questions and comments about the quality of this book, please contact us at CustomerService@Harlequin.com.

www.MIRABooks.com

Printed in U.S.A.

First printing: August 2016
10 9 8 7 6 5 4 3 2 1

In loving memory of
my sister
Victoria Graham Davant,
who loved the wonder
and beauty of the
Great State of Alaska

CAST OF CHARACTERS

FBI Agents

Jackson Crow, head of the Krewe of Hunters
Angela Hawkins, special agent and Jackson's wife
Thor Erikson, new member of the Krewe in the Alaska Field Office
Mike Aklaq, Thor's partner

Other Law Enforcement

Reginald Enfield, Special Director, Alaska
Lieutenant Bill Meyer, Alaska State Police

The Fairy Tale Killer

Tate Morley, serial killer in Kansas, recently escaped from prison

From the Past

Mandy Brandt, the Fairy Tale Killer's last victim

The Alaska Hut

Marc Kimball, owner
Emmy Vincenzo, assistant/secretary
Justin and Magda Crowley, property manager and housekeeper

Celtic American Cruise Lines—the Ship's Entertainers

Clara Avery, actress and singer in the *Fate*'s original
Broadway-style musical, *Annabelle Lee*
Ralph Martini, older actor
Simon Green, chorus member
Larry Hepburn, young heartthrob actor
Connie Shaw, actress

The Crew of *Gotcha* and *Vacation USA* (reality TV shows)

Natalie Fontaine, producer
Amelia Carson, TV hostess
Tommy Marchant, cameraman
Becca Marle, sound technician
Nate Mahoney, fabricator
Misty Blaine, production assistant to Natalie Fontaine

Other Characters

Astrid and Colin, Thor's sister and brother-in-law
Natasha and Boris, Thor's huskies

DEADLY
FATE

CHAPTER ONE

She lay in beauty.

Heartbreaking beauty, for she was gone.

There was no hope of resuscitation; she was as pale as the snow-white sheets upon which she rested. Her hair was sable brown, the color of soft fur. Her lips had been highlighted with a rich shade of red, and her features were as delicate and lovely as the intricate pattern of a snowflake.

She'd been a victim of the "Fairy Tale Killer," a man Thor Erikson had been pursuing with his partner, Jackson Crow, for months. The killer had struck in cities from New York City to San Diego, and it was in Los Angeles where they'd caught him at last. He'd been kneeling over, bending down, tenderly touching a corpse—only to turn with a Smith & Wesson pointed directly at Thor and Crow.

Thor had fired first, and then rushed to the pallet upon which the killer had displayed his "Snow White," knowing full well that they were too late; she was gone, drained of her life's blood.

Thor could still see her in his mind's eye, remember when she'd arranged a meeting with him and Crow; he could hear her sincerity as she had expressed concern about a coworker who had been dating a business executive, a man who traveled constantly. Her name had been Mandy Brandt, and she'd been so very worried about her friend, who worked at the tour center with her. He remembered the gentleness of her smile, her eagerness to help in any way...

And now here she lay, a beauty like Snow White. But no kiss would awaken her.

He turned to Jackson, who was kicking the gun from the killer's grip, checking to see if he was dead; he was not. He was still breathing.

"Saved my life—and his," Jackson said.

Thor was vaguely aware of Jackson getting on his phone, calling for medical assistance and backup.

Then the whole scene began to fog up and fade.

It was a dream that came to him again and again; a memory that played itself out in his mind when he was sleeping, when he was vulnerable. Over time it had come less and less, but sometimes, like now, it would return like the blade of a knife, digging into his mind as if piercing his flesh.

Tonight, however, Mandy's eyes opened. And she looked at him with that beautiful and tremulous smile of hers. "Thor," she said.

"Mandy!"

She reached up and touched his cheek. "You mustn't let it happen again," she told him softly.

He was dreaming; he knew that he was dreaming. He'd relived the scene a thousand times over.

And he'd wondered every time how he and Jackson and a slew of techs had managed to be just that little bit too far behind the killer...

No, he blamed it on himself. And maybe Jackson, just a little. Mostly it was his own fault. He should have known. They should have known. They shared a strange sense of...intuition, and they should have realized from the descriptions they'd received, from their gut sense of the past and time and purpose and...

Mandy had died anyway.

In his dream, he said, "Every day, Mandy, every day of my life, I still try to catch the killers, the bad guys, the sick, the evil... I am so sorry..."

She pressed a finger to his lips and sat up, then said softly, "No fault, Thor, no fault on your part. You two...you believed me, you investigated, you discovered the truth. No fault. But it's happening again. This time, Thor...this time, you must stop him."

She stroked his cheek; her eyes were immense on his...

And then his alarm went off with a jarring sense of reality and he woke up, bolting to a sitting position, reaching for the offending noise box to silence it.

He lay there for a moment; the dream had been so real he felt as if he could still smell the scent of Mandy's perfume on the air.

But, of course, he could not. He glanced at the other side of the bed. It was empty. As always. He and Janet had split up months ago and since then, he'd never brought anyone home.

He rose and headed to the kitchen of his Anchorage apartment, poured a cup of coffee from the brewer that was set for 6:30 a.m. every morning and walked out to the living room. Large windows all across the far wall gave him great views of the city.

People had a tendency to think of Alaska as the frozen frontier.

Sometimes, he wished it was nothing but a frontier filled with ice.

But Anchorage was a large, sprawling metropolis—perhaps not on the same level as NYC or Chicago, but it was still a thriving city with well over three hundred thousand residents, almost half the population of the entire state. The great thing about the apartment was it offered him a place to stay in the city— and have this incredible and majestic view of the white-tipped

Chugach Mountains rising in the distance—without having to live here full-time.

Thanks to his enterprising antecedents, his family owned a sprawl of property between Anchorage and Seward, a vast tangle of family homes, a horse farm and a sled dog–breeding facility. His sister and her husband managed the estate, so he could live in both worlds—he even had a pair of the best dogs anyone could ask for.

He was, he knew, a damned lucky man.

Albeit a haunted one, because he could never shake certain images…

Lucky, he told himself firmly. Every man out there, every woman, too, lived with things that tore at them.

He shook off the feelings the dream had wrapped around him.

In his free time, he could head out to what was still pristine wilderness. He could spend countless hours in the national parks and encounter wildlife like he could in few other places.

He wasn't a hunter. The only way he shot things in his spare time was with a camera. His day-to-day life had enough to do with violence.

He heard his cell phone ringing and headed back into the bedroom to snatch it up off his bedside table. His partner, Mike Aklaq, was on the other line.

"You ready, friend?"

"If you call standing in my shorts, drinking coffee and looking out windows *ready*, then I'm ready."

"Cool. You're always Mr. Early. Today I'm on the move. Coming to get you—got a call to rush it this morning."

"Oh?"

"Just hop in the shower quick. We're wanted down the road in Seward."

"What's going on?"

"Quit talking and shower. Put on something more than your briefs—Special Director Enfield will meet us at the airport."

"Airport? Seward isn't even a three-hour drive and only private—"

"Helicopter is waiting for us. I'm almost there. Hey, I'm pretty sure I'm along for the ride on this. Enfield thinks you're the man for this situation."

"What the hell is the situation?"

"I don't even know yet. Just get cracking, eh?"

Thor didn't say anything more; he hung up and hurried to get ready.

He managed a shave and shower in less than ten minutes. When he emerged—in his blue suit, Glock in the little leather holster at the back of his waistband—Mike was in his apartment.

"Hell, you must have been downstairs when you called," Thor said.

Mike grinned. "I was. I figured you had coffee—you always have coffee."

Mike was a big guy with broad shoulders and cheekbones to match. His dad was Native American; his mom had come up to Alaska with her father when he'd worked the pipeline. Mike was one of ten kids, all of them tall and good-looking. Thor and he made a good, colorful team, Thor often thought. He actually had Aleut blood himself. It was from a great-grandmother, while the rest of his family had hailed from Norway and it showed. He was bronzed just because he loved the sun; his hair was lighter than flax and his eyes were a blue only a little darker than ice.

They'd been partners three years in Alaska. Thor had done time in both the New York City and Miami offices while Mike had worked in Chicago and DC. Both of them had asked for the Alaska assignment—a different kind of job, for the most part. They were members of the criminal task division; in the three years they'd been working, most of their cases had been a matter of doggedly following clues and collaborating with Canadian and other US agents.

They headed downstairs. Thor knew that Mike was going

to drive—he had the official car and the keys. They both pre-
ferred their own driving.

"What time did Enfield call you?" Thor asked when they
were on the road.

"Six. He just said shake a leg and get to the airfield, and he'd
meet us there. Man, it doesn't bode well, him calling like that—
when we were due in anyway."

Thor nodded, feeling uncomfortable. The reality of the dream
had faded—in his field, nightmares occurred in the darkness
and the light. He'd always known that you had to live with the
losses as well as the triumphs. But his dad—who was still with
the Alaska State Troopers—had once put it into perspective for
him by noting, *You'll never stop the flow of evil that some men will
do, but each time you save one innocent, you make it all worthwhile.*

So he had dreams.

Nightmares.

He woke up and shook them off.

But now, the dream that had plagued him right before he had
awakened that morning seemed like some kind of a foreboding.

That feeling increased when they reached the airfield and
saw Special Director Reginald Enfield there, waiting for them.

Enfield was a solid, no-nonsense director—a good man in his
office. He'd had a kneecap shot out and knew he wasn't fit for
fieldwork, but he could analyze a situation like few other men
and collect invaluable information with his group of techs. That
he was at the airfield meant they were onto something serious.

Enfield shook hands with the men as he reached them, his
expression grim. "Your chopper is ready and waiting. You're
heading straight to Seward—there was a murder last night," he
told them.

Thor waited for him to continue. It wasn't as if Alaska was
immune to murder—far from it. According to reports by stat-
isticians at the Bureau, Alaska was the most dangerous state for
violent crime. Most of the time, murders were related to bar

fights, cabin fever, drug or alcohol abuse and sometimes, domestic battles.

Thor had a feeling none of the above applied; if so, the local
police or the state police would have been called in. Seward,
Alaska, had a full-time population of three thousand plus, but
tourism and the cruise industry could swell that number con-
siderably. It was still a quaint and beautiful town—one usually
loved by those who flocked to see the beauty of the nation's
largest, last-frontier state.

He realized they were going to have to ask questions and so
he began with the obvious. "Sir, I'm sure you plan on giving
us more. We're being sent to Seward over a murder? Aren't the
local police and the state guys on it?"

"This one isn't your typical murder," Enfield said. "We've
got agents headed here now from the DC area—it's that much
not your typical murder."

"We have a serial killer on our hands?" Mike asked.

"Let's pray that we don't," Enfield said. He glanced at Thor.
"An old partner and friend of yours is on the way here. You remember Jackson Crow?"

Thor was pretty sure that his heart missed an entire beat.

He hadn't thought about Jackson Crow in a long time, and
had only seen him in his dreams.

"Sure, I remember Crow," Thor said, hoping he sounded easy
and casual. "Great agent. We worked together a decade ago."

Enfield hesitated. "We don't know yet if there's any relation
here or not, but…" He paused and then shrugged. "You remember, of course, the Fairy Tale Killer? Tate Morley?"

Now Thor felt as if his heart had fallen into the pit of his
stomach.

"Of course I remember," he said huskily.

"Well, he's out."

"He's out?" Thor said, incredulous.

"Yeah. He escaped."

Thor felt a surge of anger. He'd been afraid of something like this—he'd said so when he heard that Morley had been transferred for his good behavior. Morley had been incarcerated first in the Feds' one supermax-security prison, but had then been transferred to max security and then a minimum-security prison—all over the last ten years or so.

Thor could never understand how the justice system allowed for such a thing to happen; the man's ninety-nine-years-plus life sentence hadn't been lessened by a parole board, and if he'd been left where he'd first been placed, escape would have been near impossible.

Enfield continued, "Seems he made himself a shank, got himself into the infirmary, stabbed a doctor and walked out easily in his white coat and with his credentials."

"When did this happen?" Thor asked.

He was pretty sure that he was speaking normally, that he moved like a sane man. But in truth, he was going insane inside, his gut clenching and his body on fire.

"He busted out yesterday," Enfield said. "He hasn't had a lot of time to get here, but it wouldn't have been impossible. Victim's name is Natalie Fontaine. She was a producer for bad TV—bad being my opinion, of course—filming in the area. Well, *Gotcha* is very, very bad. *Vacation USA* is okay. Anyway, I knew about Morley's case—everyone knew about him. I'm not sure he's the one responsible here. But Jackson Crow will be coming in along with a few of his people, and you and Mike will be taking the lead with him. He seems like an all right guy, willing to listen to the local power. Says that he doesn't know Alaska. You two do." Enfield stared at them and added, "He must be something with the main powers that be—the calls I received came straight from the top."

Thor was somewhat surprised that his old friend had the power to demand in on a case—and bring affiliates with him. But then, he'd heard about the "special" unit that Jackson headed beneath an enigmatic non-field agent named Adam Harrison. Very special. They even had their own offices.

Guys talked about it being the ghost-whispering-busting unit.

But jokes didn't last long. His old partner's team had solved too many cases to be considered a joke.

"You okay, Erikson?" Enfield asked.

Was he okay?

Hell, no. The Fairy Tale Killer was out. There was a murder in Seward that seemed to call for help cross-country.

He'd dreamed about Mandy and Jackson Crow.

Mandy was dead.

Jackson Crow was on the way.

Thor felt his sense of dread take hold again.

The Fairy Tale Killer might be back—in Alaska.

"Sir," he asked Enfield, "why would anyone believe that the murder in Seward might have been committed by the Fairy Tale Killer? Was the victim laid out to look like a princess— like Morley's victims?"

"No," Enfield said. "Like I said, we're not sure it's the same man—the display of the victim was completely different. But the Fairy Tale Killer is out there somewhere. I have all the information in your folders in the chopper. You can read on your way. Just trust me—the Fairy Tale Killer may not be at work up here, but this isn't your usual murder, not in any way, shape or form. God help you—you'd better catch this monster fast."

Clara Avery came to an abrupt halt.

She'd been running, running, running through the snow, well aware that her very life depended on reaching the Alaska Hut before...

Before the killer caught up with her.

Her breath sounded like an orchestra to her own ears; her lungs burned as if they were ablaze with an inner wildfire.

Even as she came to a dead stop, she felt the thunder of her heart.

It was the blood, the blood spattered over the snow, that brought her to the abrupt halt.

There was nothing like it, nothing like the color of blood on the snow on a sunlit day. It was a riveting hue, brilliant and vivid against the golden rays shooting down from the royal blue sky. It was spattered in a clump and led…just over the next rise.

She'd thought he was behind her.

The killer.

But…

She couldn't just stand there in indecision.

But she didn't know what the hell to do. Was the killer behind her? Or had he somehow managed to move ahead?

No, that couldn't be the case. She knew that he had seen her at the Mansion, knew that he'd still been in there, knew that he had heard her leave…

And was in pursuit.

There was only one way to go—forward. Yet she dreaded every step because now…

Now she followed a tiny trickle of blood over the next rise of snow.

Stopping had been a mistake; her body seemed to scream now at movement, even though she wasn't running. She was walking slowly and carefully over the rise…

And then she saw her.

Dead in the snow.

Amelia Carson, her raven-black hair as startling as the color of the blood against the sea of white around her. She was faceup, arms stretched out as if she were embracing the sun or making a snow angel beneath it.

With her arms only. She was in two pieces, cut in half at the waist.

Her lower body and limbs lay just a few feet away, a pool of blood separating them.

She had met Amelia Carson—celebrity hostess of many a short-lived TV show—only once. But she had met her. She knew her. And here she was...

Who else was dead?

She didn't even know! She'd seen the carnage at the Mansion and heard the movement upstairs and then the footsteps on the steps...

Clara stood still, her breath caught in her chest. She needed to think, but it seemed that her mind was as numb as her limbs. This scene had been displayed to strike fear and terror, to paralyze...

And it worked.

It was as if she was frozen.

Not your usual murder.

Though what was usual about murder?

And did it matter to Natalie Fontaine now that she had been victimized whether her death had been usual?

Natalie hadn't been killed for her money or possessions; she hadn't been sexually assaulted. It didn't seem that the act had been carried out in a fit of passion—though a great deal of thought and strength had gone into the execution of the deed.

Thor could still close his eyes and picture the room in the hotel, just as they had seen it, the body curled on the bed in what appeared to be a sleeping position. According to the medical examiner, the killer had strangled his victim before laying her out as he had, as if she were curled up...

Except her head was missing. It had been left on the dresser for all to see the minute the door was opened.

It was the head that had immediately assured the hotel staff that foul play had occurred.

The scene had been arranged like a tableau. It haunted Thor, and he knew he had viewed such a scene before...

In a picture? In an old crime scene photo?

Memory eluded him, so he'd made notes of all the facts.

Joe Mason of hotel security had come up because some neighboring guests had dialed the desk about a disturbance.

Mason had dutifully gone to the room, called out, tapped and banged for entry, and then, receiving no response, opened the door at 5:35 a.m.

The FBI offices in Anchorage and across the country had been alerted soon after.

The crime scene had filled with members of different law enforcement agencies and forensic experts. Most of their information had been gleaned slowly and painstakingly from Misty Blaine, Natalie's production assistant, who had just been getting dressed for the day in her room on the first floor. As experts learned more and more, they began to fear for others.

Law enforcement had to get out to Black Bear Island and find the people Natalie Fontaine had been scheduled to work with that morning.

A surprise had been planned for that day—not the horrifying one that had befallen her after all, but something gruesomely similar.

All in the name of reality TV.

And so Thor and Mike were now in a coast guard vessel, headed out to Black Bear Island.

"Ironic," Mike murmured.

Yes, it was. Misty Blaine had told them about the scene that was to be staged later that day. The cast of the Celtic American Cruise Line's Saturday-night performance on the *Fate* ship had been told that a film company would be interviewing them for their show *Vacation USA*. Unbeknownst to them, the cast was actually going to be featured on the show *Gotcha*, a knockoff of *Candid Camera* and *Punk'd*. Yes. Ironic.

The scenery that they encountered on their way was, in Thor's opinion, some of the most beautiful and spectacular to be viewed anywhere on earth. Crystal-blue waters, peaks of white ice rising, a sky clear and majestic.

And Black Bear Island before them.

The main problem with the island was that not even the newest, "smartest" smartphone worked out there.

Natalie Fontaine should have arrived that morning. Ready to greet her first interviewee for the day.

Four members of Natalie's film crew were also supposed to be out on the island already—cameraman Tommy Marchant, sound technician Becca Marle, hostess Amelia Carson and fabricator Nate Mahoney. Joining them should have been four members of the cast and crew of Celtic American Cruise Line's Broadway-style Saturday-night show.

Also expected were the island's caretaker, Justin Crowley, along with the property manager, or glorified housekeeper—his wife, Magda.

The film crew was not answering the radio. Neither were Mr. or Mrs. Crowley.

Thor chafed inwardly, dreading what they might find, anxious to get there.

He'd been chafing all day, he knew.

The dream; the nightmare.

And now Jackson was coming, as well.

He tried to breathe. Usually, being on the water was like receiving some kind of a cleansing balm on the heart and soul. Nowhere else in the world was the air so crisp and clean.

The wind was in his hair, the sun on his face, as the ferry approached the rugged terrain of the island. There were no roads here that allowed for cars—the ferry gave transport to snowmobiles and dogsleds, the only conveyances that could bring supplies to the island.

Pity that it was privately held; it should have been part of the national park system—a little piece of crystal heaven for the world to enjoy. It was elevated to such a height that even in summer, when the average mean temperature of Seward hovered around sixty degrees, there was often snow on the ground. Snow also covered the many peaks that rose in haphazard beauty here and there, dotted with crystal lakes, birds and animals finding refuge among them.

The island wasn't owned by the government or the public; it was the property of an absentee landowner, Marc Kimball, oil baron and Wall Street phenomenon. Enfield had assured Thor that Kimball had been advised via his assistant—a very soft-spoken woman named Emmy Vincenzo, who Enfield hoped had truly comprehended the severity of his message—that Natalie Fontaine had been murdered and police and FBI would be headed to the island in her stead. Kimball had rented the island and its properties out to Natalie Fontaine and her Wickedly Weird Productions, and was expecting their film crew this morning.

Thor had read the folder that had been left for him on the chopper to Seward—and listened to Misty Blaine's panicky and barely coherent explanation of the day of filming that had been planned. None of it was good; all of it added ridiculousness to what was already bizarre, gruesome and horrible.

As far as the film company, Wickedly Weird Productions, went...

To be fair, Thor conceded, some of their reality TV was interesting. They did shows that dealt with roadside diners, special tours that no one should miss and unusual cities or areas in the United States. He had a feeling that the real powers that be at the film studios loved history and travel—but they also needed to make money.

That meant that some of their shows were, at best, juvenile.

Those were the programs that were mostly popular with a young crowd—the kind of viewers who found fart jokes hilarious and also seemed to enjoy the distress or humiliation of those caught in the wheels of their "Gotcha!" factory.

Wickedly Weird Productions had rented two of the main properties on Black Bear Island. They included the Mansion, a sumptuous house that had begun its existence as a log cabin only to become something of a modern-day castle, and the Alaska Hut, a "rustic" lodge with eight or nine bedrooms, a huge living room, kitchen, dining room and expansive porches.

The crew was supposedly filming a piece on the Celtic American Cruise Line's entertainment venues—that's what the cast members from the ship believed, and what they thought they were signing release forms for. However, the real plan for the day had been to film a segment for their show *Gotcha*.

Other agents and the Alaska State Troopers were still busy going through procedure in Seward; dealing with the crime scene units, possible witnesses, hotel staff and more. But Thor and Mike and three officers were on this trail—hoping to find that Natalie's crew and the cast of the *Fate* were patiently waiting for their leader or already in the midst of filming.

In short, that they were all alive and well.

And it might be very difficult to figure that out.

Because, according to Misty Blaine, they were going to find a scene of carnage—blood and destruction—whether it was real or not.

Misty had supplied them with the file folder on the day's intended shoot. Wickedly Weird Productions had filled the Mansion and the Alaska Hut with bloody mock-murder scenes. Scenes meant to terrify the *Fate* cast. Of course, before anyone succumbed to their terror—the film crew would jump out and scream, "Gotcha!"

"Almost there," Thor heard. He turned around. Lieutenant Bill Meyer, with the Alaska State Troopers, approached them.

"We've got a storage shed near the docks," Bill told them. "We don't have any permanent force here—a good majority of the year, no one is out here at all. But the owner paid for the snowmobiles we keep. There's been trouble before, of course. One rush to the hospital. Wild party and a man wound up outside naked and nearly froze to death. Other than that...let's see, alcohol poisoning, a fight, one time a break-in...mostly, people behaving badly. Not lethally."

"Thanks," Thor said. He liked the cops he and Mike were working with—then again, he liked cops in general. His father had taught him from a young age that most were decent and hardworking and doing their best. Only a few were assholes—which he assumed was true in any vocation. Bill Meyer was a good guy, he knew. They'd worked together before. Bill had been assigned to Anchorage for a year and he'd spent many of his off-hours finding the down-and-outers and trying to get them help.

The Coast Guard cutter arrived at the one long dock the island offered. Captain Filmore handed out walkie-talkies to Thor, Mike, and Bill Meyer and his men, instructing them to keep close contact.

"There's no telling what you'll encounter, but..."

"We're not going to be meeting an army," Mike said.

"But, a strong man with some lethal weapons," Thor said. "Perhaps meeting up with a number of accomplices? Thing is, to escape the hotel security, it had to be someone who appeared to be part of the hotel staff. You didn't have just anyone doing that. You had someone with an extremely sharp weapon—and the strength to make that weapon cut through flesh and bone."

Someone who might not even be on the island—who might be chopping off more heads back in Seward.

Then again...

They might find a slew of dead right here. Oh, wait. They definitely *would*; he just hoped the dead were all mannequins and stage props.

"Yeah. Anyway, watch your backs," the captain said.

"Will do," Meyer murmured. Thor and the others nodded.

Ten minutes later, they were on the snowmobiles, headed to the Mansion. And then another ten minutes, riding through the snow that almost continually covered the island, brought them to their destination—and a scene of utter chaos.

Bodies strewn here and there, blood sprayed everywhere.

Thor hunkered down by the first body.

He looked up at Mike. "Mannequin," he said.

Bill Meyer had hurried on to another. "Fake blood," he called.

Thor moved through the downstairs, stopping at each body— it was all part of the staged scene that the assistant producer had told them about.

"Someone thought that this would be funny?" Mike asked with disgust.

"Apparently," Thor said, rising after his inspection of the last "corpse."

"They just had to come to Alaska," Bill Meyer muttered.

"Thing is," Thor said, "where is the film crew? And where is the cast?"

"Alaska Hut—or here, somewhere, in all this. I'll take the upstairs," Mike said. "We may find real bodies yet. Fellows? A hand?" he asked the state police officers.

They nodded and started to follow him up the stairs to the many rooms above. "Man, this is sick!" one of them muttered.

"I'm on the exterior," Thor said.

Near the top landing, Mike nodded.

Thor headed out. There were no snowmobile tracks leaving the Mansion, but there had been precipitation in the last few hours, so a path might have easily been covered.

He kept looking. And that was when he found the trail of footsteps.

And he began to follow it.

★ ★ ★

The Alaska Hut, the Alaska Hut… Help would be there, all she had to do was reach it…

It might be summer, but the snow was still thick on the ground on the rise. She was slogging through it, sinking and falling and trying to right herself. She staggered and fell—thinking of the times she had mocked horror movies, those that featured victims who seemed to trip over their own feet.

And then, over another rise, she saw it. The Alaska Hut.

Help! Help would be there.

Producer, director, fellow actors, makeup artists, costumers and…security! All she had to do was reach it.

But…was anyone left alive? She hadn't waited long enough at the Mansion to find out, not after she'd seen what she'd seen and heard movement upstairs and then…

Coming down the steps.

She'd run.

She should have stayed to help Larry.

No, how could she have helped him—against all that carnage? She didn't even have a plastic butter knife on her!

She could see it…the Alaska Hut…just ahead.

Hope allowed her to redouble her efforts. She heard the sound of her breath, and the squish of her footsteps as she ran the best she could over the snow. Her legs burned, her lungs were now pure fire.

Suddenly, a voice called out to her. She nearly lost her footing in the snow as panic swept through her anew.

"Stop! Stop now!"

Stop? What insanity was that?

She ran all the harder!

She didn't hear footsteps following so close behind her—she didn't hear or feel anything at first, just that pounding of her heart, the ragged and desperate rise and fall of her breath…

And then, it felt as if she was hit from behind by a semi.

She went down, flying, her face smashing into the coldness of the snow, a mouthful of the stuff nearly choking her. There was someone on top of her...or trying to drag her up.

And all she could picture was the blood spattered over the snow-white landscape, the woman cut in half...pieces connected by a pool of blood.

And so she fought. She fought with every remaining ounce of energy within her; she fought for her life.

CHAPTER TWO

Thor was at a disadvantage.

The young woman he tackled hadn't paid the least bit of attention to his words or his tap on her back, and she'd gone completely ballistic when he'd tried to stop her.

Now she fought and kicked like a banshee.

"Miss, miss, please!" he tried again.

Maybe she was deaf.

He was trying hard not to hurt her, but she had the athletic agility of a cat and managed a right hook to his jaw that would have done a boxer proud.

She was in panic—and he understood. But, hell! At some point she had to realize...

"Stop!" he snapped, catching her shoulders and straddling her. "Stop, please! FBI. Special Agent Thor Erikson. FBI! Stop!"

And then, she did, at last.

She stared up at him, blinked, her expression unchanging.

He immediately wondered who she was; the woman beneath him had fair skin, brilliantly blue eyes and a long mop of golden hair beneath the hood of her snow jacket—hair that tumbled around her face in wild strands after their altercation.

He found himself tensing; she looked like a fairy-tale princess, a Sleeping Beauty beyond a doubt. Her features were delicate and well-formed, her lips were full—more blue out in the cold than red, but rich and full—and he imagined they could curl into the perfect bow of a smile.

She wasn't smiling. She stared at him blankly.

"FBI," he repeated. "You're safe," he said.

She seemed to digest that for a minute and then breathed softly. "Really?"

He didn't get off her, but he sat back carefully on his haunches to produce his credentials.

She looked at them.

He had a feeling, though, that in her mind it was the fact that she was still alive more than his identification that convinced her of the truth.

"Really," he said.

She stared at him suspiciously—and stared at the documents again. "Thor?" she said.

"Yes, Thor. Thor Erikson."

"It sounds made up."

"It is made up. My parents—Heidi and Olaf Erikson—made it up when I was born!"

Again, she was silent for a minute, and then she said, "If that's the truth, perhaps you wouldn't mind getting off me? It's very, very cold."

He quickly rose and offered her a hand. She seemed to hesitate before accepting it, but then she did, trying to dust some of the snow off herself after she had risen. "Have you seen...?" she asked then.

"Miss...?" he began.

"Avery. Clara Avery," she said. "Have you seen... Oh, God. The film crew—they're all dead. Some at the Mansion...and now...here."

"Miss Avery, I was just at the Mansion. I'm afraid that you've been misled because of a sick prank. The scene you discovered there was completely fabricated by set and scene designers for an episode of *Gotcha*."

"No," she murmured. She blinked, as if unable to assimilate that anyone could do such a thing as a prank.

Frankly, he couldn't begin to understand it, either.

"Yes, Miss Avery. But, I'm sorry to say—"

"Even the—the body in the snow?"

He'd meant to tell her about Natalie Fontaine, but before he could do so, she had interrupted.

"What body in the snow?" he asked.

Her brows hiked up. "You didn't see it?"

"No. I saw you—I tried to get you to stop, to listen to me."

"You tackled me," she muttered, and she seemed to be aggravated and angry—at the film people or him, he wasn't sure, or maybe even herself—and apparently even more disgusted by the body in the snow.

"Where is this body?" he asked.

She pointed over a little rise of snow. "There," she said.

It was probably more of the horror created by Wickedly Weird.

"A body…um, two pieces," she said.

He didn't reply; he headed over the rise in the direction she had pointed.

Then he saw the drops of blood.

And then the dead woman.

A dead woman, in two pieces, as she had said.

He had witnessed pictures of a scene like this, too.

And then he knew what kicked in his memory.

The Black Dahlia.

This woman had been cut in two…and lain out just like the Black Dahlia. An unsolved murder; he had seen crime scene photos in one of the numerous classes he was always taking on criminology for the FBI.

He hoped against hope that this was another horror vignette by the *Gotcha* people.

But, as he neared the bisected body, and smelled the tinny scent of real blood, he knew that it was not.

He pulled out his radio and called back to the state police and Mike.

"We have another corpse," he said quietly. "A real one."

The city was filled with cell phones, PA systems, rapid response teams, computers, and all manner of tools and aids for investigation.

All of that was moot on Black Bear Island. Phones never seemed to work; the internet needed to be reconnected.

He had his walkie-talkie, and he had a corpse in the snow, and a woman standing so still she might have been a statue—except that she shook like blue blazes.

He shouldn't leave the corpse; he really shouldn't keep a witness standing there.

But there had to be something there that suggested how the killer had come and gone, what weapon or weapons he had used—and where the hell he was now. But there seemed to be nothing; just the victim, bisected, dead in the snow. Not enough blood for the young woman to have been murdered where she lay, so she must have been brought out here—and cut in half.

By what instrument? It wasn't easy to do—unless you happened to know how to use a French headsman's sword or a Japanese *samurai* sword, a machete or a chain saw. But a chain saw would have left little bits of flesh abounding around the body, like wood chips...

There were no prints in the snow. Nothing leading away from the disposal of the body. It looked as if the victim might have been teleported to where she lay.

It wouldn't take Mike long to get there. Thor carefully skirted the body and hiked over the little rise. The snow there was already trodden and thrown—it was where he and the shaking blond had wound up in their ridiculous tussle.

His jaw still hurt. The woman knew how to throw a right hook.

"So horrible!" she whispered, as if to herself and not to him.

"You went to the Mansion?" he said.

She nodded jerkily. "I told you that I did—and what I saw!"

He didn't know why—especially with his jaw still hurting—but he put his hands on her shoulders, causing her to actually look at him and heed his words. "And I told you. No one there is dead. Those are mannequins at the Mansion."

It took a second for that to register in her mind. He saw anger filter into her eyes. "It was all a joke for that ridiculous show *Gotcha*?" she demanded.

"Not all," he said quietly. "The woman in the snow is really dead." He hesitated. "Natalie Fontaine is dead, too."

Her eyes widened again. He realized just how striking she was then. The color of her eyes was blue, and yet a blue nothing at all like his ice color. Her eyes were deep and rich, almost a royal blue, and set against features with fine bone structure, arched honey brows and a perfectly straight nose.

Her face was flushed, of course. Reddened from their scramble in the snow.

"Natalie…and Amelia?" she whispered, as if the two women being dead was the most confusing possibility known to man.

"You knew them well?" he asked quietly.

"I had just met them. Still…"

"I'm sorry," he said.

"But, but my friends…are here. Somewhere. And if all the people at the house…if the scene wasn't real… I don't understand what's going on at all, but I know that my friends are supposed to be on the island somewhere. Cast mates, from the show we're doing on the ship. They headed out before me—they're here on the island."

The next sentences lay unspoken between them.

They are here. Dead or alive, no one knows.

The way she looked at him now, he wondered if she really believed that he was who he was—and whether he still might intend to kill her.

She seemed to shrink beneath his hold.

She lowered her head and inched back half a foot—as if anxious to be free from his touch.

Then she looked up at him and there was a hard strength that she'd forced into her features. "I came for *Vacation USA*. That's what the head of entertainment for Celtic American asked me to do. The other cast members—except for our ingenue, who is finishing up a previous engagement—came here ahead of me this morning. But that was a hoax, you're telling me? They were going to try to scare us half to death to film us for *Gotcha*. So those corpses at the Mansion weren't real. But, Amelia is really...dead. And Natalie Fontaine is dead, too. That is the real situation?"

"Yes, I'm sorry."

She swallowed hard and nodded.

"Miss Avery, have you seen anyone else here on the island—alive?"

She looked at him with alarm. "Oh, God! Oh, God, Simon... Larry... Ralph!"

She turned and started to run. He tore after her. He realized that she was headed for the Alaska Hut.

He didn't want to tackle her again. But he also didn't want her rushing into the building if there was a sword/knife/machete-wielding killer awaiting her.

"Miss Avery!"

She kept running.

No choice.

He caught her by the shoulders and they went down together again. She started to fight him but he gripped her hard.

"Wait!" he said firmly. "Let me go first—"

"My friends—"

"I have a gun. You don't!" he snapped.

She went still and nodded at that, probably realizing the folly of running into the unknown. Thor rose, not waiting for her to accept an offered hand, just pulling her back up with him. They were both covered in snow. He went first, moving with good speed through the soft snow. He heard her behind him. At the door of the rustic log cabin, he pulled his weapon, and then threw the wooden door open.

A flash of light went off.

"Gotcha!" someone shouted.

He assessed that six people were there, five men, one woman; the lone woman held a microphone, while one man held a large camera.

The woman dropped the microphone and screamed as she noted that he was wielding a gun.

"FBI," he said quickly.

From behind him, Clara Avery went tearing through, throwing herself into the arms of a tall blond man.

"What the hell…?" the man asked.

"Natalie Fontaine is dead," Clara said. "And…and Amelia Carson. She's dead—dead in the snow."

"No, no!" the woman in the group said, trying to ascertain how badly she had damaged the microphone she'd dropped. "No, it's all just for *Gotcha*. See the mic you made me drop? I'm Becca Marle, sound. It's—it's just a joke," she finished weakly.

A man at her side, slightly older, spoke up. "Tommy Marchant, cameraman, videographer… We're filming them. That's it. See, we got your cast mates before you, too—they also thought it was real. Maybe they decided to join in and scare us as well or…"

He desperately wanted his words to be true.

"No," Thor said harshly, holstering his gun and producing

his credentials. "No—the scene at the Mansion might have been for your show, but Miss Fontaine and Miss Carson are dead."

"Don't try to trick a trickster," one of the men protested. "What—are you from dial-a-stripper or something? Set up to play bad cop? Hey, don't mess with me. I'm Nate Mahoney, best young fabricator coming up the ranks. Trust me, I know I'm good. But it's for TV, it's for a show, a reality show."

Thor had to take in a deep breath. "The reality is," he said sharply, "that the two women are really dead."

They all stared at him, disbelieving.

"It's true!" Clara Avery said. "I saw Amelia."

Thor noted the grouping: the film people huddled together, and Clara in the arms of the tall blond man who somehow seemed to have "actor" written all over him. Another young man was next to him, and a third, solid man—closer to middle-aged—stood protectively by Clara, as well.

For a moment, they were all silent.

Disbelief began to change to confusion—and horror.

Gotcha. Great.

The sound of a snowmobile broke through. Thor turned. Mike—followed by members of the state police on their vehicles—were arriving at the Alaska Hut at last.

Thor pointed at the group. "Stay here, right where you are. Who else is here that you all know about?"

No one answered at first. They all just stared at him. No one seemed to comprehend the situation.

"Who else is here?" he demanded roughly.

"Um, um…the housekeeper. And the groundskeeper…the Crowley couple," the woman, fumbling awkwardly with the fallen microphone, managed to say.

"Get them, please. Bring everyone to the parlor," he said curtly. They all continued to stare at him.

"Now," he said loudly and firmly, adding, "Please!"

He wasn't sure if they moved or not. He turned to greet Mike and the others. Someone needed to draw a perimeter around the body—the body pieces—of Amelia Carson.

Forensic teams needed to get out to the island.

And they had to determine if a killer was in the Alaska Hut...

Or watching them all with glee from somewhere on the cold and windswept island.

Gotcha.

Sadly, death was the reality now.

Safe.

Clara had reached the Alaska Hut at last.

She wasn't alone—and she didn't need to be afraid. She was surrounded by policemen and FBI agents, and other scared and frightened members of her own cast and crew and the film crew.

She sat in a chair at the kitchen table, a blanket around her shoulders, a cup of hot coffee in her hands—and still she was shivering.

"Come, let's sail the Alaskan cruise, it will be different, it will be fun!" Ralph Martini, at her side, murmured. "Fun!" he sniffed. He glanced over at Clara and then winced. "Sorry," he said softly.

"No, it's all right—it *was* my idea for us all to work on this cruise," Clara said. She still felt like an ice cube even though the log cabin that was the Alaska Hut was well heated. She knew that the numbness was inside her. She was managing to speak, to sound somewhat coherent—and to take it all in.

The truth of everything was beginning to sink into her consciousness and comprehension. What was real and what was not.

The Mansion—where she had stumbled upon all kinds of horrors—had not offered anything real. She'd run from an imaginary foe when she'd left the place, too terrified to scream. Cameras had been shooting her movements. She shouldn't have been there alone, though. She should have been there with Natalie Fontaine.

Except she knew now that Natalie Fontaine was dead—but not among the carnage that had appeared to fill the Mansion. She'd never made it to the island. She was dead back at her hotel room.

Decapitated.

While the members of the *Fate* cast had traveled to the island—Ralph, Simon and Larry had come together. They'd arrived at the Mansion about a half hour before Clara. They had also screamed their way out and run to the Alaska Hut—only they hadn't stumbled upon the body of Amelia Carson along the way.

Cameras rigged at the Mansion would have captured first the terror—and then what was supposed to have been a laugh.

No one was laughing.

Because of what had happened to Natalie, Misty Blaine hadn't gone to the island, and Amelia Carson hadn't been there because she'd been dead, as well.

According to Nate Mahoney—who had spoken as if he'd become a zombie himself—it would have been a great crossover. The cast would have been featured on *Gotcha*, and then on *Vacation USA* as wonderful people who had come to work an Alaskan cruise, talking about why they loved the state so very much.

At the moment, Clara wasn't sure that she loved Alaska at all. But then, she was still in shock, she assumed.

"It really doesn't have anything at all to do with the ship," Larry Hepburn said, trying to speak lightly.

"That's right," Simon Green said. "This is someone—someone who hates reality TV. And, I mean, that's half of America. Some shows are cool—you know, where they save people or really give people jobs at the end. But, most of it…"

His voice trailed off.

"Alaska is beautiful," Ralph said.

Clara looked at the three men at the table with her. Ralph Martini, kick-ass tenor, star of many a Broadway, off-Broadway and off-off-Broadway show. Simon Green, new kid on the block, early twenties, thrilled to have his first speaking role/solo song in *Annabelle Lee*, the play they were set to perform on the *Fate* the following Saturday night. Larry Hepburn, tall, blond, bronzed—everyone's golden-hunk guy, leading man for the play.

They'd all worked the Caribbean and Mexico together on the Celtic American Line's *Destiny* ship—until a serial killer had been taken down aboard. Clara had known she was in danger on the ship, but she had never faced anything like this, nor had she stumbled upon a dead body then…a dead body in two pieces.

Not that the previous situation hadn't been awful. And naturally, after it had all happened, she'd wanted to go in a new direction.

When she'd learned about *Annabelle Lee*, her new path had seemed perfectly clear. Alaska! What could be more different from the sunny Caribbean? And the cast called for a middle-aged tenor in a great role as the father of the house—Ralph!—as well as two younger men and two younger women. Larry and Simon fit the bill perfectly for Ashley, the haunted husband, and Billie Boy, Annabelle's brother. Clara had gotten the role of Annabelle, the light and ethereal ghost still longing for life, while Connie Shaw, great dark-haired alto, was the young hero's new wife, having to deal with the ghost of the past—who just didn't want to go away.

Simon, heroically trying to save Clara's friend Alexi Cromwell when they were on the *Destiny*, had broken a leg in a fall down a flight of stairs on the ship. His injury was healing nicely, but since he was a song-and-dance man, it was great that this show only required a few ballroom-dancing numbers between the ghost and Ashley, played by Larry Hepburn. It made the part perfect for Simon while he continued working his rehab exercises on his leg.

It had seemed so good. And so they had all headed up to Seward. She'd heard about the beauty of Alaska for years from other performers with whom she'd worked. Clara had come as soon as possible—longing to see as much as she could of Seward before going into the long days and nights of rehearsals. She'd spent time at the museum, learning about the native people, the first Russians on the scene, "Seward's Folly," the quake that had devastated the area in 1964, and more. She'd been able to take a small local cruise to see the majesty of the glaciers, giant whales breeching, the power of falling ice…but there was so much more she wanted to discover. The wildlife, dogsled races, the raw geography of the area, Kenai Fjords National Park—everything that made Alaska so special and different. And, eventually, she would find the time, but then…

The time she had given herself just hadn't been enough.

Rehearsals had started, and then Celtic American had contacted her and some of the others about filming for *Vacation USA* and she had met with Natalie Fontaine and agreed to head out on the ferry and meet her at the Mansion, and then the blood and guts that had been fake and now…

Now the blood and guts that were real.

Simon, slim, young and earnest, reached over for her hand. "It's going to be all right."

"Yeah," Ralph said. "None of us blames you."

"Blames me!" she repeated, staring at him, her temper rising. "Blames me? For what? Hey—you guys were out of a job. The ship was being held for months. I found out about this opportunity and told you about it!"

"I could have been playing that new role on Broadway," Ralph said.

Clara felt the frown that gripped her brow. "That role is being played by Jeff Goldblum. I don't think you should have counted on it—no offense, Ralph. Mr. Goldblum does have one hell of a résumé."

Ralph sniffed.

"Hey—I'm happy. I'm out of the chorus," Simon said. He

smiled at Clara. "And I know I wouldn't have any role on Broadway!"

"That didn't come out right," Ralph murmured. "I'm sorry, Clara. Really. I mean, this is going to be okay. This doesn't have to do with us. This has to do with someone who really, really, really hates reality TV."

Clara was silent. She prayed it went beyond that. One woman decapitated; one woman cut in half. That seemed like a lot more than anger.

"Miss Avery?"

She looked up. It was the wall of an FBI man who had pitched her down into the snow—and scared her out of ten years of life. She realized that she hadn't been thinking FBI because these guys looked so different. He'd been bundled up in an official parka; now, he had doffed the jacket and he looked like a Norse lumberjack. He was Norse—he had said so. Norse American, obviously. He was very tall—possibly six-four or six-five—and definitely built like a logger. But then, she'd spent enough time with Jude McCoy and Jackson Crow of the FBI to know that they took their work seriously. They went to the gun range frequently, and they went regularly to the gym, since their strength and agility in the field could be just as important as tools of their trade.

"Your turn for the grill—I guess we come right after you," Ralph murmured.

She supposed that they would. The state cops who had arrived first on the scene with a second FBI man had stayed with the cast where they were grouped together at the kitchen table. Clara knew that, a little more than a hundred yards away, police, FBI, techs and whoever else, were still working on the crime scene. So far the living film crew on the island—Nate Mahoney, Becca Marle and Tommy Marchant—had been questioned at the Alaska Hut. Clara felt bad for them; she'd only met Natalie

Fontaine and Amelia Carson once. But that crew had worked with the two women hand in hand for several years.

Now, she wondered where the three of them had gone—or if law enforcement was purposely keeping them all apart.

Or, if they were lucky, and are already off this wretched island.

"Miss Avery?"

He had to repeat her name. She rose and followed him out of the kitchen. She passed through the dining room and the cozy parlor with its raw wood furniture and huge stone hearth to the office straight across from the kitchen.

There, Special Agent Thor Erikson indicated that she take a chair.

"You all right?" he asked her.

"Just great," she replied. "Nothing like being taken with a bunch of fake blood—and nearly plowing into a pool of the real stuff."

"If it makes you feel better, there was less blood than there could have been," he said. "Miss Carson was apparently killed elsewhere—and dumped where she was found."

Clara didn't react in any way; she didn't know the proper reaction to such words.

"Why were you running?" he asked her.

"Are you kidding me?" she asked.

"No," he said very seriously. "I don't kid under circumstances like this."

Well, of course you don't.

She almost snapped the words out, but refrained. "Surely, sir, you're aware that I was at the Mansion. And I believe you saw the Mansion?"

"Fake," he said. "All for the cameras."

"Yes, well, Agent Erikson, you knew that. I did not."

"But why did you run out here?"

"The hut is out here! I hoped to God I'd find friends at the hut, film crew, people—anyone other than whoever did that!"

"You acted as if you were being chased."

"I was being chased."

"By who?"

"By whoever killed all those people—I assumed," she said.

"Did you have reason to believe someone was after you?" he asked her, frowning.

"Yes, I heard something," she said.

"Heard it from where?" he asked her.

"In the house—the Mansion. I didn't go in very far. I came up the front steps. I opened the door to the mudroom, and then to the foyer. And then…then I stared in horror at what I thought was a massacre."

"You didn't call out—you didn't scream?"

She shook her head. "I was too—too terrified to scream. Then I started to back out of the house and…yes! I'm certain that I heard someone upstairs. And by what I saw…it might have been whoever did this. So I turned to run out and as I did so…yes! Yes, I heard someone on the stairs. So I started to run as hard as I could. I figured my only hope for help was the Alaska Hut. I didn't know what had happened at the Mansion, only that no one—no one living—was there to meet me. And I knew that part of the filming was supposed to be at the Alaska Hut. I figured people had to be there—someone who could help."

"What if you had found the same thing here, at the Alaska Hut?" he asked her.

She shook her head. "I didn't think like that. I couldn't think like that. If so…"

She didn't say it aloud. Maybe if she had allowed herself to think the worst, she would have just lain down in the snow to die.

"But you're positive you heard someone."

She nodded. "Pretty positive."

"Pretty positive."

Annoyance shot through her like a bolt. "Look, I'm not an

agent. I'm not a cop. I don't even like horror movies. I live alone. I like musicals and *The Big Bang Theory* and reruns of *Friends* and *Frasier* and *I Love Lucy*. I never even watched shows like *Gotcha*. I don't think I knew it existed. I was scared out of my wits and I ran, pretty darned certain that I'd heard someone and that if I didn't want to be minced meat, too, I needed to run and pray for help."

"We haven't found anyone on the island so far," he told her.

"Well, you don't think that I paused in running from the house to chop a sweet stranger in half, do you?" she demanded, her temper flaring.

"I thought you knew Miss Carson."

"I met her once. Yesterday. The first time I was out here on the island. I met with Natalie Fontaine and Amelia Carson at the Mansion and then Tommy Marchant—their cameraman— gave me a tour of the island in a snowmobile thing that seats two. I knew where the Mansion was in relation to the Alaska Hut. I know now where there are heavily forested sections of the island and where there's ice down to the water. I know the dock. That's what I know. To the best of my knowledge, you can reach this place by private boat and ferry and that's it. I'm not a regular at wild parties here, Agent. I sure as hell don't know what more you want from me!"

"Cooperation!" he exploded.

He leaned back in the office chair, hands gripping the sides. If he'd had longer hair, been wearing furs, and maybe had an Irish wolfhound at his side, he'd have looked like a conquering Viking.

"Miss Avery, as you might have noticed, there's a heinous killer at work here. Two people you knew were brutally murdered. I'd like every bit of help you can give me—if I'm not keeping you from an episode of *Friends* for too long!"

She stiffened as if she'd been hit by lightning.

"I'm trying to help! And don't you give me this holier-than-thou speech! I know how to cooperate. I've worked with the FBI, real FBI, good FBI agents! They were all there when the Archangel came on the *Destiny* and—"

"What?" He leaned forward suddenly, staring at her as if he was convinced that she had suddenly announced that she was the Archangel herself.

She foundered. "I was last supposed to be performing on Celtic American Cruise Line's *Destiny*. We never did do the show. There was a storm at sea and a killer on the ship and, thankfully, Special Agents Crow and McCoy and..."

Her voice trailed off. He was still staring at her.

"Look. I'm sorry. I know I'm being rude. I'm sure you're an excellent agent." She stopped speaking again. She was afraid she'd spill out something like *So, you see, I do know how agents should act! You think you're tough, huh. Yeah. You've got the look. You could be an actor. You'd make an excellent Viking. I could totally see you in* The 13th Warrior. *And you'd have been great in* Thor, *given Chris Hemsworth a run for his money—move over, Stellan Skarsgård.*

Thankfully, she managed not to speak.

They were both still staring at each other when there was a rap at the door and it opened a shade.

"Thor?"

Clara knew the voice; she knew it because she had depended on Jackson Crow as if he were a lifeline when she'd been on the *Destiny*.

The man in front of her blinked. He stood, recognizing the new arrival, as well.

"Jackson," he said.

Clara leaned back for a minute, just breathing. Then she, too, rose to her feet and turned to the door.

Jackson Crow had arrived. He was busy shedding a huge parka. He hadn't taken note of her yet; he walked across the room.

She'd expected that maybe such *manly* agents greeted one

another with stiff handshakes, but she was mistaken. The two embraced in a fierce hug instead.

"How the hell are you?" Crow demanded.

"Pretty good—until this morning," Thor Erikson said.

"Yeah, me, too," Crow said, and Clara was startled by the timbre of emotion in his voice.

She didn't know what was going on. Surely, neither of these men had known the victims.

They spoke quickly for a moment in a conversation that meant little to her—but seemed to make perfect sense to the two of them.

Crow first. "You heard, then."

"Didn't believe it. How the hell...?" Erikson responded.

"It's the system. Criminals who are incarcerated will find a way out."

"Damn, someone out there should have known—should have watched him better."

"Should have. But this isn't—"

"The same. No. I've seen the remains."

And then, it was as if they both realized she was in the room. They were an intriguing pair, both so tall, the one dark, the other so light. And while they were perplexed, there was also something solid and reassuring about them together—as if they were godlike sentinels of old.

Jackson Crow saw her then. "Clara, poor Clara!" He walked toward her.

She hurried to him and he encompassed her in his arms.

"I'm so sorry, so sorry," Crow told her.

Agent Erikson cleared his throat. "I'm just beginning to get the gist of this. You were all aboard the *Destiny* when the Archangel was caught."

"Myself and Jude McCoy, Miss Avery and her actor friends out there," Jackson Crow told him. Clara realized she was still clinging to Crow like a lifeline. She managed to straighten herself. Agent Erikson was looking from one of them to the other. He shook his head and sank back in his chair.

"Miss Avery found the second body," he said.

Jackson Crow looked at her. "Clara, Lord, how horrible. I'm sure you came up here to get away from what happened in the Caribbean."

Clara shrugged uneasily, aware that Erikson was looking at her as if she somehow brought bad things with her wherever she went, like an unlucky penny.

Jackson Crow looked over at Thor Erikson. "What else did you need from her?"

"Anything, everything. When you met with Ms. Fontaine and Ms. Carson, Miss Avery, were they nervous in any way? Did they make any comments of being afraid of anyone in Alaska? Did they suggest that they had received any threats?"

Clara shook her head. "We met. Natalie made sure I was aware that Celtic American was wholeheartedly for the cast joining her show for the segment—it would be wonderful publicity for them. I'd already signed all kinds of waivers for the show."

"Which, of course, you didn't really read," Thor said.

Clara stiffened but forced a pleasant smile. "Actually, I did read what I was signing. The problem is that you sign for the parent company, which meant they could use us in their silly *Gotcha* show, as well. I didn't realize it at the time—hindsight is wonderful. Have you never thought that, Agent Erikson?"

"I don't think there's anything more that Clara can give you right now," Jackson Crow said quietly. "Give her some time. If there is something, she'll think of it. And she will help in any way she can."

Erikson inclined his head.

"I need to speak with everyone involved," Thor said. He looked at Clara. "So, your entire cast was on the *Destiny* with another serial killer."

"Not the entire cast, no," Clara said. *We have one new member we haven't worked with yet—she's not on the island, though.*

She really hated the third degree she was getting. She might have been brutally victimized here—and the man behaved as if he was suspicious of a group of actors escaping the horror of what had happened.

"For your information, Special Agent, Simon was nearly killed himself while trying to save a friend of ours from the Archangel. He's still healing from a broken leg he received from a brush with the killer. He is certainly something of a hero. You have no right to treat us as if we're involved in this horror in any way. Ask Jackson—he sailed on the *Destiny*." Clara hoped her righteous indignation was cool and mature.

"Miss Avery," Erikson said, "I'm sorry for what you endured—in the past, and today. The Archangel is dead. Whoever is responsible for this butchery might have just gotten started. I'm doing my best to see that the killer is caught before someone else is murdered. If that offends your sensibilities, I do apologize. But it doesn't change the fact that you all are on an island where a woman has been cut in half. So, I will ask you all, bear with me."

How the hell could she be so right and this man still be able to make her feel like a plaintive schoolgirl?

She thanked God for her theatrical training and didn't react in the least.

"Shall I send someone else in?" she asked.

He nodded at her. "Yes, please." He looked at her keenly, and she had the odd feeling that he was inwardly shaking his head at her behavior—despite the fact that Jackson Crow had spoken so well for her.

Well, you're a jerk! she thought. *Tackling me into the snow—twice!*

"I will seriously try to help in any way that I can," she said evenly.

"There's always hope," he said. "Miss Avery, you do realize there's a key word in what I'm telling you," Erikson said.

She remained still.

"Island," he said. "Either the killer knows Alaska like the back of his hand, such that he knew how to get here, kill and leave—or he is still here, perhaps among you and your friends."

CHAPTER THREE

A deeper chill settled over Clara. That was it—of course. They were all suspects.

No, no, no. These men couldn't possibly believe that she—or Ralph, Simon or Larry!—could have had anything to do with these horrendous murders.

Jackson would quickly set him straight on that!

But what about the film crew? She couldn't believe they had anything to do with the murders. They'd all been too shocked, stunned and horrified when they'd been told that it was not a prank any longer, that people were dead.

But it was an island. And the only people here were her cast mates and the crew working for the film company.

And, of course, Mr. and Mrs. Crowley. The caretakers for the estate.

Had they been interviewed? Clara hadn't even seen them yet, though she knew that Larry had gone to find them and that they had been at the Alaska Hut.

But, no. Impossible. She'd met the couple. They were in their late sixties or early seventies. Mrs. Crowley was an attractive, slim, gray-haired woman who was, admittedly, a little odd. She was coldly—but perfectly—courteous while making sure people, even Natalie Fontaine, understood that even though she was there to oversee and facilitate, they needed to help themselves and be self-sufficient if they needed something.

Mr. Crowley matched his wife; he was still fit as a fiddle.

And strong.

Strong enough to wield whatever weapon it took to cut a woman in half?

No, Mr. Crowley was a little weird, but to her, at least, he had been as nice and cheerful as a department-store Santa.

She shook her head and let out a long breath.

Maybe she could be helpful—state some simple facts.

"It is an island, Agent. It's also heavily forested and has a ragged coastline with caves beneath ice and snow. It has little peaks and valleys. I believe there are survival caches left in various places around the island. Someone could be hiding out in the trees. Someone in a small boat could make it from the mainland in about fifteen minutes—that's about how long it took to get here when the captain the company hired brought me out. He left me at the dock, but there are a lot of shallows and little beachy areas around the southern and western sides. A person—or persons—could easily come and go from a zillion little hidden coves."

"Yes," he acknowledged. "Someone could be hiding. But we have had the state police out looking and they'll continue to look. The thing is…"

He paused and glanced toward Jackson.

"The thing is it might well be someone sitting among you like your best friend," Jackson Crow told her. "So, be careful."

"Exactly," Thor Erikson said quickly.

"Jackson," she said, "you know Ralph, Simon and Larry!"

"Yes."

"I trust them with my life!" she said.

"Thank you for your help, Miss Avery," Erikson told her. His ice-colored eyes fell on her and she realized that his tone had been somewhat gruff. Maybe, despite his calling in life, he'd been just as thrown as she by the girl they'd found dead in the snow. "Send Simon Green in, if you will."

"Certainly."

She turned to leave the room, but paused, looking at Jackson. She impulsively hugged him again and said, "Jackson, thank God you're here!"

And thankfully, he hugged her back.

"We'll catch this man, too, Clara, or die trying," he promised her softly.

She gave him a nod and a weak smile.

She didn't look back at Agent Viking, but left the room, ready to tell Simon that he was next in line.

Down to the last. Thor, with Jackson now in the room with him, just had two more interviews to go.

He was grateful for Mike—an amazing partner with whom he worked really well.

But he was even more grateful that Jackson Crow had arrived. Thor couldn't help his feelings and his hunches, and he couldn't help but believe that these murders were somehow personal.

And had to do with him and Jackson—and the Fairy Tale Killer.

The day had been ungodly long. While he and Jackson continued to speak with the others, Mike worked with the state police.

No one knew why the phones were down. The techs believed a phone line had been cut somewhere, but it would take a very long time to find out how and where. Of course, phones and electricity went out on the island often enough without help from a criminal mind.

The radios had just been gone. Taken. How or when, no one knew.

The television worked via satellite, but the internet system on the island had been through the phone company and was thus down, as well.

The island had been, for all intents and purposes, cut off.

Thor was good at reading people. At seeing ticks and nuances, the fall of someone's lids over their eyes, the way they sat—many little things that gave away a liar.

But it seemed—so far—that everyone was telling the truth. Becca Marle, a woman in her early thirties, was athletic and he had the feeling she was usually competent and capable of handling her mic and sound system on her own. She had short dark hair and a muscular, almost square shape, which made him, naturally, wonder about her strength. But, she was still stunned when they spoke; she broke into tears every few seconds, as well.

Tommy Marchant was the oldest in the group, maybe forty-five or fifty, tall with a slightly protruding middle, graying hair and a sun-wrinkled face.

He'd spent most of the interview shaking his head. "Natalie. I've worked with her—on one project or another—for nearly twenty years," he'd repeat now and then. He'd wince, and shake his head again. "Can't believe it—can't believe it."

Nate Mahoney had been the most interesting of the film crew in his initial interview. He couldn't seem to wrap his mind around the fact that the deaths had been real. He talked about being a fabricator. He could make almost anything appear to be something else. "But, these days…well, there are unions and all, but I hang around to fix fabrications, of course, but also to deal with props and help out. Film…and TV! So fickle these days. The blood and guts were all my inventions. Great, huh. Oh, God, how terrible now. The fake has become the real. I mean, I'm good at what I do, but…wow. I don't know much about self-defense. I'm scared. Should we be scared?"

Thor had told him that he needed to be vigilant, alert and

wary—and, of course, to report anything at all to him or Mike immediately.

He thought about Becca Marle again. She had spent most of the interview crying. She was so distraught she hadn't even thought to be afraid for herself, but, he imagined, soon enough, she would. Of the seven main members of the Wickedly Weird Productions team, she and Misty Blaine were the two surviving women.

The *Annabelle Lee* cast had been talkative—maybe because they all knew Jackson Crow already. Jackson's appearance was a good thing. While Thor felt that talking with Clara Avery had been somewhat of a challenge, it had been easy, thanks to Jackson, to gain trust and a comfortable rapport with the three men.

Now...

Mr. and Mrs. Crowley.

"Their name just had to be Crowley," Mike murmured, bringing the pair in. Neither Jackson nor Thor responded and Mike added, "Crowley. You know—like Aleister Crowley. The satanist."

"Yeah, we know about Aleister Crowley," Thor told him, managing a grim smile. "But, hey, it's still a pretty common last name."

"Just don't think we needed it here!" Mike said. He hesitated and added, "And they're weird! Remind me of that painting—*American Gothic*, I think it's called. Or those movies you see where the old folks are raising a tribe of cannibals who feed off travelers."

"Mike, there aren't that many travelers out here—a family of cannibals would starve pretty quickly," Thor told him.

"They're still weird!" Mike said.

He'd been to the toolshed and around the Alaska Hut with the couple while Thor had interviewed the others.

Although the police and forensic crews had been scouring the island, the how of the crime here remained a mystery. No weapon could be found; no hiding place. Of course, with not much blood at the site of the body, Thor hadn't needed the medical examiner to tell him that Amelia Carson had been killed elsewhere, and brought to be left in the snow for discovery. But how had the killer gotten her there—and gotten away—without being seen?

Unless he was among those in the house.

Ralph Martini, Larry Hepburn and Simon Green vouched for one another; they had come to the island together.

Thor had found Clara Avery running through the snow himself.

That left the film crew—unless the three actors had gone crazy and started chopping people up together, a scenario that seemed unlikely.

And then there were... Mr. and Mrs. Crowley.

According to Ralph, Larry and Simon, the first people they had seen were the film crew, when they had—screaming bloody murder over what they had discovered at the Mansion—run into the Alaska Hut. Apparently, Mr. and Mrs. Crowley had been in on what was going on.

Of course. The film crew had signed saying that they would make sure every last piece of fake blood was cleaned up, every bit of fabrication was taken away and the Mansion was left as it had been.

But the members of the film crew had arrived at the Alaska Hut at different times. And no one had seen Mr. or Mrs. Crowley until they'd been there at least twenty minutes or so.

Now Mrs. Magda Crowley sat across from him. She looked stiff and dignified, wiry and fit in jeans and a turtleneck sweater, and still—as Mike had commented—somewhat reminiscent of *American Gothic.*

"Mrs. Crowley, you're aware of the dead woman found in the snow, of course."

"Of course," she said humorlessly. "My husband and I are older—we're not deaf or stupid."

Touché.

"Where have you been all morning? You're not deaf or stupid so you must know that since you live here, you definitely fall into the suspect range," Thor said flatly.

Jackson cleared his throat.

But Magda Crowley seemed to like his tone.

"Working, Agent Erikson. Preparing meals. Justin and I live up at the main house, but we came out here early—about five forty-five this morning. We were to leave the house—my pleasure, with the way those film people rigged it up yesterday!—so that it was prepared for the people to come in and see all that fake blood and gory stuff. Justin and I have been in this house since that early hour. We made sure this place was fitting for more filming, for meals. We freshened the bedrooms, we cleaned and prepared. Period. That's it. Those film people showed up one by one, and then they laughed their asses off waiting for those actor boys to come screaming through the snow. Got to admit, they were kind of anxious when Miss Fontaine and the hostess didn't come over with the boys. After they all laughed at scaring the actors so badly, they started to argue about whether or not to head over to the Mansion, but someone said something about waiting for Clara to show up and that's where everything was when I started to hear the commotion going on. You'd showed up with that Clara girl and that was the first I knew that anything whatsoever had gone wrong."

"You and Mr. Crowley were together all the time?" Jackson asked.

"What? Joined at the hip? No. I was making biscuits. He was making beds," Magda Crowley said, looking from Jackson to Thor. "Good cop, bad cop?" she asked.

"We're not cops," Jackson said.

"That's right…you're federal men. Well, you know, this is Alaska," she said.

"I do. I'm from Alaska, Mrs. Crowley," Thor told her.

"You ought to be out there finding out what happened to that poor woman, not in here, hammering at hardworking folks!" Magda told him. She wagged a finger at Thor. "I could see something like this coming. I could. All this reality! People sitting in front of the boob tube watching other people behave badly. It's horrible—just horrible. I'm darned sorry that people were killed, but am I surprised? Hell, no! It was a matter of time."

"You didn't see or hear anything unusual?" Thor asked.

"What the hell would you call unusual? If I'd walked by that poor girl I'd have just kept on going—you saw what they did to the Mansion, right?"

"Thank you for your time, Mrs. Crowley. If you think of anything…if you see anything suspicious or can help us in any way—"

"It will help a hell of a lot if everyone just gets off the island!" she said. She stood up and started out. "I guess you want my husband now?"

"We do," Thor said.

She sniffed and left. Mike poked his head back in. "She's something, huh?" he whispered. "I'll get the husband. They should both be watched—hell, who knows this island better than those two?" Mike stepped out.

Thor looked at Jackson. Jackson was grinning. "Cranky."

"Cranky, yes. She doesn't look much like a conspirator in any kind of demonic cult," Thor said.

"And we both know looks can be deceiving," Jackson reminded him.

Justin Crowley walked in then.

It was, Thor knew, a mistake to go by looks or any preconceived notion. The man, however, seemed like the most likely suspect. He was like a weathered rock—strong against whatever might come. He also had a hard, rather sour expression—he might have a heck of a lot more bulk than the farmer pictured in the painting *American Gothic*, but he looked just as grim.

"You couldn't just talk to me and the wife at the same time?" he asked. "And how the hell long are you going to keep all these people here? Now you got all the cops and whoever traipsing in and out all day, too—hell of a thing to get these floors picked up now and everyone wanting coffee and more."

"Perhaps you won't begrudge people coffee, when they're trying to find out who killed a young woman who won't have the opportunity to work again ever," Jackson said.

"I don't begrudge them coffee—they can have all the damned coffee they want. Ain't my coffee. Film people paid for all that's in here. They just need to start taking care of themselves a little. Where's this, where's that? You don't have any of this kind or that fake sugar? This is a quiet place, most of the time. People rent it out and come and go, but there's a time limit on it, you know?"

"No time limit on finding a murderer," Thor said. "So, did you see anything unusual—besides the setup by the film folks," he put in quickly. "Did you hear anything, did you see anyone else on the island anywhere?"

Justin Crowley waved a hand in the air. "It's a private island. We know when people are due out on the ferry. Hell, just 'cause it's Alaska, doesn't mean we're not like the rest of the world! Sometimes, yeah, kids like to come out here from the mainland to the 'rich people's island,' and bring girls and beer or cheap wine, but they don't stay. We got grizzly bears in the forest and they are mean—especially the momma bears when they got cubs. If kids come, they hang out in the water, hug to the coves. In winter, you can get iced in, so no one comes then. We got generators, the missus and me, because it can freeze like a mother here and the electric can go. Did I see anyone

else today—no, I did not. Did I hear anything—no, I did not.
I didn't know one damned thing about the girl in the snow or
the woman killed back in Seward until you all came out here
today. And that's a fact—and there's nothing I can say or do to
help you. I wasn't looking out for anyone to be on the island.
I wasn't paying much attention. We were just getting ready for
the film people, sprucing this place up. Hadn't been rented out
in a while. It wasn't dirty, but it's like anything else. You don't
use it, somehow you still have to clean it anyway." He leaned
forward suddenly. "Don't you think we'd like to help you? We
live here—survive here. Thinking some maniac who likes to cut
people in half might be running around isn't a good thought,
not for my wife and me. We're a little old to be hitting an over-
crowded job market!"

"People don't always realize what they might know when
something first happens," Thor said. "After a while, you might
remember a sound or a moment or something out on the ice.
I'm pretty sure that whoever did this had some knowledge of
the island."

"Something might come to you later," Jackson said. "It doesn't
matter how small."

"Sure. So, what's happening now? You're not leaving the wife
and me out on this island alone with a killer running around?"

"No, we won't be leaving you alone," Jackson said. "You'll
have forensic crews going through everything at the Mansion
through the night."

"You and your wife are sleeping here?" Thor asked him.

He nodded. "We were planning to, anyway. Natalie Fontaine
hadn't been sure how it would all go. We were prepared for her
crew to stay at the Alaska Hut, too."

"Someone will be here," Thor assured him.

Justin Crowley nodded and set his hands on his chair. "Then
I guess 'someone' can talk to me anytime they want. You finished with me for now?"

"Yes, we are. Thank you, Mr. Crowley," Thor said. "And you know, of course, that we have search warrants that allow us to search every inch of property here, including your personal space?"

Crowley smiled. "Feel free. We're too old for any personal kinky stuff, so it will be kind of boring, but, hey, go for it."

Crowley left the room. "Hm," Jackson murmured. He looked over at Thor and grinned. "Sometimes, the older, the kinkier."

"Please, Lord, don't give me any mental pictures!" Thor told him. He leaned back in the chair and rubbed his eyes.

"What do you think—seriously?" Jackson asked him.

"Seriously—don't paint any mental pictures!" Thor said, and then shook his head, looking at his old partner. It had been over a decade since he and Jackson had worked together. They'd been good partners—great partners, really, even knowing what each other was thinking most of the time. They had an unspoken rule: there was no sense in doing what they were doing if it fell short of real humanity. They tended to be by the book and courteous until they couldn't go by the book and courtesy just wasn't in the cards anymore.

"I think that they can search this island for days and miss nooks and crannies," he told Jackson. "I think that the film crew and the Celtic American people were taken completely by surprise. Then again, the group from the ship are actors, and the film crew are in 'reality' TV. As for Mr. and Mrs. Crowley—they're either cantankerous from too much cold or just downright creepy."

"Do you think someone else is on the island?" Jackson asked him.

Thor hesitated. "There has to be someone else—or, at the very least, a cache somewhere out here. There's not even a speck of stage blood on anyone in this house. And yet... I still believe that one of them had to have seen something. Because, at some time, Amelia Carson was killed here or brought here. We know

that. We go backward from there." He looked at Jackson again.
"I can't help but believe that Tate Morley is here somehow. That
he is out there on the island. And he's watching us."

They weren't being offered any means off the island—not yet.

And it had been hours, or so it seemed. Hard to tell in Alaska
in the summer—the sun never seemed to really set. Clara didn't
wear a watch, but she knew that lunch and dinner had come
and gone.

State police—ready to draw their weapons at the drop of a
hat!—watched over them. The crew of Wickedly Weird Productions had been brought to the entertainment room in back
to wait while she, Ralph, Simon and Larry were in the parlor.

They'd all had sandwiches, provided by the police officers.
They'd been offered power bars and fruit. Ralph had complained
a bit about not having a proper dinner as time had gone on, but
she didn't think that he was even hungry.

It was a nice enough waiting area. The fireplace was huge
and the room was done with stone and natural wood. The sofas
were worn, plush leather. While the entertainment center was
out in back where the TV people were gathered, there was a
smaller screen in the living room.

There was no stopping the media; while neither the police nor
the FBI had given out any particulars, the news that producer
Natalie Fontaine and celebrity TV hostess Amelia Carson had
been murdered was plastered all over the screen.

Every news channel was broadcasting the information. Reporters interviewed other guests and employees at the Nordic
Lights Hotel. They spoke in serious tones.

Not one of them missed the opportunity to say that both
women had now become part of the sensationalist television
they had promoted during their lives. And while a man named
Enfield gave a press conference along with the chief of police,

neither let out the information that one woman had been beheaded and another had been cut in half.

Law enforcement was doing its best to see that the murders
did not become speculative gossip.

After the third or fourth program, Larry had suggested they
watch a music channel.

They had all quickly agreed.

She and her cast mates had talked for a while—a little awkwardly, since a uniformed man watched them at all times—and
then they had grown silent. It wasn't a bad silence; they were all
comfortable with one another. They were not only part of an
ensemble cast, they had lived aboard the *Destiny* in close prox-
imity, and knew each other very well. Larry and Ralph were
now partners, living together, close as could be.

And, she thought, afraid. They were all scared. Every now
and then, she caught her cast mates looking at her. Though they
were on edge, they were men—and the killer had targeted two
women.

But even she could distance herself a little. The two women
killed had been with Wickedly Weird Productions.

She was not.

Becca Marle was. Clara had heard a bit of a few of her conversations with Tommy Marchant and Nate Mahoney. They
were anxious. They wanted off the island.

Becca didn't. She felt safer here than she would elsewhere.
She liked the armed policeman watching over her amid a sea of
cops and the FBI men, who were in the house, as well.

Clara wished that Jackson was out there with them. But now,
of course, he was with the man she thought of as Agent Viking.
She hoped he was taking charge; she certainly felt more secure
when he was with them.

"It's good that Crow is here," Ralph said.

"Definitely," Simon agreed.

Larry grinned. "I don't know. That Thor guy looks pretty

tough to me. We're going to be all right." He patted Clara on the knee. "Hey, don't go wishing you were back in NOLA. Bad things can happen anywhere. Wait—very bad things did happen out of NOLA."

She frowned, looking at him. She couldn't help it; she did wish she was back in New Orleans. She had been born there, grown up in the French Quarter; her parents were there, and her younger brother was getting his master's at Tulane. Home would feel good right now. Actually, New Orleans was where she'd gotten to know Jackson Crow and his wife, Angela, and where the "Krewe of Hunters" had been formed in pursuit of a killer on a high-profile case.

And when they'd been on the *Destiny*...

Her friend Alexi Cromwell had been there, and the cast of *Les Miz* had been large—lots of friends. When they were nervous, they'd stayed together. They'd kept working.

Hell, they'd polished their nails and done all kinds of mundane things.

She reminded herself that it had really only been a matter of hours that they'd been here. Long hours, but not a full day and night.

People had died—horribly.

There'd been a few minutes when she had tried to convince herself that the whole thing was an episode of *Gotcha*. Natalie Fontaine would come walking in and announce cheerfully that wow! They had all been really gotten. Special Agent Thor Erikson would prove to be an actor/stripper and the whole thing would have been a farce in extremely bad taste.

She couldn't pretend at all anymore—if she'd ever been able to convince herself of such a thing. Jackson Crow was here now. She knew this was real.

"Yeah, you know, this isn't right," Ralph said. "Not right, and not fair. I'm reminded of *The Importance of Being Earnest*, by Oscar Wilde, you know. Wonderful quotes from that story. 'To lose one parent may be regarded as a misfortune. To lose both looks like carelessness.' Well! To be in one horrendous situation is certainly misfortune, but how in God's name did we all manage two?" he demanded. "Carelessness?" he asked.

Clara, Simon and even Larry stared at him.

"Sorry, sorry, yes, no one's fault. Still..." Ralph let his sentence end with a sigh. "I'm scared again, I guess. God! I hate being scared."

"We're all right, Ralph. Really. We're all right," Simon said. "Two things. Both of the people killed were with reality TV, not with the cruise line or the cast. And the other—both people killed were women."

He winced, looking over at Clara.

"It's okay, Simon. I had noted that fact already," Clara told him drily.

"Hey!" Simon said suddenly. "Someone else is entering the fray!"

Clara had been curled on the sofa in the parlor beneath the large picture window that looked onto the porch; at Simon's words, she sat up and looked out.

Someone was coming. A handsome man of about forty-five, medium height, with dark hair. He wore a double sweater beneath a thick parka and he was followed by a police officer and a shivering woman carrying a notepad.

The police officer with him appeared to be frazzled.

The woman looked as nervous as a cartoon rat. She was pinched thin, and wore a parka as if it were a heavy burden upon her.

The officer, the man and the pinched-rat-like woman were stopped at the door by another state policeman.

They talked for several minutes. At last, the officer in charge of guarding the front door opened it and let them in.

For a moment, the man looked around the room. Then his eyes lit on Clara. He looked confused, as if he'd seen a mannequin come to life or a ghost return from the dead. Then he smiled. "My God—it's you!"

Clara didn't have the least idea of what he was talking about.

"Hello?" she said politely. She stood; the others had done the same at the man's entry.

He smiled—a great smile, she thought.

"I've seen you! You performed a Sandra Dee character in *Grease*! You were amazing. I was a little bit in love!" the man said.

"I was in *Grease*," Ralph murmured.

No one paid him any heed.

"Thank you. And I'm sorry. Who are you?" Clara asked.

"Marc. Marc Kimball," he said. "I own Black Bear Island."

"Oh!"

The murmur seemed like a chorus line—it so perfectly seemed to come from everyone in the room at the same time.

"How do you do?"

"It's a pleasure."

"Marc Kimball!"

The greetings seemed to sail around the room.

Clara didn't speak. She felt uneasy.

She loved being a performer. She'd received good reviews and bad reviews. She'd been in casts when she'd been the low man on the totem pole, totally ignored by those seeking autographs. She'd had lead roles and signed and greeted people, as well. She'd been panned by critics and loved by critics and she'd been careful never to take any of it too seriously.

She'd been admired before, and that was nice. But something about the way this man looked at her made her feel queasy.

She tried to smile. He hadn't done an evil thing to her.

"It is you, right? I wasn't sure about all the particulars, but I heard about *Annabelle Lee* being done on the *Fate*. And, I knew, of course, that Wickedly Weird Productions was using cruise line employees for *Vacation USA*, and I had hoped..."

Simon sprang to her rescue.

"We're all in the cast, sir. Ralph Martini and Larry Hepburn are the gentlemen over there. I'm Simon Green. And, yes, our leading lady is Clara Avery," he said.

"Miss Avery!" Kimball said, walking over to her. He took her hand. She wanted to scream and wrench it away.

He kept looking at her as he spoke again. "I came as soon as I heard about what happened. They said it wasn't necessary, but... I'm so glad I'm here."

CHAPTER FOUR

"We've got to make some decisions," Mike said, joining Thor and Jackson after the initial interviews. "The groups out there are getting restless. I've still got the film crew separated from the caretaker couple and from the ship's cast, but they're all getting edgy. One of the film guys was saying he was already getting cabin fever, but his mate, Becca Marle, was saying that she didn't want to be out of sight of a cop for the next year. Are we getting them all on a boat or holding them here for a while longer?"

"None of them is under arrest," Jackson said. "We can't really hold them."

"Some of them, I think, want to be held," Mike said. "Until we find this guy."

They were all silent. It was a dream that a killer such as this could be caught quickly. Many serial killers had reigned for more than a decade before being caught.

Some never were.

"Do we have anything else? Anything more from the forensic crews?" Thor asked.

"Still not a damned thing," Mike said. "Doc Andropov has taken the body—says because of the snow, he'll try to run some tests and pin down time of death. He says that from the data he has so far, she was most likely killed early this morning, murdered and bisected elsewhere. Said it's hard to be certain because the body was packed in snow, but Amelia Carson was with the film crew last night until about eight. I just got off the walkie-talkie—talked to Detective Brennan, head on the case via the state police—Bill Meyer patched me in from the Coast Guard cutter. This is the info I have from him. They were all staying at the Nordic Lights Hotel on the waterfront in Seward," he said, pausing to look at Thor and reminding him, "Where we arrived at the investigation into Natalie Fontaine's murder this morning."

Thor nodded. "Yes, we knew that they all had rooms at the hotel—and, of course, that other than Misty and Miss Fontaine's remains, none of them were in their rooms. Thanks to Misty, we knew what we'd find at the Mansion as well, and that a ship's show cast were out here, too. That's why we came to the island as quickly as possible."

"I spoke with Brennan this morning, too," Jackson said. "Director Enfield put us together. He's the man who made arrangements to get me out here as quickly as possible. Seems like a really good cop—solid and quick. Enfield likes him."

"He is a good cop. We've worked with him before," Thor said.

"Anyway," Mike continued, "Detective Brennan has been interviewing everyone he can find at the hotel. There's a desk clerk who was on the night shift, Arnold Haskell, who says that he saw Amelia Carson up and heading out before it was really light."

"Sunrise was just about 5:00 a.m.," Jackson said.

Thor murmured, "That would have meant that morning twilight began at about 3:00 or 3:30 a.m." In Alaska, summer days were long. Because of Alaska's position near the North Pole, it was really only truly dark from about midnight until three or three thirty at this time of year. Some people couldn't stand the continuous light in summer and the equally continuous darkness in winter. It didn't bother Thor at all, but he knew that visitors often found themselves wide-awake far too much of the day.

"Did she leave the hotel?" he asked.

"He wasn't sure. She stopped to demand to know why there was no coffee in the lobby yet—he told her that coffee didn't go out in the lobby until six thirty and that there were little pots in the room. She was not nice to him." He hesitated, looking at Jackson and Thor and grimacing. "Apparently, after speaking with other employees at the hotel, Detective Brennan came to the conclusion that while Natalie Fontaine was all right—not someone you gush over, but all right—Amelia Carson was not liked by many people. She was all smiles in front of a camera, and self-centered and entitled off camera. Brennan told me that a maid at the hotel said Amelia treated her as if she was little better than a cockroach."

"Are there cockroaches in Alaska?" Jackson wondered aloud.

"There are cockroaches everywhere," Mike assured him.

"In every way," Thor murmured. "So what did Haskell say? She did or she didn't go out?"

"Haskell didn't know—she bitched at him and he did his best to be polite and explain hotel policy and she walked off. He didn't wait to see if she went up the elevator or out the door— he had paperwork and he went back to it. He did say that she had been on her cell phone, bitching at someone on the other end, even while she was bitching at him about there being no coffee for an hour or so."

"People don't usually kill people and cut them in half just because they're not nice people," Thor said.

"May depend on who they're not nice to," Jackson said.

"True," Thor agreed. "So, by this time frame—if everyone was right about time—it seems that Miss Fontaine was killed first in her hotel room. The killer apparently kept it down, though he was heard, which brought security up. Somehow he killed her, left that room as it was and got out of the hotel with what-ever he used to sever her head, and went on to meet up with Amelia Carson, catch her, kill her, slice her in half and deposit her on the snow."

"And no one saw him," Jackson said.

Thor met his eyes. "I doubt that," he said softly.

"The body was behind that snowbank or rise," Mike said. "If Miss Avery had run about fifty feet parallel from where she was, she might not have seen it."

That was true.

"Hey, I work with you daily, Thor, and you're confusing me," Mike said. "You think that there is someone on the island, and you also think that someone saw something?"

"This is all too clean—too neat," Thor said. "And here's an-other thought. What if there are two killers? One who decapi-tated Natalie Fontaine, and one who chopped Amelia Carson in half?"

"Two killers?" Jackson asked. "God, I sure as hell hate to think that there might be two such demented people in the area."

"There really are a lot of people who hate reality TV," Mike said. He was serious, Thor realized.

"You just change the channel," Jackson said. He was looking at Thor, and he knew that they were both thinking the same thing. Tate Morley—the Fairy Tale Killer—was out. These kill-ings had not been carried out in any way like the murders he'd committed before. But he had been locked away for over a de-cade. He might have changed.

Then again, Thor and Jackson might have such traumatic memories of the man's previous victims that they were ready to pin anything on him.

Realistically, there were new sociopathic and psychotic kill-ers cropping up constantly.

"Our director doesn't believe that the Fairy Tale Killer, Tate

Morley, could have anything to do with this," Thor said to Jackson.

"He basically believes that the display of the bodies is too different," Mike added.

"Well, what do you think about the people we've interviewed?" Jackson asked. "They all appear to be horrified, devastated and so on—except for Mr. and Mrs. Crowley, who didn't seem to feel one way or the other about the dead. But I've seen cold-blooded killers pass lie-detector tests without blinking."

"We do have a cast of actors here," Mike pointed out.

"Three men who left their hotel together and arrived together. And Miss Avery," Thor said.

"Maybe they were angry—someone filmed them from the bad side," Mike suggested.

"I know that group," Jackson told them. "I know Clara well."

Thor swiveled around to look at his former partner. "You know her well? How well?" It wasn't any kind of an accusation; he knew that Jackson Crow had married another agent. His old friend had never been anything other than the monogamous type. Everything about the man had always been straightforward and honorable.

"An agent I worked with in New Orleans and the *Destiny* is engaged to one of her best friends. I was looking out for that group of performers and working with McCoy when the Archangel was on the ship. I knew Clara and some of the old cast were coming up here to sail the Alaska seas after what had happened there."

Thor knew about the Archangel case.

And knew that the Archangel was dead. He couldn't help but wish that the same was true of the Fairy Tale Killer.

"So where do we go from here? Send the TV and ship's entertainment people all home?" Mike asked.

"None of them actually has a home in Alaska. The film crew

would go back to the Nordic Lights Hotel. Where has the cruise line lodged its performers and staff?" Thor asked.

"Celtic American uses the Hawthorne—about a block down from the other hotel," Mike said. "I'm assuming that, from what we've seen, the killer's focus is on the film crew and not the Celtic American people. They had to have been targeted—I think we'd all agree on that."

"They're scared. All scared," Jackson said. "I'm pretty sure they'll all do anything we ask."

"You're thinking about keeping them here?" Thor asked.

"One of them may be in on this somehow," Jackson said.

"So they need to be watched," Thor said flatly. "This TV and entertainment group could still be in danger, here on the island. So, here we are. We all know the situation, and why we're looking for a needle in a haystack. Even Miss Avery pointed all this out. Parts of the island are covered with thick woods. There are massive glacial cutouts along the shoreline allowing for a multitude of caves and caverns. State police and forensic crews have been out there all day. But the geography here is such that someone might well be hiding on the island. We haven't found a damned thing. They haven't been able to give us anything from the mainland."

"It's only been, what, about ten or twelve hours?" Jackson asked.

"About twelve since we walked into the hotel this morning," Mike said. "And a long time for scared civilians. We're going to have to arrange for Coast Guard vessels to get everyone back." He looked over at Jackson, and shook his head slightly. "Director Enfield said you weren't taking over the investigation from our end, but—are you?"

"No," Jackson said. "I don't know Alaska. You two do."

"But you had to have been on a plane two seconds after reports of Natalie Fontaine's murder hit the system this morning."

Jackson nodded. "Yeah. I guess I was waiting to hear about

something. Natalie Fontaine's murder coincided with Tate Morley escaping. I guess I'm here on a hunch," he said, looking over at Thor.

Thor smiled ruefully and told his old partner, "I had a dream last night—a nightmare, I guess one would say."

That caused Jackson to look at Mike again and speak carefully.

"About the Fairy Tale victims?" he asked.

"Yep."

Jackson nodded. "Yeah, well, I woke up shaking myself."

Mike was studying Jackson. Jackson looked back at him. "You're about to ask me something. As in, do I head a unit of ghost hunters?"

Mike grinned. "No, actually, from all I've heard, you do lead a unit of ghost hunters."

"What were you going to ask?" Jackson asked him.

"Sioux?" Mike said.

Jackson shook his head. "Cheyenne. My dad's side. Why?"

Mike shrugged. "No reason. Except pride. Inuit, here. Old Thor's got some in him, too, though you'd never know it from that thatch of platinum on his head. It's just that I think our Native American people are more open to—well, shamans have always been more into reading dreams than priests. Quite frankly, the Russian influence here brought about a ton of people belonging to their Orthodox church, but…hey, maybe it's the in thing these days to be more native. Anyway, if you two saw something in a dream—hell, I'm up to believing it."

Jackson laughed. "Honestly? I had a Scottish grandmother more into the spiritual world than my dad's family, and whatever works, that's what I believe in."

"That works for me. But let's just lay it all out. Bring me up to speed," Mike said. "Thor and I have been partners for a few years. I know his intuitions are damned good, and I don't know if he's listening to the spirit of an ancestor, a voice in the wind or his own gut. I just know that it's worth paying attention to the voices—wherever the hell they come from."

Thor looked at Jackson. "You dreamed about Mandy Brandt," he said.

Jackson nodded.

"Same dream," Thor said.

"I see you in front of me and I see him, Tate Morley, and the way he was standing over Mandy Brandt. I hear the sound… you shooting Tate Morley. And I can't help but wonder if we wouldn't be plagued by the dreams—if it wouldn't have been better—if we hadn't done the right thing and called for an ambulance."

"Bad situation," Thor said. "My aim wasn't great—I couldn't get a clear shot. We're taught to shoot to kill in situations like that. I meant to kill him." He paused; the moral quandary there was pretty brutal. He and Jackson could have finished the man off, or just let him die; even if they had just let him die, in reality, it would have been murder.

But would it have been better to have committed that murder—and possibly saved lives in the future?

"The question is moot," Jackson said, as if reading his mind. "Neither of us knew if the injury was or wasn't mortal at the time."

That was true.

Except he knew that both he and Jackson had been afraid since Tate Morley had been convicted and incarcerated. Prisons were expensive from the get-go; trials were staggering. Executions somehow cost the state far more than incarceration for life—*except that incarceration for life sometimes didn't mean life!*

"This can't be Tate Morley," Thor said. "He escaped in Kansas—I'm sure the authorities are all over finding him there. Everything about this is different. Different method of killing. Totally different display. Except…"

"Except for the theatricality," Jackson said.

"Exactly," Thor agreed.

"You mean—staging the bodies? The way they were left to horrify whoever came upon them?" Mike asked. "If I remember the newspaper reports right, the Fairy Tale Killer left his victims looking…as if they were sleeping."

Thor nodded. "Yeah, but I can't help thinking about the way we saw Amelia Carson in the snow—she reminded me of the Black Dahlia."

"Whose killer was never caught," Jackson said quietly.

"And finding Miss Fontaine this morning?" Mike asked.

"Other killers in history have left their victims in such a state—historically, when traitors were decapitated, their heads were left on poles for all to see—like Natalie Fontaine's was in her room today. Dozens of movies have been made about such murders as that of the Black Dahlia—and those who have been decapitated. There was a Florida killer who left the head of one of his victims on a shelf to greet the police when they came. It's shock value—it's theater."

"In other words, you think that Tate Morley might still actually be the killer, just taking a new direction on his theme?" Mike asked.

"It's a wild shot," Jackson said.

"Whether it is or isn't, we have a monster on our hands. I do believe that the remaining members of the *Gotcha* film crew are in danger," Thor said. "I don't know about the cruise ship cast—but they were here. Who knows?"

"Who knows what might have happened if you hadn't gotten here?" Jackson asked.

"I think we were supposed to get here," Thor said.

"You mean because of the dreams we had. Because of Tate Morley?" Jackson asked.

Thor shook his head. "We were meant to come here to see Amelia Carson's body laid out the way it was. This killer is like the Fairy Tale Killer in one aspect. He delights in what I believe he sees as his theatricality."

"His reality," Mike said drily.

There was a knock at the door. One of the state police officers opened it when Thor called him in. The man looked perplexed. "Um, Mr. Kimball is here."

"Who?" Jackson asked.

"Marc Kimball. The owner of Black Bear Island," the officer said.

The three men quickly headed out of the office and down the hall to the parlor.

Thor had seen pictures of Marc Kimball in the papers; he hailed from Santa Monica and his main residence remained there. He'd purchased Black Bear Island about a decade ago from another private owner. The man seemed to have a Midas touch; his stock market investments had allowed him to buy into oil rigs, and more investments enabled him to buy in more and more until he owned an oil company outright along with a number of other diverse companies.

He seemed smaller in person than in the papers. Medium height, medium build, brown hair, pleasant features. He seemed way too cheerful for anyone arriving at a site where a woman had been found severed in two, but he was talking to Clara Avery, and he was smiling and laughing.

"I wanted to buy the cruise line and try to hire you on for every show ever done!" he was telling her.

To her credit, Clara looked incredibly uncomfortable and overwhelmed. Her costars appeared to be baffled. A skinny, frazzled young woman stood slightly behind him, hugging an agenda, bored and anxious at the same time.

"Mr. Kimball?" Thor said.

The man stopped speaking and turned to him. "And you are?" he asked sharply.

"Special Agent Thor Erikson, in charge of the murder in-vestigation on the island," Thor said, keeping his voice level.

"Ah, yes. Of course, well, please tell me that you plan to bring this awful affair to a speedy resolution!" Kimball said. He smiled suddenly. It wasn't a warm and cuddly smile. It had as much ice in it as the glaciers that loomed around the bay.

"Indeed we do. Why are you here?"

"I own the place!"

"I'm aware of that, Mr. Kimball. But at the moment, you have rented the property out," Thor said.

"Not to the FBI."

"No, sir, to Miss Fontaine. Who is dead. This is an active and intense investigation. I'm sure that my colleagues in Seward have spoken with you," Thor said.

Thor kept his features carefully controlled. On the one hand, he was irritated. He'd met with men like Kimball before. They were accustomed to walking into a room and taking charge. Money seemed to cow many people.

But he was also amused. Thor was flanked by Jackson and Mike. He knew that they were a formidable trio and that Kim-ball was sizing them up. His zillions of dollars and attorneys could probably make many things happen, but at the moment, he was just facing the three of them.

"As this horrible thing occurred on my property, I came here as quickly as I could. I am an absentee landlord most of the time, Special Agent—Erkson?"

"Erikson," Thor said pleasantly.

"I'm here to help in any way that I possibly can. I bought Black Bear Island because I truly love it. I know it like the back of my hand. I can help you search the island. I can tell you where little caches of survival supplies can be found. There is a great deal I can do to help you."

Thor became aware that, despite the state police officers as-signed to keep everyone separated, the crew members from

Wickedly Weird Productions were also in the room watching what was going on—gaping a bit.

Along with the police officers.

He figured it was natural. Kimball was almost as rich as Donald Trump, or so the media claimed.

"Thank you again, sir. We appreciate your offer," Thor said. "I believe, for now, the best we can ask is that you settle into your home for the night. Officers will be on guard. In the morning, they'll be renewing their search of the island. If you're willing to help with that search and remain with the officers, it will be deeply appreciated."

"However," Jackson said, stepping forward, "we have to warn you that we don't know what we're dealing with—"

"She was chopped in half!"

He turned. Becca Marle was standing there, staring at Kimball in awe, and yet horrified anew as she voiced a fact of the murder.

"The point is," Jackson continued, "any search for this killer might be highly dangerous, and perhaps, for a man of your standing, not advisable."

Kimball wasn't a fool. "Agent... I didn't catch your name, sir. You are...?"

"Assistant Director Crow," Jackson said.

"I believe you're *not* referring to the importance of me in the world, sir, but rather to the fact that you don't believe I'm capable of defending myself. I am happy to advise you that I am a crack shot and have trained with some of the finest experts in the world in martial arts and various other forms of self-defense. I can provide documentation as to my prowess, if you wish."

"We'll take a signature on a waiver that you've chosen to work with law enforcement," Thor told the man.

"I shall sign that I insist," Kimball said. He looked at his watch. "Are you gentlemen aware of the time?"

Actually, he wasn't, Thor realized.

"Nearly midnight," Kimball continued. "Perhaps, with your

permission, I can assign rooms to the people here, since—even with my boat and the vessels the Coast Guard can surely supply you—it might now be better for them all to remain in the safety of so many fine officers for the evening. Let them have a few hours of sleep, at the least."

"We did have the place rented… We thought we might stay tonight. That, of course, was what Natalie wanted to do," Becca said, her words ending in a sob.

Nate might be an extraordinary fabricator of stage and scene works, but he hadn't seemed much like the demonstrative type, and he probably wasn't; he awkwardly patted her shoulder.

"There are eight bedrooms and my master suite," Kimball said. "And of course, the kitchen room, where Justin and Magda stay. I can't accommodate all the officers here—"

"The officers are here to be on duty," Mike interrupted. "We spell one another, and chairs and couches do us just fine."

"As to the others, I believe it is up to them. We can arrange for the Coast Guard to get everyone back to Seward," Thor said.

"But, they're welcome to stay!" Kimball protested.

"I'm glad to stay," Becca said. "Delighted, really. We have law enforcement here—it's safe!"

"Whatever," Tommy said with a shrug.

"Lord, yes!" Ralph said, looking over at Clara, Simon and Larry with excitement.

Clara was silent; she didn't look at all thrilled.

Simon murmured, "Sure."

And Larry said, "At this point and this time, yeah."

"Wonderful!" Kimball said. "I'm assuming that during the day you've availed yourself of the kitchen, so you're aware that the place is always well stocked. There are four rooms to the left of the kitchen and dining area and four beyond my office. Perhaps assign an officer to each hallway? Though I doubt that a cowardly killer would darken a door here, not with so many fine agents of the law in residency."

His tone and word choice were irritating beyond measure.

But his offer made sense; it was late. They'd been debating themselves the best course of action.

"I gotta say, we've been up since the crack of dawn," Nate said. "I mean…that doesn't mean anything against what happened to Natalie and Amelia, but…"

"Everyone is exhausted," Simon said quietly.

"Perfect," Marc Kimball said. "Please, help yourselves—with the kind agents' permission, of course—to the rooms. They are all fully stocked with toiletries and robes, and each has its own bath."

"We did rent the place," Tommy said. "So…"

"Trust me," Kimball said, irritation slipping into his voice despite his smile. "My contracts have clauses that give me full control of this property at any time—I believe this situation calls for my breaking any agreement with Wickedly Weird. But, that's no matter, is it? The police and the federal government are here and I believe we all agree this is best for the remainder of the night. Please. Get some rest. This is terrible, terrible."

Everyone waited after he spoke. Thor realized they were all looking at him.

And waiting for him to agree.

"At this point, it's as each individual wishes. If you are all in agreement, then we'll thank Mr. Kimball for his hospitality. Everyone here does need some rest," he said. "We'll make arrangements to get you back to the mainland in the morning."

"I can take first watch among us," Jackson murmured.

Thor was too tense to think about sleeping, but Jackson was right. When you were worn-out, you rested. That was the only way you were good to function at full capacity when you were needed.

But he wasn't ready yet.

"Mike," Thor said, "there are seven guests here—that leaves

a room. Get some sleep on something comfortable. I'll wake you in a few hours."

Mike nodded.

Thor watched as, beneath Marc Kimball's gleeful eyes, everyone moved to claim a room for the night.

He realized that Marc Kimball wasn't just pleased that his suggestion had been taken. He was nearly elated.

And he wasn't just watching *anyone* as they chose rooms.

He was watching Clara Avery.

Thor barely knew the woman. Their acquaintance came from the fact that he'd tackled her in the snow. But there was something about her...pride, humor, intelligence—the sense to be afraid? Thor hadn't realized it at first, but he was intrigued by her.

She was a friend of Jackson's—that was it.

Either that, or...

It wasn't that he was so worried about the young woman, it was that he was so annoyed by Kimball.

The man might be richer than a god, but there was definitely something discomfiting about him. As the others walked off, he heard Kimball's skinny little assistant or secretary ask, "Marc, what about me?"

Marc Kimball didn't seem to hear her.

"You have a room, little lady," Ralph told her pleasantly. "We only need three of those on our side. And, heck, we're theater people. We can sleep anywhere," he said proudly. Then he asked, "What's your name, dear?"

"Emmy. Emmy Vincenzo," she said.

"Nice to meet you," Ralph told her.

Kimball paid them no heed.

He was still watching Clara Avery as she walked down the hallway. She'd shed her parka and outerwear and wore a soft blue cashmere sweater. Long blond hair tumbled down her back and she moved with grace despite her exhaustion. She was a stunning woman, which Thor had noted before. She turned to look back at him—or maybe she was looking for Jackson. But she caught his eyes and she smiled grimly and nodded, as if grateful to rest now, and do so securely.

She looked like a princess, a fairy-tale princess, a Sleeping Beauty.

The thought sent a jolt of white ice shooting through him.

She wasn't part of the Wickedly Weird Production Company. She wasn't the one in real danger here—not from what they had seen so far. It was a stretch for him and Jackson to believe the Fairy Tale Killer might have come here, a complete stretch. This man was out for the reality TV people.

Sleeping Beauty... She would have made a perfect Sleeping Beauty...

He turned away but he saw Jackson watching him. And he knew—just as his old partner knew—that he'd die before anything happened to Clara Avery.

CHAPTER FIVE

The Alaska Hut wasn't a bad place to stay, Clara thought. Actually, while its appearance was rustic, the decor was artistically warm and comfortable.

And her day had been...

Sitting. Going from the living room or parlor to the dining room or the kitchen. Of course, before that, she'd run like a crazy person through the snow.

Stumbled upon the corpse of a woman she'd met.

Bisected.

So, maybe it wasn't such a ridiculous thing that she was both exhausted—and wide-awake.

She lay on a comfortable bed—the mattress was Tempur-Pedic, she was pretty sure—staring at the ceiling. She couldn't have begun to sleep in the darkness then and so she had the television on. The police, she understood, were still trying to find the problem with the phone line and so actual communication was out of the question unless she borrowed a police radio.

She lay there grateful that she hadn't mentioned being filmed for *Vacation USA* to her parents as of yet—if they heard about the murder in Seward and on the island, they wouldn't know that she was in any way involved.

Her mom never said *I told you so.* She just worried about her. She hadn't been so bad before the events on the *Destiny*; in fact, she had loved coming aboard the ships Clara had worked on for the last several years.

She wished, of course, that she worked at a local theater—or in New York. She had gone to an audition in New York, as her mom had suggested, and found herself in a cast on a ship. But she had loved sailing and kept at it.

She had great friends. Like Ralph and Larry and Simon. And Alexi, who she missed terribly. But Alexi was in love now, and Clara was delighted for her. Agent Jude McCoy was great; the two were wonderful together.

It was just that Alexi wasn't here.

She shivered suddenly, then wondered why. Not that it was a strange thing to do, with what she had stumbled on that day, but she knew that wasn't the reason.

She was shivering because of Kimball. Something about him made her feel slimy. His flipping hand had seemed slimy!

He hadn't come on to her rudely. He hadn't really come on to her. But she knew he intended to do so.

Maybe she'd been the only woman in the room who had appealed to him. Becca Marle was cute enough, but she was a husky girl and didn't dress in any way to enhance herself. She kept her hair short and boyish. It was probably best for her work, and Becca might just love working sound the same way Clara loved the theater.

And she truly loved the theater—being in it, seeing others in it, musical theater, comedy, drama, anything. It was good; loving theater had made her a fairly sensible and strong person. First, the *don't call us, we'll call you* element meant she knew how to be rejected without taking it personally.

And that had helped in life when her last—actually, her

only!—serious relationship had ended. Steve Jenkins had chosen a way of life over her, and she'd seen it and ended their relationship.

She sat up restlessly.

Right now, she even wished Steve was with her. He hadn't been a bad person—he just hadn't had any ambition in life other than hitting the clubs, drinking and sometimes taking his flirting a little too far. He was a talented actor who had lost too many good jobs by not being able to get out of bed in the morning. At first, his grin, his casual attitude and his charm had all swept her away. And then...

Then she'd paid the rent one too many times, picked him up outside a bar one too many times, and she'd realized that they both wanted different things and it wasn't going to change. She'd headed to New York City, gone to a number of auditions, and been called for a touring company aboard a ship.

She'd been sailing ever since. Her brother asked her once if she was trying to sail away from herself.

Clara rose. She'd shed her jeans and sweater but not her tank top or underwear; she wished she had a pair of her flannel pajamas, but while she'd found toothpaste, soap, shampoo, razors and anything a guest might have needed—including condoms!—in the bathroom, there were no nightclothes. She was, in truth, just really grateful for the toothbrush.

She found a flannel robe with *The Alaska Hut* embroidered over the pocket. Slipping it on, she cracked open her door. She didn't recognize the policeman in the hall, but she assumed he was the next shift. He smiled at her and tipped his hat.

"Are you all right, miss?" he asked.

"Fine, thank you. I just thought I'd make myself some tea," Clara told him. She hesitated. "Would you like a cup of tea?" she asked.

He smiled. "Thank you very much. I'll be on watch here in

the hall. I just came on—don't need anything. You're safe, you know."

"Yes. Thanks."

She realized that she'd been unnerved and horrified—but not really worried about her own safety. With everyone telling her that she was safe, she was getting worried!

Maybe she'd put a shot of whiskey in her tea.

The kitchen would have made a great advertisement for every new appliance out there. One machine made almost every form of coffee or espresso known to man. Another made customized fizzy drinks.

One just heated water—but a nearby box offered the widest assortment of tea she had ever seen.

She chose a chamomile and set it and the cup in the proper slots in the machine and folded her arms to wait the sixty seconds it would take.

That's when the unease settled over her—and she was certain she was being watched.

Kimball—it was creepy Marc Kimball! she thought.

But it was a different kind of feeling.

She looked over to the log-framed kitchen doorway.

She was grateful she wasn't holding a cup of scalding water; she would have dropped it.

She almost screamed.

But it was as it had been earlier; she was too stunned, too bone-deep terrified, to make a sound.

Amelia Carson was standing there. She was wearing jeans and a fluffy pink parka, the hood over her dark hair. She reached out a hand, as if she were trying to touch Clara.

"Please," she said simply.

Clara blinked.

It had to be a joke; the whole thing was still a joke, and somehow they had gotten Jackson Crow in on it. She was being filmed. Amelia hadn't really been dead in the snow...

She heard a sob.

And then, she heard the officer in the hallway call out to her. "Miss? Everything all right?"

The vision before her evaporated. Clara didn't look away.

She didn't blink.

The image simply…disappeared into mist and then into nothingness.

Where Amelia Carson had been, there was just air. Beyond that air, his face obscured by the living room shadows, was the FBI man, Thor Erikson.

She just stood there, afraid to move, afraid to give away any indication she had just seen a dead woman before her.

But Thor Erikson came striding toward her then and she saw the intensity in his ice-blue eyes. He caught her by the wrist and spoke with a deep, ragged voice. "You saw her, too."

Clara blinked at last.

They'd said that the *Destiny* was filled with ghosts. Clara knew that Alexi had seen them.

And maybe Clara had sensed things or thought that she had, but…

Alexi had seen and spoken with the dead—so she had sworn. And when she had talked about it, sometimes, Clara had actually believed in ghosts…

But…

She had never seen a full-blown image such as this, as if the dead woman in the snow had come back to life.

In one piece.

"I saw her. But you saw her—I know that you did. I saw your face. She spoke to you. What did she say?"

Clara shook her head. "I don't know what you're talking about."

"Amelia Carson."

"Amelia Carson is dead. We saw her—both halves of her," Clara said.

His eyes really could be so cold, and like ice, they could burn.

She was afraid. Afraid as she had never been before.

And too afraid to admit what she had seen.

"Let me go, Agent Erikson. Let me go, please!" she said.

He released her instantly. She forgot all about tea and hurried back to her room, closing the door behind her.

Then, just as quickly, she opened her door.

If she saw anything again, anything at all, she was going to scream. She was happy to have the door open, knowing a police officer walked the corridor.

But could a police officer save her from the dead?

Or was Amelia dead? That was it—the whole thing was a hoax. A massive hoax. She'd seen ridiculously expensive things done by *Gotcha* before. They'd hired a whole crew of actors to pose as police officers; Jackson—hard to believe as it was!—had been coerced to come in on the prank; and in the morning, Amelia and Natalie would be there, laughing at a prank done in the worst taste known to man!

She was overtired; her nerves were completely on edge.

They couldn't get Jackson Crow in on such a ridiculous scheme, could they?

Jackson was head of the Krewe of Hunters. The Krewe stepped in when the unusual seemed to be part of the horror that was happening.

The unusual...such as ghosts.

No, no, it couldn't be real. It was smoke and mirrors, it was trickery—it was the magic of film.

She wasn't even sure what she was doing when she went back out.

The officer in the hall spoke to her. "More tea?" he asked sympathetically.

She ignored him and returned to the kitchen. Thor Erikson was sitting on a rustic stool by the island counter. He looked at her, frowning.

She walked back over to the stove area, tired, and yet suddenly determined that she was going to have the truth—whatever it might be.

"I have to admit, you look good. And them getting Jackson in on it—coup d'état!" she said.

"What?"

"You know, trust me, I've been acting for years. I am not a household name, but I love what I do, and I survive at it. If that's what you're looking for, there are much better ways to get ahead. How did you come into doing this? You're really in great shape—that usually means a stripper trying to break into movies. Hey, I have plenty of friends who have tried it for a while—good money, I've been told. Allows you lots of time for auditions. But, honestly, using this *Gotcha* thing to try to break in? What, you're trying to be a television personality? Whatever, I have had it! This is it—it ends here!"

He stared at her, frowning, his expression confused at first, then incredulous, and then hard and angry.

Maybe he could make it as an actor.

"Miss Avery, I believe that even an actress accustomed to dealing in the world of fantasy should have grasped this situation by now. I don't know—"

"Stop! Both of you!"

Clara knew, before she turned, who was speaking. An eerie sensation snaked up the length of her spine and radiated throughout her.

She's here again. Amelia Carson.

But she stood there for just one moment, looking at the two of them pleadingly.

Then the officer who had been in the hall was at Clara's side, shaking his head. "Miss… Agent Erikson? Is something wrong?"

Before either of them could answer him, it seemed that a crowd had formed; Clara realized that she'd been all but shouting when she'd spoken to Agent Erikson.

They appeared like a very strange Greek chorus. Ralph, Simon and Larry bundled in the Alaska Hut robes, the cops in uniform, a very sleepy Agent Aklaq still in rumpled plain clothes and then the film crew—Nate, Becca and Thomas—coming up from the other hallway. Magda and Justin Crowley were there, looking very grumpy in their own robes.

Obviously they'd been sleeping just fine until the commotion in the kitchen had wakened them.

Clara realized that Jackson was there, as well, alert—ready to come to her defense if necessary.

"What? What? What's going on?" Mike demanded.

Thor Erikson looked at Clara as if she had just caused the roof to collapse.

"I believe Miss Avery is having trouble sleeping," he said.

"Miss Avery! Oh, my dear Miss Avery!"

Marc Kimball had joined them—his dressing gown was more elegant than the rest, made of an exceptionally fine fabric. And, of course, the minute he was out, his little assistant, Emmy, came running out as well, and more state police seemed to materialize from nowhere.

Clara felt like a deer caught in blinding headlights.

Marc Kimball broke through to set his hands sympathetically on her shoulders. "I'm so sorry. What can I do to help you through this ghastly night?"

She tried desperately to think quickly, wishing that sensations and emotions were not racing through her like wildfire. The image of Amelia Carson had just disappeared again—right when the state cop had come to stand *exactly where she had been.*

It might have been a projected image?

She lowered her head—also feeling clammy and almost *dirty* somehow because Marc Kimball was touching her, because it seemed that she breathed in something that wasn't evil, but...

Slimy.

"Clara," Jackson said, coming through the crowd. "I guess

we're all having trouble trying to get some sleep. Perhaps, since you're awake, you wouldn't mind coming into the office? I think you might be able to give me a hand with something—a timetable?"

She had lost her mind for a few minutes there. No way in hell would Jackson Crow be involved in such a farce and no way in hell would he chance anything ridiculous for his precious Krewe of Hunters.

She swallowed hard, wanting to scream and shake off Marc Kimball's touch. Thor Erikson had risen and done so in such a way that he forced Marc Kimball back.

She didn't particularly want to feel she owed the man in any way, but at that moment, she was eternally grateful.

"I'm so sorry—I had no idea I was speaking so loudly," she said to everyone. "Forgive me. Please, try to get back to sleep. Jackson, of course I'll help," she added, looking over at him.

"Come on, folks, break it all up!" Mike Aklaq said.

They all began to disperse.

"Really, Miss Avery, if there's anything…" Marc Kimball said.

"Thank you. Thank you so much," she told him. And she fled toward Jackson. She realized that her three friends—Simon, Ralph and Larry—looked at her with grave concern.

"I'm all right, I swear!" she whispered to Larry as she passed him.

Following Jackson to the office, she heard Becca speaking with one of the policemen. "Please, this is rough. If you'll really keep an eye on my door…"

"Of course, Miss Marle," one of the officers assured her.

Then Clara found herself in the office with Jackson—and Thor Erikson and Mike Aklaq. She wound up seated on the sofa that faced the desk; the three men were perched on the edge of it, arms folded over their chests, looking at her with grave expressions.

"Clara, what happened?" Jackson asked her.

"I think maybe the, uh, the film crew is still at it somehow," Clara managed. "I saw Amelia—I saw Amelia Carson in the kitchen. Twice. And she was…she was in one piece. I'm sorry. I guess I freaked out. I assumed that maybe all of you were in on it."

"She thought I was a stripper!" Thor said indignantly.

"There are many legitimate places where people work," Clara said, cringing inwardly.

Jackson and Mike both laughed. "Stripper!" Mike repeated, grinning. "Hey, there, Magic Mike!"

Thor looked at him, a brow hiked.

"I'm sorry!" Clara said again.

"No one is playing tricks here," Jackson said quietly.

Clara winced, lowering her head. "So, she's—real. As in really dead—and really a ghost?" she whispered.

She'd have given her eyeteeth for Alexi to be there. Alexi took all such things in stride; she believed that ghosts had come to help her on the *Destiny*.

"The thing is," Thor said, coming to hunch down before her, causing her to meet his eyes, "Amelia apparently thinks you can help her. She appeared before you."

"You saw her!" she told him. "I know that you saw her!"

Clara hoped he would deny it.

He did not.

"Yes, I saw her because…"

"He saw her because he can see the dead," Jackson said flatly. "Actually, many people can. Most of them never know it. Some feel a presence. Some actually see things. And some—well, I guess the dead pick and choose who they wish to speak with, just like the living. And the dead are like the living—some can barely appear. Some can learn to shift the air and make noise, even to move small objects, while some cannot. I know you're aware that Alexi has always quietly had something extra. You know about the *Destiny*."

She was surprised when Thor set a hand gently on her knee. "It's hard to grasp. When you're older…an adult. I knew very young that I saw things that others didn't. That I heard things. That dreams could be warnings, the dead entering our subconscious minds. It's hard. Truly hard. But, once you let yourself accept that while a large majority of the world might think you're crazy despite the fact that you're not at all, it gets easier."

"And you find that you can embrace it—and do a lot of good with it," Jackson said.

Thor was looking at her earnestly. She looked back at him and shook her head.

"Why?" she whispered. "Why would she come to me? Members of her film crew are here. You all are here…people she could just chat with at will, apparently!"

Thor glanced at Jackson before looking at her and answering. "She might not trust the members of her own crew."

Clara sat in silence for a minute.

"We need you to be open to her," Jackson said.

"What?" she asked.

"Amelia may well know her killer," Thor said.

Clara looked at him. She was amazed that this strong and serious man could be speaking to her about ghosts.

Then again, she'd wanted to believe that he was a stripper/actor and that it was all make-believe.

"So," she said, slowly and carefully, "you think that this ghost will just walk up to me and tell me who killed her? And then you'll make an arrest and go to court and convince a jury to convict someone on a ghost's testimony?"

"No, but if Amelia approached you, she did so for a reason," Thor replied.

She let that settle in and then she said, "You want me to go back to bed by myself and just wait and see if the ghost shows up—in my dreams? Or, um, in person?" she asked.

"Of course not," Thor said, the corners of his mouth turning

up. He actually had a nice smile. To her surprise, he kept smiling gently as he smoothed a strand of hair back out of her eyes.
"We don't mean to terrify or make anyone miserable. Do you
think you could get some rest on the couch here? Either Jackson, Mike or I will be in the office at all times."

It beat the hell out of lying alone in a shadowy room by herself!

She nodded. "If, uh…if you think I can help," she murmured.

She didn't really want to help—no, that wasn't true. She'd
love to help. She just didn't think that she could.

She didn't want to see the dead—that was the issue.

But neither did she want to be alone, not now. Not in the
Alaska Hut, where she was afraid of the dead—and made very
uneasy by the living. As in Marc Kimball.

"I'll get a pillow and blanket," Mike said.

"And we need to move back into taking shifts in the spare
room," Jackson told him.

"You go on," Thor told Jackson, rising to his feet. "Mike got
about an hour or so of sleep already. I'll sit with Miss Avery."
He smiled at Clara. "It will be getting light soon—morning
twilight, that's what we call it."

"Shadow time," Mike said. He shrugged. "You know it's all
because of the sun on the horizon. Twilight comes when the sun
is rising, and when it sets. It's right when the ball of the sun slips
down past the horizon of wherever you may be in the world."

She nodded, trying a smile herself. It was weak. "I was anxious to come to Alaska," she told him. "The pictures I had seen
were so beautiful, and friends who have sailed these cruises told
me there was nothing like it. I came up here early to see the
sights and I stayed awake the first night to marvel at the amount
of light there could be in a day."

"And darkness in winter," Thor murmured. "But, lucky for
us, it is still summer."

Lucky. Easier to catch a killer in the light? Wasn't everything easier when one could see clearly?

Just as she had clearly seen a ghost?

Mike stepped out and Jackson paused by her. "You're going to be okay?"

She nodded.

Jackson left. Mike returned with a pillow and blanket. She thanked him and adjusted them on the sofa, then lay down.

"Try to rest," Thor said.

He sat behind the desk. She realized that he was studying something on the computer—studying it so intently that he might have forgotten that she was there.

She readjusted; she didn't want to interrupt him, but she was unnerved and didn't feel much like sleeping.

"You okay?" he asked.

"Yes. I'm sorry. Just restless."

"You should try to get some sleep."

"I can't sleep."

He looked up from the computer. "Yeah, I know the feeling," he said.

"Have you always—seen the dead?" she asked him.

He hesitated, lowered his head and seemed to be smiling again. She noted that he really was exceptional.

Stripper. Great.

But she could imagine him with a Viking helmet and sword—and a bunch of furs!

"Always," he murmured, and shrugged. "I don't really know. I had one Norse grandmother I spent time with and she loved to believe that there were different places where the soul lingered once the body was gone or used up. She was Catholic—she didn't believe in ancient Gods or myths. But, like most people, she had her own way of believing. Since I was a kid, I would have hunches or gut feelings, and I would see things in dreams—real ones and daydreams. Jackson and I worked well together because…because we didn't ask each other a lot of questions. When one of us had a strong feeling, we went with it."

"When one of you talked to the dead?" she whispered.

Once again, he was vague. "Speaking to the dead—seeing or feeling something that others didn't. Whatever. It has worked for both of us. Jackson became part of the Krewe of Hunters… I've worked in my own way. Thing is, we've both always gone the way we felt we needed to go. Alaska was home. I believed I needed to be here. It's kind of a like an often frozen Wild, Wild West. And Jackson felt strongly he needed to move in another direction. It's good to see him again, good to be with him again. Especially now."

"Now—because of this?" Clara asked.

He hesitated. There was something more, and it was obvious, but he wasn't going to say. Clara wasn't sure why, but in that moment, she decided he wasn't such a jerk.

"This is pretty bad," he said quietly. "You should try to get some rest."

He was dismissing her; he wanted quiet. Fine. She laid her head down.

Then she bolted back up.

"Footage! Film footage! Everything at the Mansion was being filmed. Maybe if you get that film footage, you'll find the killer on it—find out if Amelia made it to the Mansion before she met up with the killer. You can see if—"

She broke off; her eyes locked with his.

She felt like a fool.

"You've already gone through all the footage, right?"

He smiled. "Yes."

"What's on it?"

"The Wickedly Weird crew mugging in front of various cameras to check them out, and your friends—Ralph, Simon and Larry—arriving, freaking out, screaming and leaving. And then there's footage of you. Silent—seeing the place—freezing and then leaving."

"Yes, but I know that someone was upstairs. I heard footsteps!" Clara protested.

He hesitated. "Possibly."

"What do you mean, *possibly*?" Maybe he was a jerk after all!

"The camera upstairs clicked off about two hours before you got to the house," he said.

"Yes, but doesn't that prove my point? Someone was there—someone who turned off the cameras!"

"We have tech people working on that possibility now."

Screw resting; she was angry. "I told you that someone was in there. Do you really think that I made that up, that I'm a liar?" she demanded.

"No," he told her impatiently. "It's *possible* that you were completely unnerved and imagined that someone was in there. Whoever killed Amelia Carson didn't do so at the Mansion. There's no real reason to suspect that the killer was ever in there. He might have known what was going on and had no reason to go in."

"So I just panicked and ran?" she demanded.

He sighed, trying to hide his impatience. "The main-floor cameras were working fine. You can't get upstairs until you've been downstairs. Look, this is no insult to you. I've been with the Bureau for fifteen years—that scene at the Mansion was horrific and damned real."

She knew that her eyes narrowed and her voice was strained and harsh. "I'm not an idiot who imagines things." *Except I've just seen a dead woman!* she thought.

"That isn't what I'm suggesting."

"But it is!"

"Miss Avery," he said, clearly growing agitated as well, "I don't know what to tell you. Our reports say that while the cameras upstairs did an automatic click-off, the cameras down-stairs were working away."

"Maybe there are ways into the house that aren't within cam-era range," she said.

"That is possible," he said.

Possible.

But it didn't sound as if he believed it—not in the least.

She let out a sound of frustration and anger. "Stop playing hard-core Fed—I mean, you did see a ghost, too!—and pay at-tention to what I'm saying. Someone was in that house. Right now, you have a dead woman in a hotel room and a dead woman in the snow—two different places. You don't know how either one of them wound up dead, by whose hand or why. Or even when! And I'm telling you—I heard someone in that house. It wasn't Ralph, Simon or Larry, because they'd already been got-ten. And apparently, the film crew were here, greeting them when they came screaming their way inside. And I'm assuming Magda and Justin Crowley were here, as well. So, that would mean that your killer is on the island somewhere."

"And law enforcement officers continue to scour the area," he told her.

"You'll never find him," she murmured suddenly. "This is-land… I've only seen it once before, but we all know it's full of hiding places."

He stood up abruptly and walked over to her. For a moment, his sheer size and the heat that swept off him scared her.

But he didn't touch her. He stopped at the couch.

"We'll catch him," he said. "If it's the last thing I do in this life, I will catch the bastard," he swore.

Before she could respond, they both heard a thumping sound—as if someone or something had banged against the outer log wall of the office.

She definitely didn't imagine it. She saw his frown and the tensing of his body. He turned and headed for the door.

She was up and after him in a flash.

"Get back in there!" he told her.

"I am not staying in there alone!" she said.

Jackson had been sleeping on the sofa in the living room; he was up in an instant. The officers in the hallways came heading toward them, along with Mike. By then, Thor was exiting by the front door. Clara ran after him, terrified of being alone.

He was already walking down the length of the porch and into the surrounding snow. She and the others were behind him.

He stopped and she slammed into his back. "Get back in, please, for the love of God, will you?" he demanded, shouting to the others next. "Fan out around the house. Someone was out here!"

"I'm not staying alone!" she told him as he glared at her.

"Go in with one of your friends."

"I'll stay directly behind you!"

"You're going to make me lose him!"

She stood still at that, wincing, and then turned around and returned to the house. She stood just inside the door, watching the night. One officer remained in front. The others had vanished into the darkness and shadows surrounding the house. The moon had disappeared behind a cloud—only the dim lights from within the house afforded illumination, and then seemed to play tricks on the mind, as well.

Clara was shivering.

It seemed that she stayed there for hours, keeping her eyes on the one officer left in front—afraid to look around in any direction.

If she did…she might find herself alone with a dead woman.

And then the men returned to the house in disgust.

"There was no one out there?" she asked anxiously. "Nothing?"

"Yes, there was something," Mike said.

She looked at him, frowning.

"Bear," he told her. "Some kind of bear, by the tracks. It made off into the woods."

She nodded, swallowing. Just an animal.

So, besides a crazy killer, she might have met up with a pissed-off bear out here, as well!

But Thor was shaking his head, oblivious to Clara. He looked at Jackson. "Something about it I just don't like. A bear doesn't listen at windows."

"They were bear tracks, for sure," Mike said.

"They appeared to be," Thor said.

"You think someone has some kind of a snowshoe that emulates a bear track?" Jackson asked him.

"Well, hell, idiots come up here to try to emulate Big Foot or abominable snowman tracks now and then—why not a bear?" Mike mused.

"It's impossible to search the forests in the dark," Jackson said. "We'll get all the crews started again in the morning."

He was the first to really note Clara then. He touched her cheek. "Hey, you're okay. The place is surrounded by law enforcement—guys who know how to use guns," he assured her.

Thor glanced at her, annoyance in his eyes. She was sure that he saw her as the person who "possibly" imagined things, and had slowed him down on his hunt.

She really didn't give a damn.

"Jackson, I need to get to the Mansion in the morning."

"Oh?" he asked, frowning.

"Miss Avery is certain that there's another way inside—that someone was in the Mansion when she was," Thor said.

Jackson and he seemed to exchange some kind of silent communication.

Thor continued, "So, we'll take another good look in the morning. Forensic crews have been all over the place, but..."

"But they weren't there when I was," Clara said. "And I know that I heard something. Anyway, good night, gentlemen." She turned and headed back into the room that had actually been assigned to her.

She tried to tell herself that no ghost was as bad as an agent with an attitude.

But that was a lie.

She was still terrified.

And so she lay awake with the television on and the lights glaring.

Somewhere along the line, she slept.

She felt as if someone tried to wake her then, speaking her name softly, shaking her shoulder.

She opened her eyes.

And there she was, Amelia Carson, dark hair curling around her pretty features, snow hood fallen back, a serious look on her face.

Clara nearly screamed. Except that when she blinked, Amelia was gone.

And Special Agent Thor Erikson was at her door, tapping, calling her name and—as seemed perpetual now—scowling when he looked at her.

"You wanted to go by the Mansion? Let's do it," he said. "Five minutes, please."

The door closed and she was left alone. She sat up, shivering and certain that the room was exceptionally cold, even for Alaska.

It was as cold as…

Death.

CHAPTER SIX

Forensic crews had worked through the night at the Mansion; in their efforts to find anything at all, they had removed, bagged and tagged the props in the bloody scene that had been left there by Wickedly Weird Productions.

But it wasn't the inside that concerned Thor at the moment.

While Mike was seeing to it that the remaining members of the film crew and Ralph, Simon and Larry were returned to the mainland, Thor, Jackson and Clara were walking around the Mansion.

And Clara was right: a group of Sitka spruce grew by the side of the house, all of them huge trees and some with heavy branches.

Smaller branches lay broken in the snow. Any number of birds or other animals might have caused the breakage.

But it also might have been caused by a man climbing a tree.

Thor remained downstairs with Clara while Jackson went up to a second-floor bedroom. He looked down at them, easily opening and closing the window.

"See!" Clara breathed, turning on Thor. "There was some-one in there!"

"Might have been someone in there," he said.

"Might have been!" Clara exclaimed, staring at him furiously. "I'm trying to help! I tell you things—and you act as if I'm a terrified two-year-old! Don't tell me to talk to a damned ghost—and then disbelieve me when I tell you something credible!"

She was, he thought, in her right to be angry. But she didn't understand that everything in their world was a "might be" until it could be proved as fact.

He turned his attention from the window to her and almost smiled. Her blue eyes were shimmering with indignation. Her hands were balled into fists at her sides, and she almost looked like a mud wrestler about to go into action.

"I'm sorry if I've offended you," he said. "Until something is proven, it's theory. Your theories are not without sound merit."

His answer seemed to puzzle her—at the least, deflate her.

"They're still checking the island," he told her. "We'll keep searching it. The problem is, of course, that the nooks and crannies and coves that lead to the water are as plentiful as the hiding places. In winter…well, in winter, it's doubtful this would have happened. Even the heartiest native might well freeze to death out in the wild. But it's summer. The water between here and the mainland—in several directions—is clear. Someone could have come and gone."

"Like they did from the Alaska Hut last night?" she asked evenly.

He looked back at her and nodded, not sure why she had managed to evoke hostility in him.

It was fear—fear for her. Because he'd seen Mandy Brandt in a dream again last night.

And, of course, it was the fact that both he and Jackson felt like they were on a tightrope.

Because Tate Morley was out.

Naturally, they'd kept abreast of the situation. Agents, US

marshals and police from every city, county and state were on the lookout. They were following every clue.

But Tate Morley had covered his tracks, becoming a doctor, covering up the corpse of the doctor and even signing himself out of the prison.

All done with an hour to spare before his subterfuge had been discovered.

There was no reason to suspect that he might have been in Alaska.

But there was no reason to believe that he might not have gotten here—and come specifically to kill the man who had caused his incarceration.

Thor.

He wasn't worried for himself; he knew Morley, knew how he moved, talked and even thought. He never slept without his Glock in easy reach. His home had alarms up the wazoo.

He knew, too, that Morley wouldn't want to just kill him.

He would want to torture him.

Torture would mean killing others.

Theory! he mocked himself. He'd been irritated with Clara for her assumptions, but all this was simply what he believed—conjecture, until they had proof.

"That's theory, too, at the moment," he said quietly. "We'll get you back to the mainland now, Miss Avery. I'm going to explore your suppositions as well as my own, I promise."

She turned away for a minute and then looked back at him. "You're staying here? To search the island?"

"Yes—since it's quite possible there is someone else out here."

"I'll stay, too."

"There's no reason for you to do so."

"Oh, yes, there is."

"What?"

"I am not going to be alone when a ghost comes back!"

He smiled at that. Maybe she was right. The ghost might be

the one element that could give them something that *was* fact rather than theory.

"The problem is, we can't be with you—even here on the island. I plan to head out on a snowmobile and cover all the territory, all the nooks and crannies—"

"But you can't look at night," she told him.

"You know, ghosts can come by daylight, too."

She had a stubborn look about her then. She stared at him and then winced and looked down. "I'm not as terrified in the daylight as I am at night."

"Night is only about three hours this time of year."

"Twilight comes in the early hours—and at night."

He turned away from her. There was really no reason she couldn't stay. He knew well that Marc Kimball would be more than happy if she did. And the Alaska Hut would require the presence of officers for at least the next twenty-four hours.

"All right," he said.

"What?" she asked.

"All right. If you want to be here, you can."

She let out a sigh of relief. "The others have gone, right? My only problem is that I don't have any clothing... I don't have... my things."

"So, I guess you'll have to go back."

"But you don't have clothing or your things!" she said. "You're going to have to go back, too. And Natalie Fontaine was killed, same style more or less, back on the mainland, and there will be some kind of meeting or briefing and—"

"You've been watching too much television," he said.

She smiled; it was a beautiful smile. "But, I'm right!" she said.

"Right about what?" Jackson said as he came around to meet them. He looked from Clara to Thor.

"What's going on?" Jackson asked.

"Clara wants to stay on the island," Thor told him.

Jackson seemed to weigh the information. "Might be for the best," he said.

"Might not. This is an island. Even with law enforcement running around, we're not on the mainland. We don't have the same access to services, we don't—"

"You just said all right," Clara reminded him.

He shrugged, looking at Jackson.

Thor knew what they were both thinking.

Why not? She was the one the ghost of Amelia Carson seemed to be trying to meet.

She was also right about the fact that they would travel back to the mainland that afternoon to meet with Enfield, the Alaska State Troopers and the Seward police. But first, they were going to spend a few hours scouring through the forest themselves.

"Let's head back to the Alaska Hut, regroup with a few of the officers there," Jackson said.

He couldn't argue.

"I have the team combing anew for fingerprints," Jackson told him as they headed to the snowmobiles. "I'd bet if there was someone running around in there, they were wearing gloves, but we never do know. They'd fine-tooth-comb everything from the tree to the windowsill and beyond again."

"Thank you," Clara told him.

"Of course. It's an investigation," Jackson told her, smiling grimly. "So…we head back."

Clara had ridden behind Jackson on a snowmobile to reach the Mansion. She climbed on behind him once again.

He geared his snowmobile into action.

They passed the area where the two halves of Amelia Carson's body had lain; the body was gone now, but crime scene tape remained.

It was an exasperating puzzle. No prints leading to the body; no prints leading away.

Her remains found just after the decapitated body of her producer.

Hating reality television was one thing...

Could that have something to do with these horrible crimes?

Seriously, that would be taking it to the max when all you
had to do was change the channel.

When they reached the Mansion, to Thor's dismay, Marc
Kimball was standing on the porch, a cup of coffee in his hands,
as if he had been awaiting them.

Apparently, he had been.

He ignored Jackson and Thor and spoke quickly to Clara.

"Miss Avery! I heard you stayed behind. You know that you
are more than welcome to remain with me at the Alaska Hut
as long as you choose. I'm sure you must be very frightened—
there will be officers here. And, while it is not in politically
good taste, I do admit I have been a hunter at times in my life.
I'm good with a rifle. You might well be safest here, surrounded
by officers...and watched over by myself."

Clara had dismounted the snowmobile and hung back with
Jackson. She smiled, but Thor thought it was a plastic one.

She didn't like the man. She didn't trust him.

That made Thor like her all the more, he realized. She had
the sense to realize this man thought he could buy anything.

"That's so nice of you," Clara murmured.

Thor looked around to assess the situation; Mike hadn't returned from the dock as of yet. A state police officer was standing guard on the porch. He nodded to the man, who nodded
gravely in return.

"Magda has just gotten some lunch together. Agents, Miss
Avery, can we get you something? We're seeing to the police
officers, too, of course!" Kimball said.

The perfect host.

Clara walked ahead and they entered the house.

Magda was bustling around the kitchen area; lunch was laid

out buffet-style. Thor imagined that was because no one knew how many people would be eating or when.

The food smelled wonderful and Thor realized he hadn't actually eaten anything cooked in a while. The woman had prepared a hearty stew to be served over rice. He helped himself to a bowl, thanking her and Kimball politely before taking a chair.

He noted that Clara managed to sit between him and Jackson, despite the fact that Kimball continued to wax on about her performances. She just smiled.

He and Jackson ate in silence. Halfway through the meal, Emmy Vincenzo appeared.

She asked if it was all right if she joined them. It should have been nothing but a courtesy and polite question, but Thor realized she was actually asking permission.

Her fault for staying in his employ, Thor thought.

They finished quickly; the others were still eating when he rose and Jackson joined him.

"We'll be back," Jackson said. "We'll be taking a look through the forest, Mr. Kimball."

"If I can help…?" Kimball offered.

"We appreciate that and we'll definitely let you know," Thor told him.

When they were on the way out he asked Jackson, "You got the radio?"

"I do."

"Have Angela find out where Kimball was before he came here."

"You think that Kimball is in on this somehow."

"Not really. Being a giant ass doesn't make him guilty of murder. I think we should know."

"I agree, though I imagine Enfield was already on it."

"Yeah, they would have done a check on him, but just an airport check about the plane—I'd like something a little more thorough. Guaranteed," Thor said.

"Sure," Jackson agreed. "I don't like him, either. I just don't see him as this killer."

"Elimination," Thor said.

They started up the snowmobiles again and followed the tracks they had found the night before.

Bear tracks? Or snowshoe tracks made to look that way by someone who knew that a wind or a fresh batch of flurries would make it impossible to tell?

Alaska was home to all three species of North American bears, including grizzlies, black bears and polar bears. Black bears held prominence on Black Bear Island, but brown bears made a home here, too.

But were what they had seen in the snow bear tracks?

The experts had yet to tell them.

Clara was left alone with Magda, Justin, Emmy, a few cops who were not into conversation, and Marc Kimball.

Maybe she should have left the island.

Well, she would be leaving. When Jackson and Thor returned from their mission, she would go back in with them. The only problem she had was speaking with her employers at Celtic American. She was pretty sure, however, that she didn't have to worry about rehearsals; she knew her role backward and forward and the ship still wasn't due to leave for a week.

Ralph, Simon and Larry would be delighted to have some time off. They'd probably turn into tour guides when their young ingenue, Connie Shaw, finished her last commitment and arrived in Alaska, showing her around and protecting her like mother hens. They were very safe mother hens; Ralph and Larry were now openly together—she and Alexi had convinced them that the days were gone when they had to hide, at least among friends! And Simon was the furthest thing in the world from a womanizer; he was just a supernice young kid who had been brought up to be courteous and polite to everyone.

She sat at the table with Marc Kimball and Emmy, who ate her food without looking up.

Marc kept talking. He would say something about himself, and then ask about her. It seemed that he had taken Dating 101 or some such class because he didn't monopolize the conversation, he was polite, he tried to be funny and was now and then, and seemed to be the perfect gentleman.

She just didn't like him. She felt that even his easy table conversation had been plotted out the same way he would attack a business proposition.

After a while, she begged to be excused to take a nap, yawning and apologizing.

"Of course, of course!" Marc said. "You had such a trying day yesterday, and you were off with those FBI men this morning..."

If he wanted her to explain why she had gone with them, he was doomed to disappointment.

"Yes, I'll probably just lie down for a bit, but I do need to close my eyes. Thank you again for your incredible hospitality, and forgive me," she said. "Emmy, nice to spend time with you."

"What? Sorry?" Emmy said, looking up from her bowl at last.

"It was nice to spend some time with you," Clara repeated.

"Oh, yes, lovely, of course!" Emmy said.

Clara smiled—and escaped as quickly as she could, hurrying down the hall.

That day, there was only one man from the state police in the hut. He was more relaxed; seated on a chair in the living room, he had a newspaper in his hands. It was a national paper. The headline screamed Murder in the Arctic; Horror Show in Alaska.

The officer stood as she walked by, quickly hiding the paper and assuring her he was on duty.

She thanked him and went on to her room.

She didn't want to close the door; if she did so, the officer wouldn't seem to be in easy reach.

But if she didn't, Marc Kimball might come by and feel that he should reassure her.

She wondered for a moment if she was more afraid of the living—or the dead.

She stood there debating for a while and then heard Kimball's voice.

She closed the door. Walking to the window, she threw open the drapes. The sun was pounding down hard. The windows filled the room with light.

The sunlight seemed to beat off the snow and create a dazzling display of brilliance. Glad of it, Clara lay down. Before she knew it, she was asleep.

She woke to the soft sound of tapping at her door. For a moment, she was afraid to open her eyes.

Then she did. The light was streaming in. No ghosts stood at the foot of her bed.

With a soft sigh of relief, she stood and hurried to the door, throwing it open.

An arctic freeze seemed to settle over her. She could see—with peripheral vision—that the cop was still sitting on the sofa. He was idly drumming his fingers on the occasional table at his side, and gazing at the television.

He hadn't noted that she'd opened her door.

Or that a scream was caught in her throat.

Amelia Carson stood at her door, her expression anguished. "Please!"

For a moment, Clara couldn't snap out of it. Then she heard Kimball's voice from somewhere and reached out to draw Amelia into the room. Of course, her fingers went through air. But Amelia came on in; to her own amazement, Clara shut the door.

"I didn't want to be rude," Amelia said. "Or startle or scare you and start you screaming…"

If what Clara had heard was true, Amelia didn't mind so much being rude. The woman had been very pleasant when they'd met, but Clara had heard that she could be something of a diva.

The past didn't matter much; Clara realized that she had drawn a ghost into her room and closed the door.

She stared at Amelia. "Why? Why are you coming to me?" she whispered, her voice sounding desperate. "Two FBI agents here will be able to see you—if you go to them, you'll be all right."

Amelia walked into the room, heading to look through the windows out to the bright afternoon beyond. "Yes, the tall Nordic-looking guy. I figured he could see me. I get the feeling that his one friend could, too. I was afraid. Am afraid," Amelia said. She turned and looked at Clara. "Dead, I am dead, and I know I am dead, and I am still so afraid. I don't know—can they still hurt you after you're dead?"

Clara stared back at her. She knew that if she were to describe this encounter to most people, they would assume the events on the *Destiny* had been too much for her and that she needed some serious rehab.

She shook her head. "Amelia, I don't know," she said. "But, if you know anything…"

"I know I'm dead," Amelia said bitterly. "And I never thought…oh!" she cried, sinking to the foot of the bed. "And I saw myself! He cut me in half! Right in half. How horrible, he couldn't even let me be as I was…" She paused and looked at Clara again. "And I heard… I've heard the talk. He *cut off* Natalie's head!"

Clara sat in the center of the bed, looking at Amelia. "I'm so sorry. So, so sorry. But, Amelia, do you know who did this to you? They can be arrested. They can pay."

"Alaska has no death penalty," Amelia said.

"Amelia, this person can be locked away for life and ninety-nine years—*life! Behind bars!*" Clara said.

Amelia shook her head. "That should be comforting, right?

No, I don't want whoever did this to me to live, to see the sun, to feel the breeze." She quietly began to cry.

Clara reached out—and of course, touched air.

"Amelia, who—who did this?"

But Amelia shook her head. "I don't know. I was on the phone with him. He called me the morning we were coming out to film you." She flashed Clara an apologetic smile. "We were all set—giddy, really. I hadn't seen the Mansion yet. But I headed out early. He said he was going to be on the island. He'd be a great surprise guest for either or both shows we were filming, and he could give me a story I'd never forget. To be honest, he was so mysterious and charming, I thought it was Todd Beck, the bright young actor they just hired to play in the new superhero movie. He's working it right now, you know, publicity from every angle! It was a chance, yes, but I was willing to take it. Every once in a while, someone really big does want to be on one of our shows. Oh! I was such a fool, so eager! I hired the first boat I could find at the docks to get me out here. And then I walked toward the Mansion…but I never got there. I remember feeling as if there was a rush of air behind me… and then it seemed a clamp was around my throat, I couldn't breathe…and then…"

She started to sob again.

"And then?" Clara asked gently.

Amelia sat straight, staring at nothing, shaking her head in bitterness. She had been a beautiful young woman with her dark hair, light eyes and skin, and perfect bone structure.

"Then I saw myself," she said. "And I realized that I was walking around…watching people, listening to people, trying to tell them that I was there. But they were totally oblivious to me, their attention on…the pieces of my body."

"You never saw your killer?" Clara asked. She refrained from asking how she was here as a spirit now, but hadn't seen when the killer had cut her in half.

Maybe there were small mercies in the world.

"No. The world went pitch-black…and then I was there, watching all the forensic people work around me. I saw…what he did to me."

At least he hadn't chopped her up when she'd been alive.

For a moment, there was silence between them. Then Amelia looked at Clara again. "I saw you—I saw your eyes. And I knew that you were horrified for me. Not *because* of me, but for me. And you barely even knew me. Oh, Clara! How could this have happened? Why did it happen? Was I being punished for thinking too much of myself? Am I… Will I walk around like this forever?"

Clara wasn't sure what to say to her.

I don't know, Amelia! I know nothing about being dead, yet. To the best of my knowledge, there is no Being Dead for Dummies *book out as of now.*

"Amelia, you weren't a bad person," Clara tried.

"I was nasty to people who worked with me. I thought… I thought I'd be a huge star one day. I was in tabloids!" Amelia said.

Clara didn't assure her that she'd be front-page news on most of the tabloids that existed now—and on television and every other media source in the world, as well.

"But you weren't a bad person," she repeated. "Bad people are like—are like whoever did this to you. I know that you'll… that you will find a better place."

She spoke with sudden conviction and Amelia looked at her hopefully.

"The FBI agents can help you, Amelia," Clara said.

"A little late," Amelia murmured. "I just had to have that story. Oh, and I had to beat Natalie out here! I never even knew that he'd gotten to her first. How—is there no security at that hotel?"

Clara assumed that because the Nordic Lights Hotel was small and privately owned, it didn't have the security that might be found at a larger establishment. Then again, there had been horror stories about events in larger hotels, too.

"Maybe there is security at the hotel. That's why you need to speak with the FBI members, Amelia. They can answer questions like that."

Clara heard a soft tapping at her door—real this time, and not an echo of a policeman drumming his fingers on the table.

She stood to answer it.

Amelia looked up in alarm—and disappeared as if she'd never been there.

Maybe she hadn't been. Maybe the stress…

No. Thor had seen her, too.

Clara walked over and swung her door open. Marc Kimball was there, smiling at her. "We were about to have an afternoon snack and fine sherry, Miss Avery. Would you be so good as to join us?"

It was absolutely the last thing she wanted to do.

"I…"

"Yes, of course, join us, please!" he said. "I'd be so grateful."

She lowered her head, trying to think of a good excuse, unable to do so. She heard the front door of the lodge open.

"Miss Avery?" It was Mike Aklaq, back from the docks and whatever else he'd been doing.

"Here!" she called.

A look of annoyance crossed over Kimball's face.

Clara smiled. "I'm here, Agent Aklaq!" She slipped past Kimball and looked back into her room, just briefly. But she was sure she saw a slight indentation in the bed where Amelia had been sitting.

And yet, as Clara hurried down the hallway, she couldn't help but wonder if she was suffering from whiteout hysteria on the island, along with a massive dose of stress.

★ ★ ★

"They end here," Thor told Jackson.

He was off his snowmobile and had been since they'd reached the tree line.

It had been easy enough to follow the tracks in the light powdery snow—harder once they reached the massive pines and the ground became a wet bed of earth, snow and pine carpeting.

Thor hunched down, studying the tracks and the broken branches and needles.

He'd seen prints; he'd seen broken, dislodged branches. He hadn't seen any other indication that a bear had come this way— not a speck of fur, not a scratch on a tree, not so much as the whiff of a scent of a creature marking territory.

Jackson came carefully behind him.

"Well?" Jackson asked.

"Snowshoes, I think. Custom snowshoes. Short and broad prints—hard to tell them from the tracks of a real bear, unless you find fur or droppings. Look ahead—you can see where the pine needles are cracked. Not enough to catch something like an actual footprint, but whoever came here tossed the 'bear' feet, and started through the trees. It's really dense here. I know the state police were through this area yesterday, but we're going to have to get them back. Somewhere on this island, we'll either find someone or find proof that someone was here."

"You're sure?" Jackson asked.

Thor nodded gravely.

"You've spent a lot of time out here, on this island?" Jackson asked him.

"When I was a kid, there were absentee owners who weren't so rich," Thor told Jackson. "The Mansion existed, but it wasn't like it is now and it wasn't called the Mansion. The Alaska Hut existed, too—again, not as is it now, but just as a big log cabin with small rooms to allow for heat circulation. We used to come out here without telling our parents. The island was really taboo for kids growing up here—too many places where someone could get lost or hurt."

"Bears?" Jackson asked.

Thor paused and looked back at his old partner, grinning. "Enough for me to know that a bear didn't get to the forest and stop being a bear."

"Sorry," Jackson said. "I have to admit, in all my years, I never had to wonder if it was a man or a bear that had run through the wilderness."

"What I'm trying to figure out is how this guy got into the mainland hotel, killed Natalie—decapitated her—walked out without being seen, and came out here to the island," he said.

"The cops on the mainland are looking all over for anyone with a boat—anyone who could have gotten the killer over here. So far, nothing. And the Coast Guard has skirted the place. If there is a boat here somewhere, it's incredibly well hidden," Jackson said.

"Yeah."

"Two separate killers?"

"That's a terrifying thought."

"And what was their motive?" Jackson murmured. "The main office has been scouring the records for anyone who had a beef with the company."

"I hope they find something," Thor said. "That seems the logical conclusion here—that the producers 'got' the wrong person with their *Gotcha* show."

"And still..." Jackson said.

And still, neither of them could forget that Tate Morley had escaped from prison.

Thor kept walking carefully through the pines, avoiding the broken areas, studying the trees. As they moved deeper into the woods, the world darkened; not even the bright Alaska summer sun could penetrate through the thickness of the pines and brush.

He stopped suddenly, seeing a patch of light ahead. It looked as if the pines were just as dense as ever, but there had to be something different for the sun to be breaking through.

He had to crawl over fallen branches and weave his way along.

And then, at last, deep in an area that appeared to be impenetrable, he saw the break—the place where the sun was shining through.

Taking even greater care, he squeezed between two tree branches. And there, he found it, a pool of dark liquid that had melted the snow beneath it and now darkened the carpet of earth and pine it covered.

"What is it?" Jackson called, coming up behind him.

Thor stopped dead and hunkered down again, looking around.

He reached out with his gloved hands and grasped a tuft of blue fabric.

A tiny piece of the jeans Amelia Carson had been wearing. At least, a good chance that was what he'd found.

He touched the ground.

Still damp. Dark and damp.

It was the blood pool, the place where Amelia Carson had been severed in two.

CHAPTER SEVEN

Clara didn't speak about her conversation with Amelia until she was on the little Coast Guard cutter heading back to the mainland. The officers aboard were courteous and tense, aware they were in the middle of an investigation in which many lives might still lie in the balance.

She waited until she was alone with Jackson and Thor at the back of the boat.

Even then, she couldn't shake the feeling that they were being watched. She didn't know why; she felt safe with Thor and Jackson and the Coast Guard men. Mike wasn't with them because he had remained behind on the island—the FBI officers had decided that one of them should stay there until the situation was solved.

Some situations were never solved, she knew.

This one had to be—it just had to be.

Once they were headed back to the mainland, however, she knew that she had to tell Jackson and Thor what had happened.

She knew that both men would believe her, and she dreaded that, because it meant her newfound camaraderie with a dead woman was far too real. And they did believe her; they both listened to her gravely as she spoke.

"We found where she was killed," Jackson said.

"On the island, right?" Clara asked.

"Yes," Thor told her, watching her as he spoke. "We've been in contact with Special Director Enfield and Detective Brennan. They rushed the autopsies yesterday." He paused, looking over at Jackson. "Both women were struck with hard objects and rendered unconscious quickly, and then strangled before they were—cut," he said. He glanced over at Jackson, whose lips pursed grimly. It seemed they both knew something she didn't, and they weren't sharing it with her. Even though anyone associated with the two dead women might be in danger.

"Thank God for that at least. I mean," she added, wincing, "hopefully, it was…quick. I couldn't begin to imagine if someone had been alive while being…cut."

"So, a man called Amelia and told her he had an amazing story for her—and that he'd meet her on the island?" Thor asked.

"That's what I understood," Clara told him.

"Her cell phone hasn't been found, but the phone company sent her records. Techs are chasing down her calls," Jackson said. "We may find something."

Thor nodded. "Yep, we'll find that she was called by a no-contract phone bought with cash. But it will be important to track down where that phone was purchased."

Jackson rose. "I'm going to get some coffee. Want some?" he asked the two of them.

"No, thank you," Clara said. She'd had plenty of coffee while waiting for them to return.

Thor was staring out over the water. Clara remained silent for a minute, and then decided that she'd just ask.

"What's going on between you and Jackson?"

He turned his attention to her, frowning. "Pardon?"

"What is it that you two are sharing—about Natalie and Amelia and...whatever is going on?"

He was quiet for a minute.

"Jackson and I were partners years ago," he told her.

"Yes, I understand that." She hesitated. "Did you have a bad time, or..."

He shook his head. "We were good partners—great partners. But there was a killer out there at the time. The newspapers called him the 'Fairy Tale Killer' because he left his victims' bodies displayed as if they were characters from stories—tales by the Brothers Grimm. Cinderella, Briar Rose—or Sleeping Beauty, as she's more widely known—Rapunzel, Snow White."

"I remember... I had just started college," Clara said. "He was shot by agents but he survived and went to prison and...oh. You were those agents?" she asked.

He nodded.

"But—you caught him. You saved countless other potential victims. Why do you suspect him?"

"Because he's out."

"What?"

"He's out—he killed a doctor and escaped from a prison in Kansas."

"Oh," she said. "I hadn't heard—"

"Because the news just hit yesterday morning and by the time any of us saw television out on the island, all the stations were carrying all the 'new' news on the killings that happened here," Thor explained.

"Oh, I'm so sorry. I can only imagine how you feel, having caught him and now... Do you think that this man, this Fairy Tale Killer, could be here—in Alaska?" she asked, wincing as she heard her tone, which was slightly incredulous. She went on quickly. "From what I understood back then, he left his victims looking...beautiful. As if they were sleeping."

He nodded and looked away from her. She found herself

studying him, and in doing so, and from their conversation, feeling as if she knew him better, as if they'd formed some kind of bond. Despite their bizarre beginning and the resentment she'd felt at times, she suddenly felt close to him—like an old friend. More than a friend. She looked down quickly, realizing that in an instant, something inside her had changed, and she felt an almost overwhelming attraction to the man. He'd become so human.

They were talking about incidents of horror and terrible things that plagued the soul.

And yet, what she wanted at that moment was to touch him and assure him that she knew—she knew from knowing him—that at every turn he'd done the right thing, and that he couldn't blame himself for anything.

"You know Jackson Crow," he said softly, looking back at her. "And you know about the Krewe of Hunters."

"I know that they saved us on the ship and I know..." She broke off, feeling a little breathless.

Ghosts.

While many reports on the work done by the Krewe of Hunters had speculated on their unorthodox methods, none had ridiculed them—they had brought too many highly unusual cases to their conclusions.

They'd locked up a hell of a lot of bad guys.

"Yes, I know something about the Krewe," she murmured.

Thor stared at her. Apparently, he'd decided just to explain—and she could take it or leave it.

"The last victim was a young woman named Mandy Brandt. She'd come to the Bureau and told us that her friend had been dating someone she found to be questionable. We had a zillion such reports at the time, but I believed Mandy—so did Jackson. So we started tracking the man she was talking about and it was Tate Morley. We even went after him right away, but..."

He paused, and he looked out to sea again, shaking his head. "Not before he got Mandy."

"And you feel responsible," Clara said. "But...you said you and Jackson started right away, working on her information."

"Not fast enough," he said.

"I can only imagine how you feel. But you might have saved countless other young women. He was creating his own line of fairy-tale princesses. He could have killed for years and years."

"Yes, we both know that," Thor said. He offered her something of a wistful, rueful smile. "You see, we both knew Mandy."

Clara nodded at that. "I'm sorry. So sorry." She inhaled deeply. "And now this man you and Jackson caught...is out."

She hadn't heard Jackson returning, but he was right behind her.

"That's what brought me," he said, taking a seat again by her side. "I got the news about the killing of Natalie Fontaine at the hotel right after we received the reports that Tate Morley was out."

"And the thing is..." Thor said, glancing at Jackson.

"We both had dreams about Mandy," Jackson said.

"As if we were watching movies of the time we found her and shot Tate," Thor said.

"So...you think that Mandy's spirit came to you in dreams and warned you that Tate Morley was out and killing again, and you linked it with these murders?"

Jackson and Thor looked at one another again.

"Yes," Jackson said.

"That's about it," Thor agreed.

"Oh."

"We're the only ones who think that, by the way," Jackson told her.

They were waiting—waiting for her to speak.

"I just... Well, from what I've read...and seen," she said, not able to forget coming across Amelia's body in the snow, "these murders are very different. I mean, you two are the agents. You've been through years of working with killers…but this just seems the work of someone different."

"Yes," Thor agreed. "But, maybe not. Tate Morley was in prison for ten years. He escaped by coldly killing a doctor and walking out with his credentials."

"He stabbed the doctor in the throat with a shank he managed to create from a ripped-out piece of toilet plumbing," Jackson told her. "The Fairy Tale victims were strangled."

"These victims were strangled before he took a knife to them, or whatever weapon or tool he used to cut them," Thor said.

"The killer likes sensationalism," Jackson noted.

"Like reality television," Thor said.

"Theatricality," Jackson said. He let out a breath and looked at Thor. "I just learned from the captain on the ship that the media already has a name for this guy. 'The Media Monster.'"

Thor winced. "Great."

"So, you really think that this might be the same man. Then if you saw him, you'd recognize him, right?" Clara asked.

"Yes," Jackson said. "Unless…"

"Unless he's disguised himself in some unknown way," Thor said. "Then, of course, we might both be crazy. Tate Morley might be thousands of miles away."

"Maybe not," Clara said, having no real idea of what she was thinking at all. She could see that they were approaching Seward. She stood, watching the approaching shoreline. The different areas of the port were busy; the charming and colorful waterfront businesses were filled with shoppers and businessmen and women moving about on their workday.

There was no snow in the city; the temperature felt much warmer than the island, as well—perhaps somewhere between fifty and sixty.

It all seemed so normal. People were surely talking about the horrible and grisly murders. But they were distanced from them.

They would be aghast at what had been done to the women, but it wouldn't touch them intimately.

Parents would keep close watch on beautiful daughters. Husbands would watch their wives. They would all bitch and moan about the police and the FBI—and wonder how they had not yet caught such a horrid killer.

And still…

Seward would feel much more normal than Black Bear Island!

"You wish to go straight to your hotel?" Thor asked her. "The Hawthorne?"

"Yes, please," she said. "I… Yes."

"You don't need to be afraid," Thor told her. "We'll have an officer with you at all times."

She gave him an awkward smile. "I rate personal protection?"

"Yes."

His answer wasn't reassuring. But a woman had been murdered in a hotel room. She was sure that few visitors to Seward were treading hotel hallways alone.

They were met at the dock by a tall gray-haired man with a lean, fit physique and a grim, bulldog face.

He was, Clara learned, Special Director in Charge Reginald Enfield. He didn't speak much in the car, but saw to it that Clara was brought to her hotel and that she was escorted into the lobby. There she was introduced to Officer Kinney, who would be watching over her hallway while she was in her room. She thanked Kinney and watched while Thor drove away.

Officer Kinney was from Nome, had attended Northwestern and was now back in Alaska. He'd missed his home state; he'd always known he wanted to be a cop.

He checked out her room before he left her to stand guard in the hallway.

She rushed for the shower, despite the fact that she'd had one that morning. She was anxious to shower *and* put on her own clean clothing.

It was while she was in there that she heard a voice. It startled her so that she slammed her head against the tile.

A shiver seized her as she remembered she was locked in her room—and a cop was on duty outside.

"Yoo-hoo… Clara?"

She closed her eyes. The ghost of Amelia Carson was out in her hotel bedroom.

Wrapping her towel around herself, Clara came out. Amelia was perched on the bed, her hands folded around her knees.

"I'm sorry. I didn't mean to be rude. Yes, I was known for it, but… I'm learning how to be nicer," Amelia said.

Was Clara crazy? Weren't ghosts supposed to haunt certain places? As in, the place where they had been murdered?

"How did you get here?" Clara asked.

"The boat, of course. I was on the boat."

She had felt as if she was being watched.

"I didn't see you."

Amelia shrugged. "You weren't looking."

"Why didn't you come and talk to us? I told you—you need to speak with the FBI men."

"I know. I'll try. But, I figured it wasn't really the right time."

"But it is the right time for you to pop into my room?"

"I'm sorry. I will knock, always, in the future," she promised. Her eyes seemed to cloud with pain. "Honestly, do you think that I was murdered for being…rude?"

"Amelia, I think you were murdered because someone out there is a sick son of a bitch. And I only really know you from one meeting and the tabloids. I'm sure you're a good person at heart."

"I was. Really. At heart. And now, I'm going to prove it. I'm going to watch over you."

"Nice," Clara murmured.

Clara jumped and nearly dropped her towel when her phone started ringing.

It was her mom. And it wasn't an easy conversation. Her mother was all but crazy with worry; Clara assured her over and over again that she was fine, that personnel from a television company had been involved and not the cast from the cruise ship. She told her that officers were guarding the hotel hallways and that she really couldn't be safer.

Amelia tried to look away while she spoke.

Then Clara's dad got on the line—and Clara went through the whole thing again.

Naturally, they wanted her to drop everything and come home.

She convinced them that she couldn't, that she was doing well, and that as soon as the *Fate* had sailed a few times with the new show, they had to come aboard.

"Personnel," Amelia murmured when Clara had hung up. "I'm personnel for a different company."

"Amelia, I'm sorry. I had to say something to my parents."

Amelia nodded. "My mom died when I was kid. I haven't seen my father in fifteen years. Bet he'll be crying for me now, though. That will put him on the news."

"I truly am sorry."

"Guess it's best that there's no one out there to really care," Amelia said. "I never even had any real girlfriends. Natalie was the closest—we were both ambitious. That made us pals, I guess."

"Amelia…" Clara hesitated, feeling ridiculous. Oh, God! If she ever told any of this to a shrink, they'd lock her up forever. But…

"Amelia, we're friends," Clara said. "We didn't have time to know each other well, but we're friends."

"Think we could have talked about guys and done pedicures together and stuff like that?" Amelia asked her.

"Sure."

"I should have done things like that," Amelia murmured.

There was a sharp rap on Clara's door. "Hey, Clara! It's Simon!"

"Hang on, two minutes!" she called, hurrying over to her drawer for clothing. "Friend of mine!" she told Amelia, and she paused to smile. "Another friend," she said softly, and ran quickly back into the bathroom to dress.

When she emerged, however, she didn't see Amelia. She was glad in a way; she wasn't sure that she could keep Simon from seeing how weirdly she was behaving if Amelia had remained and kept talking to her.

She opened the door. Simon looked at her expectantly. "I had to pass muster with the guy in the hall," he told her. "You okay?"

"I'm fine. Come on in."

Simon did so.

"Everyone is as jumpy as Tennessee Williams's *Cat on a Hot Tin Roof*!" he said, finding a perch at the foot of the bed—almost where Amelia had just been. "And you're worrying me," he told her.

"I'm worrying you? Why?" Clara asked him.

She had just met Simon when he'd joined the chorus of *Les Miz* on the *Destiny*—his first chorus role, one he'd never gotten to perform. He had a really nice voice, good movement, and she'd been thrilled when he'd been cast in *Annabelle Lee*.

He had a great look—long, lean and thoughtful—which boded well for his career. He was caring, too—he'd taken some major chances trying to save Alexi on the *Destiny*.

"Well, Amelia Carson was really gorgeous—and I see you that way, too," he told her.

She smiled. "Thanks. But look around. There are a lot of pretty young women in the area."

"I don't know. I mean, we're associated with all this. It was the day we all thought we were just doing *Vacation USA* that this all happened." He sighed deeply. "I guess I'm glad our new girl isn't here yet," he murmured. "Long dark hair—cute as a button."

"Simon, don't worry."

"Don't worry. We were just on a ship with the Archangel killer!"

"Yes, but…that was different."

"Yeah. We're not on a ship. Alexi isn't here. I guess I'm scared because… I don't know. I was watching television. The reporters caught Misty Blaine coming out of the police station. She's terrified! She said so. They have cops all over now, though, at the Nordic Lights Hotel. And she's…she's kind of a frazzled-looking little thing. Like Marc Kimball's assistant. Man, someone should tell that guy that slavery and indentured servants went out over a century ago! Jerk, huh?"

"Yes, an amazing jerk," Clara agreed.

"Good. I was afraid you might be unable to withstand his adoration, and money, power, all that rot."

"Simon! I'm not that shallow."

"Shallow? Hell, you endure a guy like Marc Kimball for a year, get a divorce and walk away. Now, I guess that's shallow. But what good business sense."

"I have a job—I'm a lucky actress. Not a household name, but working in theater, which I love. I don't need a fortune."

"Yes, but…well, anyone could use a fortune, right?"

She shook her head. "Simon, he is a creepy jerk of a man. I will remind you of this conversation when creepy women are after you, okay?"

"How creepy?"

"Argh!"

He grinned. "Well, at least I made you smile. Seriously, though, watch out for that guy."

"I will. I promise. I don't trust Marc Kimball at all."

"Want to have dinner with Ralph and Larry and me and talk about people?"

She grinned at that. "Sure. I'm here until the Feds go back."

Simon's smile faded. "Why are you going back? You should be here with us—recuperating, as the bosses see it."

"I just feel that I can help."

He bit his lip, lowering his head. "You hang on to the FBI guys with everything you got, okay?"

She nodded.

"Okay, downstairs in an hour?"

"Downstairs in an hour," she said.

He left; she looked out in the hall. Her officer was still there. He'd gotten a chair, at least. He smiled and waved to her. She smiled and waved, too.

Turning back into her room, she almost walked straight back into Amelia.

"I really like him," Amelia said. "Wish I could have gotten to know him."

"Simon is a good guy," Clara assured her. She wished, however, that Amelia would have stayed gone awhile longer; she needed some private time.

Her wish was going to be fulfilled—the ghost began to fade.

"Oh!" Amelia said.

"What's wrong?"

"I don't know. I just… I fade sometimes and I think I sleep and… I really can't control it yet," she told Clara.

"Then you need rest," Clara said.

"I'm a ghost!" Amelia said indignantly.

"Maybe even ghosts need rest!"

Amelia didn't reply. She was gone. Clara tossed herself back on her bed and closed her eyes.

She really needed a little rest herself.

The task force meeting took place at the offices of the state police. There were dozens of officers in attendance along with representatives from every conceivable law enforcement agency and the Coast Guard.

Special Director Enfield was there, and so was Detective Brennan.

There was a fine air of determination in the room. Every officer just wanted answers, and the killer caught.

They began with what they knew about the murder of Natalie Fontaine. Natalie was last seen the evening before her death in the lobby meeting with her crew, including Amelia Carson, Becca Marle, Nate Mahoney and Thomas Marchant. She had seemed excited—according to the surviving members of her crew, it was because they had just returned from "setting" Black Bear Island for the day to come.

The call about a commotion had come at just about 5:00 a.m.— minutes after the desk clerk had briefly seen Amelia Carson on the phone in the lobby.

The only cameras at the Nordic Lights Hotel were in the lobby and at the ATM.

Every boat captain at every point was being queried about Amelia Carson; the captain who had gotten her across to the island could not be found. Speculation was that the killer did indeed have a boat and that he perhaps got her to the island, strangled her, removed her to the pine forest for bisection and then displayed her where she was found.

The medical examiner, Dr. Andropov, who had been the lead on both bodies, stated the women had been strangled and were dead before being decapitated and bisected. Before being strangled to death, they'd both been struck with a blunt object, the nature of that object unknown. The tool used on the bodies after death, he believed, had been either a custom or specialized spade or woodsman's ax or hatchet; a broad weapon with a honed blade. He displayed various sketches of what he believed the weapon to be, emphasizing the fact that it wasn't easy to remove a head—it required a sharp instrument and a fair amount of strength—and that it was even more difficult to cut a human being in half.

Detective Brennan reported on his interviews, a member of each forensic crew reported on their findings or lack thereof, and Thor gave a report of what they'd discovered on the island.

"Can you tell us anything else?" someone asked Dr. Andropov.

"Yeah," he said. "This killer is one sick son of a bitch."

"Who doesn't like reality TV!" someone else cracked.

"Taking it to the extreme!" another officer said.

"Yeah," Andropov said quietly. "Problem is, this guy isn't the kind who stops. Whether reality TV triggered him or not, I've been around long enough to know that it's not like shooting a pal in a bar because he changed the station on the sports screen. This kind of killer—he keeps going. Until he is caught."

There was silence.

It was Thor's turn to speak.

Since the ME and forensic members had done a fair job on reporting the facts, he described hearing what sounded like something falling against the house, their search in the darkness—and then their search by the light, which allowed them to discover that the killer had used "bear" snowshoes to escape the house and changed them in the pines, and that the discovery had led them at last to the small clearing where the murderer had bisected Amelia Carson.

"Naturally, our technical crews are doing their best to determine the movements of all of the people on the island when Amelia Carson's body was found, as well. A number of law enforcement officers scoured the surrounding areas after the discovery of the body and no one was found, though that doesn't mean someone may not still be on the island. The timing means it is possible for one killer to have murdered Natalie Fontaine, called Amelia Carson to set up a meeting, gotten out to Black Bear Island and killed her. On the other hand, it's equally possible that we have two killers working in tandem. Therefore, it's incredibly important that we do know where everyone involved was at any time. While we all know that eyewitness reports can be shaky at best, we need anything that we can get. The information is out—the killings were so horrendous and so many civilians were involved, the media caught hold quickly. Townspeople and tourists will be frightened. All information that we have is being shared nationwide and, of course, with our Canadian neighbors. Please, no matter how small any piece of information may seem, we need it reported. We're keeping joint force members—police and FBI—out on the island at this time, and the Coast Guard is continuing to monitor the shores of the island."

An officer raised a hand. Thor acknowledged him.

He introduced himself as George Hardwick and said, "We're all aware that the Fairy Tale Killer murdered a doctor and escaped from Kansas. We've heard there is speculation that he's here. Do you have any reason—of which we're not aware—to think this man might have come to Alaska? From what we've seen, there's no indication that the man was ever in Alaska or knows anything about Seward or Black Bear Island."

"There is no forensic reason at this time to believe that the Fairy Tale Killer has come here," Thor said. "Kansas is a long way away. The man wouldn't have had a full day to reach Alaska and he's being sought by law enforcement agencies everywhere. Our victims' display doesn't resemble the displays of the Fairy Tale Killer in any way." He hesitated. "However, in theory, it is possible that he's come here. It is possible that his end goal in displaying his previous victims wasn't to make them beautiful, but to cause sensationalism and earn a moniker. I believe the press has already dubbed this killer the 'Media Monster.' We all know that talk on the street compares the positioning of Miss Carson on Black Bear Island to that of the Black Dahlia—impossible to see her without that image coming to mind. As to Natalie's murder, we think he had something in mind. Unfortunately, there have been a number of decapitation murders in history, so we're not sure if he is or isn't going for a theme that has to do with history, or perhaps movies—or gruesome historical murders that have been portrayed in movies."

"You mean, you really think this guy—this Tate Morley guy—might have gotten up here?" another officer asked.

"No, there's nothing that says that it is him. But, there's also nothing that says that it's not him. At this point, anything is speculation. We have to keep our eyes open, be exceptionally vigilant and, yes, warn young women," Thor said.

"We'll be doing that in a press conference this afternoon," Enfield told the assembled crowd. "Right now, we're keeping eyes on the Wickedly Weird Production Company, and—to a lesser extent—the folks who were to be interviewed on the island. Unless all three men with the theatrical company suddenly became sickly homicidal together, they're in the clear—background checks on the three come up with nothing but clean slates. We're keeping an eye on them for their safety."

"You have all received sheets on Tate Morley. They have gone out across the country," Thor said. "He is capable of being a physical chameleon. He escaped one of his scenes dressed as a nun, one as a clown, and another as simply stoned out. Again, there's nothing that suggests he did come here, but, again, be vigilant."

When the meeting was over, they spoke with Brennan and Enfield briefly.

Enfield believed that Thor was right; they needed a representative on the island from now until it was determined to be unnecessary.

"Get techs checking up on Marc Kimball for me, too, please, will you, Director?" Thor asked.

"Kimball?" Enfield was surprised.

"He's back on the island," Jackson said.

"I know, of course. Detective Brennan told me that Kimball arrived at the police station soon after the news of a death on the island reached him. Very distraught. You realize that legally, it's all very complicated. He owns the island. Wickedly Weird rented the island. We can claim parts of it as a crime scene, but—without brute un-American force—we are beholden to him to cooperate as far as searches and use of the Mansion and Alaska Hut are concerned. Legally, I'm not sure what happened with the Wickedly Weird Productions crew's contract. Best at the moment to get done what we need to get done with the cooperation of Wickedly Weird and Marc Kimball."

"Sir, with all due respect," Jackson said, "we understand that. But it is curious that the man showed up so quickly."

"Amen," Detective Brennan muttered.

"I simply believe that his whereabouts immediately before the deaths would be nice to know," Thor said.

"Absolutely. We are running a time check on Kimball," Enfield agreed.

"When he's in Seward, he usually heads out to the island immediately—that's what the tabloids tell us," Detective Brennan said. "So where was he when the killing was going on?"

"I'm pretty damned sure you're barking up the wrong tree with Kimball," Enfield said. "A man like that...odd behavior would have been reported by now."

"Describe 'odd behavior,'" Thor murmured.

"Criminal behavior," Jackson said.

"Let's face it. He's on the list of the world's wealthiest men—he can buy a lot of discretion. Still, it's not a matter of me suspecting him—it's really a 'let's eliminate him' quest," Thor said.

Enfield looked at Jackson curiously. "I'm interested, Crow. You manage your own team of investigators now—several units, I believe. Shouldn't you be managing them? No disrespect meant, but I have to assume you're here because of Tate Morley, too?"

Jackson nodded. Watching the interaction, Thor realized that Jackson had reached to the top for permission to come out here and involve himself in this investigation. Enfield had to be wondering what kind of pull Jackson had to get his way so quickly in a Bureau often filled with red tape.

Jackson smiled. "Yes, sir. When it comes to Tate Morley, I have to be hands-on."

Detective Brennan studied Jackson and shrugged. "If it could be this man and you've hunted him before, I say all hands on deck."

"But," Enfield asked, "wouldn't it have made more sense for you to be hands-on in Kansas?"

Jackson gave him a rueful smile. "I can't say that I do know where Tate Morley is now, sir, but I would bet my eyeteeth that he's no longer in Kansas."

"No one is here for a pissing match," Thor said. "Sir—"

Enfield laughed. "I've heard about the Krewe of Hunters. Unorthodox methods—using the dead for witnesses, some say. Intuiting from ghosts or revenants or whatever. Well, I know you are an assistant director—field director—in your own right, taking a backseat here since you know Thor and don't know the terrain and he knows it especially well. And I don't care if you talk to walls, dogs or elephants. Get this guy—whoever the hell he is." He hesitated. "We'll have forensic teams on the island for another few days. I don't know why the killer would hang around now, but if you still seem to think it's important to be out there, I'll go with your instinct."

"We found where he butchered Amelia Carson, sir. I think we may find his hideout, as well," Thor said.

"We're working on recovery of the video from the hotel— my guys are cleaning it up and enhancing it now. It will be ready in a few hours. You might want to see it before you head back," Brennan said.

"We will want to see it. Thank you," Thor told him.

"I've looked at it—poor quality," Brennan said. "Nothing but people coming and going, all looking fine and normal. But the video doesn't even cover the elevators. Still, one man may see something that others don't." Brennan's face tightened with an edge of aggravation. "And the island is covered for the moment at the least. Mike Aklaq is there, right? And I have people finishing up at the Mansion with hours and hours of film to process, only to prove it's all fake!"

"Thank God for science and talented techs," Thor said. "Thing is… I know that island. I was once one of those obnoxious kids who liked to sneak out there and drink beer and build a bonfire. If there is anything out there, I believe I'm the one who can find it."

Enfield nodded. "All right, just take it in shifts, and make sure you report to me, as well." He shook his head, eyeing them both. "I'm no clairvoyant," he added, "but I've been around awhile. Killers like this don't suddenly see the light. Do whatever you have to do. Use any method. Stop him—before he kills again."

CHAPTER EIGHT

Clara couldn't help looking around the restaurant. She was afraid that Amelia Carson was going to make an appearance.

But Amelia was not in the restaurant. She and her cast mates ordered their food. Clara began to relax, but she only half listened to the conversation going on around her.

She hoped that Amelia wouldn't arrive. She wasn't afraid of the ghost anymore. Amelia was lost—she needed help. Clara wanted to give her that help.

She just hoped that she didn't wind up appearing to talk to walls herself.

"I really hope that we actually get to do this show," Simon said wistfully.

"Of course we'll get to do the show," Clara said.

"We didn't get to do the last one," Ralph reminded her.

"Yes, but that was different," Clara said.

They all looked at her. "It was different!" she assured them.

"I guess so. I was so happy to be here! See Alaska," Simon said.

"Well, we are seeing Alaska," Larry reminded them.

They all fell silent. Larry drummed his fingers on the table. "So. You're going to go back and stay on the island, huh, Clara?"

"Yeah."

"Just watch out. I mean really watch out. Not just for the killer—watch out for Kimball! He's looking at you like he's a wolf and you're a lamb," Ralph warned.

"Ralph, maybe the guy just appreciates theater," Clara said.

"He didn't pay any attention to me," Ralph said.

"He might have realized you and Larry were a duo," Clara told him.

"No, no, I'm not a duo with anyone and I'm heterosexual and I can tell you—wolf looking at a lamb," Simon said, nodding his head sagely.

"Well, don't worry. I can't stand the guy," Clara said. "He gives me the creeps."

"Yeah, but he's staying on *his* island, right?" Ralph asked.

Clara shrugged, feeling acutely uncomfortable.

"She's got Jackson and Thor—she'll be all right," Simon said.

Ralph grinned. "Jackson—and Thor. So, last time, she gets the married agent. This time…hey, what do we know about this Thor guy? And who names their kid Thor?"

"He's of Norse descent," Simon said. "Probably a common name. Like Jesus if you come from a Spanish-speaking country."

"He looks like a Thor," Larry said.

"You look like a Thor!" Ralph told him with pride and affection.

"Um," Larry said, smiling. "No, but, I mean, he really looks like a Thor."

"You two are kind of beautiful together," Simon said. "Really," he added, laughing. "You're both just exceptionally cool-looking people. And he's not married."

"Guys, please!" Clara begged.

"Sure. Tell me that you haven't noticed the man!" Simon said.

"I've noticed the man. I noticed him—right after I noticed a body in the snow!" Clara reminded him.

Ralph waved a hand in the air. "Clara—bad things happen in life. But we move forward. We seize what moments we can!"

"That's kind of melodramatic," Simon told him.

"Life is melodramatic!" Ralph claimed.

"Both agents are excellent—wait! All three agents are great. Mike Aklaq is cool, too," Clara said.

"Ah, yeah, but it's different with you and Thor," Simon commented, taunting her with a subtle smile.

"I don't know what you're talking about," Clara said.

"Well, of course she doesn't. She's Clara!" Ralph said. "Dear, dear, dear child! You never notice. Now, of course, you have noticed Marc Kimball because he practically drips slime when he's around you. But! You should see it when you and Special Agent Thor Erikson are together!" He demonstrated, flicking his fingers in the air. "Sparks! You share something." He leaned toward her, his elbow on the table. "Let it happen, Clara, let it happen. I'm telling you…"

"Stop. We started off with him tackling me in the snow and he really hasn't been all that nice. Kind of a dickhead, really," Clara said. "He's pretty cold. Hard-core FBI."

"Damned good-looking dickhead," Larry noted.

"I found him to be very courteous," Ralph said. "Just passionate—which is very good. He's looking for a killer."

"It is quite simply basic nature," Simon told Clara. "Men are horrible because of biology—scatter as much seed as you can with anyone. Women are selective. They have only so many eggs—gotta get those puppies fertilized by the best there is. And I've heard that a man's scent is something that kind of warns a woman if he'd fight for her or not. Supposed to be huge in the chemistry of two people."

"Sparks, sparks, sparks!" Larry said.

"And he does smell really good," Ralph said.

"Guys! Stop with the smells and the sparks. The waitress is

coming!" Clara said. And, with her cheeks reddening, she realized that she'd never been so happy to see food arrive.

But while the others forgot their teasing conversation, Simon did not. He reached across the table and took her hand.

"I'm being serious now. We like to tease you about Erikson, yes. But hang with him and Jackson, please. And watch out for Kimball," he said quietly. "There's something about him...well, there's something about him that just isn't right."

Jackson and Thor left the station.

A company car had been left for their use.

Thor slid into the driver's seat and looked at Jackson. "You have Clara's number, right?" he asked.

Jackson smiled. "I do. You're driving—I'll call."

Thor listened as Jackson asked questions, since the phone wasn't on speaker. "An officer is still on duty in the restaurant? We'll be no more than another thirty minutes."

Jackson nodded, repeated the questions and relayed the answers. "She's fine. She's having dinner in the Hawthorne's restaurant with her friends, the officer is great—and she's anxious to speak with us."

"Does she know something else?"

Jackson asked the question and turned back to Thor. "She repeated that she's having dinner with her friends."

She didn't want to speak in front of the others, Thor realized.

"We'll be there soon," Jackson said.

"Let's go straight to her. I can go by my house to get a few things after we see her," Thor said.

Jackson smiled slightly, looking down.

"She could be in danger," Thor said.

"She didn't sound as if she was in any danger. She's at the hotel with three friends and an officer on duty. She'll be all right," Jackson said.

"Let's get her anyway—it never hurts to make certain of any-thing."

"Of course," Jackson said. "I'm surprised Enfield didn't argue about her coming back out there with us."

"I think you'd manage to one-up his authority if it came to that," Thor said, glancing over at his old partner. Crow was a decade older, but he hadn't changed much. Even as a young agent, he'd been cool and cautious—able to act in the blink of an eye, but just as capable of thinking.

"It's not me," Jackson told him, half smiling as he looked over at him. "The acting director of the Krewe—Adam Harrison—answers only to the director of the FBI. Adam was finding the right people to get things done around the country before he became official and started the Krewe. I was his first guinea pig. Adam had his eye out at all times for the right people. He is a bit of a red tape magician—when we need something, we turn to him." He was quiet for a minute. "Adam knew about Tate Morley, and he knew about my role in that investigation and that I'd been partners with you. So, there it is."

"Well—nice," Thor told him. "I knew a bit about the Krewe. Good that you're here."

"Right or wrong as far as the Fairy Tale Killer goes, it's good to be working this with you," Jackson said. "And… I'm glad I'm here for Clara."

Thor glanced at him quickly. "You are just friends, right? I mean, I'm not missing something here that I should be seeing. I heard that you were married to a fellow agent. I don't imagine the man I worked with not being…monogamous."

Jackson didn't take offense. "We're just friends, good friends—I guess circumstances made it so. And yes, I'm married to a fel-low agent, Angela Hawkins. She's a whiz at management, at finding what is needed, at sending the right agents out to the right place at the right time. When I need information that the local people can't give me in seconds, I always call back to the

Krewe offices." He hesitated. "I've actually thought about you in the last years, even discussed you with Adam. But while we work with a few satellite offices, Alaska wouldn't be in the mix right now."

Thor was silent.

He thought that Jackson—and the mysterious Adam Harrison—might ask him into the unit.

It was something he would consider.

Except...

He kept thinking that he had to find the truth for Mandy, who had haunted their dreams, and for the other victims.

And most important...

There was Clara Avery.

They reached the Hawthorne. They stepped out of the car and hurried into the old hotel. It had been built in 1905 by an Emile Hawthorne, an old New Englander who had come to Alaska to work on the railroad line right after Seward had been founded. Hawthorne had fallen in love with the scenery—unbeatable almost anywhere, with the rugged mountains rising to one side and the glistening beauty of the waters of Resurrection Bay on the other.

While it didn't offer much in the way of security, the Hawthorne did have charm. The lobby offered the comforts of an old lodge—worn leather sofas and chairs, a massive stone hearth and tables where guests could engage in chess, checkers, cards and other nonelectronic games.

It was only two stories tall and had thirty guest rooms, but the restaurant, off the lobby, served locals as well as lodgers and tourists.

Thor made straight for the restaurant.

The cop sent to watch over Clara was rigidly on duty, staying just inside the restaurant, right next to the giant stuffed grizzly that stood as if he were a maître d', ready to welcome patrons.

Thor and Jackson nodded to him; he gave them a thumbs-up sign and pointed to a table in the middle of the room.

Jackson went to speak with the police officer.

Thor paused a moment, watching the table group.

Clara was smiling at something Ralph Martini was saying.

Her smile was infectious, he thought. She was young and beautiful, in her late twenties, he thought, lithe and toned. There was something natural about her, as well. Or maybe *sincere* was a better description; perhaps both words applied.

But, he knew then, it wasn't really that at all. He felt something for her that he didn't remember feeling; somehow, he'd lost the ability to let himself become involved years before. He wasn't a fool or blind; she was lovely and arresting and the kind of woman to draw attention and desire without ever realizing the power of her appearance or character. Anyone would be attracted—like a moth to a pretty flame.

She wasn't just good-looking. She was somehow personal now, as well.

He shouldn't get personal; he knew that.

But he hadn't really gotten personal with Mandy Brandt. Actually, it had never been a matter of attraction with Mandy—he had simply liked her. And admired her. Her life had been filled with tragedy. Her mother dead of cancer when she was about five, her dad in a car crash when she was eighteen, and her only brother had been killed in the armed forces. She had told him once, *You can only cry so much before the soul is dead inside.*

That was because Mandy had been so worried about her friend—but in a very matter-of-fact way. She'd never suspected that she herself was the one Tate Morley had been after.

He hoped that her soul was alive and well now; he liked to believe that she was in light and happiness somewhere.

Still trying to help…and that would be why she had entered their dreams.

Clara Avery looked up then and saw him. Something in her

eyes changed; she was actually glad, he thought. Then again, she might have been glad to see her friend—Jackson Crow.

The others at the table turned to see him and Jackson arriving, as well.

He kept his voice low and level as he greeted them all. "Everything all right here?"

"Right as rain," Ralph said, rising to greet him and Jackson. "Officer Friendly over there seems to be a great guy. He wouldn't join us. Said he's on duty and eating a burger takes two hands."

"Ah, well, he'll be off in a few minutes," Thor said.

"I'll grab you a chair," Simon offered.

He was about to say that they should get going, but Jackson sat down at the table then and suggested that they should get something to eat quickly. "You know the staff around here?" Jackson asked him.

Thor grinned. "Yeah, I do." He'd eaten at the Hawthorne often enough. He knew Ali Norman, the waitress serving the table, because he'd helped out when her son had been arrested for drugs, getting him into rehab instead of jail.

Ali was quick to see that he and Jackson were promptly served the house specialty—venison stew—and to assure him that her son Tyson was doing well, working, and even engaged to a girl he had met while doing community service.

Thor told her how glad he was.

"Anything new?" Simon asked anxiously when Ali was gone.

"I'm afraid not," Thor told him.

"The cop goes when Clara goes, right?" Larry asked.

Thor nodded. "I'm afraid that law enforcement is being stretched thin here."

"We're good," Ralph said. "The *Fate* has security. The ship is still undergoing some work before our appointed sailing time, but we've been told we're welcome to take our cabins. Most of the crew is already aboard. We're set to sail in less than a week."

Thor wasn't sure why that wasn't a comforting thought. If she sailed, Clara would be far away. Far away from Seward, murdered women and, hopefully, the killer.

No, this killer—this killer had to be caught before the week was up!

"So, you three are going to board," Jackson said. "That's a good choice." He looked at Clara. "You're sticking with us for the time being?"

Clara nodded.

"Crazy!" Ralph said. "The killer was after the television people—and maybe us."

"Not crazy," Simon said. "She'll be with the FBI guys. Let's admit it, Ralph, you can play a great cop, but you aren't one. And no one in his right mind is afraid of me, which has been proven."

"I just look big and tough," Larry said regretfully.

"It doesn't matter," Clara said. "I feel I have to stay—for a few days at least. I'll be with you guys soon enough." She glanced over at Thor and Jackson. "Nothing new?" she asked weakly. "Nothing at all?"

"At least, no new bodies, right?" Ralph asked.

"Right," Thor said. He wasn't sure why—just agreeing made him uneasy.

"So," Jackson said. "What's the show about?"

"A ghost," Simon said, shaking his head.

"Yep, a ghost," Clara murmured, and then she smiled. "It's really charming. Shades of *Blithe Spirit* mixed with an older movie about an Irish castle. Love, falling in love, learning to fall in love again, all that."

"Sounds good," Jackson said. "Just the four of you?"

"Five of us. I'm the old wife, and there's a new wife," Clara said. "Connie Shaw is joining the Celtic American lineup. She was working on a ship that ended a cruise in Seattle. She's due up here anytime."

"I think she's due today," Ralph said. "But she's not staying here. She rented a cottage on the outskirts of town for the few days she planned on being here. Says she's seen Seward and wanted more of the rustic feel of Alaska."

"Do you know where this cottage is?" Jackson asked.

Damn—was he also feeling uneasy?

"No, but you can get that information easily enough. Head of entertainment for the ship knows everything," Ralph said.

Jackson rose. "I'll get the info," he said.

Thor rose, as well. "We need to get going. Clara?"

"My things are at the desk. I've checked out," she said. "I figure I'll go on to the ship, too, when—when it's time," she finished lamely. "Anyway, see you guys soon."

"Soon, my love!" Ralph said as she rose to leave them. Simon and Larry stood, too. She hugged them all; Thor waited patiently.

He followed close behind her as they headed to the front to meet up with Jackson.

"Don't think the place is far from your house, Thor, not by the addresses we have," Jackson said.

"The McGinty place?" Thor asked. One of his closest neighbors—close being about ten acres away—was old Theodore McGinty. He left during the summer to visit his daughter in Fairbanks and always liked to rent his place.

Jackson raised an eyebrow and rattled off an address. "Is that the McGinty place?"

Thor nodded. "Yeah, it's an old cottage—nice little place. Old, but he has the best heating system in the world and all kinds of computer gadgets and a great entertainment center."

"We'll see if Miss Shaw has checked in. You know this young woman, right?" Jackson asked Clara.

"Yes, not well—not like the guys. But we met at the auditions for the show and had a meeting after the casting, along with a blocking rehearsal and some readings of the script," Clara told him. "She's very nice, a petite dark-haired woman."

"But you do know her well enough," Thor murmured. "That's good."

They reached a black sedan. Thor slid into the driver's seat. Jackson opened the passenger's door for her in the front and slid into the back himself.

They drove through the town of Seward. Clara had gotten to walk a great deal of it; Seward was a wonderful small town, offering so much in a compact area. Floods throughout the years had been devastating, but Seward meant to thrive. The drive from Seward to Anchorage was supposed to be one of the most scenic to be found. She was fond, however, of the town itself, where many of the buildings were in different and complementary pastels, which seemed to be—along with the shimmering water, the cruise ships and other vessels at port, and the fantastic mountains—uniquely Seward. Uniquely Alaska.

Thor was driving quickly but skillfully, making good time.

She leaned forward. "You're afraid for Connie?" she asked. "But..."

"It's not a rational fear—it's just a situation we should check out," Jackson said.

"Well, we're driving awfully fast," Clara said.

"We'll just make sure everything is all right," Thor said.

She knew that neither of the men thought that everything was going to be all right. She felt her own stomach pitch.

They left the city behind, remaining beneath the shadow of snow-tipped mountains, hugging a road that cut through dense forest. Thor then turned down what looked like little more than a dirt road. In a matter of seconds, a little cabin appeared, with a board porch and a cheerful striped umbrella over tables on the veranda.

It seemed that the motor was still running when Thor and Jackson stepped out of the car; both men jumped out quickly and headed for the door to the cabin. Clara followed them up the steps to the porch.

Thor tapped hard at the door. "Miss Shaw? Miss Shaw?"

A frightened whimper came back to them. "Who is it? Who's there?"

"FBI, Miss Shaw. Are you in distress, is anything wrong—"

"Connie, it's me, Clara Avery, and these men are FBI," Clara called.

The door swung open. Connie Shaw stood there in purple sweats, dark hair pulled back in a ponytail, her features drawn and pale. She threw herself in Clara's arms.

"Connie, what happened? What's going on?"

"Someone was out there—someone in back. I... I'd left the back door open. I was out on the porch, looking up at the mountains. There were deer, two of them, right back there! I came in for my phone and I heard someone...whispering my name!" Connie said, her speech hurried and barely coherent.

Jackson was already gone, heading around back. "Stay with her—I'll go through the house to the back!"

"I'm not a chicken, not a chicken, not a chicken, but... Not right, not just a person, not just a visitor... He was there, he would have gotten in... I'm so scared!" Connie babbled. "I got here and heard about the murders—Natalie Fontaine... Amelia Carson... I didn't think they'd be after us...but I'm so scared. I thought...well, their kind of reality TV, they might have really pissed someone off, but I just act on a stage... I don't do anything evil to anyone, except, you know, maybe by accident and that wouldn't be evil or mean, just..."

"Connie, calm down. It's all right," Clara said. "Sh. These men are FBI. You are all right now."

She wondered if she had been like this—this hysterical, this scared—when she had found the body of Amelia Carson.

Yes, yes, she had been.

She swallowed hard. Two very competent, strong, well-armed members of the FBI were with them. They were all right.

No, not really, the killer was still out there.

They wouldn't be all right, none of them—not even the big, strong members of the FBI—if this killer wasn't caught.

She mentally renewed her passion to do whatever was necessary to help.

She also heard Ralph's voice in her head.

Sparks!

Sparks…flying between her and Thor Erikson.

Connie was still talking, she realized.

"What's happening, Clara? Oh, my God, what's happening? And I was so excited to be on the *Fate!*"

"Sh, sh, it's all right," Clara repeated.

Was it? They'd all been so excited about the *Fate*.

And now they were all here…fated to be here?

She was suddenly angry; really angry with herself. Nothing was truly predetermined; they were all architects in their own destiny.

This was the fault of a horribly sick, heinous and cruel murderer. And she was going to do whatever it took to help the FBI catch him, even if that included becoming best girlfriends—a bit belatedly—with Amelia Carson.

"It's all right," she repeated firmly. "We're with the FBI. And they have guns. Big ones," she added, and smiled to herself.

She had no idea of the size of their guns.

There was no one in the house Connie had rented, but when Thor stepped out the back door, he studied the lock.

He frowned. It appeared that someone had been trying to jimmy it—which didn't really make sense, not if Connie Shaw had left it open.

She'd said that she'd heard someone whisper her name.

Had she—or had she been afraid and imagined that she heard the whisper?

The possibilities shot through his head. She hadn't expected to be so alone, even though she had opted for nature and privacy, so maybe her imagination had run rampant. Maybe the lock had been jimmied long ago—even by the owner, who might have forgotten his keys.

Bull.

Staring at the jimmied door, he pulled out his cell phone and flicked the screen to contacts, finding Theodore McGinty. He called the older man—a close friend of his dad's, and a stern disciplinarian with all the neighborhood kids when he'd been young.

"Mr. McGinty, this is Thor Erikson."

"Thor, hey! Ah, hell. It's not a social call, is it?" McGinty asked. "I thought I was okay—gave the place to a sweet young woman for a week. What, she have a bunch of frat boys in? They cutting up and doing drugs in my house?"

"No, sir, nothing like that."

He heard McGinty's groan. "What's the matter with me?" McGinty asked. "I keep forgetting you're FBI, boy. This is no minor thing. Lord, I've been seeing the news on the murders. Please tell me that…that it's not as bad as it could be."

No, it wasn't as bad as it could be. A killer could have carried out his plan to kill and mutilate a beautiful young woman.

"I wanted to let you know that Miss Shaw isn't going to be staying here. We're taking her where she'll have police protection. We're watching out for everyone involved with that TV show and Miss Shaw's cast was being interviewed the day the murders took place. But I also wanted to ask you—have you had any kind of problem with an attempted break-in at any point?"

"Boy, why would anyone break in on an old man who has nothing but great memories?" McGinty asked him in return.

"Looks like someone tried to jimmy your lock."

McGinty was silent for a minute and then said, "You get that girl out of there, then, Thor. You see that she's safe. You tell her she'll get all her money back from me. No, no, sir. No one has tried to break in on me. But, when I'm there, old Oslo is with me, and no one messes with my dog."

That was true. Old Oslo was a "chusky"—a new designer mix of a chow and a husky. Oslo was huge; he wasn't to be messed with.

"Do you need me to come there?" McGinty asked.

"No, sir. Thank you. If I do need you, I'll call."

"Don't hesitate," McGinty told him.

"I won't," Thor promised, and hit the end button.

Someone had been out here—someone might have been here even as they had come driving up to the place.

Just the same as at his family's property, the backyard disappeared into a forest of trees that, especially during summer, seemed to have a life of their own, intruding on the lawn or yard. Thick and heavy—with a million places to disappear.

But how could someone have gotten out here? Where would they have left a car? There was no snow on the ground so a snowmobile or dogsled couldn't be stashed anywhere. Some people did have wheeled sleds that they used in summer, keeping their dogs fit. But, if there were dogs, they would hear them. He'd sure as hell never heard a silent dog team.

Logical conclusion: someone had been here. Perhaps they had first tried to jimmy the lock. But that had proved to be unnecessary when Connie Shaw had left the door open.

How would they have known that Connie would be here?

It wasn't privileged information, but it wasn't advertised online, either.

When a criminal wanted information, they tended to be good at getting it.

Jackson came walking back from the tree line.

"Anything?" Thor called.

Jackson shook his head with disgust. "If someone was here, that someone heard us when we turned down the road to the house. You'll know better than me if someone crashed through that pine forest. I went all the way back—there's a dirt service road out there. I guess it's used by police or rangers or the trash company? Nothing out there and it doesn't seem to lead to anything, but there could be a small vehicle back there. I'd have heard a motorcycle, but if someone drifted out of there in Neutral before I was actually into the trees, I wouldn't have been able to hear them."

"So, she could be hysterical and nervous because of what she heard, or someone might have been back here," Thor said, adding quietly, "Which would mean the murderer isn't just after the women who had to do with the television crew."

"She can't stay here, that's for certain," Jackson said.

Thor told Jackson about the jimmied lock on the door and his conversation with McGinty.

"No, Connie Shaw can't stay out here," Thor agreed. "Not that I think she would now."

"Let's try talking to her again," Jackson suggested.

Clara had gotten Connie Shaw to sit down in the living room. She looked up gratefully when Jackson and Thor arrived. Connie sprang off the couch and flew into Thor's arms. He disentangled himself gently and sat her back down.

"We're here. We're not going to leave you. You're all right. What I'd like for you to do is tell me when you got here and everything that happened after that," he said.

"I came in this morning—snagged a ride in on another ship," Connie said. She looked at Clara. "I should have stopped and met up with you all, but I figured that this might be like…well, you know, like my afternoon! I drove out here about an hour ago—I was in love with the place. It was just what I wanted. I turned the television on and heard what had happened…my mom says I should listen to news and not music all the time! But, I… I had on satellite radio, singing all the way! When I saw the television, I was horrified. My coffee was outside—I saw the deer. Then I thought about how what happened all had to do with Wickedly Weird Productions and I realized that people might be trying to get in touch with me. So I came back inside to get my phone...and that's when I heard it!"

"Heard what, exactly?" Thor asked.

"The whisper. It sounded as if it was coming from the back windows. Someone was saying my name—saying it all softly and like, like...eerily! 'Connie... Connnnnniiiieee... Connie... Shaw.' I heard it, I swear I heard it. I was in the bedroom, the back bedroom, where I was going to sleep. I wasn't imagining it! Then, of course, I realized that the whisper was out there—and that I hadn't locked the back door! I was flying out to the kitchen when I heard the rap on the door!" Connie said. She stared at them and added quickly, "I need a drink!"

"Did you bring anything?" Clara asked her.

"No!"

"Check the little cabinet above the refrigerator. McGinty usually keeps a bottle of Jack there," Thor advised her.

"Yes, please, please, I can't stop shaking!" Connie said.

"You really don't want to be blitzed right now," Thor advised.

"Yes, I do!" Connie said.

"No, but one shot..." Thor said, nodding at Clara.

Clara headed into the kitchen. Thor could hear her there, finding the bottle, opening it. Connie kept murmuring about the way the person had been saying her name. "It was creepy, so creepy!"

He heard the rattle of glass, the opening of old man McGinty's foot-powered trash can.

Clara came back into the room.

She was the color of the snow on Black Bear Island.

But, she set the glass down in front of Connie Shaw and said,

"Thor, can I see you in the kitchen for a minute? Just want to—
check with you on the bottle. Connie, if you want to wait—"

Too late for that. Connie had swallowed the shot.

"Oh, God, no! You don't think it was poisoned or anything,
do you?" she asked, holding the glass away and staring at it.
"They weren't poisoned…they were strangled. The women from
Wickedly Weird. And then cut up. But they weren't poisoned."

"No, no, Connie, I just want Thor to make sure I remember right what the label says—so that we can replace it," Clara
said. "Thor?"

He followed her into the kitchen. She was, to her credit, dead
calm and not even shaking—despite the fact that she was white
as snow—as she pointed to the trash can.

"I didn't touch it," she said softly.

He opened the trash can with his foot and looked down.
There was only one item inside.

A book page offering a historic photo.

It was laid out at the bottom of the can, carefully placed on
the white plastic liner.

It was a photo of an old crime scene.

A woman lay dead in it.

She was barely recognizable as a woman. Even in black and
white, it was an image of unspeakable carnage.

Thor closed his eyes for a moment.

He knew the photo; he'd seen a copy in one of the Bureau's
criminology classes—seen it as a PowerPoint image on a large
screen.

They'd been studying Jack the Ripper.

The photo laid out in the trash can was that of the body of
Mary Kelly, the Ripper's fifth and last victim, according to most
criminologists and Ripperologists.

Mary Kelly had been killed indoors, where the killer had spent
time tearing into her, enjoying himself at his leisure.

And the whole of the surface of her abdomen and thighs had

been ripped away; her insides had been torn out; her breasts had been removed...

This was just an image, a page taken from a book, he thought. Not ripped out, but carefully cut out. Not crumpled, but smooth and clearly visible.

But someone had put the image in the trash. Someone had been in the house.

Someone had intended, he was certain, for Connie Shaw to die...

And to take the form of Mary Kelly, infamous victim of Jack the Ripper.

Mutilated...

And about whom many a movie had been made.

CHAPTER NINE

Clara couldn't help it; she engaged in a heated argument with Thor just beyond Connie Shaw's realm of hearing—right after she learned that he was grouping her with Connie and the others, determined that she be apart from everything that happened from that point on.

Jackson had kept silent.

According to Thor, she should be on the ship. She should be on the *Fate* with Connie, and both women should be assigned full-time guards in addition to the ship's security.

"That makes absolutely no sense!" Clara said. "After all, I'm the one with the connection—Amelia keeps coming to me. She's looking for something that she never had in life."

"And what's that?" Thor demanded.

"Friendship. All she had was ambition. Now that life is gone… I think she knows what she missed. It doesn't matter. What matters is that we have something going in the communication arena. You need me. I can help you! Hey! I'm the one who seems to have her finger on the pulse of what lies below the surface. You can't just dismiss me!"

"I don't want you to get yourself killed!" Thor exploded in

turn. "We don't need you enough to risk that. You know Jackson—you know about him. He's frigging ghost central! We don't want you to die—and become a ghost trying to communicate."

Jackson listened to both sides, and then told Thor, "There's no way out of it—she is in on this. And, in that vein, I prefer that Clara be with us—we can depend on one another and Mike as we can no one else. Not to mention that the island is also still crawling with police, should we choose to go out there again. In truth—I'm not so sure that Connie Shaw has been targeted. I think she was convenient. And I think the Mary Kelly image in the trash was a message to one of us. If we hadn't come when we did, Connie might well have died. But I think she would have died as a matter of convenience. Because the killer found out about her—and that she intended to be alone out here."

Thor lowered his head, shaking it slightly in hard anger. "You mean that Connie would have been ripped to shreds, and he would have left that picture for us to discover just in case we missed the connection? Because, otherwise, the killer had no idea we would look in the trash."

"I do believe we interrupted him," Jackson said. He smiled at Clara. "And that's a good day," he told her. He turned to Thor. "You called this in?"

Thor nodded. "Detective Brennan and a forensic crew are on the way out—they'll look for anything they can find. But hell, this is Alaska. This guy is wearing gloves. And who notices anyone buying gloves in Alaska? If they were even purchased here." He shook his head in frustration again. "There's something out on that island—but whether it was actually now or sometime before, the killer was here."

"We're both thinking Tate Morley," Jackson said.

"But how the hell the man could have spent years in prison, gotten here, killed here, gotten a boat and gotten out to the island, then back here..." Thor broke off, looking at Jackson.

"You're thinking two again," Jackson said.

"He had to have had a connection here," Thor said.

"Someone he's been communicating with while in prison," Jackson said.

"We need to—"

"I'll call Angela—my wife. As I've told you, one of the best people I know on any kind of research. Not to mention she can put other Krewe members on the case. Angela will dig until she finds out everything there is to know."

Thor grunted his agreement.

"I still think there's something out on that island. We found his cutting ground, at least. But I believe there's more to find out there," Thor said.

"But we know that someone was here," Jackson reminded him. He was silent a minute and said, "There are good agents here, good police. Good police on the island, too. There's no way to know the right move. Is someone in the near vicinity now—someone who left that picture in the trash? Probably. But he may not be here long. We're not the only competent people working the case, but you have been given lead. So, it's a matter of where you think it's most important to be, Thor."

Thor spoke slowly.

"You're right. He was here—now he's gone. Forensic teams will do what they can. Brennan will do everything he's able to do. Enfield and a dozen other men with the Bureau are here. We need to get back to Black Bear Island." Thor shook his head, as if he wasn't sure himself why he was so convinced that they needed to be on the island—when the killer had more recently almost struck here.

Or—one of the *killers*.

"Take the car to your family's place so you can pack up for the next few days. I'll stay here with Miss Shaw and meet with Detective Brennan and the forensic unit," Jackson said. "Brennan might have something more to give us. Get set, we'll stop by the police station to see if there's anything that resembles evi-

dence or a clue, and we can see the security tape from the Nordic Lights Hotel. Then we'll head back as planned and search
the island again. We can let Mike come back to Seward and get
some sleep."

Thor nodded and headed for the car.

Clara raced after him. He stopped, swung around and looked
at her. "Wait here. With Jackson and Connie Shaw."

"You're trying to get rid of me."

"And, apparently, I'm not doing well at it."

"May I at least talk to you while we head to your place?"

He didn't say yes.

He didn't say no.

He turned and kept going. Clara hurried after him and slid
into the passenger's side of the car.

She was going to talk him into keeping her close—and she
wasn't even sure what her own reasoning was.

She was crazy, ghost or no ghost; she needed to be in the safest place possible.

He drove in silence.

"You live out here?" she asked.

"I have an apartment in the city, too. But yes, I have a home
out here. At this point, it's easiest just to shower and change and
pick up a bag out here."

"Out here" wasn't even half a mile from the road that stretched
down to the McGinty house.

But, while they headed toward a place that was similar to
the McGinty cottage, it was different in size and scope. It was
a compound. There were a number of houses, stables, kennels
and other outbuildings.

A stone fence encircled one house; steps of the same stone
created a pathway that led to a porch and much larger log cabin.
Beyond the fence, encircled by a ring, was a large stable and what
looked like a kennel. Past those were more buildings.

"I thought you lived in the downtown area of Seward," she said.

"I have an apartment downtown," he told her.

"But you come out here, too?"

"Whenever I can."

She looked at him as he drove. "This is all yours? You have stables of horses—and huskies?" she asked.

He shrugged. "It's a family compound."

"Your family is out here?"

He shook his head. "My sister runs everything out here—my dad is a cop and he and my mother live in Nome most of the time. They have a cabin here." He pointed at a house far to the other side of the stables. "My sister's place. She and her husband and kids care for the horses and huskies. They race. They've won all kinds of mushing awards. They are heavily involved with the Iditarod each year."

"Are you a musher?" she asked him.

He shook his head. "No, I don't mush. But..."

"But?"

"I do have a couple of huskies," he told her. For some reason, he then smiled and shrugged and decided to become more forthcoming. "Boris and Natasha," he said. "You'll meet them. I just hope you're not against a lot of husky fur as an accessory."

"I love dogs," she told him. And she did. "My parents have always had dogs and cats, and growing up we had mice and all kinds of other creatures, as well. I'm fine with fur as an accessory."

She was glad that she did love animals. She thought that he might be putting her to the test, because he didn't speak a word to the big huskies when the door opened and Boris and Natasha immediately rose to greet them and be greeted in return.

They had evidently known that their master was home from the time that Thor had turned down the drive to the house.

They jumped about like children, but woofing and howling, seeming almost to speak.

Clara greeted them cheerfully. She was thrilled at the way they behaved—like dogs, just eager for affection. Being there, with the two huskies all but crying with excitement, suddenly made the world seem good again.

"They're not great as far as being watchdogs goes—they love everyone," Thor said. "My grandfather started breeding them for special friends. Now the family is known to breed some of the finest huskies anywhere. And my sister…my sister has a contract with buyers to make sure that our dogs are never mistreated in any way. We take back any animal we've sold or given away if there's any problem whatsoever. Astrid and Colin have a number of special charity situations in which we give dogs away. As far as my pets here, they kind of chose me. Boris is a little too big to be show quality—though he is a hell of a sled dog. Natasha is his sister. They were inseparable from the time they were puppies, so when I decided to take Boris, I took Natasha, as well. They're my pets, and I don't get to see them often enough, so they live here on the property. The stable manager and her husband live in a place just behind this one, and they look after Boris and Natasha and everything else around here."

"They're beautiful!" Clara said. "I love them!"

She'd been so involved with the dogs that she hadn't seen the house; she looked up at a sound and realized that from the front, she could see down a hallway all way to the back. While the "log cabin" look was still in effect, the back room had huge plated windows. There was a set of double doors between the windows, and a tall, very blonde woman could be seen through the glass, tapping at the door.

Thor strode through the house to let her in, greeting her with a kiss on the cheek. Clara heard them murmur something to each other and then they came down the hallway. "Clara, this is my sister, Astrid. Astrid, Clara Avery."

Astrid was quick to smile and offer Clara a hand. "Nice to meet you, Clara. So sorry to hear that you're involved in all this trouble."

Astrid was elegantly light and had an almost ethereal look to her; her handshake, however, was like steel.

"A pleasure to meet you," Clara said. "The dogs are magnificent!"

"Huskies are pure personality," Astrid said. "These two—they are loyal to Thor to a fault. Boris is as strong as an ox, and Natasha…well, Natasha is the mediator. Most of our dogs are sled dogs, which means there's a lead dog, and when Natasha is on a sled, she's kind of like the mom, putting everyone in his or her place." She smiled. "You'll have to come when we're preparing for a race and it's just crazy, dogs everywhere, excited, barking, set to go!"

The back door opened and closed again and a tall man with dark hair came walking down the hallway. "Thor, hey, glad you're here, sure you're in a hurry, but—oh!"

He stopped speaking, seeing Clara there.

"Hello," she said.

The man glanced curiously at Thor and then smiled, giving Clara his hand.

"Hello."

"Clara, Colin, my brother-in-law," Thor said quickly. "Colin, this is Clara Avery."

"How do you do, Clara? Lovely to meet you!" Colin said.

Clara wondered if Thor was afraid that his sister and brother-in-law thought that she was there because she was someone special in his life, because he very quickly explained who she was.

"Clara was there, on Black Bear Island, to be interviewed when all this happened. She actually found Amelia Carson."

"My God," Colin murmured, looking at Clara. "We've been keeping up with the news," he said, slipping an arm around Astrid's shoulders. "That's why I was surprised to see Thor here—

figured he'd be tied into twenty-four-hour-a-day work right now. Just wanted to see if there's anything we can do to help, seeing as how you will be busy."

"And careful, of course," Astrid said, looking at her brother anxiously.

"Always careful," he said. He hesitated. "I hate to say this, but in this particular case—"

"You're worried about your family, too," Astrid said. "Yeah, Dad called and said that you would be. We're alert, wary, and we're good." She turned to Clara with a small smile. "My brother thinks that our dogs are big babies, but they're not. I know when anyone is anywhere near the property, and whether they belong here or not. They were back in the stables with me until a few minutes ago. We knew that Thor was here—they made a beeline for their dog door into the house."

"She trusts the dogs," Colin said to Thor, shaking his head. "I'm a crack shot, and Astrid grew up knowing how to handle a gun, as well. We're okay here," he told Thor. "You go out and find the son of a bitch."

"I just need to clean up, get a few things," Thor said. He started to walk and then paused, turning back to speak to his sister and brother-in-law. "Thanks for taking good care of Boris and Natasha."

"Hey, it's what we do!" Astrid said. "And don't worry about Clara—I'll make tea and we can get to know her."

"Ohhhhh," he groaned, shaking his head. "Don't worry," he said to Clara. "I'll be out before water can boil."

"Even you are not that fast!" Astrid told him.

"Come on into the kitchen. So," she said, leading the way. "This is Thor's part of the complex. My parents only had two kids, him and me. My dad is a cop in Nome, so he and mom are almost never here. My great-grandfather was the guy who created the family biz, and now, Colin and I run it. My mom was the dog woman before me. Guys in this family seem to like being cops or agents or marshals—my uncle was a marshal. Anyway, not to worry, we're not alone here, either. We have two couples who work with us, and they have families...altogether, we have ten horses and twenty-four dogs at the moment, so... so, anyway, what about you? Where are you from, what do you do—something interesting, right? You were going to be interviewed, so, I figure..."

"Actress, musical theater. I work for Celtic American Cruise Lines," Clara said.

"Wow, cool!"

"Are you good?" Colin asked, grinning as he met them in the kitchen, a room that artfully joined a few state-of-the-art appliances with logs and an old-fashioned hearth, and copper pots that were hung from the rafters.

Clara laughed, liking Thor's sister and brother-in-law very much.

As well as Natasha and Boris, who trotted in behind the three of them.

"Good is always in the eyes of the audience," Clara said.

Astrid poked a button on an electric kettle on the counter and set about taking cups out of a cupboard. "We'd love to see your show," she said. She paused, looking at her. "I take it the show is only on the ship?"

Clara nodded.

"Well, hopefully you'll be out to sea and performing soon. But, hey, when you're not on the ship, you live here, in Alaska?"

"New Orleans," Clara told her.

"Oh, oh, too bad," Astrid said, looking over at her husband.

"Why? It's a great city, really," Clara said.

"Oh, NOLA is super," Colin agreed. "We just wished that you were here."

"Um, well, thank you."

"Except, of course," Colin added, "that it's terrible you're involved in this...this horrible, awful situation. Be careful, please."

"Do whatever Thor tells you, no matter how paranoid or ridiculous it may seem," Astrid said.

The water had boiled. Thor wasn't out yet. Astrid began to prepare the tea. "So he's going back to the island. And you're going back, too? Why?"

"I found the body... I was involved," Clara said a little lamely.

"Maybe you shouldn't be on the island," Colin said.

"Why not—I mean, where is safe?" Astrid asked. "That one woman was killed in her room in a busy hotel!"

"Maybe Clara has a more personal bodyguard," Colin murmured.

Clara was startled, certain that he was suggesting that she and Thor were a twosome. "Really," she murmured. "We just met. I mean, he seems to be a really great agent, but—"

"You're gifted," Astrid said.

"What?" Clara said, startled.

Astrid shrugged. "Thor—since he was a kid—has, well, a knack. An instinct...a way of seeing things." She smiled "I'm horrible at this. I can't say *sight*, because it's not really sight. I mean, sight is seeing, right? And sometimes, it's an intuition, or hearing, or knowing...going to sleep and waking up and knowing something. He doesn't talk about it much. But I'll never forget when he worked with Jackson Crow. The two of them together, they were something. I'm not making any sense, am I?" she asked.

Yes, actually, you are, Clara thought.

But the words that came to her lips were, "Jackson Crow is here. I know Jackson. I mean, I knew him before he came here. He was..." She paused and took a deep breath. "I was on another ship when there was an incident. I met Jackson on that ship."

They both looked at her. Boris made a noise that was partially like a howl, and partially a whimper—a reminder that he and Natasha were there and needed to be in on whatever was going on.

The dogs provided a great break.

"Treats! They need treats!" Astrid said. She looked at Clara and said, "Oh, Lord, I am way too impulsive. It's just that… please, don't tell Thor that I made him sound…strange. Out there… Oh, I'm so sorry! You know what I mean."

"Astrid!" The name was spoken from behind Clara—by Thor.

Clara spun around. Well, the water might have boiled, but he was fast. His hair was still damp from the shower. He was dressed in jeans and a casual sweatshirt and he was shaking his head.

Astrid winced; Boris and Natasha woofed happily. Thor reached for a cabinet and a bag of savory dog treats and told his sister, "It's okay, Astrid, she's strange, too, so if you made me sound strange, she might just be a happy person."

"So, I was right, and you're going to help?" Astrid asked.

"We didn't actually agree on that," Thor said.

"We didn't disagree," Clara reminded him.

"And she knows Jackson!" Astrid said, nodding gravely, as if that mattered tremendously. "And Jackson is here. Thor, I can't see where you have a choice. And we'd love to see Jackson, of course."

"Astrid," Thor began.

"When this is all behind us," Colin said, putting his hands gently on his wife's shoulders.

Astrid impulsively hugged Clara. Clara hugged her back.

The huskies barked.

Thor groaned. "Hey…we've got to go."

"Of course, sorry, we're just so delighted to meet you, Clara," Astrid said. "Thor never brings people here, so—"

"Goodbye, I love you," Thor said, giving his sister a kiss on the cheek. One of the huskies woofed; he bent down and both dogs came to him, tails wagging, smothering him with affection. He spoke to them both softly.

They both sat then, tails wagging.

To Clara, it almost looked as if they nodded, agreeing that he needed to go on to work.

Clara was hugged in turn by Astrid and Colin; the huskies were allowed to tell her goodbye, too, and she and Thor were finally out the door and heading back to the car.

She couldn't help but smile as she slid into the passenger's seat. He glanced over at her, frowning slightly.

"What?"

"I don't know. They just made you human."

"You didn't think I was human?"

She was still smiling. Looking straight ahead, aware of him watching her, she shrugged.

"They made you more human."

He grunted and drove and she turned in the seat to study him. "Thor...it's what you do for a career. I imagine it's not just work. So you deal with bad things all of the time. How do you not let it rule everything in your life?"

He glanced at her, head at an angle, and he smiled slightly himself, as well. "Most of the time, you don't bring it home. There is no way not to care, but you have good days, too. Like today, really. By the happenstance of your group talking about Connie Shaw, we might have saved her life. Maybe we're wrong and a horrible trickster had stalked her—I don't know. But putting the pieces together, this might have been, as Jackson said, a really good day."

"So...you're in the city most of the time?" she asked him.

"Depending on what's going on," he told her. She thought that he flushed slightly. "I love my sister. My brother-in-law is great. And I love riding—and watching them with the dogs when they're training. I come here often. I see my folks in Nome. We still...live. But, in this case..."

"It's what happened with Tate Morley?" she asked.

He nodded grimly as he drove. "Most men and women in law enforcement have that one case...the one that seemed to rip

you up, even if it did come to a legal conclusion. Morley was
that case. We'd been hunting for a magician, or so it seemed.
Someone who could disappear at will. Mandy Brandt came to
see us—she came to Jackson and me. She gave us the first via-
ble clues. Nice kid, really nice kid, just concerned for someone
else. We followed up on what she told us and started a search on
this guy her friend was dating. He was going by Thomas Jones
at the time—he knew it would be a good choice of name because there are probably thousands of men with that name. The
man is something of a magician, or an actor. He also wore cos-
tumes sometimes when he abducted women—never the same.
He was a clown at a birthday party once, a 'cowboy, new to
town' when he picked up another of his victims." He paused,
shrugging. "He wore a suit and tie and picked up one victim as
an FBI agent. He'd go from glasses to none, a bald look to long
hair, different clothing all the time. We followed dozens of leads.
Anyway, we'd finally gotten a tip on where he was supposed to
meet Mandy's friend. But while we were heading off there, he
was busy killing Mandy. We found him. She'd told me things
about him in conversation that suggested he was heading to a
museum with her. We found her—and he was still with her.
But, Mandy was dead."

Clara sat in silence for a minute. "I'm so sorry."

"Thing is… I just always wonder now about 'the book' and
what's right and wrong, morally. I shot him, but I didn't kill
him. I was actually shooting to kill—that would have been
by the book under the circumstances. But I had to take a wild
shot. Still, it was just Jackson and me there then. We could have
killed the bastard—no one would have known that we didn't
have to take a second shot. But we didn't take it. He was down.
We called for backup. He went to the hospital—Mandy went
to the morgue. I watched the case every day. He wound up in
federal court because he'd crossed state lines. They debated the
death penalty. They decided on maximum security. Now, he

should have stayed—the sentence was harsh enough. There was no chance of parole. But…"

"But, he's out. And you believe that he is killing again, and killing here."

"And I could be crazy. They could catch him in Kansas or Nebraska tomorrow."

They had arrived back at the McGinty house. Jackson was waiting at the end of the walk with a tall man of about forty-five with short-cut hair, in a plain wool suit.

The place was busy now; Clara could see a number of vehicles there. Writing on the vans identified them as belonging to forensic crews.

Jackson walked down to the car with the tall man. By the time they reached the vehicle, both Thor and Clara were out of it, waiting. She saw that Thor knew the tall man; they greeted one another briefly.

"Erikson," the other man acknowledged.

"Detective Brennan," Thor said, and introduced Clara to the man.

He eyed Clara curiously and then said, "You had quite a bad time, so I understand," he said.

"I found Amelia Carson, yes," she said. "And naturally I'm passionate that we find her killer," she added softly.

"Will you be heading to the *Fate* now with Connie Shaw?"

She hesitated, aware that Brennan might protest her determination, and insist that non–law enforcement personnel must not be involved.

"Clara is returning to the island with us," Jackson said.

"She was given a tour of the island when she arrived and witnessed a great deal that may help us now," Thor told him.

"And," Jackson added, "Marc Kimball has seen her perform. He's a huge fan."

"She's been quite a help easing into any access we might need," Thor said. "We were at the Hawthorne Hotel today

with Clara and her cast when we discovered that Connie Shaw
was out here."

Brennan was grave. "You're willing to do all this, Miss Avery?
You can just board your ship and be with your cast mates, away
from all this. I have men watching over your friends. We don't
usually allow civilians to place themselves in danger."

"I won't be in danger, sir. I've been asked to be a guest by
Marc Kimball—I believe that I can work as a liaison."

Brennan nodded. "I'm not a Fed, so it's not really my call
anyway. And however it happened, you might well have averted
disaster here today. But, we do have two actual murder sites.
And, I thank God everyone is in on this because we do need
all the manpower we can get."

"We're going to stop by the Seward station—we'd like to see
anything new that your officers might have gathered and, as you
know, they were working with the video from the hotel when
we were there earlier," Thor said.

"All right. I've had techs working over on the island today.
Phone service is still pretty nonexistent, but we've got the internet going, so anything that you can manage by Wi-Fi is up." He
hesitated. "My officers are having difficulty dealing with Mr.
Kimball. He's played the outraged citizen on them. He doesn't
want his house invaded."

"As she mentioned, Clara can help us with Kimball," Thor
said.

"That's good," Brennan said. "But, if you have any difficulty
with him as far as access to what you need, let me know. There's
not a judge out there who won't give us warrants for a search
of any real property on that island under these circumstances."

"Will do," Thor promised.

Brennan shook his head with exasperation. "FBI, police, Coast
Guard—so many people working on this. We have to come up
with something. It's almost like this guy is a space traveler—
he's here, there, gone. He knows that there's no security other

than the desk at the Nordic Lights Hotel. He knew when people would be on the island. It's uncanny. Unless of course—"

"We have two killers," Thor said.

"Working in conjunction," Jackson added. "We are working that angle," he said.

"Get out to the island, then. We have communication now—please keep it going," Brennan said.

"Will do," Thor promised.

They headed back to the car; Thor went to the driver's side. Jackson opened the door for Clara, giving her the front passenger's side. She murmured her thanks.

They had been driving a minute when she noted that Jackson and Thor seemed to be silently communicating; Thor glanced into the rearview mirror now and then.

And at last, Jackson said, "Yeah. Two. Has to be."

"But who is calling the shots?" Thor wondered aloud.

"Tate Morley," Jackson said flatly.

"With a local, someone with local access, someone who knows Alaska—specifically, Seward and Black Bear Island," Thor said.

They reached the police station. Officers nodded and acknowledged Jackson and Thor—and looked curiously at Clara, smiling at her politely.

One officer led them through a maze of desks to a small office in back. A young woman in uniform quickly rose from her desk to greet them.

"Sally, great!" Thor said, reaching to shake her hand. "Jackson Crow, Clara Avery—Officer Sally Martinelli. She's one of the finest tech people you'll find anywhere."

Sally was small with curly dark hair and eyes to match; she smiled quickly and ruefully. "Once, I thought I wanted to make great movies. I'm not the best tech around, really, but when it comes to video…anyway, their 'security' cameras at the Nordic Lights Hotel are almost older than I am. It's not digital, it's all film. But I think I've cleaned it up pretty well and I have it set to go to the screen—there."

"Perfect, thanks," Thor told her.

"Hit the lights—you'll see better. Almost like the movies," Sally said lightly. "If we only had popcorn. I'll start from the beginning of the day…moving it along until we get to later in the afternoon."

The room was darkened. Sally hit buttons on her computer; images sprang to life on the screen.

The camera angle had taken in the check-in counter, the concierge and some of the lobby. The hallway to the elevators disappeared into shadow.

For the early part of the day, Sally fast-forwarded. People moved about like ants. Thor, Jackson and Clara all stared at the screen. They saw Natalie Fontaine meet with Amelia Carson and the rest of her crew—Becca Marle, Tommy Marchant, Nate Mahoney and a young woman Clara hadn't met, but who Jackson pointed out as Misty Blaine, Natalie Fontaine's production assistant.

They saw that Natalie seemed to be giving fierce instructions to her workers, and the faces Tommy, Becca and Nate made as they listened and then turned—backpacks and suitcases in hand—to head out to Black Bear Island to prepare the Mansion.

They watched as Amelia and Natalie seemed to have a heated argument. Misty Blaine stood back—definitely not wanting to be part of it.

The tape slowed as night came on. Misty went to the elevators. Amelia went to the elevators. And then Natalie went up at last.

"That's the last we have of everyone but Amelia Carson—we see her in the morning, berating the desk clerk," Sally said.

Clara glanced at Thor. He seemed uninterested in that. "Go back," he said quietly. "Go back, please, to where the crew is leaving."

Sally did.

Clara had no idea what he was seeing. The Wickedly Weird people were there, talking, involved in what they were all saying to one another.

A woman with a poodle was standing near the counter, apparently waiting for someone to come from the elevators to join her.

A group of businessmen was checking in. A couple was studying a brochure. An old man with a head of white hair, wearing a black coat and a slouched hat, was seated in a chair near the front door, reading the paper.

"What's the time line on that shot?" he asked.

"Six forty, early evening," Sally said.

"Slow motion on his face, please. Back it up a bit, zero in on him," Thor told her.

Sally did as requested. Clara heard Jackson's intake of breath as the man looked up. He was wearing little horn-rimmed glasses and the lower part of his face was obscured by a white beard.

Clara looked at Thor. He looked back at her.

"Tate Morley," he said. "That's him. Tate Morley is here."

CHAPTER TEN

The freeze-frame image of the man Thor was convinced was Tate Morley was printed out several times and sent around.

Not everyone who viewed the image necessarily believed that the man pictured in the rough footage was Tate Morley. Enfield himself was uncertain; Detective Brennan was hesitant to agree, as well.

Jackson, however, believed, as Thor did, that the man definitely could be the escaped convict and serial killer. He could easily change his appearance with different hair lengths and colors, facial hair and hats, glasses and all kinds of accessories.

Thankfully, Enfield and Brennan had enough faith in Thor to see to it that the man's picture was plastered all over the local news, with the warning that he was known to change his appearance.

Thor looked at the footage over and over again—to the point where he thought even Jackson might lose patience—and yet Jackson and Clara sat with him in silence as he did so.

The problem was that no matter how many times they watched the tape, the man managed to disappear.

Not into thin air, but into a large group of people who arrived for what had apparently been some kind of a pharmaceutical convention. He was obscured by a large cardboard cutout of a smiling young doctor pointing to a host of reasons to take a new drug.

The group went by, pausing in front of the man, laughing and chatting for a moment, and then proceeding to the check-in counter.

And then the man was gone. Whether he had headed out of the hotel or toward the elevators, they just couldn't see.

His disappearance was frustrating; at the least, Thor could be grateful that his superiors believed in him enough to warn the public about the possible appearance of a serial killer in their midst. Of course, the Seward population—actually the *Alaskan* population—was already on alert.

Before they left the station, Sally gave them her office space so that they could videoconference with Angela Hawkins at the Krewe headquarters.

She was perfect for Jackson, Thor thought. A woman who appeared to be extremely competent and, best of all, not just attuned to what he did with his life, but totally a part of it.

"I'm going through everything," Angela said over the computer screen. "It's difficult, because we're tracing some calls through the routers. And his mail! My God, you wouldn't believe the amount of women out there who write to men in prison! They think they're the ones who can change them, or they're the ones who understand them. I swear to you, we'll get through all the letters and calls as quickly as possible. Luckily Will Chan is working in the office, and you know how great he is with computers and film, and people who are trying to hide with disguises or pay-as-you-go phones. We need a little time, though—please bear with us."

"Of course," Thor murmured. "Grateful that you're there."

"Thanks," she said brightly. "And I'm grateful that you're there—Jackson has talked about you quite a bit."

"Scary," Thor said.

Angela laughed. "All good. Anyway, I'll do nothing else but this until I have something for you," she promised.

"Angela, what about Marc Kimball?"

Thor hadn't realized that Clara Avery was as close as she was until she spoke; neither, apparently, had Jackson.

He'd forgotten, too, that she knew Angela—that she had spent time with her in New Orleans after the Archangel affair.

"Clara! I'm so sorry you're involved in all this," Angela said.

"It's okay. Hey, I'm with the best of them, right?" Clara said.

"Don't you two dare leave her alone," Angela said firmly.

"Don't worry. I won't let them. But what about Kimball? He's freaky-scary-slimy, even if he isn't a crazy murderer," Clara said.

"Ah, yes, Marc Kimball!" Angela said. "His business policies are certainly questionable—especially everything I've read regarding the treatment of his employees. They've had protests, they've tried boycotts…but, people need jobs. According to reports, he was flown via his private jet from New York City to Alaska yesterday morning after learning about the terrible crimes at his property. All I know for sure is that his jet did leave NYC for Alaska. I haven't found an eyewitness account of him getting on or off the plane. Private jets at small airports fly by different laws than commercial liners, so finding someone at a small airport isn't easy—especially when it comes to a very rich man who has always seemed concerned about his privacy." She paused. "We have proof that the plane left NYC, and we have proof that it landed. But we interviewed the pilot and he never saw Kimball. Doesn't even know what he looks like. He was given his directions via an email the day before he flew, and through the intercom on the plane. He was in the cockpit before Kimball boarded. Since I didn't accept anything about the plane at face value, I can't say for a fact that he was on the plane as he claimed. But I can't say that he wasn't. There are no reports of his having been in Seward until he arrived at the police station there."

"Thanks, Angela," Jackson said.

"Yeah, sure," she said, her voice dropping low and husky. "Be careful, guys, please. This sounds like a really rough situation. I mean, yes, investigating is what we do, but..."

"Of course," Jackson said softly.

"How is your research going on the others?" Thor asked her.

"No felonies among your television crew," she told them. "Becca Marle has some unpaid parking tickets. Tommy Marchant was reported once for domestic violence, but witnesses said that his ex-wife was the one being abusive. Nate Mahoney—once again, we're not looking at anything more threatening than parking violations. He had a juvenile record."

"Really?"

"He robbed a convenience store with some neighborhood toughs—they pretended sticks were guns. The judge put him on probation...his father had just died. Apparently he's been clean ever since. Graduated from NYU film school and apprenticed with one of the top special-effects companies in LA. He took the job with Wickedly Weird Productions about two years ago. None of them sound as if they have the makings for murder and dismemberment. But we all know that might not mean anything."

"No history of anyone tying firecrackers to cats' tails, throwing stones at dogs or chopping up lizards?" Jackson asked.

Angela shook her head. "Ups and downs in life. Tommy apparently had a very nasty divorce. Poor Becca was literally left standing at the altar. Nate dealt badly with the death of a parent—a situation that is definitely not unprecedented."

"What about the couple at the house?" Thor asked.

"American Gothic!" Clara murmured, and Thor glanced at her.

My thoughts exactly, he told her in silence.

She smiled slightly.

"Ah, yes, they're interesting. They've worked for Marc Kimball since he bought the property. Alaskan natives, both of them. They had one child who died in infancy. Neither had much of an education, but they are, apparently, the only people who don't kowtow to Marc Kimball. They watch his place, they cook and clean, but—I searched a lot of Facebook pages for this, by the way!—they move about Kimball in something like silence, they don't suck up to him or his guests. In fact, Ginger Vixen—of Ginger Vixen Cosmetics—wrote on a page, 'I feel like I've entered a Victorian manse when I'm there. The servants don't talk or even crack a smile.' Apparently, she said something to Kimball about them. 'They're the best at leaving me to my privacy and keeping a true eye on this place,' Kimball told her. As for a criminal background—no. Not even parking tickets!"

"Okay, thanks. We'll get on it here," Thor said.

"I'm still working. I'll be in touch with anything, no matter how small," she promised. She said goodbye to all of them. The screen went to gray.

"We'd better get going," Jackson said.

Thor nodded and looked at him. "I think we should speak with the hotel clerk who was on duty—Arnold Haskell, if I remember correctly. And the production or production assistant who worked for Natalie Fontaine. Misty Blaine. Let's see how she's doing. We spoke when we arrived at the crime scene, but she was really hysterical. Maybe she's calmed down some. I figure she's still at the hotel?"

"Yes. None of the Wickedly Weird crew is leaving yet— they've been asked to stay. I'll check it out, find out where they both are," Jackson said.

He turned aside to use the phone. Thor found himself looking at Clara. "You do know that this investigation could go on a very long time, right?"

She looked up at him with her incredibly blue eyes and smiled.

"No, it won't," she said. "You and Jackson won't let it take a long time."

He hesitated. "He might have come to Alaska because of me. For revenge. That puts anyone near me in danger."

"No," she said. "I know Jackson, I know some of the Krewe—and now I know you. I'd be in danger if I weren't with the two of you. And you won't convince me otherwise," she told him.

He nodded. "Well, for now... For now," he told her. "It's true that we just might need you. I'd really like to avoid a vicious fight with Marc Kimball and twiddling my thumbs while we wait for a warrant if we need something that requires one."

Her expression faded slightly. "He really does give me the creeps."

"And I really do want you to keep your distance," Thor said.

She laughed suddenly. "Suck up to him from a distance."

"Yep, that's it," he told her.

Jackson finished with his phone call. "Our hotel clerk, Arnold Haskell, is at the front desk at the Nordic Lights. Let's head over."

At the Nordic Lights Hotel, the day manager was quick to come and take over for Arnold so that he could speak with them. The four of them headed over to a little group of lobby chairs; Thor noted that Clara was silent but that she was an attentive listener. He had the feeling that she'd be able to remember everything they heard—almost as if she were studying personalities or learning a script.

Arnold Haskell was a young, eager man in his early twenties. He started off by telling them that he'd already spoken to the police; he wished that he could give them more, but he could only tell them what he had seen, and what his dealings with people had been.

Thor showed him the image printed from the security footage.

Arnold Haskell frowned, studying the picture.

"Did you see this man?" Thor asked him.

"Yes, I did," Haskell told them. "But he wasn't a guest here at the hotel."

"You're certain?" Jackson asked him.

"Well, to the best of my knowledge. We're a fairly small, local hotel. There are only six of us desk clerks altogether, covering all shifts. You can check with the others, but if he were a guest here, I believe I would have seen him coming and going. I only saw him the one time."

"And it was the same evening Miss Fontaine was killed?" Jackson asked.

Haskell nodded, his eyes growing larger as he stared at Thor. "Yes," he said quietly. "I remember that Miss Fontaine was giving instructions to her people." He hesitated. "I don't think I would have liked to work for her. The evening Miss Fontaine was killed here, he was sitting in that chair while she and her staff were talking. I remember seeing him because I thought he was a bit strange looking—kind of like I'd imagine Marc Twain to look, except that would have been a long, long time ago!"

"Did you see him leave the hotel or head for the elevators to go upstairs?" Thor asked.

Haskell frowned, thinking hard. "A whole pack of people came in—there's a drug company having their annual meeting here. They kind of overwhelmed the desk when they first arrived. They had my attention…but I think he did head toward the elevators!" Haskell said suddenly. "I mean, maybe. You know how you see things from the corner of your eye? I looked at this poster thing the drug company had. And it seemed like it was moving oddly—it jostled! I think he went behind it, toward the elevators!"

"This is important, Mr. Haskell," Thor said. "Can you remember if he was carrying anything?"

Haskell let out a sigh. "I'm sorry. I didn't even really see the man, much less if he was carrying anything."

If the white-haired man had been Tate Morley, how the hell

had he beheaded a woman if he hadn't gotten upstairs with a weapon?

Unless the weapon had been left for him.

"I didn't see or hear anything out of the ordinary that evening or even in the morning—until all hell broke loose. And I was here from about six until after the cops came the next morning. We work twelve-hour shifts," he explained. "Everyone loves it—gives us three days off each week."

"I'm sure it's good," Clara murmured, offering Haskell a smile. He smiled back at her, a little smitten.

He looked at Thor then, and he seemed even more passionately earnest. "I really want to help you in any way. This is so horrible. And the hotel is so great. Seward is great! I don't want people to stop coming here, you know?"

"They won't," Clara assured him.

"You were still on duty through the night and the next morning, so you saw Amelia Carson before she left?" Jackson asked.

Haskell nodded. "Oh, yeah. I didn't just see her. I heard from her. She was just irate that we didn't have coffee out! I wonder what it is about people who come to Alaska. Well, I mean, I suppose I should understand. We're used to so much darkness and so much light. But Miss Carson, she just couldn't believe that I could do anything about there being no coffee. The concept of 'hotel policy' meant nothing to her!"

Thor thanked him for his help, gave him his card and asked him to call if he thought of anything else. Then they rose and asked about Misty Blaine.

"We moved her to the concierge level—easier for a cop to stay up there and guard the hall," Haskell said. "I'll put you in the elevator to the top. You need a key."

Up on the concierge level, Haskell nodded to the police officer on duty, who nodded back and acknowledged Thor, Jackson and Clara.

"She's in her room?" Haskell asked.

The officer nodded and Haskell tapped at the door.

"Who is it?" came a scared voice.

"It's Arnold Haskell, Miss Blaine. I'm with some people from the FBI. You can check your peephole."

"It's Thor Erikson, Misty. We spoke before," Thor said.

Apparently, Misty trusted no one. "Show me your badge!" she said.

He pulled his badge from his pocket and put it up to the peephole. A moment later, the door opened.

Misty Blaine and little Emmy Vincenzo, Marc Kimball's assistant, seemed very much alike, in Thor's opinion. They worked—and had worked—for people who cowed them. They were hesitant, ready to shrink into the shadows.

Misty was a plain woman, medium in height and size. She moved with her shoulders slumped and her eyes darted nervously about.

"Who are they?" she demanded suspiciously, looking at Jackson and Clara.

"I'm Clara Avery," Clara offered quickly. She had an innate ability with people; she stepped forward and reached for the other woman's hand. "I was on the island. I'm so, so sorry."

Misty nodded, nervously pumping Clara's hand. "Horrible, horrible, I can't believe… They gave me something to sleep. I still couldn't sleep."

"I understand," Clara said, and turned to Jackson. "This is Jackson Crow. He's with the FBI, too. These men are going to find out what happened. But they need your help."

"I—I've spoken to them. I don't know… I said good-night to Natalie when we came up. We were on a different floor…all of us had rooms here. But the others…they were going out to the island. It was just Natalie and me in the hotel after they were gone. She wasn't afraid… She didn't know anyone here. I don't know how he got in. We didn't talk to anyone but each other, I don't think. Oh, I don't know, I don't know!" she said. "I just went to bed. I woke up, and Natalie... Natalie was...oh!" She started to shake, big tears welling in her eyes.

"You're sure that Natalie didn't speak to anyone, tell anyone that they could come up?" Jackson asked her.

Misty shook her head. "Natalie was all about Wickedly Weird. She was married once—so I heard. I guess she scared him away. She's very intense. Oh! She *was* very intense. She would call me at three in the morning sometimes. She really loved *Vacation USA* best. But when she had an idea for *Gotcha*, she would call at any hour of the day or night and tell me about it, and she'd be so excited." She paused, shaking her head. "'Did she have any enemies?' That's what they asked me! Of course, there were people who didn't like her. But just because someone doesn't like you doesn't mean that they'd do something like this! And the people she deals with aren't here in Alaska. And this was... sick! If someone is mad at you, maybe they'd smack you or at worst shoot you or..." Her voice trailed and she just stared at them, stricken.

"Misty, did you notice anyone paying special attention to her or any of you? Think about it, will you?" Thor asked gently.

"Special attention?" Misty said, perplexed. "I mean, everyone here was super nice to her, even when she was a little bit short. I mean, I guess a lot of people think that reality TV is cool, you know? Alaska—Seward!—was going to be on *Vacation USA*."

"Anyone besides the hotel people," Jackson said.

"You're observant, Misty. I'll bet that's why you're great at your job," Clara said. "Did you get into a conversation with anyone else, say, on the street, or anything like that?"

"Anyone who looked at you strangely," Thor said patiently.

She looked at him and shook her head, but then began to frown. "I only remember the man...the man in the chair!"

"What about the man in the chair?" Thor asked.

"She kind of brushed by him. I just thought he was kind of funny looking," Misty said. "We were hurrying toward the elevator—the place had suddenly filled with people and she wanted to get up and away from the crowd. And she brushed by his knees. She kind of absently apologized or said 'Excuse me,' or something like that. He looked at her for a moment and said, 'Not at all. No worries.' He was polite… It just seemed to take him a minute to talk." Her eyes suddenly became huge. "You mean it could have been him?" she demanded.

"Misty, we don't know anything yet. We're going to keep investigating," Thor told her.

She nodded again. Her eyes filled with tears. "Both of them! Natalie and Amelia. I can't believe it! I just can't believe it. My mother warned me that people might not always like getting gotten, but I never imagined…"

"Misty, we think that this is just a very sick and cruel human being," Thor said. "And nothing would have changed what he wanted to do. Normal people just change the channel. Thank you—you've been a tremendous help. Lock us out."

"Oh, I will, I will. The officer is still in the hall, right?" Misty said.

"Yes, he is," Jackson assured her.

"I'm here. I guess for now. They asked that we stay a few days. Of course, we have to stay. The cameras, the props, the equipment…the police haven't cleared us to pick up the props. Tomorrow morning, I think. I can't wait… I can't wait to leave. Except when I leave, I won't have an officer in the hall. So, right now, I'm glad to stay. I mean, you have to get him. You have to. How will any of us be able to go to sleep at night?" she asked.

"We'll do everything possible," Thor assured her.

Now that she'd let them in, she didn't want to let them go.

"You will. And you're here, right? If I think of something else, I can…well, you can call me. Anytime of day or night. I'm used to it. I was used to it. I don't know what will happen now. I mean, Natalie was Wickedly Weird Productions… Amelia was our media presence…it's so horrible."

"Yes, yes, it is," Clara said. "There's nothing we can say to make it better. We're just so very sorry."

Misty suddenly hugged Clara, gripping her tightly. Clara allowed her to cling. Then she gently disentangled herself.

At last, they were able to leave.

Thor, Jackson and Clara headed out of the Nordic Lights Hotel. Thor wanted to make one last stop: the airport.

They were able to find Ben Greenhall, head of security, who directed them to the hangar where they could find Ash McGruder, the pilot of Marc Kimball's plane.

McGruder was playing a game at a desk at the far rear of the hangar with Vince Beardsley, a mechanic. Both were interested in speaking with them—asking the usual questions when a scandalous tragedy had taken place in the area.

Thor and Jackson answered the questions carefully first, and then asked their own, wanting to know if either man had actually seen Marc Kimball on the plane.

"I never saw him," McGruder said. "His car is always here for him when we arrive. I'm in the plane at the time—he clicks a button to tell me to leave. I've already been questioned, you know. I didn't see Marc Kimball or his little minion when we took off. Or when we landed. Not in the flesh and blood. Look, he pays me and pays me well. I fly the plane at a moment's notice—else I'd be in a bar right now or enjoying a good time seeing whales or watching salmon jump or something! It's good money, I'm a good pilot, and I'm paid to fly and mind my own business. It's what I do."

He was sincere. They all thanked him; Thor gave him his card and asked him to call if he thought of anything. Then they left.

As they drove, Clara murmured, "It still doesn't mean anything. I mean, don't we all have to watch out for the fact that we really dislike Kimball?"

Thor glanced over at Jackson, who smiled.

"Yes, we have to be aware of that," Thor said, and he put a

call through to Enfield, who arranged for a Coast Guard vessel to get them back out to Black Bear Island.

Tate Morley was here; Thor was certain of it—just as he was certain now that the man wasn't working alone.

"It was him," Jackson said flatly. "It was Tate Morley sitting in that chair. He might have targeted Natalie already, but he made up his mind when they interacted in the lobby."

As they left the dock, Thor noted that Clara was looking at the many vessels there—including the Celtic American ship the *Fate*.

"We can go back. I can get you aboard her anytime," he said.

"She's a beautiful ship, isn't she?" Clara said, smiling. "I loved being hired on by the company. They take such good care of their ships. And, of course, all of the company's ships are old and historic. The *Fate* dates back to World War I. She was a hospital ship and avoided a number of torpedoes. She was also used to carry South Vietnamese families to safety at the fall of Saigon. She's really a grand old dame and…"

"And?" he asked.

She shrugged. "I was just thinking that it's ironic that my role in this play is that of a ghost." She studied him. "Amelia really likes to just hang out with me. Talk and all," she told him.

"And you're not afraid anymore?"

"Not of Amelia," she told him.

"Amelia just wants help," Jackson said, studying the *Fate*, as well. He turned to smile at Clara, then directed his attention at Thor. "He's here—we both know that he's here. He's changed over the past decade. I think you were right when you said that it wasn't so much the fairy-tale thing that he needed, but the dramatics of it. The theatricality. First fairy tales. Now infamous murders. The first, the Black Dahlia. And, I believe, he would have killed Connie Shaw in a manner like the Ripper's murder of Mary Kelly. As to what we believe to be his first murder, I'm not sure."

"They weren't caught," Clara said.

"What?" Thor asked.

"The Black Dahlia killer was never caught, and neither was the Ripper. Do you think that he's replicating killers who were never caught—maybe even suggesting that you can't catch him now?" Clara asked.

Thor and Jackson looked at one another, and then at Clara.

"What?" she asked.

"I think you've got it," Jackson said. "I'm going to try to Face-Time Angela before we get out to the island."

He left them, pulling his phone from his pocket, turning it in different directions.

Thor and Clara remained by the rail, watching as they left Seward behind.

"You really love Alaska, don't you?" she asked him.

Thor said, "I do." He turned and smiled at her. "Alaxsxaq—that's the native word and it means 'the Great Land.' The first Russians in the area also referred to it as 'the great land to the east.' It is a great land. So much is still natural—back at my family's property, you can have moose and caribou walk up to the front door. The landscape is magnificent, carved out by the many glaciers. You can come to dozens of different places to see fantastic sea life. You really come to believe in something greater than yourself out here. Russian influence is still heavy, in a beautiful way. You have the gorgeous orthodox churches that are scattered about many cities. Man being man, by the mid eighteen hundreds, hunters and trappers had killed off a lot of the otters and the seals, and Tsar Alexander II saw the country as a liability that just wasn't offering much profit anymore. The US was about to engage in the Civil War, so congress wasn't that interested in buying what looked a bit like a frozen wasteland that wasn't paying off for the Russians anymore. But in 1867, William H. Seward, then secretary of state, gave his all to see that the United States purchased Alaska. 'Seward's Folly' was the term used by many, but the United States went ahead and bought it for about seven million dollars—less than Marc Kimball paid for Black Bear Island. I think it was reckoned that we spent about two cents an acre." He grinned. "There's another expression they used for Alaska at the time that I like—'Uncle Sam's Attic.' It's a great attic. And, in time, it proved to be one of our great assets."

"Ah, spoken like a native son," she told him, grinning. "You'd never consider leaving."

"I have left—and who knows? I could leave again. But I'll always come back. It will always be my home." He felt a little twist inside. "It can be a violent state. There are huge distances that are still wild. Sometimes the law is hard to maintain. But we're also a place many, many people want to visit—pristine, fascinating. It kills me that..."

"That Tate Morley has come here," she finished for him.

He nodded.

A long strand of her hair blew about in the wind; she went to pull it back. He found himself reaching out to help her.

His fingers grazed over her skin. She didn't back away; she looked at him, a slight smile on her face, and he realized that it might have been that moment when they both realized something.

That they were both young and healthy and sexual creatures. He been attracted to her since he'd seen her, since he'd actually talked to her, seen her move, the way her eyes lit up when she was angry, glistened when she laughed...

Yes, she really was beautiful and charming and he hadn't been immune, he'd been sexually attracted in every way.

But was there was something deeper than that?

He liked her, he knew. Really liked her. The fight in her, for one—the great right to the jaw she had given him when she had thought herself in danger. She would never let life pass her by; she would always reach out for what seemed important to her.

"I really wish you were on the *Fate*," he said. "Actually, I wish you were a couple thousand miles away, safe at your home in New Orleans."

She smiled at that. "One thing I've learned—there is no place in the world that can be guaranteed safe. And if someone is coming after you, you can't keep running. You have to stop them, unless you want to run forever."

The air was so cool and fresh around them. The snow glistened on the mountains. The sea appeared as if it was dotted with a million crystals, and she seemed to be everything beautiful about the world as she stood beside him. He longed to touch her, just bend down and feel her lips with his own. Because there was so much that was good in the world, and she seemed such an incredible and seductive part of that beauty as they stood there.

"Look!" she said suddenly, pointing to the water.

It appeared that a spray of diamonds suddenly burst above the surface of the sea.

He smiled.

"Salmon," he told her.

"Salmon?" she asked.

"Hey. Alaska is famous for its salmon," he said. "You see them everywhere in these waters. They jump, and they make the scenery even *more* magical. And you can see whales breeching. When you're close enough and they come up, it's amazing. But, let me warn you—when they send air out their blowholes, it can be nasty. Bad breath in whales!" he said lightly.

"You're joking."

"No."

"I still love whales!" she told him. There was a breath of excitement in her words. They'd forgotten murder and dismembered bodies for a moment.

He wanted to put an arm around her and hold her close and just look out at the spectacular scenery, the glaciers in the distance reflecting the water and the sky, the ice appearing to be a spectacular shade of blue itself.

Jackson walked back to them, distracted. "Hey."

Thor tamped down the idea of setting his arm around Clara.

Jackson pocketed his phone and said, "I reached Angela. She found a case that matches Natalie's scene. Happened in the late 1920s. Jeannette Warren, thirty-two, was found in a hotel room in Chicago, her body curled on the bed, her head displayed on the dresser. The killer was given a moniker—the Deadly Dancer—because Jeannette was a dance-hall girl and she'd been ripped up. The police at the time thought a few other disappearances might have been due to this man. He was never caught. It didn't hit the media the way it might have now, and while some police officers suspected that Jeannette's killer might have had other victims, it was never proven."

Thor looked at him and slowly nodded. "So, this is what we theorize at the moment—there are two killers. Tate Morley is one of them. Somehow, in prison, he communicated with someone who became his accomplice. Morley, we believe, was in the Nordic Lights Hotel, and killed Natalie Fontaine. His accomplice was out on the island, either ready to meet up with Tate Morley, or ready to commit the second murder. The accomplice knows Alaska and Black Bear Island. One of the two was back on the outskirts of Seward today, and terrified—and possibly meant to kill—Connie Shaw. The displays were to appear as close as possible to the murders carried out by the Deadly Dancer and Jack the Ripper and the killer who murdered the Black Dahlia. But there's one thing I can't figure out."

"What's that?" Jackson asked.

"Where the hell are the weapons? It's one thing to strangle a woman with one's bare hands—it's another to cut up a body."

They were all silent. Black Bear Island was just before them, snow-covered, wild and dense, and, in Thor's mind, hiding the secrets that could lead them to the truth.

Marc Kimball's behavior was oddly like that of a father who was distraught with a college-age student's tardiness when coming home at night.

And he seemed to be all theirs that night; the Wickedly Weird crew had made arrangements to return the next day and gather the last of their property from the Mansion. Kimball told them that he had asked them all to stay the following night.

But tonight it was just them.

As usual, he made Clara uncomfortable.

"Miss Avery! My God, thank goodness you've come back here. I mean, this is the right place for you to be right now. We're isolated—in a good way! In this house, you have police all about you." He looked from Thor to Jackson. "Anything? Anything at all? Are you any closer to catching this heinous criminal?" he asked.

"We like to believe that every lead brings us closer, Mr. Kimball," Thor told him. "And we remain grateful for your complete cooperation with law enforcement."

"Of course, of course. I'm horrified that this took place on my property. I should have known better. I don't really watch television much, except for the business news now and then. I saw a show by *Vacation USA*, though, and thought it was quite good—that's how I allowed my business manager to make arrangements with the television people. Ghastly business! I hadn't realized that they planned to terrify people with such a grisly scene as the one they fabricated at the Mansion. One can't say 'how fitting,' because it's absolutely horrible."

"Ironic," Mike Aklaq said, arriving in the living room to stand behind Kimball.

Clara liked Mike. He was a patient man, and that was excellent for an agent; he'd wait until he got what he wanted, come what may. And he waited now for an update from his partner and Jackson, not at all anxious or ready to speak in front of others.

"Ironic, yes," Kimball said. "Well, Magda has something of a late dinner prepared. Agents, you weren't about to head out now, were you? Even here, in Alaska, the light won't last much longer."

"Actually, dinner sounds wonderful. I hadn't realized myself how late it had gotten," Thor said.

"It's the hours of daylight," Jackson said.

"Yeah, but I'm accustomed to days that are light forever," Thor said.

"Magda!" Kimball called. "Our guests are back. Dinner!"

He wasn't polite; Magda didn't care. She wasn't polite, either.

"It's stew. I'll set the pot in the middle of the table. There's rice, some salad. Tea and sodas are on the sideboard. You'll help yourselves. Mr. Kimball, you do know your way to your own liquor cabinet," Magda said.

Marc Kimball was oblivious to her tone, as well.

"Shall we?" he said cheerfully. "This is a horrible situation, but we must eat. And, of course, you gentlemen deal with bad things all the time. I mean, you must eat and laugh and all, right?"

"Yeah," Mike Aklaq said, "haven't you noticed? I'm a regular comedy club."

Clara saw that Mike, Thor and Jackson exchanged looks. She was certain that while their faces bore no real expression, they communicated.

Nothing that had happened today was dire. They could wait to exchange notes.

They gathered around the table. Clara saw that there were settings for herself, Thor, Jackson, Mike, Marc Kimball—and one more.

She remembered his timid little assistant, Emmy.

But, Kimball pulled out her chair and seated himself.

"Where is Emmy?" Clara asked.

"Emmy? Oh, Emmy," Kimball said, waving a hand in the air. "She prefers to be alone."

Apparently, Magda hadn't known that. And Clara had the feeling that Emmy didn't really want to be alone—Kimball just ignored her as he would a pen or a pad he used when it was needed and forgot when it was not.

"Oh, but I'd love to talk to her a bit!" Clara said.

"I'll go knock on her door," Mike Aklaq said, smiling at her.

"Great!" Clara said, smiling brilliantly at Kimball. "The more the merrier, right?"

Kimball took his seat. Jackson and Thor waited.

Mike returned with Emmy, who looked pleased and flushed.

"I was just working on some data…and I was actually just realizing that I was hungry," Emmy said.

Mike held her chair for her. She took it and Mike, Thor and Jackson seated themselves.

Magda appeared from the kitchen. "I'll scoop," she said, and proceeded to do so, dishing out hearty helpings of stew.

"You doing all right, Magda?" Thor asked her.

"Right as can be," Magda assured him.

"Nice, good to hear it," Thor said.

She glanced at him and shrugged. "I need to get back in the Mansion. Those scientist people are just finishing up. We need to get those TV crew people back here after, too. Pick up their stuff. Bloody awful junk, if you ask me. Apparently, all that fake gore they have is expensive—props!" She shuddered to convey her disgust.

"We'll get them out as soon as the cops give their okay," Kimball said. He turned to Clara. "You don't work with awful stuff like that, do you, Miss Avery? You do beautiful, wonderful, cheerful musical things all the time, right?"

"All musicals aren't entirely cheerful," Clara said, accepting a bowl from Magda. "I love *Les Miz*, but it's not all cheerful. I've also done *Jekyll & Hyde* and a few other shows that aren't all a laugh a minute."

"But nothing like that horrible TV!" Kimball said.

"No, nothing like that," she agreed.

"Mr. Kimball," Thor said, "we really do want to convey our

thanks for you being not only cooperative, but so hospitable. We're grateful that your business ventures allowed for you to be able to come out to the island so quickly. We appreciate how valuable your time must be."

"Yes, well, there are situations that require one to forget about business, right?" Kimball asked.

"You really arrived quickly—that was exceptional," Thor said.

"I happened to have finished an important deal the night before. Naturally, when I heard, I sent instructions to the pilot immediately," Kimball said.

"You must be exhausted," Jackson said.

"Yes, of course. But, I sleep on the plane," Kimball said.

He made a point of turning away from Thor and looking at Clara. "So, Miss Avery, I'm sure you must hate Alaska after this."

"I don't blame a place for what a horrible person might do," Clara assured him. She went on to talk about the things she had been able to see and the things she wanted to see, aware that the agents around the table listened—and seemed grateful that she was keeping it all rolling. Emmy commented that she'd have loved to see more.

"You're lucky you see anything," Kimball said. "Very lucky that you work for me!"

"Of course," Emmy murmured.

Clara glared at Kimball, her dislike for him heightened by his rudeness to his employee.

She saw expressions of disgust on the others, as well. Emmy looked at her and shrugged and shook her head; she didn't want anyone coming to her defense.

The stew was delicious, which Clara mentioned to Magda. "Venison," Magda told Clara. "And don't go thinking we killed Bambi! You have to watch the population or the poor critters starve to death!"

When the meal was over, Clara yawned—and not with any point. She apologized quickly.

"It's late," Kimball said, dismissing her apology.

"Very late!" she said, looking at her watch.

They all rose as if on cue. "Can we help you pick up?" Clara asked Magda.

"Justin and I have this—you all just get out of our way," Magda said.

She meant it; Clara thanked her and Kimball for the dinner.

"Good night, then," Clara said.

Kimball took her hand. "I'm so happy you're here. I'm not really sure why you've agreed to stay for law enforcement, but I'm so glad that you did."

Clara shrugged, glancing at Thor, and wanting her hand back.

"There just might be something I can say or do or remember about…about Amelia," she murmured. She hoped she didn't sound too lame.

"So caring!" Kimball said.

"Yes, well, I am really exhausted," Clara said.

"Of course, of course. The same room is yours," Kimball said.

"I'll walk you there," Thor said, smiling as he set an arm on her shoulder and turned her around to head down the hallway.

As they left, Jackson made a point of engaging Marc Kimball in conversation regarding a print on the wall.

They stopped in front of Clara's door.

"Get some sleep," he told her softly.

She looked at him and nodded.

There had been that moment on the Coast Guard boat when he had touched her…

She didn't want him to leave, she realized. She wanted to draw him into the room. What happened after that…

Sparks!

"Yes," she murmured.

"And don't worry—one of us will be here," he said.

"Just whistle," she murmured.

"Whistle, yell—scream blue blazes," Thor said, and smiled.

She thought that he would touch her again; she wanted him to touch her.

But, of course, they were standing in a hallway. The others were just down the hall, in the living room with its great hearth, animal heads, and warm and cozy decor.

"Just whistle," he said softly. The hall was shadowed, but she thought that there was a glint of amusement in his eyes.

"I love old movies," she said. *"To Have and Have Not,"* she said. "Lauren Bacall—great lines in that movie, and terrific performances."

"Ah," he said softly.

On impulse, she stood slightly on her toes and pressed her lips quickly to his, then backed away, flushing. "Thank you," she said. "Thank you for making me feel useful—and safe."

He grinned. "You kissed me."

"I did. I'm sorry. I know you're working and—"

"No, no, I was just thinking about *To Have and Have Not*, and a few of the other lines," he said.

"Oh?"

He leaned closer to her and whispered near her lips, "It's going to be better when I help."

He opened her door; she went into her room, closing it behind her, leaning against it.

Sparks.

Oh, yes, good God, they were definitely there.

There was a knock on her door. She was startled by the way her muscles quickened—by the way her heart seemed to leap into her throat.

He'd come back. And her heart was thumping too quickly.

She threw open the door.

It wasn't Thor Erikson.

It was the ghost of Amelia Carson.

CHAPTER ELEVEN

Thor and Jackson met with Mike in the office.

Mike listened to everything that had happened back in Seward and environs; he told them that he'd spent his time watching over the house—though there were still four police officers assigned to that duty—and searching the woods.

Thus far, he hadn't found anything else; a forensic team had spent hours combing the area where they had found the blood spill, but as yet, no one had found the weapon or tool used to cut Amelia Carson into two halves.

"I was thinking of heading down to the cliffs next," Mike said.

"Tomorrow," Thor agreed.

"So, this guy really broke out of prison in Kansas and came here," Mike said.

"I just don't believe I'm wrong," Thor said.

"So, we are looking for two killers."

"That's what we believe," Jackson said.

Mike nodded. "Makes sense. Well, the most sense." He stood up and said, "You're here—I'm going to get some real sleep. But I don't need to leave the island. Not if Enfield and Brennan are working everything in Seward. I can stay here, Thor. No offense to Jackson, but you and I know this place, and I can help search. Better than you going it alone."

"That's what we hoped," Thor said.

Mike nodded. "Thing is, though, where are these killers now? Here, or on the mainland. Or, are they still split up?" He hesitated. "There have been cops or teams around the Mansion and the Alaska Hut since you've been gone. It's cold at night here. If someone has been hanging around, where the hell can they be without freezing their buns off?"

"That's the question," Jackson said quietly.

"Unless of course," Mike said, "one of the killers happens to be someone who is in this house."

Thor nodded at that. "Kimball is pretty slimy."

"Bears watching," Mike said.

"The two of you can feel free to search," Jackson assured him. "You don't need to worry. I'll be watching him. And Clara, of course. Actually, the two go together, since Clara may need watching because of him."

"Fine. I'm going to get some sleep," Mike said. "Thor, we'll start about eight in the morning?"

"Eight it is," Thor told him.

"I'll read a book in the living room for now," Jackson said.

"All right. I know the cops are on, but I'm going to take a walk around the place and maybe check on Clara," Thor said.

Mike opened the door and they all left the office. Mike headed to a room. Jackson talked to the officer on duty in the living room; Thor slipped out the front door.

He saw someone leaning over the rail on the long porch. Someone tiny—Emmy Vincenzo, he thought.

And it was.

He walked over to her. She turned as he did so. For a moment, she looked frightened. Then she smiled hesitantly, reminding him of a frightened Chihuahua, always hopeful for a bit of affection while being afraid of a hand slap at the same time.

"Hey," he said. "Enjoying the night? A bit cool, I guess, if you're not from here. It's warmer—really nice, actually—in Seward. The freeze here all the time has to do with the altitude," he told her.

She pulled at the neckline of her windbreaker.

"I guess it is a little cold," she said. "But I like it out here. I've been here with Mr. Kimball a few times before. I've never seen much of Alaska—just the airfield and then a car and a boat and Black Bear Island."

"The island is special, though. I mean, usually. You can see moose and caribou and black bears and brown bears—including grizzlies—out here," Thor said.

She nodded. "I know. I woke up one morning and a moose was looking right through my window! I didn't try to go near it. Mr. Kimball said they can kick the life right out of you."

"That's true. They are big and powerful. But, they're not vicious animals. Give them their distance, and you'll be just fine. Like, don't try to tug at one or rope it in," he said.

She didn't smile. She looked at him gravely. "Oh, I would never!" she said.

"So, I guess you work closely with Mr. Kimball," he said, casually leaning on the porch rail as well and looking out over the night.

"Closely?" she asked.

"You're his assistant, right?"

She glanced toward the house, as if fearing that the walls had ears.

"He'd never bother to see what I was doing," she murmured, and then looked at Thor. "Minion. I'm just a minion," she said.

"Ah, but you flew here with him," Thor said.

She made a sound in her throat. "With him? No. I was in my seat in the front of the airplane. I assume he was sleeping in back. I didn't actually see him until he got in the car at the airport." She shrugged. "If he's sleeping, the steward doesn't even come in the back. I get a loudspeaker announcement that says we're taking off and to buckle up, and then that we're landing, and we should buckle up."

"Really?" Thor said.

"He's like that. When he doesn't want to see anyone—he doesn't. I never know when he'll pop up, or what he expects I should have known, or whatever."

"You're the one who informed him about the situation, though, right?"

She laughed. "I was in an office. I don't know where he was. I called him on his 'red' phone, though, and he did answer right away. Then I called the pilot. And the plane arrived and I don't even know when he got off the plane. I just met him in the car."

"Why do you work for him?" Thor asked her.

"Money," she said flatly. "I need the money."

"Surely there's something else you could do."

"Maybe. But, you might have noticed—I'm just not that charming. I clam up in an interview. I just sit there and freeze. I'm actually shocked that he hired me," she said.

"If you found a job where there was mutual respect, Emmy, you would probably find out that you had more confidence."

"Great. Find me a job."

"Let me think about it," he told her.

Once again, he looked out on the landscape, feeling a tinge of guilt. He'd come to get information from her, because she was a little mouse. He'd gotten some details, and now he wanted to turn her into a lion.

But, he still needed more information.

"So, Emmy, in truth, you really don't know that Marc Kimball was even on the plane you took to get here, right?"

She looked at him, puzzled, and then she shook her head, laughing a little. "Agent Erikson, you've got to be kidding. He would never, ever have put me in his private plane by myself. Oh, no, if he were just sending me out here, I probably would have been on a mule train."

"But you never saw him before you left New York, or on the plane?"

"No, sir, I didn't. But I'm used to that. I'm just the hired help. But then again, no one really sees Marc Kimball—not unless he wants to be seen."

"You're alone," Amelia said to Clara. "You really shouldn't be. I was alone. And…you don't know what's coming. Suddenly, he's behind you and his hands are around your neck and you're fighting and kicking and screaming, but…he's strong. You can't breathe—he has your windpipe. And the harder you try to fight, I think the faster you use up your air. It's horrible…so horrible. Everything starts to go dark, and your lungs are burning…and, you really shouldn't be alone. That's how he gets you."

"Amelia," Clara said gently. "I'm not alone. There are many people here. There are cops here, Mike Aklaq is here, and Jackson! And Thor."

Amelia sat at the foot of Clara's bed. Clara leaned against the rustic, raw wood dresser.

Amelia smiled, her expression a strange combination of wickedness and wistfulness.

"You're alone. In a room. Talking to a ghost," she said. "I'm grateful that you are talking to me. I want to believe that you'll find my killer and help me—without dying yourself. But, frankly, as far as the not dying yourself goes, I don't think you're doing very well."

Clara was surprised to feel somewhat irritated by the ghost of a young woman who had been brutally murdered. "I'm doing all right, I think—since I am alive," she said, and quickly regretted her aggravated response.

Amelia's expression immediately became one of sadness. "At least, when I was alive, I knew how to live," she said softly.

"I'm sorry—truly," Clara said.

Amelia smiled at her. "I know you are. You're actually a nice person. I wasn't a vicious person—I just thought that I... I thought that I would live forever, becoming more and more adored and famous! Ah, well. I will go down in the history books. I wanted people to remember my name. Now they will when they talk about horrible killers in history. I probably already have thousands of hits on the internet."

"Oh, Amelia," Clara murmured. She wasn't sure what she should say.

"I think you should hop right on one of those FBI guys," Amelia said.

"What? Hop on?"

"Oh, please!" A mischievous smile crossed Amelia's face. "My God, how old are you? Mid to late twenties? Where have you been? *With* one of them. At all times. Through the night. How do you know that the killer isn't in this house? Do you want to wake up with your throat slit or hands around your throat, choking the life out of you? You need to pick one—and sleep with him. Oh, my God! If I were the living one, I would have done so by now!"

Clara stared at her, completely taken off guard. And then she began to laugh.

"Amelia, honestly, and say what? Hey, buddy, I'm here, and since I am, I think we should sleep together?"

"Really? And you're an actress!" Amelia said.

Clara inhaled, smiling. "Amelia, I just came from another bad situation. I was working on a ship, and people were killed. Jackson Crow was there and—"

"You slept with him!"

"No, he's married."

Amelia studied her nails and sighed. "Well, I have to admit—

that never mattered to me. Do you think that's why I'm float-ing around here? Am I on my way to hell? Do you think that there is such a thing as heaven, or…will I just float over the ice and snow and pines and watch others live forever? Maybe that is hell," she added softly.

Clara moved across the few feet that separated them and sat next to Amelia, wishing she could put an arm around her shoul-ders and comfort her.

"Amelia, I don't know any of the answers. But I can't believe you were evil—you might have been a bit selfish and maybe self-centered." She winced. Wrong thing to say. Amelia looked even more pained. "But I do believe—especially since I am sit-ting here talking to you—that there's more. And, honestly, I believe you're here to help us catch the killer. You will help us. I know that you will."

Amelia looked at her. Clara wondered how the woman could be nothing more than heart or soul or whatever it was that made an individual a revenant or an energy that remained—and ap-pear to have huge tears burning brilliantly in her eyes.

"Yes, I will," Amelia said with conviction. "Yes, I will." She seemed to brighten. "Okay, so you and Jackson Crow are best buds—but the married thing bothers you. So that leaves Mike Aklaq and tall, blond and handsome. Seems to me like you and tall, blond and handsome have something going. Oh, honey, I wouldn't have blinked!"

"Okay, okay, I think lots of people survive bad situations without sleeping with one another," Clara said.

"But I saw you kiss him."

"I am discovering that I like him. Very much," Clara said.

"So?"

"So I'd like to see where that goes, if anywhere."

"Watch where it goes later. Sleep with him now," Amelia said. "Oh, seriously, do come on! You're an actress—surely you've played some kind of strumpet or harlot or the like somewhere along the line! And you kissed him. I saw it, I saw the way you looked at him, the way he looked at you… You know that you want to. He's like a frickin' perfect creature!"

Clara had to smile. "Yes, I like him very much—now."

"You mean there was a time when you didn't?"

Clara waved a hand in the air; she didn't want to explain. And she realized that she was still smiling because talking to Amelia was fun. And she was sorry that the woman was dead— even though she seemed to be getting a newer, nicer version of Amelia.

Death had changed her. Death, Clara figured, could do that.

"So, should I have this honest conversation?" she asked Amelia. "Tell him that, yes, this is really an awkward situation. Two women are dead and we're trying to find their killer before he strikes again. Oh, and I know you're obsessed—thinking it's a killer you put away who has escaped and is killing again—but, in the meantime, let's sleep together?"

"It would work for me," Amelia said.

"Hm. Just tell him that it's a great stress reliever?" Clara asked.

"Yes, absolutely!" Amelia said.

"I was just kidding," Clara said.

"That's too bad. You shouldn't be kidding. You should do it."

"There are other people all over this house!" Clara protested.

"Cops and agents, and the creepy couple. And creepier Marc Kimball. Hey, I'd sleep with the FBI guy just to make sure that Kimball doesn't come in. No, *you* might sleep with him just to make sure that Kimball doesn't come in. Kimball isn't all that bad looking, and he's rich as an Arab oil nation. I might have slept with him," Amelia said with a shrug. "Anyway…for me!" she said softly. "Be careful. Be really careful. Let me help you live. Maybe I'll redeem myself."

"But—"

"Do you really think any of the people guarding the place are going to say anything about Thor Erikson being in here?

Do you think the cops will pay any attention? They'll just relax, thinking he's watching over you. And," she added, a sparkle in her eyes now, "I promise you, I knock before I enter!"

She began to fade then and added, "Not to mention, I only last so long! And I might have been the hostess of *Gotcha*, but in real life, I'm not a voyeur. I liked living too much. Hey, I just said *real life*. That's funny, right, ironic? For me, there is no life."

"Oh, Amelia," Clara murmured, reaching out.

She touched air. Amelia was all but gone.

"Get out there and enjoy your every minute, Clara," Amelia said.

And then she was gone. There was really nothing there but air.

Clara had to wonder if she hadn't gone a little crazy—if they hadn't all lost their minds a little bit. She might just be arguing with herself, the sane side of her mind trying to tell her why she shouldn't do exactly what she wanted to do.

Sleep with the man.

Thor tried to analyze what he knew—and didn't know—logically. He threw what he believed to be true into the mix. That was theory, but he was going to assume at the moment that theory might well be fact.

Tate Morley had escaped from maximum security in Kansas by killing a doctor and taking on his identity.

He had an accomplice; someone with whom he'd been communicating in prison. Letters in and out were scrutinized. Angela Hawkins at Krewe headquarters was fine-tooth-combing the letters now.

It appeared that Tate Morley had gotten to Alaska. He knew about Wickedly Weird Productions. He probably knew as well that Thor was working in Alaska. Morley definitely hated him; he might also hate reality TV.

Fact—Thor really disliked Marc Kimball. Disliking the man had nothing to do with whether or not he was a killer. While

Morley's partner might just be supplying him with information and transportation, it was possible that the accomplice was a killer, too. Morley had been in the hotel lobby; Morley had interacted with Natalie Fontaine.

If he'd killed her in the early hours of the morning, he would have been able to get out to Black Bear Island by some kind of private conveyance and await the arrival of Amelia Carson. He could have killed both women.

Whoever had killed Amelia had dragged her into the woods to bisect her. Had he been worried that he'd be seen by Justin or Magda Crowley or one of the film crew who were eagerly awaiting the arrival of Natalie and Amelia and the poor cast members from the *Fate*?

Or was the killer someone on the island?

One of the Wickedly Weird crew or one of the just plain weird workers at the estate, Justin or Magda?

Or was it Marc Kimball himself?

Had the man been here all along and pretended that he had arrived via his private jet?

Due to his suspicions, Thor had been casual with little Emmy Vincenzo, but talked her into going inside and locking herself in her room.

He asked the police officer on duty in the house to make sure that he kept an eye on her.

He wondered, though, if Emmy wasn't safe.

Tate Morley had always killed beautiful women. Emmy was too much of a mouse to be considered beautiful.

He spoke briefly with Jackson in the living room, telling him that he was going to check on Clara Avery.

"Feel like sleeping in front of her door like a Doberman, huh?" Jackson asked.

"I'm still not happy she's here."

"She might be in danger anywhere. We really don't understand what's going on," Jackson said.

"Yeah," Thor agreed. He turned to head down the hall.

"Thor," Jackson called after him.

"Hm?" he said, turning back.

"Don't worry. I swear, I'll have my back to the wall like a Mafia capo—I won't let anyone near her while you and Mike are out tomorrow," Jackson promised.

"I know you will," Thor assured him.

He started to head down the hallway to Clara's room and then paused.

There was someone in the hallway. For a moment, he wondered if the ghost of Amelia Carson was lingering in the shadows, but it was not Amelia. Whoever was there was tall and broad-shouldered—a man.

"Who is that?" he demanded, speaking loudly for the person to hear, but glancing back with a questioning frown for Jackson and the officer who was positioned against the wall heading toward the other section of the cabin.

Jackson was quickly on his feet.

"No one walked here by me," he said tersely.

Thor strode the distance to the man.

"Hey!" came a voice of protest. "It's Marc Kimball, and I own the place!" Kimball said, coming into the glow of light in the living room.

"But how did you get there?" Jackson demanded, coming to stand by Thor.

Kimball was silent, just looking at them belligerently for a moment.

"I said good-night to you. You went up the stairs to your room," Jackson said.

Kimball shrugged. "It is my house, gentlemen, and I am free to move about it as I choose."

He had been coming to knock on Clara's door, Thor was certain.

He was amazed at the cool control in his voice when he spoke.

"Of course you are, Mr. Kimball, but we're trying to protect everyone in this house. If there are secret stairways, we need to know about them."

Kimball pointed down the hall in the direction from which he had come. "No secret stairway—you just push the panel. Go on up and it leads to my private rooms. Well, it leads to another panel, and then my private rooms."

"Why were you sneaking down the back stairs?" Thor asked.

Sneaking. Wrong word.

"Special Agent Erikson—I do not have to sneak anywhere in my house," Kimball informed him.

The door to Clara's room opened and she stepped out, blonde and beautiful in a silk bathrobe.

"Hey!" she said. "Is everything all right?" She gave them all a dazzling smile. "I'm incredibly lucky—all of you keeping watch like this. Thank you, Mr. Kimball. With these gentlemen, it's their work. You're going above and beyond—hospitality, and guard duty. It's all truly appreciated. I feel wonderfully safe here at night. Thank you!"

Kimball turned his attention to her. "I was hoping not to wake you, but I did want to make sure that you were all right. You are my guest—I'd loathe for any danger or any ill whatsoever to come your way in my house."

"So kind," Clara murmured. She looked them all over again like a sweet Southern belle. "Thank you all, and good night."

She went back in her room and closed the door.

The three men in the hallway stood there in silence for a moment. Then Kimball cleared his throat. "Well, then, good night."

He went back down the hallway. The panel he'd referred to looked like part of the wall. When he pushed it, however, it slid open. Then he disappeared into darkness.

"I don't like it," Thor said.

"At least we know it's there now," Jackson said.

"I don't like that he came down here."

"He makes no bones about the fact that he's attracted to Clara," Jackson said.

"I don't care what he says about it being his house—he was *sneaking* around in it," Thor said.

Jackson didn't argue that. He thought that Clara was probably a good actress; she'd managed to still a possible fight with down-home Southern charm.

He didn't have to ponder it long; her door opened again and she stepped out, looking anxiously at them. "He's gone?"

They both nodded.

She swallowed. "He could have been coming to…well, it was slimy one way or the other, whether he wanted to kiss or kill me."

"I'm coming in. I'll get a chair and sit in front of the door while you sleep," Thor said.

He waited for her to argue.

She didn't.

"Now I'll be looking in both directions," Jackson said. "The two of you, get some rest. If anything goes on from here, the cops and I will handle it. Good night, Clara."

He walked back to the living room. Clara had already turned to head into her room. When Thor entered and closed the door, she swung around to face him. "Amelia was here. She was here for quite a while."

"And you learned…?"

"Nothing new, I'm afraid. Except, of course, that she thinks Kimball is after me, too, and that, considering the amount of money he has, she might have slept with him. And that she's worried. She's afraid she's just stuck here because she wasn't a very nice person. She loved living—and she's just watching everyone else live."

"It would be nice if she could help," Thor said. "But maybe she will. Somehow." He wondered what kind of wisdom it was to insist that he keep watch over her by being here, in her room.

So close. She stood just feet from him and, looking at her, he felt his lips burn…with the memory that she had kissed him. The slinky bathrobe covered her completely, yet draped around the curves of her form evocatively. Some women might have known just how they looked. He didn't think it was any kind of a ploy with Clara. She had thrown the robe on to open the door. It was her own robe, silky, comfortable.

Clara Avery didn't need any kind of a ploy. She stood so close he could breathe in the delicate tease of her perfume.

"Well," he said, determined that his voice wouldn't be too husky, "you should get some sleep. And I'll doze a bit here and there. I'll take the chair from the dressing table and just put it by the door."

"You need to sleep, too," she said. "More than I do. I have to say, though, that I will sleep better with you in here."

"Good," he told her.

They still both just stood there.

"Amelia gave you nothing else?" he said.

"She told me that I should sleep with you," Clara said, smiling drily. "Actually, she said I should sleep with one of you. And I explained that I'd known Jackson and that he was married and she wasn't sure that would have bothered her, and…anyway, the upshot is that you're the one she really thinks I should be sleeping with. She would have."

"Oh," he said. "And what did you tell her?"

"I tried to tell her that I wouldn't sleep with anyone just because of circumstances."

"No. You wouldn't, would you?"

She shook her head.

When she spoke again, her voice was low and soft and as silky as the robe.

"I would sleep with you," she said. "Not because of circumstances. But because…"

The simple sound of her words sent something electric sweeping through him, arousing him ridiculously. They weren't even touching.

He smiled, coming a step closer to her.

"You would sleep with me because...?"

"Because you are...you," she said softly.

He loved the way she said it.

He took another step.

"Great answer," he told her. "Very seductive."

"It's my answer. I mean, Amelia would have slept with you because of...being afraid, I believe, whereas..."

"What makes you think I would have slept with her?"

"I think she believes it's easy to persuade any man."

"Really? That doesn't say much for men."

Clara smiled. "I don't think she meant it as an insult. Just biology. But I don't believe that I... Well, I don't think I'm quite as...persuasive."

"Hm. And you were doing so well with your Southern charm, mollifying Kimball."

Another step closer.

"I'm sure Amelia would have done better," she said.

"Ah, well, I'm not so sure I would have slept with her. Honestly."

"Oh?" she said softly, looking at him.

"No. Not even if we had met under normal circumstances, I mean. She's not..."

"Your type?"

"I don't think I have a type. She just isn't someone I would have felt attracted to."

"Ah." She was quiet a minute. "And me?"

He smiled at that, taking the last step and taking her into his arms. "Do you really need me to answer that?"

"Actually, yes," she told him.

He ran his knuckles down the soft side of her cheek, looking into the sky blue pools of her eyes.

"Am I attracted to you?" he whispered. "Actually, yes."

She smiled. A huge smile. "So…does that mean that if I kiss you, you could help, as well?"

"Yeah, I could try that." He paused, serious for a moment. "You know, we don't have to sleep together, even kiss. I intend to protect you with my dying breath, whether we sleep together or not," he told her.

His knees, he realized, were trembling. He hadn't felt like this in forever.

He hadn't let himself. Caring for people seemed to put them in danger.

But this, he couldn't stop…

"Oh, my God," she murmured, and she moved closer to him, so close that he could feel the heat and shape of her against him, causing the trembling in him to stop and a heated constriction to begin.

"I'm not good at this, am I?" she whispered.

Oh, no, you're very, very good! he thought. But she was speaking; she needed to speak. He savored the feel of the burning within him and just held her as she went on.

"We did talk about this, Amelia and I. She said that I was an actress, surely I played the part somewhere along the line. And I have played the part, but this is real life, and when it comes to real life… I guess I should tell you that I'm a little out of practice, it's been a while, I am career oriented, well, not really, not above all else in life, just that my last relationship—with an actor, go figure—didn't go so well, and onstage playing a part is one thing, but when it's really you… I'm sorry, I'm ridiculously nervous, and I can't seem to stop talking. I'm woefully out of practice, not that I haven't thought that someone would come along somewhere along the way and I've stayed on birth control pills… That may be more than you wanted to know, and oh! Well, I mean, really, I'm trustworthy and I—my God! I'm still talking and I—"

"I can help you stop!" he told her, and he pulled her closer, molding his mouth down over hers, tasting sweet and seductive warmth and a hint of peppermint. Her lips parted to his and he made the kiss slow and leisurely, as if he could come to know her, really know her, through the depth of a kiss. When their lips parted, she said, "I talk too much."

"I can take care of that," he murmured.

And he kissed her again. Her arms encircled his neck, her fingers playing at his nape. "And when I first met you, I just thought that you were a..."

"A what?" he murmured, his lips teasing at her throat then.

"Well, I thought you were trying to kill me, and that..."

He lifted her hand and teased the palm and wrist. "You do have one mean right hook," he assured her.

"And you do have a way of sweeping someone off their feet," she said.

"You ain't seen nothing yet!" he teased.

And swept her off her feet.

Her arms curled around his neck and they lay down on the bed together. He felt her lips tease along his neck and a sweet raw ache began to tear at him. He rose above her, lowering his mouth to hers again, sweeping aside the silk of the robe, moving his lips and tongue over her collarbone, down to the valley of her breasts. The silk she wore created a heightened sensuality to each touch, and yet it was in the way; she slid her hands beneath the soft wool of his sweater, running them up his midriff, and he paused to pull the garment over his head. She laughed then, fingers on the buttons of his shirt.

"My Lord," she murmured, "you do have enough clothing on!"

"It's Alaska!" he reminder her.

"Difficult," she said.

"Trust me, we find a way—we do find a way!" he said.

She was determined to help; she slid her fingers beneath the waistband of his jeans; they ran over his bare flesh and sent schisms of electricity racing through his hips, and down below his belt. But he eased back from her, removing the Glock and its holster from the back of his waistband and setting them next to the bed, reminding them both briefly of why they were there. Their eyes met for a moment; the movement might have given them pause, and it did, but her hand slid down his arm and she told him, "Amelia did remind me that I haven't really lived in a long time."

He lay back with her. "In some ways," he said, "I don't think that I ever really did."

He fumbled out of his shoes and socks; she helped and hindered as he removed the rest of his clothing, and they laughed breathlessly at the effort. Finally, he was naked beside her.

She was in the silky robe. He straddled her and began to kiss her, lips caressing her flesh through the silk—slender throat, breasts, belly and below. He ran his fingers along her thighs, planted more kisses at her knees and above.

She writhed beneath his touch, rising and twisting, finding his lips again, kissing them with hot, wet intensity. Then she pressed him down to the bed, sliding against him, seductive with every inch of her body, arousing him with each brush of her hand, feathering of her fingers, and searing tease of her tongue. His hunger burned, centralized—and shot through his limbs. But the burn was as evocative in anticipation as it might be in fulfillment, and he held back, savoring the way they exchanged touching...stroking...caressing...tasting.

The silk robe slid from her flesh, and yet he felt that her skin was as soft. Her eyes... So deep a blue, as if the passion and the fight and the sweetness that had so compelled him to her were alive in that sea of blue.

He didn't remember feeling this way before, as if he'd burn alive in desire without her, as if the woman he touched was why the basic instinct existed.

They laughed and rolled and kissed and touched anew, so intimate in every move, and then suddenly the laughter faded with the heat of passion. He groaned softly, sweeping her up, finding her mouth again while he thrust into her at last. The waiting culminated in a pleasure that was almost unbearable—instinct, need, desire and something more...

Her face. Her beautiful face, the way she looked at him...

Easing from him, crawling atop him, straddling him, looking down at him. "'Fasten your seat belts, it's going to be a bumpy night!'" she teased.

"Bette Davis, *All About Eve*," he returned.

"Impressive!" she said.

"Me or the quote?" he demanded.

No answer. She laughed softly and kissed his abdomen, and moved down.

He drew her to him, finding her lips, whispering against them.

"I'm going to take that to mean *me*!" he said.

"Ah, confident, Special Agent Erikson!" she whispered back.

"You make me so," he said.

And she did.

She swept the past away. She made the present urgent. She encased him in a way he was sure he'd never known.

Climax swept through him as if he had been lit on fire—explosive, gripping the length of him, shooting through with something erotically wild and hard and exquisite. She arched wickedly against him, creating the shock waves over and over again until he lay beside her, heart thrumming a million miles an hour, a fierce echo in his mind. He was at her side, drawing her against him...

Just breathing.

And after a while she said softly, "So much better..."

"Better...? Than what?"

She looked up into his eyes. "So much better…when you help, of course," she said.

He kissed her lips very gently. "Why, thank you, ma'am. Thank you so very much."

He held her, suddenly very glad of the night, of the Alaska Hut—even of Marc Kimball, since it was because of Kimball that he'd been so damned determined not to leave the room.

CHAPTER TWELVE

When Clara awoke, Thor was gone.

She'd slept deeply, exhausted and in a state of sheer comfort and security; Thor had slept beside her. Thor had held her. She'd been able to forget everything.

Showering and dressing, she wondered how she was going to feel when it was over…whatever it was. She was a musical theater actress; he was an Alaskan FBI agent.

And yet…

She'd never felt anything before like she did when she was with him.

She argued with herself, of course. They really hadn't known each long; in fact, it was a ridiculously short time.

Sex was…sex. It didn't mean an undying commitment—it didn't even mean two people would ever see each other again. It had happened; she'd wanted it to happen. But…

What did the future hold?

She dug through her purse to find a hairbrush. As she did so, there was a light tap at her door.

Amelia, she thought.

She hurried over to open the door.

Not Amelia; it was Marc Kimball. "Good morning, Miss Avery! I've had Magda whip up some of her amazing omelets. I didn't mean to disturb you, but I thought you might be hungry."

"I was just coming out," she said. With her peripheral vision, she could see that Jackson was there, standing in the living room, just feet away from her.

She smiled. She felt safe.

"I'll be there in one minute," she promised Kimball.

"Of course," he told her.

She closed the door and hurried back for her brush; she'd have a mad tangle of hair when it dried if she didn't brush it out first.

Almost immediately, she heard another tap.

This time, Amelia just seemed to appear before her.

"I'm not being rude, am I?" she asked. "I mean, I knew he was gone. Did you do it? Did you sleep with him?"

"Amelia!"

"Ah, you did! Good for you! Was he great, was he amazing? I'll bet you he's great in bed!"

"Amelia, honestly—"

"Oh, come on! I'm living vicariously through you—in a very real sense!"

Clara turned to the ghost and smiled. "He is amazing in bed."

"I knew it! Yes, say thank you, Amelia, for egging me into it. Because, Clara, you're really just too much of a prig to do things on your own."

"I am not!" Clara protested. "Okay, thank you. Now I've got to go out—Kimball has already summoned me to breakfast."

Amelia shuddered. "He's a creep! I don't think that I would have slept with him—even if he does have a zillion tons of money and could have catapulted me into being a household name."

"What did he do creepy now?" Clara asked her.

"He talks to himself," Amelia said.

"And what does he say?"

Amelia shrugged. "Actually, he was talking about ways to get to you. Trying to figure out how to shake the cops and the FBI and everyone else. To be alone with you."

A prickling sensation skipped along Clara's spine. The way that Amelia looked at her, she knew that they were wondering about the same question.

To get her in bed? Or to kill her?

"Don't worry about me, Amelia," Clara said. "I'll make sure that I'm never alone with him."

Amelia nodded. "Good deal. Well, I guess it's time to go to breakfast."

"You're coming?" Clara asked her, frowning.

"Wouldn't miss it!" Amelia assured her, smiling mischievously.

Sighing, Clara set her brush down and headed out. Amelia followed her.

She didn't have to worry about it being just her, Jackson and Marc Kimball—the crew of Wickedly Weird Productions had returned.

Just returned. Nate Mahoney was handing his coat to Magda when Clara reached the living room, Becca Marle was speaking animatedly to Jackson, and Tommy Marchant was just coming through the door.

"Clara!" Tommy said, seeing her across the room. "Hey, you're here. Nice to see you. I heard the cast was on the *Fate* now."

Everyone turned to look at her. "I'm still here for the moment. I'll be joining the cast soon enough."

There as a moment of silence in which it seemed everyone waited for an explanation.

Except for Magda.

"Hey, wipe your feet there, Mr. Marchant!" she said. "This isn't a barn!"

Tommy wiped his feet and everyone shuffled. Marc Kimball came out to the living room looking less than pleased.

"You're all here," he said.

"The police have told us—more or less ordered us—to get out here and pack up at the Mansion," Nate Mahoney explained. "And they escorted us here. I think they wanted one of the FBI guys with us as well while we packed up our things."

"Yes," Jackson said. "I believe we have breakfast and coffee ready here, then we can all head on over."

"Yes, do come on in," Marc Kimball said. "Every day will be a step closer to finishing with this ghastly business."

"When we catch the killer," Jackson said, "that's when we'll be finished with this ghastly business."

"Of course," Kimball said. "Come in. Magda, we'll need more plates." He forced a smile.

Clara couldn't help remembering that he'd come to her door in the night; she tried to slide by him and head into the dining room and sit at the end of the table.

No good; he found his way right after her.

But she was going to be all right. She heard a whisper at her ear.

"Don't you worry, I'm watching the rich weirdo!"

Amelia was behind her.

Black Bear Island was actually small, a piece of earth and rock shot up by ancient volcanic activity and cut and carved by the movement of ice and glaciers.

That day, it seemed huge.

Thor and Mike rode snowmobiles to the forest and went through it bit by bit. They found bear markings, a hungry moose and dozens of bears.

Nothing more.

They'd sectioned different areas and each started from opposite ends; they'd comb the ground until they met in the middle each time.

It was in the midst of dense pines—leaves and branches so

thick that the sun barely made its way through—that Thor suddenly stopped.

He stood dead still, looking, listening.

There was someone ahead of him in the forest. A dark shadow. But the shadow didn't move, nor make a single sound.

He moved forward. It seemed a single ray of sunlight penetrated the green darkness.

He stood still again himself, his heart beating.

He was imagining things, he thought. Mandy Brandt was really gone; he'd never encountered her as a ghost. He'd only seen her in his dreams.

But she was there today. Caught in that single ray of sunlight.

Words tumbled from his lips; words he had said a hundred times.

"I'm sorry, Mandy. So sorry!" he said.

And he thought that she smiled. She came toward him and lifted her hand, setting it gently on his cheek. He felt the touch softly.

"It's all right," she said. "You are not to blame. You must keep going. You know the island. You can find the truth—you can stop him."

The ray of sunlight was suddenly gone. He was standing by himself, talking to a large pine tree.

Mike reached him, unaware.

"Nothing. Damn it, nothing at all," Mike said.

"The cliffs and caverns," Thor said, turning to him. "I know the Coast Guard has been patrolling, but we can get into the cliffs. There's a weapons stash here somewhere, and we're going to find it."

Not about to stay with Kimball, Emmy, Magda and Justin Crowley, Clara joined Jackson and the crew of Wickedly Weird Productions.

She'd wondered if Amelia would come to the Mansion.

But Amelia disappeared at some point after teasing both her and Jackson during breakfast, trying to make them appear to be talking to themselves. Clara had followed Jackson's amused cue and ignored Amelia.

The Mansion had changed drastically from the morning when Clara had walked in looking to meet up with Natalie and Amelia and the Wickedly Weird crew and seen nothing but bodies, body parts, blood and guts.

The stage blood had been cleaned from the floors.

The body parts and props had been piled up in a tangle on the beautiful hardwood living room floor.

Forensic teams hadn't actually cleaned up; they had made sure that all the blood was stage blood and they had garnered all the property that was meant to horrify, inspected it thoroughly and deposited it where the crews could look through it.

For their part, the Wickedly Weird people had brought the canvas totes and boxes that held the expensive prop pieces.

Nate Mahoney bemoaned the condition of what he considered some of his finest work. But then he looked up miserably.

"Wow. I'm sitting here thinking that my artistic talent was wasted—and Natalie and Amelia are dead. I feel like a horrible person."

"You are a horrible person," Becca said. "Oh, I just meant that as a tease, Nate. You're not a horrible person."

Clara hated seeing them so unhappy. "Hey, it's just a bad situation."

Jackson was behind her. "I'm sorry, but this entire prank was in really bad taste, as well," he said.

Becca sank down on one of the living room's sumptuous, plush sofas. "It was Natalie's idea," she said.

"And Amelia embraced it," Tommy Marchant added. He sat down, too. He was holding a bloodied piece of leg, but didn't seem to notice. "I was so excited when we first came here. I mean, here is the thing about Natalie. She really loved doing

Vacation USA. She thought that our country was wonderful and that people didn't realize how diverse. They didn't need to have the money to run off to Europe or South America, they just needed to know what was right in their own backyard. I remember when I got to come up here on the site inspection for Black Bear Island. When old Justin Crowley brought me about on the snowmobiles, I was so ecstatic! Such a cool, unusual and beautiful place!"

"Then, of course, Natalie came out. And she was whining about production money—as usual," Becca remembered.

"And," Nate told Jackson, "saying she couldn't understand how the money for *Vacation USA* came from *Gotcha.*"

"When she was out here herself," Becca said, "that was when she came up with the idea of inviting the actors from the *Fate* over. She could get one of her well-sponsored *Gotcha* segments—and then showcase the beauty of Alaska!"

"What happens now with the company?" Clara asked.

Nate waved a hand in the air. "Well, Natalie was CEO, but there are stockholders. I guess we didn't even worry about that yet."

"They'll make Tommy CEO, I'll bet," Becca said. "He's older. He's been around."

"Thanks," Tommy murmured drily.

Becca didn't seem to notice. "We're not that big a company, but we do have a board—mostly slightly rich guys who like to have a hand in television, play like they're big producers, you know? But, Tommy is the only one who really knows how to pull shows together. Oh, there's Misty, of course, but she's kind of a follower, you know?"

"Maybe we ought to be looking for jobs instead of moping around," Nate said. "Of course, I really think that I'll be fine. I'm good at what I do."

"I'll vouch for that," Clara murmured. "Well, do you want some help?"

"You want to help?" Nate asked her.

"I'm here—sure. What do I do?" Clara asked.

"Here," Nate said, handing her a leg. "Peel this stuff off…it's just garbage. We'll preserve the leg."

Clara took the leg and stared at it blankly for a moment.

But she'd said that she'd help. So she sat there, peeling the dried "blood" off the plastic leg.

She noted that Jackson wasn't amused by any of it; he had brought a laptop with him and she assumed that he had accessed the internet the police techs had gotten working.

At any rate, he frowned while he read.

Looking at the stack of props on the floor, Clara thought that it was going to be a long day; it was good that she was helping.

She started back at it, thinking of the plays she had done, the dramas and the tragedies.

Nothing ever quite this gruesome…

She looked up to find that Jackson was staring across the room.

Amelia had reappeared.

She seemed to waft through the space. And she sank down beside Clara.

"There's something…" she said. "I feel that there's something familiar that I'm kind of getting a sense of now…something that sparks memory." She looked at Clara a little helplessly. "I can't figure out what it is. It's important—I know it."

"Think!" Clara told her.

"Huh? What?" Becca asked.

"Oh, nothing. I was just thinking…um, what the heck is this stuff, anyway?"

"Mostly red dye and corn syrup—gone sticky in the days past," Nate said morosely. He paused and added, "Honestly, hard to tell from the real stuff sometimes. I think you have a fly caught in there, too." He was quiet. "Really like the real stuff, I guess," he added.

They all fell silent; they all went back to work.

Amelia remained, an image, perhaps, in Clara's mind, looking perplexed.

And Jackson stared at the two of them.

The cliffs and caves on Black Bear Island were treacherous. Some formations were hard ground, hard rock, piled with earth and snow. Some were just ice. And some were just snow. A wrong step could bring a man crashing down to die on a jagged crop of rock or ice.

But both Mike and Thor knew the landscape—and knew to respect it.

They left the snowmobiles behind the high ledge on the southern side of the island and began the slow descent through the crystal-white cover down to the "beach" below.

There, caverns and glacial ice—carved out in the earth long before the coming of man—stood in what was truly fairy-tale beauty. The ice and snow shimmered in the sun. The water glistened. Sea birds flew overhead and the ever-present Alaskan salmon jumped high now and then, creating magical diamond-like dances on the horizon.

Snow and rock crunched beneath Thor's feet as he walked along the shoreline. About fifty yards from where their descent ended, the caves began.

They were mammoth, appearing—from the water—like giant back mouths, waiting to consume the unwary into darkness forever. They were treacherous; at high tide, water filled the beds beneath them, except in winter, when they were solidly frozen. At low tide, the water was gone, and inside, they offered a spectacular view of natural formations.

Boats could catch on jagged rock and ice—and the inhabitants might well be left in freezing water, helpless to escape. Thor knew that, when early explorers had first come to the island, they had found the bones of many a lost sailor caught within the snow and ice and rubble.

It was low tide. He looked at Mike; they had several hours to explore.

He turned on his heavy-duty lantern, illuminating the first cave they entered. Mike did the same. Light filled the darkness, but created eerie shadows in the depths of the formation.

"I'll go left," Mike said.

"I'll take the right."

Thor moved in carefully, raising the light, looking everywhere. Police officers and Coast Guard men and women had searched, but there were nooks and crannies abounding here—it would be easy to miss a clue, especially when you weren't really sure what you were looking for.

"Beer cans!" Mike called out. "Rusty—they've been here awhile."

"Yeah, I found a broken flashlight. Been here awhile, too, though—all rusted out."

"Hey, Thor! Come over here," Mike called.

Thor did so, making his way around a spike of rock that seemed to grow like an oak, straight up from the earth.

"What do you make of this?" Mike asked.

Thor hunkered down while Mike held a light up high.

There were splotchy, circular dots on the ground. The color was a deep crimson, almost brown.

"Blood?" Thor wondered.

He walked carefully to the last bit of trail and looked beyond. There were more of the spikes of rock heading toward the rear of the cave. He moved around them and came to what appeared to be a wall of rock and ice.

But there was a break in it.

He slid around it. A crevice—almost like a closet-sized room—had been naturally created there.

He shone the light.

And he found what he was looking for.

A rough brown blanket lay on the ground.

And on top of it...

"Mike!"

He picked up the spade that had been left there. Once upon a time, it had been an ordinary farming spade. But it had been altered. It had been sharpened and honed until it was...

"Sharp enough to slam down and cut through a woman's body," Mike said from behind him.

There was a large butcher's knife beside the spade.

It, too, had been sharpened and honed.

"Especially if you use both tools," Mike said quietly. "I'd say these are the weapons or tools that our killer used," he added softly.

"Yep. Especially when you consider the fact that they're still covered in blood."

Forensic crews were busy as the afternoon wore on.

By early evening, Thor came by the Mansion; he'd been in touch with Jackson, so Clara knew that he had found something—the weaponized tool that the killer had used to bisect Amelia.

She was sitting on the porch with Jackson when Thor parked his snowmobile and she hurried out to meet him; he looked tired but grim and satisfied. He greeted her with a smile and, as she reached him, set an arm around her shoulders and waved to Jackson. "You okay?"

She nodded. "The crew from Wickedly Weird is staying tonight. They're showering now. We cleaned and packed a bunch of their props and bloody creations," she said. "It was a quiet afternoon." She searched out his eyes. "You found...what...was used?" She wasn't sure why she couldn't just say *the tool that bisected Amelia*. She never knew when Amelia might pop up. And she just didn't want the young woman hearing her—even if she knew what had happened to her.

He nodded. "I thought something had to be here somewhere. Forensic teams are out again; God knows, maybe we can get a bit of trace evidence somewhere."

"Okay, but you know that Tate Morley is here—you just need to find him," she said.

"Yes."

"But you don't know who he might be working with, and it's illegal to just run around and take people's blood or ask them to spit—right?"

He grinned. "Something like that," he told her. He was looking out toward the trees; she felt him straighten, and for a moment, she thought that he had seen someone he mistrusted—or perhaps the ghost of someone walking in the trees.

But he lowered his head and said softly, "Hey, take a look. Be quiet, and he'll hang around awhile. There's a moose over there."

She turned slightly. And she was awed by what she saw. The animal wasn't a hundred yards away from her; he was beautiful. And huge. She'd seen a moose before—in a zoo. But it had been a little one, and it hadn't been standing in the snow by the beautiful rich green canopy of a field of pines.

"You do have to be careful with them. They're very powerful, and if they're frightened…" Thor warned.

"Do you know, the last thing on my mind is thinking of a way to bug a moose," she said.

He grinned. "We get them by the compound, and some of them come up for scraps now and then. But, sometimes, people just want to feed them and they do it awkwardly and they wind up getting kicked, and a kick can do you some damage. Wildlife is just that—wild life."

"He's fantastic," Clara said, and she studied the strong lines of his face. "You love Alaska, don't you?"

He looked back at her. "I do love it. It is my home. I've lived away from it. I may live away from it again. I am a Bureau guy—when I need to move around, I do. But there's always a little Alaska in my heart. You?" he asked her. "Do you love home—New Orleans?"

"Magical and unique, and yes, of course, I love it. But... I do what I do. I leave when I need to." She grinned. "Yep, and there's always a little NOLA in my heart!"

He seemed lighter that evening. He'd found a tool that had been sharpened and honed and used to chop a woman in two. She knew that he cared about the victims of crime, and cared deeply.

And still, he somehow seemed a bit lighter.

She liked to think it was because of her. And the night they had shared.

And it was, or so it seemed. He gave her a wry grin and said, "Hm. Kind of like one of those old magazine articles my mom used to read—'Can a charming Southern actress and hard-nosed Alaskan G-man find happiness somewhere in between?' Anyway, I guess that's for the future," he added huskily. "There are so many men working this damned thing, you'd think that we'd turn up more than what we're finding."

She nodded, entranced by his words—and yet he had quickly changed in demeanor.

"Any sign of anything on the mainland?" she asked him.

"Not that I know of yet," he told her. "Shall we see what's up with Jackson? I could go for some hot coffee—it's been a long day."

She looked over at the moose one more time. The majestic animal was watching them in return. She smiled and turned to Thor. "Yeah, we should go in. But...he's amazing. The moose. He's just watching us."

He grinned. "Something like that. Yes. Down by you, the gators just watch, right?"

"Out in the bayou. Honestly, I haven't seen one walking down Bourbon Street lately."

His arm still around her shoulder, he led the way to the porch so they could join Jackson.

Jackson said, "Let's get somewhere private. FaceTime with Angela—she has some reports for us."

A police officer was reading a newspaper in the living room; they headed through to the office that Marc Kimball had allowed for their use, glad to see that Kimball wasn't about.

Jackson headed to the desk and tapped on computer keys until Angela's face appeared before them.

She greeted them quickly. "We're still tracing letters to and from Tate Morley when he was in prison. Some went to women we've found around the country," Angela said, and shook her head. "It never ceases to amaze me—the amount of men and women who fall in love with serial killers, many of them believing that they are the one who can cure a bad boy or girl. At any rate, we're following up on a few leads where someone was mailing from a drop box in Los Angeles. There was nothing about killing, meeting up with one another, escaping—anything like that—in the letters. But Will is working on this—you know his computer and illusion skills!—to figure out what is really being said."

"Same LA address on a number of exchanges?" Thor asked.

"Yes, and they're all about finding God, whiteness, purity, and leading a new life in all that's pure," Angela said. "Thing is, we should be able to track whoever these letters are going to and coming from, but…it's a mailbox. And it hasn't been paid in a few weeks. It was rented to—and you're going to love this—Jane Doe."

"Someone just rented a box to someone named Jane Doe?" Jackson asked. "Really?"

"Yep. Hey, a lot of people don't really care. Said the woman had ID that seemed legitimate. Of course, it wasn't," Angela said. "We have people down there."

"Los Angeles," Thor murmured. "That would go back in the right direction—someone involved with Wickedly Weird Productions."

"How well would any of them know Alaska?" Clara asked, mystified.

"Ah, glad you asked!" Angela said. "Actually, the entire group here from the Wickedly Weird Production Company headed north about three months ago—site inspections and all."

"The only two women left alive who are with the company are Misty Blaine and Becca Marle," Thor said.

"Then again, it might not be a woman," Clara put in. "And maybe the letters aren't love letters at all—they may be coded, as you said."

"Anything is possible," Angela said. "But, best educated guess is that Tate Morley is there *and* working with someone he's been corresponding with for some time. Again—go figure on people. As I said, some women think that they can change a man. Some are just accomplices in crime. They are just as perverted and mentally deranged and cruel as the men they find in life, or in the prison system."

"And then again—as you pointed out, Clara—we can't take anything at face value," Thor said, studying her. "You could be right. It could be anyone." He looked back at the computer screen. "Angela, anything more on Marc Kimball?"

She shook her head. "Marc Kimball might as well be a wraith. As far as any eyewitnesses go, he just appeared in the Seward police station."

"What about past history of our friends on the island?" Thor asked.

"We've kept searching, but so far, nothing we've found stands out in and of itself. Anything could mean something. Becca Marle could hate men—she was left standing at the altar, but one of our agents out there spoke with a coworker from a previous project who said that Becca had been unsure about the marriage herself. She was embarrassed, but over it quickly. Tommy Marchant had an abusive wife—he could really hate women, except that he's supposedly been happy as a lark since he's become his own man. Has he ever done anything that would suggest he was ready to go out and kill and mutilate women? No, not that we can find. Friends say he's a nice guy—a little leery now when they try to fix him up with someone they think would be nice. Our agents have done extensive work on the backgrounds of the Wickedly Weird people, and we have nothing. Then again, men like Bundy and Gacy were liked by their neighbors, so that doesn't mean really mean anything. We have Will working on discovering if there is some kind of a code in the letters; we also have people in Los Angeles. I'll let you know the minute that we have anything, anything at all. You know that."

"Thanks," Jackson told her.

"Stay safe," she said.

As the connection was broken, Mike Aklaq joined them; they brought him up to speed.

"We still have people in the caves and caverns," he told them. "They've got camping gear. They'll work through the night."

"They have techs and cops out there," Thor said. He looked at Clara. "The caves and caverns are extensive. Beautiful when times are good. Ice is so powerful…it's like you're in haphazardly designed crystal palaces. The killer has taken advantage." He glanced over at Mike. "They've enough of a police presence still, right?"

Mike nodded. "Yep. They'll be working in shifts, police guards on and off. Though to be honest, neither Brennan nor Enfield seem to think that anyone in a group is in danger—they believe that the killer, or killers, watch carefully, and strike when a woman is alone." He looked around at Jackson, Thor and Clara, and said, "I'm famished. Anyone else?"

"Let's see if the Goth Magda has gotten something together for dinner," Thor said, and asked Clara, "Has Kimball been around?"

"I don't know," she told him. "Jackson and I were with the Wickedly Weird people."

"According to the cops, he's been upstairs all day," Jackson said.

Leaving the office behind, they discovered that Magda Crowley, as sour-faced as ever, was in the living room, looking for them to announce that dinner was being served.

"And if anyone cares, you can check on those film people," she said. She said the words *film people* as if she were speaking of an inferior alien race.

"They were all cleaning up and taking showers," the police officer on guard in the house told them.

"They should be out by now," Clara said. "I'll check on Becca, just in case she is ready."

"I think she said she was going to take a nap," the on-duty police officer told her. "I'll just knock on their doors. You folks go ahead."

He headed on down the hallway to the left. Marc Kimball arrived—coming from his "secret" door and the right hallway. He greeted everyone politely and gravely and, as they headed for seats at the table, he asked Thor and Jackson about their discovery on the island.

"I know that you found the weapons. Or tools. The man's actual weapon was his hands, right?" Kimball asked matter-of-factly. "So tool, I guess, is the right description."

"Yes, that's what we found," Thor said. "Tools," he added quietly.

"Does this mean…that you'll finish soon here on the island?" he asked.

"We will move with all possible speed," Thor promised.

Jackson stepped in diplomatically. "Again, Mr. Kimball, both the police and the Bureau thank you for your cooperation and hospitality."

"Of course, of course," Kimball said. He lowered his voice. "As of tomorrow, those film people will be off the island. I should have known better than to rent to anyone involved with reality TV! As for tonight…well, please, do sit down. Magda has come up with her amazing chicken Marsala for the evening. Right, Magda?"

Magda gave him a sour look. "Getting cold, too," Magda said with a sniff.

Emmy Vincenzo came hurrying out. She looked around as if she'd been afraid no one would notice if she wasn't there. Clara greeted her warmly.

She gave Clara a warm smile in return.

Marc Kimball didn't acknowledge her presence.

"Ah, here come the Wickedly Weird!" Kimball announced. "And now, we can all take our seats!"

Kimball pulled out a chair for Clara; she accepted with a murmured thank-you, aware that he would sit next to her. Jackson pulled out a chair for Emmy, and Mike for Becca.

The men all took their seats. Kimball started right out by addressing Tommy. "You've finished—completely finished?" he asked. "Naturally, I will be making an inspection to see if my property was damaged in any way."

"Nothing has been damaged—everything is picked up and clean. We've made sure that your Mansion is spotless," Tommy said tightly. "We have all of our props and equipment in suitcases and boxes in our rooms. We'll be ready to vacate the island for good in the morning."

"Your property is absolutely fine," Becca burst in, and added, "Our hostess and our producer are not fine—they're dead. In pieces," she added.

There was a silence around the table, but Kimball wasn't going to allow it. "Has it occurred to you, Ms. Marle, that some people don't think that your humor—in which they are made to feel terrified and dreadful—is funny?"

Becca made a sound in her throat. Tommy looked as if he was about to jump to his feet and deck Kimball.

Thor spoke up quickly, and with a sobering authority. "Mr. Kimball, the state of taste in television is not at debate in the capture of a deranged criminal. Some people don't like sports—they change the channel, they don't go on a spree killing quarterbacks. We believe that these victims were chosen because of opportunity—and, perhaps, even because of your tremendous wealth and presence. Display and publicity mean a lot. The killer revels in every tiny news article on his deeds."

"Yes, and I understand you had him—and lost him," Kimball said.

He was trying to bait people, Clara knew. And she wondered why.

Was he guilty in some way—or was he just enjoying his power to be cruel?

She was aware that something in both Jackson and Thor changed; tightened, or grew darker. Yet neither man's expression flickered, nor did they make any movements to show that the words had indeed affected them.

"It's the Fairy Tale Killer," Magda said flatly, setting a bowl of steaming rice on the table.

"Quite possibly," Thor said. "And, yes, he was put away. We don't manage the justice system. That is something you'll need to bring up with your congressmen and senators, and they can ponder during their legislative sessions."

"No, well, of course you don't manage any of that. And of course I'm happy to offer the safety of this house—with so many fine officers surrounding it—while you deal with this most tragic situation," Kimball said. He turned his attention to Clara. "My dear, when this is all over, you must see more of the true splendor of Alaska. It's a huge state! Coming here for me is amazing—leaving the dirt and buildings of New York City behind, seeing the sky…beautiful!"

"Yes, it's all beautiful," Clara said. She hated being pleasant to the man in any way, but the others at the table were now so heated that she was afraid someone was going to wind up brawling out in the snow. "We saw a moose today—for someone who is not from here, it was a breathtaking moment."

"Ah, well, you can see black and brown bears, too. Grizzlies!" Kimball told her. "Have to watch out for them, but, luckily, bears are actually kind of shy. You have to be careful not to get between them and a food supply, but other than that, you can really see them best on a tour. I've only seen a few, even here on the island."

He continued to extoll the virtues of the island and Alaska.

Clara noted that although Becca said something now and then, neither Tommy nor Nate offered a word of conversation.

Emmy was silent throughout as well, keeping her head down as she ate.

Dinner seemed to last forever. And then it was over and Thor and Mike and Jackson spoke about sleeping arrangements and who would stay awake in the living room when.

Clara escaped to her room quickly and waited, certain Thor would come when he could; from the little bit of conversation she heard, he was keeping first watch.

She showered, paced and realized that she was growing tenser with each passing minute. She needed to breathe, to calm down and…stay sane.

Thor had taken a few hours of the first watch. She had to be patient.

She expected the ghost of Amelia Carson to make an appearance. She did not.

At last, there was a soft rap on the door. She started to open it, remembered that Kimball had been the one out there before, and waited until she heard Thor speak. "Clara, it's me."

Then she nearly jerked the door from its hinges, and when he entered, she barely let him in before she threw her arms around him.

Of course, after that first moment, she drew back slightly, thinking that she'd almost knocked him over, and she murmured, "I'm sorry, I..."

She didn't finish. His arms were around her, his lips were crushing down on hers, and her limbs seemed to burn with the liquid heat that fired their kiss. She held back long enough for him to deal with his gun and holster and then, together, they began to divest clothing so that it lay in a tangle on the floor. She felt the fiery wet sear of his kiss as they fell upon the bed in the remnants of their clothing, a sweet, erotic pressure as his mouth moved from hers and over her flesh. The air was cold; his touch seemed to be thousands of degrees, and even as she clung to him urgently, he continued to caress her naked flesh with his tongue and lips and a feathery and then firm touch. She responded in like fashion, both of them reaching out to touch more of one another, and still he managed to move his lips over the length of her, down her midriff and torso, along her inner thighs, into and over her in such a way that she climaxed even as she grew aroused again. Time and space transcended. There seemed to be nothing more than the desperate and vital urgency to be together. He moved with such luxurious sensuality; his form seemed to be all that filled her, the room, the night, the world.

And then there were the moments afterward when they just lay there together, breathing. They didn't speak then and it didn't matter; they touched one another again and again...and the night went on.

They slept.

And then, Thor began to toss and turn.

Clara bolted up, trying to touch him, trying to stop him from his thrashing.

His eyes opened and he stared at her without seeing her. He said a single word.

"Mandy!"

"Thor?" she murmured. It wasn't with fear or jealousy; she knew who Mandy was.

And Mandy was dead.

He blinked, seeing her, and he suddenly held her close. "Something is happening," he said. "Something has happened!"

CHAPTER THIRTEEN

Thor was up with jeans on and Glock in his waistband in seconds; Clara was almost as fast.

He got to the door, but then stopped and turned back. She knew his sense of urgency—and knew as well that same sense meant he wasn't leaving her, not for a second.

Wrapped in one of the Alaska Hut's heavy terry robes, she was behind him in a split second.

They were down the hall and in the living room in a few breathless steps.

And there, Thor stopped dead, confused, worried.

Mike Aklaq was seated on the sofa, reading a magazine, sipping coffee.

An officer in uniform leaned against the wall. Light from the outside was streaming in; Clara reckoned that had to mean it was about six thirty or seven in the morning.

Mike stood; the officer pushed away from the wall.

"Where's Jackson?" Thor asked.

The question had barely left his mouth before Jackson came down the hallway, as if he'd been mentally summoned long before words had been spoken.

"Thor?" he asked.

Thor nodded to his ex-partner and Clara realized they'd shared something again that others weren't going to understand.

"Marc Kimball," Jackson said, heading for the stairs.

"Mike, have you seen Magda and Justin yet?"

"No, I made coffee myself," Mike said.

"Find them," Thor said. He looked at the state policeman on duty and read his badge. "Officer Grady, check with the men outside. Find out if they've seen anything unusual—anyone around here at all, other than those supposed to be in the house."

"Yes, sir!" the officer said, and went to do as bidden.

Thor was then headed to the doors in the hallway, banging on the door to Nate Mahoney's room. When he heard Nate call out in startled surprise, he moved on to Tommy's door.

Clara hurried past him to Becca's door. She raised her hand to tap on it, but paused for a second; it was just a fraction of an inch open.

Clara held still for a moment, then pushed the door.

The curtains were drawn over the windows; they were heavy, made for a place where the sun barely ever set for a season.

It was bright outside—but not in here. All that illuminated the room was the very pale glow of light that filtered in from the hallway.

She looked in. There was a form she could just make out on the bed.

It appeared that Becca Marle was sleeping peacefully. In fact, Clara almost stepped back out of the room, thinking that Becca was fine and needed that sleep.

But something compelled her to move forward.

She walked over to the bed, becoming aware of a strange odor, something that had a wet smell about it.

As she neared Becca, she almost balked—she was suddenly afraid of what she would find.

She froze in the middle of the room.

She tried to scream; her first effort was pale. She managed to shout out one word at last.

"Thor!"

He was there in a moment; a light flashed on in the room as he hit the switch.

And she saw what she wished she had never seen...

It was a tableau, set out to shock and to horrify.

Becca was there... Rather, the remains of Becca were there, and yet it was hard to say for certain that it was Becca.

Her nose had been slashed. She lay to one side. The bedside table held...things.

Body parts and pieces.

And all she could do was remember the picture she had seen in the trash basket at the cabin rented by Connie Shaw.

A picture of a long-ago murder.

That of Mary Kelly...known as Jack the Ripper's last victim.

Except that this hadn't happened long ago.

Becca Marle had been killed and mutilated in the hours just passed...

With her and Jackson and policemen and women...just a hundred yards away.

She screamed; her scream was loud and piercing and filled with horror.

And it took a long, long time after Thor rushed in, held her, shook her gently and spoke over and over again, for his words to sink in.

"It's not real, Clara. Not real. It's staged. This isn't Becca Marle. It's a dummy. It's staged—this is another scene that has been staged!"

He turned her around to look at him, to see the truth in his eyes. "It's not real, Clara. It's not real—it's not real."

Thor was furious at himself, as were the others.

Whatever the hell had happened, had happened with all of

them right there! With police patrolling the property. With a cop in the hall, an agent on the sofa!

"It's not fucking real. Another staged scene. Why the hell would Becca do such a thing?" It was Tommy Marchant who exploded with the words.

He just as quickly rescinded his words. "No! Becca wouldn't do this!"

It had only been minutes since they'd discovered the "murder" scene in the bedroom. Since there hadn't been a scream, a sound—*nothing at all heard by anyone outside the room*—the logical assumption was that Becca Marle had created the scene herself, and then slipped away.

But had she? Or had someone somehow gotten into that room with her?

"But what the hell, how the hell…and where is Becca?" Tommy said.

Thor was furious and frustrated. And he knew that Jackson and Mike were feeling the same way—even while being grateful that the scene that had been left for them *wasn't real*.

It had been artfully staged. Just like the carnage the Wickedly Weird crew had set up at the Mansion. The woman left in Becca's place—chopped to ribbons and covered with stage blood—had been a fabrication. Thor had done a cursory inspection of the room while Mike had watched over the inhabitants of the Alaska Hut and Jackson had searched outside.

No prints. There had been a powdery snow last night—light, but enough to cover someone's tracks. Someone who knew Alaska and had probably known the weather report for the island.

Thor cursed, because he hadn't seen or heard anything. He tried not to hate himself too much because he knew that there had been a policeman on duty *right there in the hallway*.

Mike Aklaq had been just feet away from the door.

One of them had been there through the night.

And he still wouldn't have known—none of them would have known—if it hadn't been for his dream about Mandy Brandt.

A dream he had apparently shared with Jackson; once again, he knew it. He saw it in his ex-partner's eyes.

"Becca didn't do this—she wouldn't do this!" Nate swore. "You can think what you want about reality TV and bad taste, but we're just the workforce. Most of us have worked on movies—good movies, some that mattered. This is just what we do for a living, what we're told to do. The whole blood and guts thing was Natalie's idea, not ours! Becca wasn't into it from the start. And that said, you ought to be worried about her. I know I am."

"We are worried. We're heading out to find her," Thor told him flatly.

Nate and Tommy began to protest, both speaking over one another. Thor looked at Jackson and Mike and then nodded to the policeman to stay on top of everyone as he moved back into the room. Jackson, he knew, would head out and speak to the officers on patrol around the house.

Mike would stay with the cop, watching those in the room.

Whoever had been in the room wasn't invisible; no one had gone by the cop or Mike Aklaq as he'd set himself up for hours of guard duty on the sofa.

That meant the window.

Thor cursed himself for not reiterating over and over again that the windows should be kept locked at all times. Then again, if Becca had created the setup—which seemed most logical and plausible—she had opened the window herself to escape.

The window was not locked.

A forensic team would now have to come into the room and try to figure out whether Becca had been in the room alone or not. He couldn't take the time to try to discover what had gone on, nor did he have their technology or training.

He needed to get out on the island. He needed to find Becca Marle...

Dead or alive.

Moving back into the living room, he saw that Jackson was just returning.

"One man stands guard in front, one does rounds," Jackson said. "Neither of them saw anyone come or go after Mike entered the house last night. The rounds are every twenty minutes. Either someone was in and knew how to keep watch of the rounds, or Becca..." He paused, looking at Nate and Tommy. "Or Becca knew when to create the scene and leave the house."

Tommy and Nate began their protest anew. Clara, sitting pale and quiet for the most part, spoke up to try to reassure them.

"I'll sue her. I'll sue the little bitch!" Marc Kimball said.

Justin and Magda Crowley stood there, watching and listening.

"Are we supposed to be cleaning that up?" Magda asked.

"No!" Thor assured her.

"Becca, Becca, Becca," Tommy murmured.

"Tommy, I'm sure she's fine. Maybe she was just...just really angry with one of us...someone," Clara said.

"Let's pray she did this herself and that she's on the island somewhere," Thor said. "If not..."

"Oh, my God! If not...he silenced her somehow. And maybe he made her watch as he set up that tableau, what he eventually intended to do with her..." Nate murmured.

Thor turned to Jackson and Mike; for the moment, he even had to ignore Clara. He made a motion indicating they needed to talk.

"Stay here—no one move a muscle, and Mr. Kimball, that damned well means you, too," Thor said. He strode through the living room to the office space they'd been using.

"I've seen to it that Brennan and Enfield have been informed," Jackson said.

"The island is already swarming with forensic teams and police," Thor said, feeling the grate of his teeth as he spoke. He winced, knowing that they had to be dispassionate to a point, cold and logical. "You'd think it would be impossible for a woman who really doesn't know the island all that well to disappear. And," he added, "if the killer did come through the window and do all that, it should have been impossible for him to escape the house with a captive!"

"What if it was someone in the house?" Jackson asked. "Thing is, you were out there for a few hours, Thor. Then I was, and then Mike was. And a cop was out there. No one came down the hallways, but what the hell? Someone could have gone out a window—just as someone went out a window from Becca's room."

Thor cursed softly. "We have to get out there now. Has to be Mike and me—Jackson, you just don't know this place like we do."

"Agreed," Jackson said. "There are no tracks. There were some fresh powder flakes this morning, covered everything up. Go figure. Snow, in summer."

"Late summer, almost fall. And it's the elevation of the landscape and…" He let it go, still swearing to himself. "It is what it is. Either Becca Marle is out there on her own, or she's been taken. If she is on her own, Mike, we ought to be able to find her."

"I'll watch here," Jackson told Thor. Thor nodded to his friend and ex-partner. He knew that Jackson would watch over Clara.

"It had to have been Becca who did it herself," Thor said. "If it was the killer…"

"One of the killers," Jackson interjected.

Thor nodded. "He had time—he had her silenced. Why not kill her?"

"Unless Becca did it herself. She was angry—really angry—at Kimball at dinner last night."

Thor nodded. "We'd better move. It's amazing how quickly someone can disappear when they've chosen to do so."

Once again, Thor and Mike were gone.

Clara had watched them for a while; they were out front with members of the police who had arrived. Thor was tense as he pointed out different aspects of the landscape, assigning men to areas of search, she assumed.

Then he was gone.

And she was left with Jackson Crow, Marc Kimball, the cheerful duo of Magda and Justin Crowley, Emmy Vincenzo, Tommy Marchant and Nate Mahoney.

To Clara's surprise, it was Emmy who spoke first. She cleared her throat. "Um, may I fix myself something for breakfast?" she asked.

"There is coffee already," the police officer offered.

"No one mucks around in my kitchen," Magda Crowley said. "No one but me."

"I think breakfast would be good," Jackson said.

"Am I allowed to be in the kitchen alone, with Justin?" Magda asked.

"This is still my property!" Marc Kimball said angrily. "And if I say that you may work in the kitchen, you may do so."

"At the moment," Jackson said quietly, "I will be calling the shots, Mr. Kimball. I'm afraid that *your property* is involved in all this, whether or not you are directly involved yourself."

"My God! How dare you—" Kimball gasped, staring at Jackson.

"It is what it is, Mr. Kimball," Jackson said.

"I'll have your badge," Kimball said.

"You must do what you must. But, for now, really—don't do more than sneeze without my permission. Magda, Justin, the officer will accompany you to the kitchen. We'll just enjoy sitting here together."

Kimball was quiet for a minute as the officer and the Crowley couple headed off.

"I don't know why I'm paying the price for these horrid people!" he muttered.

"Having spent some time with you, I'm not sure how we're horrid people at all," Nate said evenly, his eyes on the man.

"You'll be off this island—off my property for good—the moment I can get an officer to make it happen," Kimball assured him.

"It will be our pleasure," Tommy assured him.

Clara said quietly, "Please, we're in the middle of really horrible and confusing circumstances. If we're all civil, we'll get through the hours here far more quickly."

"Just what is the plan?" Kimball asked Jackson. "We'll all be prisoners here together because that bitch of a woman decided to create another of her horror scenarios? This is ridiculous. I am calling my lawyer—and the mayor. And the senator. And—"

"Mr. Kimball, I'm expecting that my coworker will back with answers in a few hours. Hopefully, Miss Marle was angry—staged the scene and perhaps even panicked about our reactions. If not—someone was in the room with her. Someone has her now. And we'll hope for the best. My next step is to see that you're all brought in for questioning. We can hold each or any of you for up to twenty-four hours for questioning before charging you—more, under certain circumstances, if necessary. Mr. Kimball, I'm sure you're not accustomed to the living facilities provided at our establishments."

"There just needs to be an end to this!" Kimball muttered.

"Yes," Jackson agreed.

"Maybe I can help with breakfast," Clara said. She stood quickly.

"I have to pee," Kimball muttered. "You going to hold my hand while I go, Special Agent Crow?"

"Please, Mr. Kimball, feel free to use the facilities as needed," Jackson said. "We will, of course, be just outside the door."

Clara fled to the kitchen.

It was sad to leave the one group for the other. The police officer stood with his arms crossed over his chest. Magda was at the stove, working on a large batch of eggs.

Justin manned the toaster.

"Can I do anything?" Clara offered.

"Grab some table settings," Magda said.

"She's a guest," Justin said.

"No guests no more—just all of us in a cage," Magda said. "Go ahead, Miss Avery. There's a pack of us here. Don't mind you helping out."

Clara nodded and made a quick count. Jackson, Emmy, Kimball, Tommy and Nate. She knew that Magda and Justin wouldn't sit at the table. Nor would the police officer on duty eat with them. The most any of the police had taken while on duty was a cup of coffee.

She was setting the plates on the table when she heard a commotion in the living room; moving out there, she saw that the forensic team had arrived—along with another officer. They all had little to say; they headed straight for the room that had been Becca's—and the scene that had been created there.

Jackson had apparently just spoken with them; he beckoned to Clara to follow him.

They went into the office.

"I've got Angela online," Jackson told her. "I got a message from her. I thought you might want to be with me for this."

Clara hurried over to the computer screen. "Thank you!" she told Jackson.

He reached over her, keying in what was needed; Angela's face appeared.

She looked tired; she had probably been up as long, or longer, than any of them. She offered Clara a nod and said, "I want you know that I've reached Thor. He's on police radio and I've gotten through to him fine."

"Okay, why? What's happened?" Clara asked, looking from the screen to Jackson.

"We traced some of the letters at last. There are no cameras at the mailbox facility where the bulk of letters—between Tate Morley and who we believe to be his accomplice—were going. But our agents there found a survivalist who takes pictures of anyone using the same mail company. A kook, I'm assuming, or, who knows? Maybe they believe Big Brother should be watching. I'm amazed we got anything, but…we sent someone persuasive. No corkscrews—just a lot of charm," Angela said. "Clara, Tate Morley has been carrying on a letter correspondence—romantic correspondence—with Becca Marle. She called herself Jane. They've been exchanging letters for more than a year."

It took Clara a moment to speak. "Was that research? Was she hoping to start her own reality show? Or—was she crazy? One of those women smitten with a killer?"

"We don't know her thinking on the matter," Angela said. "She wrote to other convicted killers, so maybe it was research. But, her most ardent letters were to Tate Morley, so…he was either her main focus of research or…or the one who responded to her best. And she is an accomplice."

Clara digested the information. "Then Becca set up the room herself. And she's gone to meet up with him?"

"Possibly," Angela said. "It's hard to tell. We found other letters to him, and email—it truly is frightening to see how some men and women become obsessed with such killers. Some because they believe they can 'fix' them, and some because they're suffering some kind of mental disease themselves and admire the work of serial killers. Law enforcement is often after people like that," Angela added softly.

Clara swallowed. Thor was an agent, a representative of the law. He put his life in danger every day. He had chosen to do so. He was very good at what he did. But now, Tate Morley himself might well be out there, a trap set, along with Becca! And, apparently, both were damned good at…killing. If, of course, Becca was his accomplice.

"They know this, right? You said that Thor and Mike and the other police and agents…they all know this?"

"They know," Angela assured her. "But remember, too, that alone would never stand up in a court of law. We know that she's been corresponding with him, but he corresponded with others, as well. Still, with this information, we're going to process the room at the Alaska Hut, and then let you and Tommy and Nate leave the island. We'll get you on the *Fate* with the rest of your coworkers."

"I see," Clara murmured.

"Jackson will go with you, and I'm heading out either this afternoon or tomorrow myself."

"Angela, that's great!" Clara said. "I mean, it's not great that the case is so bad, just that…" Just that there was nothing like having another agent close to her—a woman she knew, liked and trusted completely.

"I passed the academy, too, you know," Angela said, smiling. "I've always wanted to come to Alaska." She was silent and looked toward Jackson. "And I'll be glad to see this man put away—for good this time."

Tate Morley's victims had haunted both of the men who had pursued him.

Clara understood; Angela needed to be here.

"What are they saying to the others?" Clara asked. "I think Kimball will feel justified. Tommy and Nate won't accept it easily."

"We're not making this common knowledge. They're still looking for Becca. We're just saying that the decision has been made to bring all visitors back to the mainland. That's our official line for the moment," Jackson said. "Enfield is assigning a man to stay here on the island. If we don't have anything with which to charge Kimball, he and Emmy will soon be free to return to New York or go wherever Kimball wants to be. And, as far as Tommy and Nate go..." He shrugged. "We don't have anything on them, either. You're all right with everything?"

Clara scarcely remembered why she was in Alaska...what she did for a living. She'd almost forgotten that next week, she was supposed to be taking part in *Annabelle Lee*, and that she loved what she did and the people with whom she worked.

She nodded at Jackson. Yes, she was ready to board the *Fate*. And sail far away from the cold and the fear and the...death.

If only she could.

She managed a smile for Jackson. "With any luck," she murmured, "we'll actually do this show." She nodded. "And Angela is coming."

"She's always wanted to see Alaska," Jackson said. "I don't actually think that she meant like this."

Thor had law enforcement members assigned to specific areas across the island.

Everyone had been advised that they had connected Becca Marle to Tate Morley. Nothing had proved yet that she was involved in the killings, but her behavior at the Alaska Hut certainly made her suspect.

Thor had chosen the back woods—leading out from the rear of the Alaska Hut and down toward a glacial peak above a group of caverns—for himself and Mike. A number of people had been thirty to fifty feet away at all times, but if Becca had done the work herself—or been instantly incapacitated—it was understandable that nobody had seen anything.

But no one could have passed the front of the Alaska Hut. There was a clearing before the woods; even if a police officer had done some blinking, it would have been nearly impossible for someone to have gone that way undetected.

Of course, that person might have skirted around the woods from the back and gotten just about anywhere. But Thor didn't think so. Becca couldn't know the island that well, and if someone was dragging along her lifeless body, they just couldn't have moved that quickly.

"Being pissed off at Kimball—I can see that," Mike commented as they moved into a section of the woods. "I can see her wanting to hurt him, maybe even proving what they can do. I don't know. I just didn't see the woman as a killer."

"Did you see her carrying on a letter romance with a serial killer?"

Mike shrugged. "Well, frankly, I don't see anyone doing that. But people do."

They'd moved deep into a pine forest. Mike paused, taking a breath, pointing to a tree. "Grizzly territory," he noted.

Slash marks had torn away the bark. Great.

Thor nodded. "Yeah. Let's not tick off any grizzlies, huh?"

"I'm with you, my friend."

They both stood still for a moment. Looking high above the trees, Thor saw circling vultures. He pointed them out to Mike.

"Aw, crap," Mike said.

They began to stride in their direction and found a break in the trees.

And there she was.

Birds were flocking around the corpse. A timber wolf was moving in.

Mike reached for his gun and fired a shot into the air. The birds and the wolf moved off.

"I guess she wasn't a killer herself," Mike said.

"If…"

"If?" Mike asked.

"If that is Becca Marle."

Thor walked toward the corpse. He winced as he hunkered down, and he thought about the display in the woman's bedroom at the Alaska Hut.

He knew that Clara had been shocked by what she had seen. It had been hard for him to convince her that what she saw was a display and not real. But he'd known in an instant. He was far too familiar with the tinny scent of real blood. And here, in the woods, with the buzz of flies…

With the work of buzzards and insects and hungry wolves. Yes. The Alaskan wilderness creatures had been at the corpse.

But…

The killer had meant to display it…

Just like the tableau in Becca's room at the Alaska Hut.

She lay on her one side, an elbow up, her face gone. Flesh had been stripped off her naked thighs and much of her body. Lumps…her organs and breasts…had been laid strategically around her, except that now…

Some parts had already been dragged away, a meal for hungry carnivores.

One daring and hungry blackbird remained, pecking at a bloody mound.

"Holy Christ!" Mike said, crossing himself.

The killer had found a "Ripper" victim.

This time, he'd been able to carry through with the deed.

CHAPTER FOURTEEN

"Kiss me one last time…
A whisper of memory
To the sweetness of the past
Love, my darling, is all that can last
Kiss me one last time…
I'm that whisper of memory
That rustle in the trees
Love, my darling, is all that can last
Kiss me in your heart
Locked away in the past
Where I shall be…
Oh, there in the stars, twinkling by night
Beautiful, bright, and there…in your heart."

Clara finished her last love song as the ghost of Annabelle Lee;
she hovered where she stood, as directed, and then made her
way fluidly and swiftly to where Larry Hepburn—playing Annabelle's widowed husband—stood waiting. She brushed her
fingers against his cheek, placed a kiss like air on his lips, and
turned and floated from the stage. She smiled as she exited stage

left; Larry called out, reached out, and then fell upon his knees and began the song that would bring his new wife into his arms. It really was a beautiful finale.

Clara hurried off the stage, passing Connie Shaw, who gave her hand a squeeze and whispered, "Heartbreaking!"

The director—Tandy Larson, with whom Clara had worked before—would have a few notes for her, but she knew that she could sneak down to the audience where Jackson had been watching.

It had been nice to be greeted with an enormous wave of enthusiasm when she had arrived at the ship that afternoon; she'd felt almost like a prodigal daughter, as if the fatted calf would be slain for her. She quickly found out it was because a full rehearsal had been planned onstage that afternoon—and her understudy had realized, even as the ship sat at dock, that she wouldn't be able to sail.

She'd gotten horribly seasick. Clara had been needed.

Of course, it was still nice to be needed. And it was wonderful, for the moment, to concentrate on the show, on music... movement, direction. To interact with an ensemble cast she loved.

Connie Shaw was doing well. She'd hugged Clara as if they'd known one another forever when Clara had arrived to take up residence in her cabin on the ship.

She was very grateful to be alive; worried that the killer had yet to be caught.

Of course, they were all worried. And they would remain that way. That, of course, hadn't kept Ralph, Simon and Larry from quizzing her about Thor Erikson and teasing her. She had merely shaken her head at their antics.

Clara paused on her way to the backseats of the ship's large theater, turning to observe as Larry and Connie Shaw finished up the play in one another's arms.

It was a good production, she thought. Very charming, with

songs that were not just right for the show, but catchy, as well. And the ending was bittersweet; it was about the memories of love that made it possible to love again.

She hurried to the back of the theater as the others came from the backstage areas to chat and applaud one another's performances, and Tandy called for a break before notes.

She noted the beauty of the theater. By the early 2000s, when Celtic American had purchased the *Fate*, the ship had been all but abandoned and rusting in a shipyard in Liverpool. But she'd been painstakingly restored. The theater now had elegant balconies draped in velvet; the stage itself had been revamped for excellent lighting and acoustics. The antechamber to the theater was decked out with art nouveau and art deco posters, a handsome cherrywood bar and antique tables. The final evening of each voyage offered the Broadway-quality show and a true experience for those who had sailed.

Jackson stood as she neared him, clapping. "That last song… really beautiful," he told her. "You're going to create a few damp eyes out there when you perform it for your audience."

He spoke lightly—saying the right things, of course. But she could see that he was grim.

And she knew.

"Jackson, you know something."

He didn't lie to her. "We don't think that Becca Marle did that setup in the room herself. They think that they've found her."

"They think?" Clara asked.

"Where she was left…in the condition she was left…well, the ME has her now."

Clara sank into one of the theater seats.

And Jackson nodded. "Thor has gotten back and talked to Misty, Tommy and Nate. Apparently, they knew she was corresponding with not just one convicted criminal—she was communicating with several of them."

"Oh, no. Because they were planning some kind of show—*using convicted killers*?" Clara asked him. "Oh, God, no."

He nodded. "So, we're not really sure what to think. Assuming that the corpse is Becca, even if she wasn't in on the killings, we believe that she did know about Tate Morley. And she kept her mouth shut—even after Natalie and Amelia were murdered—because she was afraid she might have been the one to bring it on. Except that she had been careful, in her mind, at least. She'd always called herself Jane when she was writing to the men she was studying."

"So. No closer," she murmured.

"No, we are closer. Every time something happens…"

"We're down a suspect," she said bleakly.

"But, there's more that we know," Jackson told her. He offered her a tight smile. "We've been working on the logistics of it all, the problem being, of course, that the only time we know exactly where Tate Morley was is the hours before Natalie Fontaine was killed. We believe he committed that murder—we also believe that he could have done so in time to reach the island and kill Amelia. But as far as being on the mainland again to try and kill Connie Shaw…we're not sure."

Jackson was thoughtful. "We think he had inside help. We think that someone has been involved, getting him messages somehow, letting him know what law enforcement has been doing and thinking—and helping him, like last night. Someone who knew all about the Alaska Hut and Wickedly Weird Productions. We thought the prison letters were our best clue, and still think they are. But if we are talking about someone being involved, it would have to be the surviving members of the Wickedly Weird staff—Misty Blaine, Tommy Marchant or Nate Mahoney—or, someone directly involved with the island, and that would mean Justin or Magda Crowley, or Marc Kimball himself, or even his assistant." Jackson paused, indicating the stage. "I think you're being summoned."

She was. She hurried down to the stage, pulling out her script, ready to take her notes. Tandy had a few blocking changes for her and little else.

The director—a wonderful woman with crisp iron-gray hair, bright blue eyes and slim, energetic form, smiled at her, shaking her head. "You're doing fabulously as a ghost! Just like someone who loved life, suddenly lost it and grows through the show to deal with her own death. And realizes that she wants the ones she loved so much to move on as well and be happy. It's almost as if you had some kind of experience in the field! I love it, Clara!"

Clara smiled weakly.

She'd had some insight into the subject matter, yes.

Which made her wonder just where Amelia Carson had gotten to. She didn't know if she wished that she would—or wouldn't—make an appearance on the *Fate*.

The Alaska State Troopers, along with a group of young agents—native Alaskans who knew the area—arrived on Black Bear Island.

It was an impressive troop of men and women, and Thor was well aware that with their expertise and their numbers, they far outweighed anything that he and Mike could do alone. And still, he and Mike joined in the intense search on the island. Hours went by; units of men combed the forests, the shoreline, the cliffs, the caverns—and the Alaska Hut.

Nothing.

Since they'd first seen the image from the lobby of the Nordic Lights Hotel of the man who had appeared to be Tate Morley, APBs had been out on the man. Enfield had wanted to play it safe, not certain that they needed to terrify an entire community—despite the fact that they were already terrified due to the murders—when Thor had first identified the man. Now, word that the escaped serial killer was believed to be in Alaska was out in every form of available media.

The ME had taken the body. The only thing recognizable about the dead woman for an on-site identification might be the clothing she was wearing; Nate Mahoney or Tommy Marchant might be called upon while they awaited positive forensic results. Or, it was possible that Misty could help—but Misty had never come to the island. She remained holed up in her hotel room, terrified. While the circumstances dictated that the body did belong to Becca, it was impossible for them to be certain. There just wasn't any face left and the body…well, she'd lain out in the open for many hours. There wasn't enough left of that, either—that hadn't been ripped up by the killer, or consumed or mauled by beasts.

By the time he and Mike returned to the Alaska Hut, the others were gone.

Except for Magda and Justin Crowley.

Thor had known that Nate and Tommy were leaving; they'd return to the Nordic Lights Hotel for the time being.

Becca's room was still designated a crime scene and a police officer still looked dutifully over it. The door was open—the window was locked.

Thor had also known that Jackson was going to see to it that Clara arrived safely back at the port at Seward, and aboard the *Fate*. He'd been in constant Wi-Fi contact with Jackson, who'd assured him all was well and that a rehearsal was in full swing.

What he hadn't known was that Marc Kimball and his little Emmy were leaving, as well; according to Magda, Kimball never told her what he was doing until he did it, but he'd had a private launch take him and Emmy back to Seward. Thor had assumed Kimball would still be on the island, watched by the police—and far from Clara Avery and the others.

Thor didn't like it that Kimball had disappeared.

"Important man, you know," Magda told him, removing glasses from the dishwasher. "He says so himself," she added. Magda wasn't much on betraying emotion, but there was definitely a dry note in her voice. "He said you can't trust the police or the agents—he's safest back in the city. Seems he tried to leave altogether, but as important as he is, he's been asked to stay for the moment. Your boss—some guy named Enfield—saw to it that he can't fly his plane out."

Thor nodded, lowering his head to hide a smile. Enfield was a good man; he didn't give a damn if you were rich or poor—an investigation was an investigation.

"Well, if no one knows where he is, he could head to Anchorage and get on a commercial flight."

Magda sniffed. "That man on a commercial flight—they don't make a class of flying that's 'first' enough for him."

"So, where do you think he went?"

Magda paused in her task and turned around to look at Thor. "I have no idea. The man tells us what he wants when he wants it. Most of the time, we don't hear a word from him. When he bought the place, he gave us explicit instructions on what kind of water he drinks—some brand-label stuff, and it's no better than what we use!—and how he likes his bed made, all kinds of little things. Never to call him direct… We're servants, Special Agent Erikson, and that's it."

"Sounds like a hard man to work for," Thor said.

Magda shrugged. "He's a pompous bastard, is what he is. But there's one good thing about him."

"What's that?"

"He's almost never here. Justin and me, we put up with him for about a month a year, altogether. We call the cops on kids maybe three or four times a year. Other than that, we live in heaven. Crystal pure water, lots of wildlife…and a quick ride over to Seward when we need to shop or feel the whim for a dinner out or a movie…not many of those I want to see these days! Salmon jumping…whales here and there…a moose at my window now and then. I love my life, sir, that I do. And if it comes with a pompous ass for a few days here and there, so be it."

Thor nodded. "Well, then, let me thank you for all the meals here and all you've done for us and the people affected by this." He paused and asked carefully, "You're not afraid of being out here now?" he asked. "Cops will certainly be around awhile longer, hunting, searching, but..."

"You might not have noticed something about me," she said lightly.

"What's that?"

"I'm not exactly a young beauty. Of course, come to think of it... Becca Marle wasn't exactly a beauty. But, that Natalie Fontaine—she was an attractive woman. And Amelia...she was gorgeous. I still think it's the pretty, young ones that he's after. So it seems. Or, hell—those that make reality TV. Quite frankly, how anything you can just turn off could piss someone off so much, I don't know. But, hey, this guy is deranged, right?"

"I'm not a psychiatrist," Thor told her, "but in my mind, yes, anyone who can do such a thing to another human being is seriously deranged."

"And you know who this guy is, right? You'd think you'd just pick him up on the street," Magda said, shaking her head. "The Coast Guard is patrolling, there are cops everywhere—you should have gotten him by now. I mean, where the hell has he been staying? Even such a guy has to eat, right? If he's on the island, why hasn't he been caught by now?"

Justin Crowley, lean and all-*American Gothic*, walked in as she spoke, a hard look on his face. "Magda, how can you ask such a thing?" He looked at Thor apologetically. "This is, in truth, the last frontier. I don't think that anyone has ever explored all the ragged edges, the caves, caverns—or even the forests." He looked at Thor. "I've been around a fair amount now, but when I'm not with a cop looking for an obnoxious teen, I don't go far from where I should be," he said grimly. "You've seen for yourself, Special Agent Erikson. Finding anything on this island..."

He paused, shrugging. "Hell, Kimball owns it—and I doubt he knows that much about it."

How much *did* Kimball know about the island? Had he discovered some secret nook or cranny among the many caverns and caves carved out by ice that others had yet to discover?

Day had waned to evening; Thor was exhausted. He was suddenly determined to find out exactly where Kimball had gone. He reminded himself that he couldn't harbor suspicions on the man because he outright disliked him.

But logically, Kimball stood in the line of possible Tate Morley accomplices.

And if they could get the accomplice, they could get the man.

He thanked Magda and turned away. Outside, he put a call through to Mike.

His partner would keep searching the island.

Thor was going to find Marc Kimball.

Clara lay down on her bed in her cabin—in what had once been the "Irish" section when the *Fate* had brought immigrants to America. She was tired, but wired. Jackson Crow had been set up in the cabin next to her and she'd join him in about an hour to have dinner with him and the cast. But she was in a restless mood.

Another woman was dead. Horribly. They believed two people were guilty; even if one person had done the killing, that person had help. Help that was close to home.

Would Thor come here tonight? Was there something between them? Would this all end when the killer was caught?

And most important, would the killer ever be apprehended?

Her cell phone began to ring—something that actually happened now that she was off the island!

Expecting Jackson or a friend—or even Thor—she answered it quickly.

For a moment, there was nothing. She wondered if her connections had gone on the fritz again.

"Hello?"

"Hello, Miss Avery."

"Yes, hello. Who is this?"

It was only then that a strange sense of dread settled over her.

"We haven't met, formally. But I've seen you."

"Who is this?"

"I am God, I am the Devil. I am both rolled into one. In a past life, I was the Fairy Tale Killer. Now I see myself as the Media Monster. Some fool at a newspaper gave me that moniker. I suppose it's as good as any."

She sat there frozen for a second, wondering if it was real, trying to remember from crime shows what she should do.

Hang up?

Keep him on the line?

He kept talking; thank God—she didn't need to think of her response.

"I don't understand how they're missing all this. Yes, it's my purpose now to bring to light memories of some of the greatest murderers known to man." He paused to laugh softly. "Jack the Ripper, the Black Dahlia killer and, yes, the Deadly Dancer."

Keep him talking? Isn't that what you're supposed to do?

But for what? There was no recording device on her phone— it was just a cell phone.

"Frozen to silence, Miss Avery?" he asked.

"No," she managed. "I was just thinking that they weren't the greatest murderers of all time. You had many killers out there who committed more atrocious crimes—by number of victims, by ingenuity of form..." She was on her feet as she spoke, racing out to the hall. She tried to bang on Jackson's door without the sound being heard over the phone.

"I haven't even begun to leave behind my trail of victims," he said, his voice low and chilling.

Jackson quickly threw his door open; looking at her, he apparently read her face and realized the killer—or someone purporting to be the killer—was on the line.

He drew her into his cabin, pulling out his own cell as he did so. He motioned to her to keep talking as he stepped aside and made a call. She could barely hear his voice. Tense, hushed, concise—she wasn't sure who he had called or what he was asking for, but perhaps there was a way to follow through on the satellites being used by her phone.

"You're also not unknown. You're Tate Morley. You've been arrested and convicted and you'll wind up dead or back in prison. You're no great genius who has gotten away with his crimes," she told him.

She thought she'd lost him; he went silent for so long. She had annoyed him. His tone was peeved when he spoke again. "No. When I end my reign of terror, the police and G-men and what have you will all be looking like a pack of ice spiders busy racing over the ice with nothing—nothing! I come and go at will. I disappear into the white mists of the snow. They'll all be standing with their little dicks in their hands. I will reign as long as I choose, Miss Avery."

"No," she said quietly, "you are nothing."

"Ah, bravo, bravo, Miss Avery! But, then, of course, you are an actress—a real one, at the least. Not like those pathetic 'reality' stars. Quite frankly, the nation should thank me," he said, and laughed as if deeply pleased with his own joke. "Yes, I was lured by the promise of my fifteen minutes of fame, and what a lovely circumstance it proved to be! A perfect killing field, perfect victims, and the bastards who put me away all there, all ripe for the taking! But don't be so very, very pleased, Miss Avery. The show doesn't always go on. I see you right now— you've run to Special Agent Crow—yes, yes, laugh, laugh, *Special* Agent Crow. He's special, all right! He's there, he's listening and he's trying to get a tab on where I might be calling from.

Well, duh, we all know I'm near, right? And his partner, ever so *Special* Agent Erikson, is running around on the ice right now, certain that he—great old tracker that he must be!—can find me in a snowbank. Pardon the crudity, but, yes—dick in his hand, dick in his hand! Oh, wait, I guess you'll fix that for him later."

"I'm hanging up now," Clara told him.

"You don't hang up on me. I hang up on you."

Clara looked at Jackson. He nodded.

She clicked End on her phone and the call went dead.

She looked over at Jackson worriedly.

"It will ring again," he said.

He was right. The phone began to ring.

"Let it ring several times. Not too quickly," Jackson said.

Sixth ring. Jackson nodded.

She answered it. The man she believed to be Tate Morley began to speak, furious and cursing and spitting words.

"How dare you—how dare you! Every state in the Union wants me. You're behaving as if I'm not the most important person in the world, and you know that I am. You know that you need me—any contact with me."

Clara glanced at Jackson, shaking, but ready to do her best. "Don't be ridiculous. You're talking to me because you believe we can't get an exact fix on you through my phone. I don't know if we can or can't. I know that all you want to do is taunt me. Well, I don't want to be taunted. You're being rude and obnoxious and full of yourself. I think you're a bitter little prick of a man who's a sociopath and a psychopath all rolled into one."

"Oh...oh...oh! Miss Avery. You do have claws. Nice survival instincts. I almost wish I was still the Fairy Tale Killer. What a beautiful Sleeping Beauty you would make! Or, if I had to stretch—I mean, no one's hair is that long these days—you might be Rapunzel. You do let down that long hair, don't you? Ah, but you're not with lover boy right now, are you? You see, I know where Thor is and I know that you're with Jackson Crow.

Yeah, like I said, I see all! I've not decided exactly where I'm going next…there are still a few tasty ideas rolling about in my mind! You shouldn't make me mad."

She glanced at Jackson, not sure who he was now on his phone with—and really having no idea if anyone could trace this kind of cell phone coverage in any way, shape or form.

"You're a cruel human being. You've stolen all that matters in any way—you've stolen life. You're horrible, worse than the lowliest crawling bug, because even a bug does good things, and you…"

He broke in. "Oh, really? I've ended some bad TV!" he said, and seemed to think that his words were hilarious. He started laughing.

"Well," he said finally, and she could hear a deep inhale, as if he was trying to get over his spurt of mirth, "you don't need to try to pinpoint my location, Miss Avery. I'll be happy to tell you where I am," he said.

"And where are you?"

"Closer than you can begin to imagine!"

Because communication could be so patchy—even with Wi-Fi and their walkie-talkies—Thor wanted to see Mike Aklaq before he left the island.

He had the feeling that the killer was no longer there. He held the firm belief that the actual killer was Tate Morley—whether he had been abetted by Becca Marle or someone else, Morley had done the killing. He'd had an accomplice who had known Alaska, known the Alaska Hut and Black Bear Island. He was able to come and go easily. With the amount of law enforcement officers looking for him, he should have been caught by now. He knew how to disappear at will. Be here when he chose, escape when he chose. He wasn't using the docks; that meant some kind of a small conveyance he'd been able to pull up onto the shore—and hide.

That meant a cavern.

Though *how* he was managing to come and go was a mystery, Thor wasn't sure solving it would help, except that he'd quit being torn as to where he'd best be putting his own efforts. Thor knew how good an agent his partner was, but he still wanted to see him before he left. Because while his gut told him that Morley was no longer here, the latest victim had not been discovered long ago.

Taking one of the snowmobiles, he headed past the forest toward the southern tip of the island where the icy cliff jutted up from the sea and an ancient wall of ice had carved out the peculiar landscape.

He could see that there were snowmobiles and the larger snow sleds used by the forensic teams present at the base, closest to the shore and cavern entrances. Men and women in uniform moved about the area, looking like ants from a distance and growing larger as he approached.

One of the crime scene investigators he knew waved to him and indicated that Mike was in one of the caverns. Thor waved his thanks and hurried on down.

The cold here seemed to be exceptionally fierce; people breathed as if they were dragons as they worked, spouting steam rather than fire.

He almost slid down one icy ledge, caught his balance and righted himself, and arrived at what might be considered "the ground," where the ice crunched beneath his feet. He could see Mike was back speaking with a few of the officers—asking them, Thor was certain, to see that no crevice remain unseen.

"Thor—thought you were leaving," Mike said. He smiled suddenly. "You have to trust someone, my friend. You can't be everywhere."

"I am leaving. I'm going to find Kimball," Thor told him.

"Kimball is off the island?" Mike asked, surprised.

"Apparently, he left with the others. None of us can be trusted.

He wants the protection of being in the city. Or so he told Magda."

"Maybe he is afraid," Mike said with a shrug. "Hey, the man is an ass. You know as well as I do that being an ass isn't illegal."

"No, but something about him…"

"He treats people really badly."

"Yeah. Anyway…"

Thor broke off, blinking. The sun had shifted just slightly, casting a different light onto the scene. He felt his muscles tighten; the fierce sun could play tricks on the mind. And for a moment, he could have sworn that he saw Mandy Brandt standing there, a shimmer of white mist in the ice and sunlight. And then she was gone, but, of course, he still stared at the place where she had been standing.

While there had been people there since they'd first discovered the killer's stash of cutting tools, and the ground was well trodden, Thor was pretty sure he saw a strange line in the crunched ice ground.

"What?" Mike asked.

"There it is," Thor breathed, because, where Mandy had stood, he thought he saw what he had been seeking.

"There what is?"

"His trail."

"What are you talking about?"

"A boat. Look at that line. He's been using a boat himself. Something incredibly small, but must have a motor or he'd never make it here or back. He dragged it here—it's how he kept any of the patrolling Coast Guard vessels from seeing it. I'm willing to bet if you head further to the west you'll find marks like this, as well. That one strange line that only shows under a direct ray of the sun. He's come and gone with ease, Mike. And I'll bet he is off the island now. He chopped up his latest victim and headed straight back into Seward."

"We'll search with a fine-tooth comb, farther to the west," Mike assured him.

"I'm heading back to Seward," Thor said. "Now."

"I'll find what there is to find," Mike promised quietly.

Thor turned, left Mike and drove the snowmobile straight for the docks. Just as he reached them, his phone—via the Wi-Fi hookup—rang. He glanced at the caller ID, and was grateful that the call had come through.

It was Jackson. Thor answered quickly. "Yeah?"

"Morley called Clara."

"What?"

"Yes, he's actually called her twice. I have our techs working with her cell provider, finding satellite usage, pinpointing a position. We've traced the number—"

"And it goes to a pay-as-you-go phone?"

"No. That's just it. It was a business line purchased by one of Marc Kimball's companies."

"Kimball's companies?"

"Yep."

"Morley threatened her?"

"He's taunting her—not a direct threat. You know. Defending his actions, touting his prowess—and letting us know that he's near."

"Kimball is off the island," Thor said. "And Tate Morley was on the island. But I believe he's off it now, too. I'm heading to the docks right now." He hesitated. "Has anyone checked? Did Kimball come aboard the *Fate*?"

"Passengers haven't boarded yet," Jackson said.

"Marc Kimball can buy his way many places," Thor reminded him.

"There were no orders out not to let the man board a ship," Jackson said. "I'll look into it."

"Thanks."

"Yeah, get here, Thor. I've called the Alaska State Troopers.

They'll get a man down to me so we can sandwich Clara out of here. I'm going to get her to the station."

"Perfect. I don't like this. I'd like to know that she's safe—in a place filled with law enforcement and with guns all around. She needs to be at the station. I'm on my way, heading to Seward— get there as fast as physically possible. I'll call when I'm near so I know where to head to meet up with the two of you."

Thor left his snowmobile and hurried down the docks.

A Coast Guard cutter was there, along with a captain ready to sail him across the water and back to Seward with all speed. Thor scanned the shoreline of Seward and the docks.

It wasn't until they had nearly arrived that he saw something that made him pause. "There! Can we pull up?" he asked the captain.

"There?"

"That little motorboat, the one tied poorly," he said.

No one who really knew how to handle a boat—or gave two figs about it—would leave a boat tied with a simple bow; any sailor worth his salt would have secured the little vessel.

The water was always somewhat rough; waves lapped at the cutter and the rowboat. Thor trusted his coordination and his years living in the wintry waters and wilderness and leapt from the one vessel to the other.

It was dotted with bits of something red. He hunkered down and touched it.

Blood.

He'd found the killer's way on and off the island.

Off—the killer was here now. In Seward.

He looked up and when he did, he saw a number of the cruise ships down at the distant cruise port.

Among them, the *Fate*.

"Thor!"

He heard his name spoken softly and he looked up to the dock. The sun was shimmering down; it was late afternoon…maybe even evening, but the sun was still a powerful entity in the sky. Streaks of gold seemed to highlight someone standing there.

Mandy Brandt.

She didn't say more; she seemed to look at him with infinite sadness. She pointed at the *Fate*, and then she was gone.

And Thor turned to look at the captain of the Coast Guard cutter.

"Get me to the *Fate*, immediately, *please!*" he said.

"Special Agent Erikson, there is protocol and there are restrictions—"

"I'll fix them. Just get me on that ship. Now!"

There had to be some kind of protection training learned at the FBI; Jackson finished his conversation with headquarters and then after his brief exchange with Thor went into immediate action. "There's no real proof, but it seems that the satellite signals cross right here—on the *Fate*. Seems like he's come here—or he's very near here," he told her. "We're going to head into the police station."

Clara nodded. "Whatever you say," she told him.

"Kimball is off the island, too. He may—he may be trying to follow or find you."

She tried for weak humor. "He does seem to like a good musical comedy."

Tate Morley was aboard the *Fate*.

How the hell had he gotten on?

Passengers weren't boarding—they wouldn't be for days.

But Jackson Crow didn't seem to be surprised.

"Morley—how?" she asked, trying to remain calm and in control.

"Morley is a master with fake papers and disguises that make him look like an 'everyman,'" he told her briefly. "Security is coming down the hallway now—we'll be off the ship and over to the police station as quickly as possible. A state police officer is heading this way. At his arrival, he'll lead and I'll follow until we're off the ship."

Clara felt as if the great glaciers themselves had found a way into her bloodstream. Even with everything happening, she hadn't felt this sense of intimate personal danger until now. She swallowed and nodded; she was with Jackson. He had been her protector before; he had seen her through a bad and dangerous time. He would do so again.

"As soon as an officer gets here, we'll head off the ship," Jackson said.

"Well, you're with me. I'm sure we could—"

"We'll wait. If you want to gather a few things, it might be a good idea," Jackson said.

"I'll just grab my toothbrush and a few clothes," Clara murmured.

She walked into her small bathroom. As she reached for her toothbrush to pack in a little toiletries bag, she was stunned to hear a scream—one so loud and piercing that it seemed to tear through the bowels of the ship.

She burst out of the bathroom. "Stay!" Jackson said. "Lock the door when I'm gone—the second I'm gone. Don't open it!"

He headed out. "Wait, Jackson, don't leave me!" she said.

But he was already walking away. He turned back. "Lock it!"

He left; she locked the door.

Pacing, she realized she was safe. She was almost below the waterline. No one was going to enter by her tiny porthole. The only way was the door.

And she didn't intend to open it.

But Jackson had been gone only a matter of minutes when something slammed against her door.

She jumped, then she heard a voice. "My God, please, Clara! He'll kill me. If he can't talk to you, he's going to kill me!"

She looked out the tiny peephole in her door.

And she saw Emmy Vincenzo, tiny, shaking—looking as if

she'd been beaten with dark smudges beneath her eyes...a heavy bruise on one cheek.

And blood trickling down her forehead.

"Please, oh, God, please help me, Clara!"

She screamed, and seemed to slam against the door again as if she'd been stabbed.

Clara opened her cabin door.

Emmy Vincenzo was not alone.

CHAPTER FIFTEEN

Thor called Jackson immediately—no answer.

He continued to call him all the way to the ship. He tried to tell himself that there were logical reasons that Jackson didn't answer.

Clara didn't answer her cell, either.

He reached Enfield, who had told him there'd been an incident aboard the ship that Jackson was investigating; they were sending men out.

"Incident? What kind of incident?"

"I don't know yet—screams reported. Crow is there. As soon as I know, I'll get back with you."

Yeah, Crow was there—but not answering Thor, either. At least the road was cleared for him when he reached the ship. He was ready with his credentials. He stopped at the ship's one entry to meet with security, words on his lips before he could be asked the first question. "Special Agent Thor Erikson, here with the investigation into the recent barbaric murders in Seward and Black Bear Island; I have reason to believe that someone involved with the case is on this ship now."

He left the security officer just staring after him and he realized that the man had already been notified. The ship had gone on lockdown.

He dialed Jackson as he hurried aboard.

Still no answer.

Swearing, he hurried along to the main salon of the deck he had entered. Once there, he caught hold of the first young woman he saw in a crew uniform.

"The ship is on lockdown," the woman informed him. "Sir—"

"Special Agent Erikson," he told her briefly. "The cast of *Annabelle Lee*—where are they?"

"Waterloo Deck. Elevators are over there and the stairs are just to the left."

He nodded his thanks and ran down the stairs.

When he reached the Waterloo Deck, he found it empty.

And he cursed himself for not having Clara's cabin number. He stood in the hallway and shouted her name at the top of his lungs.

As doors cracked open around him, he felt as if he'd entered a bad version of *A Streetcar Named Desire*.

Except that those who peeped out looked thoroughly frightened.

Ralph and Larry Hepburn were among those who appeared. Thor turned and gripped Larry by the shoulders. "Where's Clara?"

"Cabin 827," Larry said. "She came back here with Jackson. Then there was this scream that was horrible…we've been asked to stay in our cabins while the sound was investigated. Thor, hell…what else?"

"I think he's here. I think the killer is on the *Fate*," Thor said. "Get back in your cabin."

"Clara?" Ralph said, a catch in his throat.

"I'll find her," Thor said.

He ran on down the hallway to 827.

The door stood slightly ajar—the latch hadn't caught.

No, it was…open.

For a moment, he felt a keen and terrible sense of déjà vu. He remembered that day now long past when he had opened another door and seen Mandy Brandt…

She lay in beauty.

He shoved the door open, his Glock in his hand.

The room was empty.

Emmy Vincenzo had fought long and hard; she and Marc Kimball both seemed to have battled ten rounds in a boxing ring.

"Please!" Emmy had choked.

She hadn't entered Clara's room—but then, Emmy was entangled with Marc Kimball, who had stared at her like a man possessed. He and Emmy were arm in arm. It seemed he was trying to speak but could not—and was letting Emmy do the speaking for him.

"He says you must come. He has a knife to my ribs. Oh, Clara, I'm so sorry… Clara, Clara…please. I'm so scared!" Emmy had seemed to choke on her words. "He's already killed a cop—he stabbed him right in the throat…oh, Clara! I should have let him kill me. I shouldn't have been such a coward!"

She had cried out; she and Kimball had been so tightly crushed together that Clara could only assume he was pressing a blade into her side.

"Emmy, it's all right," Clara had said, amazed by her own courage as she stared at Kimball. "I'll go where he wants me to go. Marc—you sick, arrogant bastard. Don't touch her again."

And so she walked ahead of the two.

Down the hallway where cast and other entertainers were first housed, though now they had moved into another layer of the ship—where a maze led to machinery and storage and, she could only assume, at one time, the lowest of the lowly servants and workers aboard.

Clara hadn't seen a single soul; whatever the source of the scream that had impelled Jackson to leave the cabin had caused an alert on the ship.

But, surely, help would be coming. If the ship was under a code-red alarm, it would soon be crawling with police and security and...

Jackson had told her not to open her cabin door. And she had. But Marc Kimball had abused Emmy Vincenzo as an employee; now he was taking it to another level.

"This isn't right," someone said softly.

You think?

Clara glanced to her side. Amelia Carson was now walking along with her, frowning as she glanced back at the pair behind them.

"It was that Tate Morley man... I mean, he called you, right?" Amelia said.

Tate Morley. The Fairy Tale Killer. The Media Monster...

What bizarre murder does he intend to emulate from the bowels of a historic ocean liner?

Clara swallowed. She didn't know where they were going; maybe Morley had made Kimball beat and threaten Emmy Vincenzo to use against her. Maybe he'd known Clara couldn't bear to watch another woman killed in front of her.

"Where have you been? Did you see any of this?" Clara asked softly.

"Watching...the wrong place at the wrong time! I have to do something," Amelia said. "I have to do something..."

She turned around. Clara paused, as well. The other two staggered right into her. Amelia put her hand to her face; she looked as if she cried.

Emmy screamed again; Kimball must have prodded her with his knife.

"Who were you talking to?" Emmy demanded, tears in her eyes, words hopeful.

"Amelia Carson's ghost," Clara said flatly.

Emmy screamed again.

"Jerk! I'm moving," Clara said. "Quit hurting her!"

She turned and started walking again.

The ghost of Amelia Carson was gone.

Thor found Jackson working over the body of a prone officer in a cabin down the hall. He fell to his knees by his old partner and friend.

"Knifed," Jackson said briefly, using a ripped-up piece of the man's shirt to put pressure on his wound and stop the blood flow.

"Clara—" Thor began.

"Locked in her cabin—827."

"She's gone."

Jackson blanched. "Find her," he said. "I got this—find her."

Thor rushed back into the hallway. He could hear a commotion rising on the decks above; help had arrived. Jackson wouldn't be alone—help would come for the bleeding officer.

He hurried out into the hallway. He didn't know which way to go.

Then he saw Amelia Carson.

"This way!" she beckoned.

And he followed.

Clara was suddenly shoved into a room. There was a desk with piles of papers on it, an inbox and an outbox, a computer and other modern office accoutrements, all set against the hardwood Victorian desk of an earlier era.

A man sat behind it.

He rose as they entered.

He was in a steward's white-and-blue uniform, and for a brief, shining moment, Clara thought they had stumbled upon help.

Then he smiled.

"Miss Avery! My lovely, lovely Miss Avery. How very nice to

meet you in person. You really are quite something. You know, I wish we could have met under other circumstances. I'm really a charming man. You would have enjoyed knowing me."

"I doubt that," she said.

Emmy and Kimball seemed to retreat—still as one—to a corner of the room. The desk was between her and Tate Morley. She couldn't help but note that there was a letter opener on it.

She wondered about the possibility of grabbing for it—and stabbing Morley.

That left poor little Emmy in the same position.

But how could she help the woman if she was dead herself?

"I won't get to know you, but… I'd love to know how you managed all this," she said.

He was a truly nondescript man. Maybe five foot ten, with watery blue eyes and sandy short-cropped hair. His build was medium. There was nothing about him that stood out, and Clara assumed that made changing into whatever he wanted to be easy enough.

"You're a sad little man that no one notices, aren't you?" she asked softly.

"They all notice me!" he said, a note of irritation in his voice. "They all notice me. I bring the adrenaline of fear and excitement into their lives. And those women… I made them famous. I made them beautiful as they had never been."

"Your last victim didn't even have a face."

He flicked a finger in the air. "But the first! Ah, that I might have remained the Fairy Tale Killer!" Something hardened in his expression. "Your lover boy and Crow ended that for me. But, now…reality TV! They wanted reality—I gave it to them. And it was so convenient. With the resources and knowledge to come to Alaska, I not only got to begin again, but as an added bonus, I got those arrogant FBI bastards, as well. And, any good killer knows, a signature is needed…but! With your blonde beauty…all I can think of is a fairy tale! The fairest of the fair."

"You know you're on a ship. You know that police and FBI will be crawling through it within minutes."

"And I'll be gone. You see, I've had opportunity to learn all that I need to know. Please, Miss Avery! I've come and gone like the wind."

"Let Emmy go!" she said.

"Let Emmy go... I don't think so."

She'd been eyeing the desk—waging her chances.

If he wouldn't let Emmy go...

No choice.

She made a dive for the letter opener.

Thor followed the apparition down and along the hallway at breakneck speed. Then, just as Amelia Carson seemed to disappear into thin air, he heard voices.

Tate Morley's voice. And the man was talking about fairy tales...

He heard Clara's voice; it was trilled slightly with fear—it was heavier with anger.

He tried to determine who else might be in the room—and then he heard something like a war cry and he had no choice but to swing around the corner and into the room.

Clara was holding her own. She was down on an old Victorian desk, grappling with Morley and a letter opener.

Emmy Vincenzo was locked in a hold with Marc Kimball.

"Stop!"

He fired his Glock into the air.

For a moment, it seemed that everyone in the room froze; as if he had created a tableau.

But then, Morley let out a scream of fury, and slammed against Clara, wrestling the letter opener from her and raising it over her head.

Thor aimed and shot in less than two seconds.

"Emmy!" Clara screamed, scrambling from beneath the dead man.

But poor little Emmy had found her courage at last. She'd

freed herself from Kimball. She had the knife; Thor saw Kimball's eyes widen and his mouth open, as if he would make one last derisive comment—fire her, perhaps!—before her knife landed in his gut.

Kimball crumpled to the floor and Thor rushed forward to take Clara into his arms.

CHAPTER SIXTEEN

The following two days were, for Thor and Clara, a mass of reports, further investigations and dodging the press. Questions remained. Had Kimball been corresponding with Morley? When had Morley determined how, where and when Clara should be brought to him? Theories abounded on paper; they didn't have all the answers. They were still putting together puzzle pieces.

The state police found the ship's officer whose life and identification Tate Morley had stolen two days later deep in a forest that bordered the road to the state park.

It would have been his first voyage on the *Fate*, and therefore none of the other employees had known him to be anyone other than who he had presented himself to be.

Marc Kimball had simply booked passage for himself and Emmy Vincenzo, something that hadn't meant a thing to Emmy at the time—everyone knew that Kimball had a massive stage-crush on Clara.

Emmy was able to pull a number of strings for them, though, because of her position with Kimball. She had done bookings as usual. Of course, at the time, she'd had no idea of what was going on.

She'd cried copious tears at first, so finding out anything from her had been very difficult.

Thor wasn't a psychologist—and psychologists and psychiatrists would have a heyday with it all. He'd taken enough criminal behavior courses to speculate that it had been power both men had been after. For Kimball, money had given him tremendous clout, but it had never been that power over life and death that Morley had wielded. How and when the correspondence between the men had begun, Emmy had no idea. But she knew about secret drawers in Kimball's desk, and those drawers had led to a wealth of letters. They were coded, of course—they wouldn't have left the prison walls if they'd included instructions on how to come to Alaska. Cryptologists in the department would be given the task of deciphering just what the letters and phrases had meant.

They would never have all the answers, because both men were dead. Thor's shot had been a kill shot this time—he had no doubt that Morley would have stabbed Clara with an urgent desire for his last kill if he'd been given the least chance.

And sheer terror had seized Emmy, she had told them—between bouts of hysterical and copious tears—and she was both grateful to be alive and horrified that she had killed a man. She wouldn't be released from the hospital until this evening or tomorrow. There would be no charges against her—she had killed in self-defense. None of them knew if Kimball would have killed her in an ultimate defiant act or, with Morley, his puppet master, dead, if he would have just let her go.

"I have never been so terrified!" she'd told Thor, shaking in her hospital bed.

She'd been pretty roughed up. Apparently, Marc Kimball had been ordered by Morley to bring Clara Avery to him. She didn't know what the plan had been to escape the *Fate* once they'd gotten Clara. Maybe Kimball had been promised in on her—time to indulge in whatever sick fantasies he had, going along with what had appeared to be his absolute infatuation with her. Emmy didn't know that much. She only knew that Kimball had called her in, slammed her head against a door and put his knife to her throat to make her do what he wanted. He'd made her scream when he'd killed the officer on the ship—that way, they could disappear down to the cast cabins while law enforcement went to investigate the scream. He forced her to speak for him—work for him even through his deadly activities. He seemed to think, in a very malicious and sardonic way, that it was funny. And it would help show that his true intent was indeed lethal.

"What will I do now?" she asked, looking lost.

"Well, you'll get out of the hospital first," he told her. She had a nervous habit of working her fingers on the sheets.

She was going to need a lot of therapy, he thought.

"You never had any inkling—I mean, you worked with him closely. You had no idea he might be homicidal himself? He never behaved strangely?" Jackson asked.

"That's just it—he always behaved strangely," Emmy told him remorsefully.

"Strange, all right," Mike Aqlak said. Thor wondered if his partner—there from the minute he could have been, dealing with red tape, the press, acting like a bulwark in many ways—meant Kimball himself, or the whole thing, or even the meek little woman who had managed to kill her boss in self-defense.

Oddly enough, Kimball had finally met his match in the little woman he'd treated so badly for so long.

"What is it?" Mike asked when they left.

"I don't know," Thor told him.

Mike thumped him on the back. "You did it. You got Morley again, for good this time—and that bastard, Kimball. You called it with the caverns on the island—you found the damned boat he was using. Hell, my friend, you did what an agent is supposed to do!"

Thor thanked him for his support; Mike grinned and told him he knew that he would be leaving—and that it would be okay.

"Hey, partners meet up again, don't they?" Mike asked Jackson.

"It can happen," Jackson said.

Thor wished he felt a little better—he should have been in on the somber celebrations and congratulating that went around among law enforcement. The murders had been brutal and horrible; those women still lay at the morgue, disfigured, disjointed, decapitated and bisected. A ship's officer had been killed, as well. What had happened had been terrible; but the killer and his accomplice were dead.

He should have been more relaxed. He just wasn't.

Maybe it was the fact that the manhunts, the searches through the snow, the speculation and the wondering had been so intense, it was impossible to just let it all go.

The media furor wasn't going to die down for a long time.

What few cabins hadn't been sold on the *Fate* went at a premium. Yes, there were areas on the ship that were a crime scene, but the crime scene units and specialized cleaning units would be finished before the set sailing date.

The *Fate* would keep her deadline—after all, she was the *Fate*!

Thor had a number of conversations with Clara about that. But she was determined she would sail on the ship. There was no reason she shouldn't.

"It's over, Thor. And this is what I do for a living. It's a good show. Tate Morley and Marc Kimball stole lives. Now they're dead. They can't keep stealing. We can't let them."

For the next two nights, he had Clara staying with him at his family compound. He could easily reach the offices in Anchorage when he needed, the hospital in Seward and the state police. He was present at the press conference that Enfield gave, announcing that the FBI and state police were still piecing together the puzzle, but that they were satisfied that the Media

Monster—aka Tate Morley and the Fairy Tale Killer—was now dead. The country was astounded that he seemed to have been aided by and worked in collusion with the multimillionaire Marc Kimball.

Thor tried not to watch the news.

Anyone who had been close to Kimball could seize the media and fifteen minutes of fame now, if they chose.

Thor was glad of the time he could take at the compound; glad to be there with Clara.

She was a natural at his home. The dogs loved her. They were somewhat insulted when they were locked out of the bedroom at night, but a couple of treats ended the problem of them scratching at the door.

It was a day and a night after the incident on the ship; he'd dealt with the tangle of the Bureau's investigation and had his first mandatory psychiatric appointment—necessary after the shooting. He'd had a long talk with Jackson, who'd warned him, *We can never be too careful with those we choose to love. Did I have to leave when I did—yes. Did Clara have to open that door— yes. That's who she is. It's why you're with her. Can you change that and make life safe? No. We do our best in every circumstance and have faith in those around us.*

Thor was thinking about that conversation when he and Clara were alone together that second night, after they'd played with the dogs all day and learned to "mush," and he knew that Jackson was right. Clara was capable of intelligent fear—the kind that went along with survival. But if she had a chance to put herself at risk to save a life, she would.

Now they were naked and damp and hot-skinned from the shower, sunken into the plush freshness of the sheets and the softness of the down. And all he could think then was that having her hair fall around him was like being wrapped up in gold silk. The taste of her flesh was the sweetest he had ever known. He kissed her and teased her, hands and lips upon her mouth, her throat, breasts, belly, thighs and in between, and she was like a wild nymph in turn, touching him as he was certain he'd never been touched before, doing things with the shimmery slide of her tongue that he'd never felt before and driving to him to a state of hunger and desire that seemed to defy the universe—much like the climax that ripped through him volcanically. He wondered if sex was that incredibly good just because they were both alive—but no, sex was that incredibly good because there was something there, deeper than human instinct, richer than perfection. He loved her smile when, gasping, she strode atop him, tossing her hair. He reached for her, drawing her down beside him. "I'm due time off."

She tensed slightly and he worried, wondering if this was just great "I'm alive" sex for her, if what they'd shared before had simply been a result of all the tension and fear that had plagued them both.

He smoothed back her hair and continued, "I was thinking of a cruise."

"Oh—an Alaskan cruise?"

"I wouldn't want any ordinary cruise. I'd want a historic ship. Something with a rich history. A ship that has survived war and trauma at sea—one that has carried thousands of immigrants. And, of course, been meticulously refitted."

"Like a Celtic American cruise."

"Hm, just like."

"I hear you'll never get a cabin."

"Ah, sometimes people are willing to share."

She crawled atop him again, all smiles having faded, her eyes deep and bluer than the day and night together, beautiful. Touched with emotion.

"You can't give up anything for me, Thor. You need to be here, and right now… I can't have another show fall apart and—"

"I have time coming!" he assured her. And he hesitated. "I may be transferring. I get a transition period, too."

"Transferring?"

He nodded, his hands running down her sides. "I was with Jackson and Mike today—two guys who are great, two super agents. But…"

"But?"

"But…you knew that Amelia led me to you?" he asked softly. She nodded; he'd told her that. They'd both been trying to think of a way to thank a ghost.

"Not that many people really get to speak with ghosts—especially people who have graduated from the academy and have had a good decade plus of work in the field. Jackson and I were especially good together because we could read one another's minds—not so much ESP, but knowing how we both thought. He's talked to me about his Krewe of Hunters."

"Oh!" she said. "But you love Alaska!"

"It will always be home."

She smiled at that and curled next to him. "I love New Orleans, too. Right now, though…"

"You know, the DC area has some of the finest theaters you'll ever find."

"Does it mean that much to you—that we stay near one another? Not just now, but…"

He cradled her head and drew her close to kiss her lips. "Yeah," he said softly.

"I know an actress who would be happy to share her cabin," she whispered against his lips.

They made love again. Physically exhausted, still half-aroused, deeply comfortable in his own bed in his own home, Thor drifted toward sleep. Clara moved against him, murmuring, "Something isn't right."

"What?"

He realized she'd been half-asleep when she roused and looked at him, puzzled.

"Something isn't right with me?" he asked.

She shook her head and grinned. "No. You're perfect."

"Perfect?"

She smiled and lay sleepily against him again. "Okay, not perfect. But damned close."

"You are perfect," he whispered to her.

"Oh, so far from it!" she said. "No, it was something that Amelia said."

"Amelia?"

"She was walking with me…and then she said 'something isn't right' and went to find you, and bring you to me," Clara said, and she rose again and kissed him, and he held her tight.

Eventually, they slept.

Life was good. The future loomed ahead.

A future that included… *Fate.*

Clara slipped out of bed as silently as she could. She collected her things and smiled as she watched Thor still sleeping—he really was a perfect man, arms tossed about where she had been, limbs entangled in the wealth of the covers, profile striking against the sheets.

She hurried out lest she be tempted to stay.

In the shower she savored the hot water cascading around her, thinking that he might rise to join her. But he didn't. She dressed and went out and stood on the front porch first. The temperature was somewhere in the midfifties—cold for Louisiana standards! But so beautiful here.

She closed her eyes for a minute, incredibly grateful to be alive. So much adrenaline—fear? Fear for herself, for Emmy, for all of them? Anger, or a combination? A determination that she wouldn't go down without fighting?—had filled her first hours, she hadn't even really comprehended what had happened. The hours afterward had made it sink in. She'd faced a monster. And she'd come out of it okay.

Heading outside, she took a moment to really appreciate the

compound. It was so handsomely arranged and filled with such beautiful creatures. Astrid and Colin kept massive and gentle draft horses as well as the dogs. The paddocks now were filled with the animals, running about, grazing, doing what horses did. She could see Astrid toward the main paddock, working with a group of puppies, and she walked over to her.

"Good morning! Did you sleep well?"

"You bet. What a beautiful group you have here!" Clara said.

"They have professional names," Astrid said. "But, I call them Rolly, Polly and Fat Stuff!"

Clara took a seat on a bench by the kennel runs and smiled as the puppies came racing to her.

"Very social dogs," Clara said.

"There's always an alpha—I think it's going to be Fat Stuff, in this group."

"Bring me to your leader—Fat Stuff!" Clara said lightly.

Astrid took a seat by her side. "We're so grateful that…"

"We're alive?" Clara murmured. "I know I am!"

"More than that," Astrid said. "Tate Morley… I think the case haunted Thor forever. Now it's at an end. It's hard to believe that it really is at an end!"

"I guess it'll feel more real day by day," Clara murmured.

"Yes, I imagine. Well, anyway, hopefully getting back to work…boarding the *Fate*! I know you're working, but I hope you have a wonderful time."

"I think your brother is going to take the cruise. Time off— and the cruise."

Astrid nodded, grinning. "Yeah, I think so," she said.

Clara's phone rang, startling them both. Clara excused herself to take it.

Ralph was on the other end. He wanted to see if she and Thor wanted to meet up with him and the rest of the cast for dinner. "We've got our lovely young Connie Shaw joining us.

I thought we'd all welcome her here. This has got to be unsettling for her."

She grinned. Leave it to Ralph. She was the one who had been in the hands of a killer. But she was glad Ralph thought of her as the strong one!

"Sure," she said. "Well, I'll be there. I'll have to check with Thor." She went on to tell Ralph that she thought Thor was going to take the cruise. He was thrilled and told Larry, who was equally delighted.

When she hung up and her phone rang again immediately, she thought that it was Ralph calling back.

It wasn't.

But it was another invitation—or favor.

She jumped up. "Astrid, could I possibly borrow a car? I'm going to run into town and do a friend a favor. I don't want to wake Thor—especially since he never sleeps."

"Sure!" Astrid said. "Mine is the Subaru. Keep it as long as you like."

She tossed Clara her keys, and Clara asked Astrid if she'd mention dinner with her cast to Thor. "I don't know if he is going into work today or what his plans are. Anyway, dinner will be later."

"Of course," Astrid assured her.

Smiling, and thinking it was a way to really do a good deed, Clara headed out on her errand of mercy.

Thor should have slept well.

But Mandy Brandt was in his dreams again.

She seemed to hover over him, as if she was worried.

He reached up to gently touch her face and tell her that she could rest in peace. "We got him, Mandy. This time, he'll never kill again."

"No, he'll never kill again," she said, and she brushed his face with a gentle caress, as well. But she didn't smile. She was frowning. "Something isn't right, Thor. Something just isn't right."

He woke with a jerk. Mandy Brandt was not with him. He felt a warm body at his side.

With something definitely not right.

An excited half howl and half whine told him that the warm body was that of his husky Boris—and not Clara.

He couldn't remember when he'd slept so deeply and so hard. He was usually awake in a heartbeat at any sound. "Hey, boy!" He scratched the dog and arose, padded into the bathroom and the shower, and dressed for the day. He figured that Clara was already out with his sister and the horses, dogs and creatures that made up the compound.

He was glad that Clara exceptionally loved huskies. He wondered if he could ever really live without one in his life.

No one was out in the kitchen or the dining room. He headed outside and saw that Astrid was putting one of her new puppies through a training session.

"Hey!" he called to her.

"Hey!" she called back. She stopped what she was doing, told the puppy to sit and walked over to him, studying him anxiously. "You really okay, Thor? You guys seem great, but…"

"We are fine. Really," he assured her.

"You slept! You never sleep."

He smiled weakly at that. "Where is she?"

"She was going to go into Seward. Apparently, a friend called her. A friend in need. Anyway, she's off to do a favor, and she wants to know if you want to meet up with her cast mates for dinner. I don't need my car back, so whatever you want to do is great."

"Who is she doing a favor for?" Thor asked, puzzled, and damning the fact that he'd slept so well.

"I don't know—she didn't say. She just mentioned dinner. Call her cell."

He did so.

She didn't answer.

There were a dozen reasons she might not answer. She might be driving. She might have forgotten her phone; it might have run out of battery. It could be in her purse, or it might have fallen on the floor.

Didn't matter; he didn't like it.

"How long has she been gone?" he asked Astrid.

"About an hour. What's wrong?" Astrid asked him. "You got Morley," she said quietly. "And the guy working with him."

"I don't know," he said. "Something isn't right..." His voice trailed off, and then he remembered the words.

Something isn't right!

The ghost of Amelia Carson had said the words to Clara before she'd come to find him.

Mandy Brandt had said the words in his dream.

He suddenly knew what wasn't right.

He was dialing his phone again, even as he ran through the complex to meet his car. He jumped in and found that he'd been followed; Boris and then Natasha plowed in right behind him.

He started to command them out...

What the hell. It might be good to have them, though they were wagging their bushy tails, howling softly in anticipation of a car ride.

"Down!" he said simply, and revved the motor.

Something wasn't right at all.

It was very, very wrong.

CHAPTER SEVENTEEN

Emmy Vincenzo was waiting for Clara when she came around in the hospital driveway; she was smiling and waving—grateful to have her there.

"I can't thank you enough!" Emmy told her.

"It's my pleasure."

"Really, I mean, we hardly know one another. I suppose—and I don't mean this in a mean way—you're doing this for me because you are a nice person."

"Emmy, it's no problem. I have to be back on the ship for good tomorrow, but I wasn't rehearsing or anything today. It's fine, really. Now, where am I taking you?"

"Oh, I guess I can go anywhere!" Emmy said. "He's not going to be here to say 'Vincenzo! You're three minutes late. Vincenzo, I told you the office, not the flat. Vincenzo!' Oh, I must sound like such a terrible person. I mean, he's dead. And I killed him."

"Self-defense," Clara said.

"Yes, of course, it's all right in self-defense, right?"

Clara wasn't sure how to answer that.

"Well, you can go anywhere. Where would you like to go?"

"I should be planning to go home, right? New York. Home.

I'll need a new job. I still have a few things on the island so I should have you take me to the dock. I don't think I can go back to the island alone."

Clara glanced at her watch. An hour out, an hour there—and an hour in. She'd have plenty of time before meeting up with the others and Thor. She lowered her head, trying not to smile.

Thor would be on the ship when it sailed.

"Could you? I mean…wow, would you?" Emmy asked.

"I don't think we have the Coast Guard at our beck and call anymore," Clara said.

"That's not a problem. There are dozens of little boats around, ready to take people for a bit of a spin. It's a moneymaker," Emmy said drily.

When they reached the dock with plenty of little local boats, Emmy stepped out to hail them a ride. Clara dug around for her phone, but couldn't find it. It was in her bag, she was certain.

"Hey, I've got a guy! Hurry, please, he might not wait long. We'll get out there, I'll grab the few things I need…maybe that witch Magda will feed us!" Emmy said, and made a face.

"Oh, she's just grim. She's all right," Clara said. She figured she'd call as soon as they were under way.

The ride to the island was choppy and the little boat they took was small. Clara tried to appreciate the quick beauty of the trip, but the gorgeous whitecaps were throwing them around too much.

It didn't seem to bother Emmy and the Native American boat master.

And it wasn't until they were on the island, and it was too late, that she realized she'd never made her call. That was all right; she'd reach him via the Wi-Fi once they were there.

She couldn't have let Emmy come alone.

She knew that as she looked at Black Bear Island and realized that she'd never, ever wanted to set eyes on the place again herself.

★ ★ ★

Emmy Vincenzo had been released; the nurse in charge didn't know where she'd gone.

None of the security personnel knew, either; she wasn't being watched for any reason. Once she'd been questioned and interviewed and her statement had been taken, she'd been free to go. No charges were being pressed.

Why should they be? The woman was a heroine!

Thor had gotten ahold of Enfield, Jackson and Mike.

Mike was heading to the hotels in the area; Jackson would take the ship and Thor would study the security tapes at the hospital and assure himself that Clara had picked up Emmy; Enfield had seen to it that every officer in the vicinity was looking for Astrid's car.

A view of the footage of the hospital entry showed that Clara had gotten Emmy; Emmy had waited for her and been ready to hop right into the car when she had driven into range.

On the phone with Enfield, Thor was tense. They needed to find the two women—fast.

Enfield was skeptical. "I don't get it—so she went to pick up Emmy, a young woman who was browbeaten for years before Kimball beat her up physically and she fought her way free."

"Something is not right," Thor said.

"What? I'm sending all these men out to find two women— because something isn't right? You were there, Thor. You saw it all."

"I saw what Emmy wanted us to see. Kimball didn't help Morley—*Emmy* did. She was the one who screamed—she told us that. The scream took Jackson away from Clara. *She* slammed herself into the door and made Clara believe she was in danger."

"But Kimball was at her side!"

"With her knife in his side, not the other way around. Kimball never said a word—I asked Clara over and over again. He never said anything. Emmy *pretended* he was calling the shots.

She'd already stabbed the ship's security officer. Kimball knew that she'd kill him. He was playing for time—desperate to save his own life. In the end, she killed him anyway. She must have really enjoyed doing so."

"But we're studying the letters she told us about—"

"Letters *she* put in the secret drawer. Letters she'll claim were correspondence between Kimball and Morley."

"Thor, this might be crazy."

"Trust me, it's not!"

One of the police officers called to the hospital was approaching him quickly. Thor turned to him.

"We've found your sister's car," he said.

"Where? Did they find Clara and Emmy?"

"No, but we found one of the charter-boat captains who saw them—they were headed out to Black Bear Island."

It was strange to be back in the Mansion; Clara could remember the first time she'd seen it—covered in fake body parts and blood—and the second time, working with the film crew to pick up the fabricated gore.

She didn't like it—the house might have been beautiful, but there was no way she would ever feel comfortable here. While she idly paced the living room, waiting for Emmy, she remembered the magnificent moose she had seen on the island.

But then she remembered running and running in terror.

Seeing Amelia Carson—dead in the snow.

And she remembered Thor, catching her, tackling her down to the ground while she beat furiously at him, trying to fight him off until she'd believed at last that he was with the FBI.

Alaska was home to Thor.

And she still loved Alaska.

She just didn't think that she'd want to return to Black Bear Island again.

"Emmy, are you about ready? Did you say that we had to get some things at the Alaska Hut?" she called.

At her angle, she could see all the way up the stairway, not that Emmy knew that.

And there was Emmy—weak, terrified Emmy—quickly sliding bullets into a gun in the upstairs hallway. And she had a knife tethered to her jeans.

To Clara's self-disgust, she stared at the woman several seconds in confusion. And then, little things suddenly seemed to make sense to her.

Marc Kimball looking like hell.

Marc Kimball never saying a word.

Marc Kimball, so close to Emmy she believed that he was holding the woman at knifepoint...

When it had been the other way around.

"Be right there!" Emmy called out.

Clara made her way quickly to the door. To her vast dismay, she realized that it was locked.

Locked from inside. Locked with a key.

Who knew the island? Who had watched the press on Tate Morley, fallen in love with a serial killer? Who would have planned it all for him? Gotten him everything he had needed, and even with a plan for herself if things had started to go badly? Yes! It was all right there—use Marc Kimball, a man she hated! A man who had abused her...

Morley would have used her, with gentle words and encouragement, but now...

Gunfire suddenly exploded; Emmy's bullet thudded into the front door.

Clara made a flying leap and threw herself from the entry to the living room and behind a sofa. She could hear Emmy coming down the stairs.

She had six shots.

Wait! What made Clara think the woman had six shots? She

must have watched too many old Westerns. Guns could have all number of bullets in them now...

But, it was a self-loader. One of the pistols that people kept because the beloved wildlife could still be dangerous. She was pretty sure that most had six rounds and one in the chamber. Or something like that!

What difference did it make if *one* bullet found home?

What the hell to do?

"Aw, come on, Clara—we can play hide-and-seek all you like. You're so predictable, though. Self-sacrifice! How could you watch me being tortured—how could precious Clara Avery not do the right thing? What you saw was a vicious Kimball making me speak for him. Me! Claiming he had a knife on me, while I had a blade right there against his ribs. I told him he was a dead man if he didn't play along perfectly, and—coward that the bastard was—he wasn't about to take a chance. Funny, because he had such a thing for you, but, hey, the poor sucker wanted to live and so he did as I commanded him. Kimball! Oh, that was priceless. He was so scared. The saddest thing is that he believed that I might let him live. He walked, walked the way I said, shut up the way I said—and would have done whirly-jigs if I had said. Nice, after the way he treated me. Maybe I've done the world a favor. The money goes back to his first wife. She's a decent sort—she was kind to me." Emmy paused to giggle. "Lawyers and the like will be descending here soon—then all will be hell. But, of course, they'll know by then that it isn't over. I'll shoot myself somewhere nonlethal, of course. And I'll cast the blame on another mysterious man!"

Emmy was coming down the stairs. Clara looked desperately around the room. Emmy spoke her thoughts almost before she could think them.

"Oh, Clara! On the *Fate,* I had to work with a knife—better than strangling, that's what I say. But a gun is better than anything. Stay at a distance. Bang, bang. Tate needed it to be personal. He had to feel the life go out of someone. That was all well and good for him—he was a medium size, yes, but oh! His hands—you wouldn't have believed the feel of his hands!"

She was coming closer. A small statuette of an old totem pole was on the coffee table nearest Clara; she picked it up and tossed it across the room, in the direction of the door to the kitchen.

As she'd hoped, Emmy immediately fired, thinking it was Clara in the kitchen, not having seen her jump behind the couch. One bullet, two, three. Clara winced at each heavy sound as the bullets crashed into wood.

Emmy moved toward the dining room. "Clara, come on out, wherever you are. Here's the thing. You were key in taking away the man I loved—so, now, you really have to die. Oh, yeah, and you think you're an actress? Wait until you see the performance they're going to get when they find you dead in the snow and me mortally injured! Come on, say something, Clara! Your guy killed Tate—killed him in cold blood! He has to see you killed the same way." Emmy paused to giggle again. "Cold—get it? I mean, there's not much other way your blood could be, huh, out here."

Clara tried to stay calm, tried to assess her situation. She wasn't getting out the front door; Emmy had the key.

There was the side door—out of the kitchen. But she'd just sent Emmy in that direction.

She suddenly wished that the bloody props remained—there would have been lots of body parts to throw Emmy's way.

If she didn't think fast, she'd soon be body parts herself...

A whisper suddenly sounded against Clara's ear; she was so startled she nearly cried out.

Thankfully, she didn't. The whisperer was Amelia.

"I knew something wasn't right. I mean, Kimball was a strange man, but, man...the way they were walking, all bundled together. And her doing the talking!" Amelia went on.

She was hunched down by Clara, behind the sofa. Hiding, as if Emmy could see her, too.

"But, watch this, Clara. I'm getting good!"

Amelia Carson headed toward the stairway. She slammed her hand and her side against the wall.

And she made a sound—a soft sound.

"Ah, Clara, upstairs?" Emmy called out, her tone aggravated. "You know, it's not that you're a heavy cow or anything, but I'm a little thing. Dragging you down those stairs again—it's not going to be easy. You should show yourself. You don't want me pissed off at you—you really don't. Because I can shoot you in the jaw first, maybe knock off an elbow. Knees are supposed to be especially painful."

Clara stayed perfectly still and stared up at Amelia. Amelia looked back at her and smiled proudly. Clara nodded her appreciation.

Emmy headed for the stairs.

"Come out, Clara."

When she reached the point on the stairs where Amelia was standing, she paused for a second. Amelia had a look of absolute loathing and disgust on her face. She drew back a hand and slapped Emmy.

Of course, her hand just went through Emmy's face.

But it must have done something. Because Emmy stood there for just a moment; she sucked in her breath.

But then she said softly, "Is that you, Tate, my love? Is that you? I'll finish what you started. I swear, so help me God, I will finish for you, before I lie beside you in eternity!"

"In hell!" Amelia muttered bitterly.

Emmy couldn't hear or see her. But, once again, she felt something. She shivered; the gun wavered slightly in her hands.

Amelia ran on up ahead. In the upstairs hallway, she managed to make another sound.

"Come out, come out, wherever you are!" Emmy called. She continued up the stairs.

Clara waited; she rose and nearly flew across the room for the kitchen—and the door from which she had once left the Mansion before...

To run across the snow for her life.

Thor arrived at Black Bear Island alone—and not alone.

He had Boris and Natasha.

Jackson and Mike would be heading out as soon as possible, but he couldn't wait for them. Enfield had wanted to arrange police and Coast Guard assistance—Thor had pretended they'd lost the connection.

He couldn't wait for anyone.

He'd snagged the first boat he could find; luckily, it was with someone he knew well, a weathered older man of Russian and Native American descent—as rugged, worn and hardy as the landscape itself. Thor didn't have to say a lot to the man; he moved at the greatest possible speed as they made their way across.

Every minute of the ride was agony for Thor.

He'd quit trying Clara's cell. She already had a dozen messages from him. If she had her phone, she'd call him back.

He tried to tell himself that Clara was fit—working the theater had kept her so. He realized that neither of them knew yet what each other's daily routines were like, but he was pretty sure that she was young enough for roles that called for a certain physical prowess, and that she went to a gym on a regular basis. He thought about her when she was at his family compound, playing with the dogs, the laughter in her eyes when she looked up at him with delight. He didn't know that much about her.

He knew, however, that she meant everything to him now.

Boris and Natasha jumped onto the dock before the boat was

even tied; Thor didn't wait, either. He thanked the man who had brought him across, overpaid him.

And ran, the dogs moving ahead of him.

He didn't have keys for any of the snowmobiles; he had to run the distance. But he kept pace with Boris and Natasha, glad the snow was no deeper than a few inches.

He felt his lungs burning but that didn't slow him.

He should have known! Should have known when he talked with Emmy that she had stayed with Kimball because she needed the job to carry out the plan—and that her hatred for him had grown and grown. She was a prime target for a man like Tate Morley. A young woman who was never appreciated by anyone else, who desperately needed love. She would have had all the possible business resources to begin and carry on a correspondence with Tate Morley in prison—scrambled emails, throwaway cash phones and letters…all those coded letters the Bureau had combed through. From so many maniacs corresponding with a killer—Jane Doe or Becca Marle among them and also Marc Kimball…but really, Emmy Vincenzo. As long as she toed the line, Kimball wouldn't have questioned business expenses; he had enough correspondence himself.

All carried out by his assistant.

He doubted that Emmy had actually committed the murders; she had merely made the arrangements. Maybe she'd fallen in love with him, watching his trial, reading about him, seeing him on television. She had set everything in motion for him to arrive; she had arranged for warm clothing and tools and a place to stay. She'd known timing; she'd known all about the reality show.

And she'd known Black Bear Island.

He should have seen it!

She had killed Kimball, right when help had come. Of course, even the Bureau's top psychologists would have thought that a normal reaction. Bullets had flown; the moments were filled with high anxiety. She had been terrified; she'd already been beaten and abused.

But he should have seen it.

Running, running, running...they reached the Mansion.

"Boris, Natasha! Secret!" he said.

The dogs crouched low and stayed behind him as they approached the house.

The front door was open; he carefully walked in. He knew almost instantly that no one was there; the house had a feel—cavernous and empty.

"Boris, Natasha—search!" he told them. He said the last with pain.

What if Clara was here? What if she was already...

He wouldn't say it; he wouldn't think it.

The dogs ran up the stairs and throughout the house; Thor quickly checked the downstairs rooms. In the kitchen, he saw the open door there.

Clara had found her way out.

She was alive, and she was out there.

Clara ran...

And ran.

She was afraid to look back and she didn't do so for the longest time.

Emmy was far shorter than she was—and Clara was a good runner.

But while she could outrun Emmy, she couldn't outrun a bullet, so she had to dodge her way across the terrain as she headed for the Alaska Hut.

She'd done so once before, run in sheer terror for her life. And now she was doing it again, her footsteps crunching in the snow, her breath a billow before her, body on fire against the cold that curled around her.

She heard a shot; she plowed ahead, leaping over a snowbank, then slammed down to the earth, her heart thundering. She held still for a split second and looked back. The shot had been wide. She found herself counting bullets…

Why? Who the hell knew what kind of a gun Emmy had?

Looking back, she could see that the girl was still far away. And she was looking for her now—she didn't see her ahead. Emmy might have mapped the island and seen to it that Tate Morley had everything he needed here, but she didn't seem to be much of a tracker. She wasn't looking for footprints—she was staring across the distance.

She was halfway, Clara thought. Halfway to the Alaska Hut, where she'd find Justin and Magda. They would help her…they would let her in.

Justin would have a method of defense.

She had to get there; she had to reach it. But, as soon as she rose…

She heard another shot; had Emmy seen her? She crept along, facedown in the snow.

She lifted her head and peered into the distance; Emmy had paused. She seemed to be studying the gun. Clara decided that she had to take the time and run again.

Had the gun jammed? Pray God!

Clara stood and she began to run and run…

The Alaska Hut was just ahead of her.

She was suddenly aware of barking and baying…

Dogs!

"Clara!"

She turned around. Now Emmy was looking backward— looking at the two large huskies bounding at her. Clara could hear someone shouting; she heard a gun go off…

Suddenly, she was running in reverse.

Thor was there; his FBI Glock aimed at Emmy as the dogs raced up to her, barking a warning.

But Emmy raised her gun anyway.

She wasn't going to shoot; she was going to slam it down on Natasha's head.

Clara was amazed by her own renewed burst of speed.

Emmy never had a chance to raise the gun against Clara. Clara landed on her in a fury. Natasha went for the woman's wrist. Emmy let out a scream and released the gun.

And then Thor was there, pulling Clara up against him, reciting something he'd been taught by the FBI to Emmy, who just lay on her back in the snow.

"Shoot me!" Emmy pleaded. "Shoot me—let me be with him!"

They heard another voice. "Shoot her! Shoot the stupid, wretched little bitch!"

It was Amelia Carson, standing there in the snow. The breeze seemed to move her clothing and her hair. She looked so beautiful and so sad.

"Living is the most horrible punishment for her," Thor said softly.

Boris and Natasha let out their husky howls.

Clara sank down to her knees in the snow. She simply couldn't stand anymore.

EPILOGUE

Clara finished her goodbye song to Larry Hepburn. She was gratified that there was a beat after the song ended when no one moved.

She was offstage and could smile when she heard a sniffle from the audience.

Nothing like it.

Well, and then the thunderous applause that followed.

There were another three to four minutes until the play ended; she stood in the wings waiting for the curtain call.

As she did, she thought she heard another sniff—right by her side.

"That was beautiful. Really beautiful," Amelia Carson told her. Clara could feel the softness of the ghost's touch on her shoulder.

"Thank you."

"I mean," Amelia said, "everyone felt it. The love. The sadness." Amelia was silent a minute. "No one really loved me. I guess my own fault. I wasn't looking for love—I wanted to be famous. World famous!"

"I'm sure you were loved."

"Not like that. Not like you're loved," Amelia said, and before she could sound too morose, she quickly added, "not that your kindly nature didn't almost get you killed—twice!"

"Ah, but you helped save me, you know."

"I did, didn't I?"

Clara nodded. "Amelia, I know you're loved. You have family, gone before you. I know they loved you. And Natalie Fontaine—you two were close, great friends!"

"I have a feeling that I have to leave, and I'm so afraid," Amelia said. "Talking to you…it's getting harder and harder. And I feel that I'm fading, that I should be turning… Is all that stuff about walking into the light true?" Amelia asked hopefully.

"I think so," Clara said.

She heard the sound of applause again; time for their curtain call. She hurried out at the appropriate moment, meeting up with Larry Hepburn, taking his hand.

She received all kinds of beautiful flowers, and she, Larry, Ralph, Simon and Connie all congratulated one another as they headed to their dressing rooms. The director called out her satisfaction regarding the show.

Thor was waiting for her in her dressing room. He wasn't alone.

She'd known he'd be with Jackson and Angela; Angela had met them before the *Fate* had sailed.

Jackson was basically his own boss, and apparently his office of special units ran like clockwork—it was like an ensemble cast, Jackson had once told her. The Krewe of Hunters all worked together.

She knew, too, that Thor had accepted an assignment with the Krewe.

What she didn't know was that there would be another guest in her dressing room—an extremely distinguished elderly gentleman with silver hair, a perfectly tall physique and wonderful

light eyes. He seemed to have a strange combination of authority and kindness about him.

"Adam Harrison, Clara Avery," Thor told her. "And Josh,
his son."

She glanced around at Josh. He was a thin youth who appeared
to be seventeen or eighteen. He had a quick smile, slightly tou-
sled brown hair and a great manner. "How do you do," he told
her. "You were brilliantly cool, by the way."

Clara went to take his hand; only then did she realize that
he was a ghost. She swallowed hard—what? You saw one ghost
and the floodgates opened?

She thanked Josh then and asked them to make themselves
at home and apologized—the dressing room was very small.

"No, no, we apologize. We need to get out of your hair,"
Adam Harrison said.

"Adam is our great and fearless leader," Angela Hawkins told
her.

"Ah, yes, well, I knew about people like you because…be-
cause, well, Josh was always especially talented. I started putting the right people on the right project years and years ago
and then, well, friends at the Bureau and I got together and
formed the Krewe."

"I see. Wonderful, and a true pleasure," Clara murmured.

"Actually, I have a proposition for you, Miss Avery."

"Clara, please," she murmured.

"Just let me show you something," he said.

He pulled an iPad from his jacket and touched it a few times,
then offered the screen. The facade of a magnificent Victorian
theater leapt onto the display; wide, sweeping marble steps led to
an outer patio, stained-glass windows led into the foyer. Adam
ran a finger over the screen; she could see the audience, the mez-
zanine, the orchestra pit and the balconies. He touched the iPad
again—she saw the size and majesty of the stage.

"It's a beautiful theater, fantastic really! Where is it?"

"Alexandria, Virginia. Easy access from DC and Northern Virginia. People even come up from Richmond for performances," Adam told her.

"It's beautiful," she said, waiting. Had Thor finagled her a position at the theater? "Is it public, or private, or…"

"I've just purchased it," Adam said.

"Oh!"

"But it needs management—an artistic director. Frankly, I just wanted to buy it. It was up for sale, and it could have gone the way of many a beautiful old historic property."

"Well, I know something about running the books, but—"

"I believe we can hire a bookkeeper. But! We need someone who knows plays, who knows actors and actresses, a casting process…and, of course, someone who performs, themselves, someone who can make children love theater."

Clara looked at Thor, amazed, worried. "You are joining the Krewe, right?"

"I am," Thor said.

"Did you…did you ask Mr. Harrison to buy a theater because…"

"Oh, no, no—I bought the theater a few months ago," Adam said. "And now these strange cases, and a call from Jackson… and here Josh and I are, aboard the *Fate*!" He had such a great smile and he shrugged with one of those grins. "I mean, hey, seems like *fate* to me, right?"

"Oh, thank you! But, I… I'm afraid! That's major—"

"I haven't seen you afraid enough not to fight, ever," Thor said lightly.

"Are you kidding me? Say yes!"

She hadn't realized she hadn't closed her door. Ralph, Simon, Larry and Connie were just outside, listening to every word.

Ralph walked in and introduced himself boldly, saying he'd be delighted to help with such an enterprise and that they were an ensemble, ready to really give every bit of energy and talent they had to make a go of such a place.

Then Larry and Simon were in the room, and everyone was talking and somewhere in it all, she said, "Yes, yes! As soon as we finish out our contracts here, of course."

Everyone was kissing her—even Josh, with a cool brush on her cheek.

There was champagne; people talked and talked. She finally changed, and they met on the Promenade Deck and talked some more.

And finally, very late, she wound up out on the deck with Thor. They could see the crystal glaciers rising by the ship's light, because even in Alaskan waters, it was nearly dark by then.

They kissed.

"We'll both be away from home," she murmured. "Hm, maybe home is where the huskies are?"

It seemed impossible. They'd both start life anew. Even Jackson, in his way.

"You are home to me," Thor told her, his lips close, his whisper sweet, and it all ended with a fantastic kiss in the gentle chill of the night air and the strange display of light and shadow that was an Alaskan late summer night.

Clara was seeking just the right thing to say as their lips parted, but she never had the chance.

They were interrupted.

"Sweet! Oh, yeah, how almost flippingly nauseatingly sweet!"

Of course, it was Amelia, looking faint and pale.

Clara laughed and said, "Oh, Amelia. Join us!"

Amelia came to them. She'd been wearing one of her cocky expressions, but that wavered and her eyes were wide when she said, "I'm scared."

Clara noted then that Thor was looking outward—toward the glacier. He shook his head. "Strange," he said. "There's a ray of light. It doesn't seem to be from the ship. It's not moon-light, and I don't see what else…"

He broke off. Clara knew why. The light was different from anything she'd ever seen. It seemed to pour in a glittering and golden line toward them.

She heard Thor inhale and say softly, "Mandy."

She saw the woman, too. She was part of the light. She was beautiful with dark hair and large eyes and a face that was serene and perfect. And she smiled and reached out a hand.

She wasn't looking at Clara—or even Thor.

"A friend," Clara said softly. "Amelia, you don't need to be afraid. You have a friend—you won't be alone."

"Oh!" Amelia said.

"Just go forward. Take her hand."

Amelia turned to look at Clara. "You would have been such a great friend. But I'd have been too stupid to know it…to care."

"You never know," Clara said. "I feel I'm saying goodbye to a friend."

"A good friend," Thor said.

Amelia hesitated a minute longer and then shrugged. "Maybe they have a form of television up there. Oh! You do think I'm going up?" she asked nervously.

"Mandy is definitely going up," Thor said. "And she's wait-ing for you."

Amelia nodded. And she moved forward and took the hand offered to her—the hand of Mandy Brandt.

Thor slipped his arm around Clara. It was an Alaskan sky, yes…

But the light show that they saw then seemed to rival any-thing, anywhere in the world.

And then it ended, just as magically as it had begun.

Thor's arms tightened around her. She leaned against him for a moment, and she smiled. And she had to wonder if meeting him here might have really been...

Fate.

★ ★ ★ ★ ★